BOUND
&
BARBED

THE FATED CREATIONS

BOOK ONE

SAMANTHA R. GOODE

First published in the United States of America 2022

First edition

Samantha R. Goode, LLC

P.O. Box 581 Columbia Station, OH 44028

Copyright © 2022 Samantha R. Goode

Internal design © Ari Annachi/Samantha R. Goode, LLC

Cover Design © Moonpress, www.moonpress.co

Artwork © Etheric Tales & Edits/Saumyasvision

Typeset by ProDesign, Etheric

Edited by Ari Annachi

979-8-9867539-1-1

For my Papa, who broke his own "No interior lights on when I'm driving!"
rule to let me read Twilight during our middle of the night road trip.

You always told me that nothing would ever be impossible for me,
if only I put my mind to it.

I wish you were here to see the outcome of doing just that.

AUTHOR'S NOTE

Please read content information (TW) at
www.samanthargoode.com
before reading this book.

You can also submit a suggested content note (TW) to the
Submit a Content Warning button.

Wicked Mountains
Correnti
Neomaeros
River
Merwinan
Madierian Sea
Mad Strait
Rominia
Srot

BRASSILLION
KEMBERTUS
VESTARIA
LOMANDRAH
DOW MAKER PLAINS
BLUSH BAY
KROMEAN SEA
N SEA
LEGEND
KINGDOMS
ROUTES

CHAPTER ONE

Evaline

I had never pickpocketed a woman and, still, I knew that men were the easier target. The rationale could be traced all the way back to the birth of this kingdom, where men were notorious for underestimating women. Whether it's because they believed us to be inferior, or just incapable of manipulation, I'm not sure. But stealing from the men in Kembertus had been effortless.

Apart from today. Today was difficult.

I'd done it a thousand times. In the rain, during snowfall, and when the sun was bright in the sky. I was a shadow of deceit flitting about the streets of Kembertus. No one questioned why the niece of the rulers of this kingdom, Lord Elijah and Lady Therese, so actively attended the weekly markets. No one looked at me twice, except the men attempting to court me; they were a nuisance my aunt encouraged.

I shook my head.

I'd become accustomed to waving off their advances – had choreographed the perfect backstep from any situation – while remaining as polite as my perpetual scowl allowed.

But I didn't want to dwell on that. Not when the breeze of a too warm spring wind swept past me, nor when I could feel the sun's heat on my cheeks. It was the first truly beautiful day in Kembertus since winter first claimed us for the year, and I was trying enjoy it as much as I could.

Considering.

With our kingdom so close to the Wicket Mountains in the north, the chill of winter often remained long after spring should've begun. The market was prime with potential marks all out enjoying the weather.

On market days the storefronts lining this walk were closed. The Lord and Lady encouraged the people of Kembertus to gather and connect for a united kingdom rarely dealt with uprisings. It was why my aunt and uncle celebrated even the most meager occurrences, if only to justify a Ball. During the warmest time of year they would occur once a month. The next event would kick off that season in ten days. It was meant to honor Arlomandric, the God of Terra, for his blessing over the crops to be planted soon. Truly, though, it was more an excuse for the kingdom to overindulge.

I strode along the main avenue of our city that stretched from the castle to the inn, which held the markets once a week.

Plenty of businesses attended the market today; their owners likely arrived in the night to fight over the best shop site. Many hoisted a slab of wood over two standing barrels to create a makeshift table. For the less affluent businesses, that slab of wood was a door from their home. The merchants whose dealings were small, such as the jeweler or the grocer with his spices, simply displayed their items on wooden carts that could be pushed from their shop.

"Riles, keep up with me." A mother snapped at her child. I watched as she clutched his hand in hers, and yanked him toward the baker's table. I turned my head to blink away the fresh tears. Not for the way she treated the boy but for the memory of my father and I in the kingdom I grew up in; Neomaeros.

Southwest of Kembertus, it was a better city in every conceivable way, and they too held weekly markets. My father would take me with him and let me pick out a pastry each visit, then I would help him decide which blade to buy from the blacksmith.

I cleared my throat to dissipate the lump that was forming. Where had the time gone?

I diverted my path away from the baker and headed for the opposite side of the street. The smell of the freshly baked muffins reminded me too much of my father.

Sweat pooled on the back of my neck beneath my braid and I cursed myself for wearing a long-sleeved blouse. While made of airy linen, the extra fabric covering my arms was unwanted in the direct sunlight.

Focus, Evaline. I chastised myself. I had to pay closer attention. It'd only take a few more marks to meet my savings goal. Today had to be the day I banked enough money.

I slowed my pace to match that of the horde milling between stands, feeling the brush of a hundred bodies past me. The street was too crowded for comfort but the closeness made for ideal pickpocketing conditions. I scanned the crowd and my gaze landed on my first target.

He was of average height for a man, slightly taller than me, which would make reaching into his pockets simple enough. He was an elder to even my aunt and uncle, but I recognized him. A rich landlord who took advantage of his tenants and put whole families on the street for one missed payment. He was friends with my Uncle Elijah.

The landlord was sweaty. The vest he wore was meant to button over his torso, but hung open, venting the garment. I smirked; I could see two cinched purses in the inside pocket, their blossomed fabric hardly peeking out.

He eyed the young woman at the soap stand, eyes darting over her form and making my stomach churn. My father would often remark on men who eyed women in such a distasteful way. "Have you ever noticed that the men who do the most gawking, are often those who receive the least attention from the women they leer?"

I'd snicker and agree, but as his words filled my head, I couldn't find it in myself to even smile. Not today.

This landlord was an ideal target. Wealthy, uncomfortable, and distracted. Being a creep didn't make a difference, other than justifying my actions. I followed the sweep of the crowd toward him and watched as he paid no mind to the people passing, letting them jostle his form while he continued ogling the woman.

Perfect.

When I met his side, my hand shot out while my eyes remained forward. I pinched the purse with two fingers.

Within a breath the bag was clutched at my side, before I slipped it in the pocket of my pants. In another exhale the crowd carried me past him. I never looked back. I knew he hadn't realized yet or I would've heard his shouts. Even if he did notice, there was no way he'd ever catch me. There were too many people in the street to ever pick out one culprit.

Usually, I'd stay and pick at least one more purse, but the weight of the one in my pocket was greater than I expected. Much more than anyone usually carried with them in such an open and reckless manner.

I decided not to push my luck, and turned, heading straight for the castle. It was where I rested my head each night, but I would hesitate to call it my home. The Lord and Lady of Kembertus were more than my aunt and uncle, they were my guardians. Even though I was twenty-four and more than capable of having an occupation and living on my own, that's not how society ran for a member of the family in power. Especially a woman.

They flaunted me to the men of the city, and those from kingdoms not too far, as a prize for marriage. I'd been successful in warding them off for the two years I'd been in their care, but the sand was slipping quick through that glass. I didn't have much time left until they found a suitable match, or at least, one that suited them.

My father would've hated how they treated marriage – as if it was a business deal, not a sacred joining of two hearts.

Sacred is how he regarded his marriage to my mother, before she died during my birth, which was an unfortunate event that could've created a cold, callous man but instead forged a caring and protective father.

"Miss Evaline, what has you crying this fair morning?" A man's voice cut through my thoughts, and I jerked at the sound. On my right was

Antony. His warm brown eyes held a smile that was impossible not to immediately recognize. They perfectly complimented his ochre skin, which was dewy from the heat.

I hadn't noticed I was crying, but with how fragile my emotions were today, I wasn't surprised.

I faked a smile and wiped my cheeks. "Nothing, Antony. Thank you for asking."

He smirked down at me as we continued walking toward the castle. The crowd had thinned since we were out of the reach of the market.

"Surely there must be something wrong when a woman as stoic as yourself is caught crying." I think he meant the words to sound kind, but men in Kembertus almost always a hidden agenda beneath every word.

My left arm was nudged, and I turned to see flushed cheeks under a mess of red hair, contrasting pallid white skin. Unmistakably, he was Antony's friend, Nikolas, who winked at me. The bridge of his nose and crest of his forehead were beginning to turn a dark red from the sun.

I pursed my lips with a shake of my head and turned back to Antony. "It's nothing I can't handle. I appreciate your kindness in checking on me, though."

"Of course." He nodded with a tight smile. Men in Kembertus also weren't used to my less than enthusiastic responses, or my disdain for courting.

I turned to Nikolas. "How is your family? Your sister is entering her first courting season, isn't she?" I asked, offering him a smile.

His chest shook with a short laugh. "Yes, she is. And it's all I've heard about for the last month. The rest of the family is well." He shrugged and looked toward the castle. "Just busy helping her get ready for the upcoming season." His eyes cut sideways toward me. "As I have been preparing as well."

I clenched my jaw and averted my gaze, as I was reminded that both Antony and Nikolas had likely only approached me to gauge my interest in dancing with them at the Ball. For the rich and powerful, these parties were the heart of courting season. It was where most matches happened, which only added to my distaste for the events.

"Listen, Evaline," Antony said on my other side. "With the Spring Solstice Ball quickly approaching, I'm sure you're busy, but I was wondering if you might—"

"So busy. I must go meet my aunt now, actually." I cut him off while diverting my path to the left to begin ambling up the gardens that encircled the castle. I'd lied. Nikolas leaned toward me before I could turn away.

"Perhaps at the Ball you and I could—"

I threw them both a smile. "I've got to run, my aunt will not be happy if I'm late. I'll see you both around." I turned and headed toward the castle, throwing a hand toward the sky. "Enjoy the beautiful day." Even as I said the words, and remembered that the weather was pleasant, I knew for me, the day was far from enjoyable.

I'd known from the moment I woke up that the day was going to be a long one, but it was barely noon and the only thing I wanted was to crawl back into bed.

The weight of the last two years since I'd entered Kembertus, alone, hung heavy.

CHAPTER TWO

Evaline

After a nap, and more than a few tears, I left the castle again as the sun neared the western part of the sky. I smiled to myself and let a slight bounce into my step as I descended the staircase to the front entrance. After such a somber morning, I was wary that the mood would take over, but after counting the landlord's purse, I could've squealed with excitement. It was far more than I'd ever imagined pickpocketing.

For a moment I felt guilty. Guilty that today, of all days, I was feeling excitement and joy and hope for my future. But I pushed away the unease. This is what my father would've wanted. For me to be happy and to get out of this wretched kingdom as quickly as I was able. Being stuck here since his death was never my choice, and wouldn't have been his, but I didn't have any other options. It was the closest city available when he was killed, and we knew they'd take me in. I just hadn't known that they'd never let me leave.

But I would change that.

The bustle from this morning was gone, the main street was now barren of everything but pieces of trash blowing about and a few shopkeeper's tables left behind.

The sun glinted in my eyes as it descended in its arc, the golden hues of its rays leaving the street swathed in a painted light. The stone and brick buildings lining the avenue glowed, and it reminded me that sometimes this kingdom could dazzle.

Kembertus wasn't always awful. In truth, most of the people were good. But it was not like Neomaeros. There, the rulers were kind, and it wasn't just an occasional façade. They took care of their citizens and provided more than luxurious parties. Women were treated as men were, able to hold positions of wealth and power. My father taught me that all the Madierian Kingdoms resembled Neomaeros in that effect, but the Kromean Kingdoms did not.

For centuries, women unfortunate enough to be born close to the Kromean Sea had been treated as second class citizens, used for their abilities to further lineage and to manage a household. It had gotten better in recent years – they were allowed jobs and there was some autonomy now – but those privileges still didn't extend to a woman in the ruling family.

Fury heated my cheeks and I took a deep breath. Kembertus was not like Neomaeros, but it was better than Vestaria.

At least here they were making the attempt to evolve. Even if it was so clearly in response to the kingdoms by the Madierian Sea refusing trade until the treatment of women progressed to mirror their own.

Perhaps someday Kembertus would reflect the society of Neomaeros. While I remained, I tried to aid that vision, but I would leave eventually – when I'd gathered enough supplies, weapons, and money to fund my travel.

The main street ended and the city inn stood at the intersection. I turned right at the corner to continue my way toward the orphanage. It lay at the end of this street and might've looked like an old home, with vines crawling up each side, if not for the sign hanging in the front yard.

Kembertus Orphanage.

The cold metal gate was rough in my hand as I thrust it open. It creaked from the movement, and I cringed against the unpleasant sound, closing it slowly to avoid the second squeak.

I smiled at the handful of children playing in the front yard. Little hands held jump ropes, dolls, throwing balls, and nets. They were clearly enjoying the first warm day of the year.

"Evaline!" Jacqueline shouted from the porch. I turned toward her and smiled, waving. She drew the back of a golden hand over her forehead, wiping the sheen of sweat from there. The movement made sunlight bounce off her blond waves.

She took a seat on one of the porch chairs and invited me to join her. I felt the weight of the purse rest against my thigh as I sat.

"What brings you by today?" She asked, turning her green eyes on me.

I smiled at her. "Do you even have to ask anymore?"

I dug my hand into my pocket and gathered the purse, doing my best to shield it as we reached for each other. She covered my hands with hers, patting the top of one as she did so, and said something about having a long day. To anyone looking from the street we would only appear to be two friends embracing in a gesture of familiarity.

No one knew I pickpocketed, not even Jacqueline. But I always took the majority to give to the orphanage when I did. It made the immorality of stealing weigh less on my conscience, even if I did only steal from the well-off.

Her eyes widened when she felt the weight of it, taking only a second to tuck the bag in the high waist of her skirt.

"Evaline, this is too generous." She said, her voice hushed.

I shrugged. "Kembertus needs the orphanage and if this helps keep it running, then so be it."

She didn't know where I got the money from, and never asked. I only instructed her to never tell a soul that I donated.

If I ever did get caught I'd only have to convince my guardians that my uncle gave me the money for the orphanage in one of his drunken stupors, which occurred often enough that my aunt would likely believe me without much explanation.

"Well, we thank you."

I looked toward the children playing. There were twin brothers chasing each other, their steps making their black curls fly up. A lilting giggle pulled my gaze to a young girl named Aliya, she was squeezing a bear in chubby arms, and her pale cheeks were reddened from the heat.

Jacqueline was a teacher at the orphanage. She was my friend before I knew she worked here, so I always gave her my donations to pass along to the orphanage's owners, a married couple named Lillian and Monte. Technically it should've been something the Lord and Lady owned, but they were more than happy to pass ownership to whoever offered to run the place. The less responsibility for non-profitable ventures my guardians had to take, the better – in their eyes at least.

Jacqueline was married to Aurora, who owned the most popular boutique in town, and Aurora's father, Nathaniel, was the wealthy owner of several businesses; the inn, the tavern, and the gambler's den. He'd raised Aurora to have the same entrepreneurial spirit as he did. He preferred to manage his businesses hands on, so he spent much of his time circulating between them.

Jacqueline had always wanted to be a teacher, and she knew the orphanage was the best place to start that change after Kembertus announced the new initiative to begin teaching girls the same as boys. She and Aurora had been taught to read by their respective parents. Because of how many decades had passed without allowing women literacy, Kembertus had a lot of catching up to do. Jacqueline, with volunteers, were working through that list of women and children to teach, and I had offered to help.

I preferred to conduct lessons at the orphanage since it gave me time away from the castle, and I got to see my friends, but my guardians had other motives. The optics of the legal ward of the Lord and Lady teaching children to read in the ornate castle library were simply too valuable to pass up. Thus, when I gave lessons, someone would escort two young girls up to the castle and I'd spend the day teaching them.

"Evaline!" Megin shouted and ran up behind me. I knew based only on the voice that it was her. I turned around just in time to see her reaching for my braid. "Your hair is so pretty–"

"No!" I said, a little too harshly, and pulled my braid out of her grasp. I quickly fixed a smile on my face and took her outstretched hand. "I'm sorry, I just don't like when people touch my hair." I lied.

She nodded and came around to stand in front of me, her pin straight blond hair falling over her shoulder.

"Are you here for a lesson?" She asked and I shook my head. She had been one of my two private students for months.

"No, unfortunately. I only stopped in to say hello."

One of the kids playing on the lawn called for her, she shot me one last smile and ran toward them.

"I'm sorry about that, Evaline." Jacqueline said beside me. I turned to her and shook my head.

"It's not a problem at all. When you grow up with white hair you get used to others making comments about it." I looked back to the yard where Megin played with the other children. I enjoyed the days when I got to teach Megin, and Priscilla, but still preferred to leave the castle whenever possible. I was allowed to do so whenever I wanted, unless there was an event being hosted in the castle, and as long as I was back before dark. The latter condition didn't take much convincing; I hated the outdoors at night, even though it hadn't always been that way.

The thought cast my eyes to the sun that dipped lower toward the horizon. I stood and ran my hands over my thighs, loosing the wrinkles that formed in my high waisted pants while I sat.

Jacqueline stood and waved toward the house. "Please, stay, have dinner with us. It should be done soon. The children always look forward to spending time with you."

I smiled and shook my head. "I appreciate the offer and would normally love to. But I want to go see my father's grave before dark."

Her eyes softened and she reached out to pull me into a hug. "I'm so sorry, Evaline. I've been insensitive."

I squeezed her back then pulled away, shaking my head. "You have not. I just haven't had a chance to go yet today, and I need to."

She nodded. "Two years is a long time, please let us know if you need anything." Then her eyes widened with a thought. "Oh! Wait one moment."

She ran inside, and re-emerged after a moment, running straight for a rosebush. She grasped a handful of the blood red roses and cut them with the shears she'd retrieved. I felt my heart give a painful lurch as she cut them and offered them to me.

I accepted the flowers and thanked her. I cast one last glance to the children still playing in the yard, but all of them were oblivious to my exit.

The sweet scent of the flowers drifted up around me and it took a moment before I realized the thorns were digging into my hands. I sucked a drop of blood from my fingertip before turning for the cemetery.

The thing about losing a parent is that a whole half of your world fades into nothing but memories and faintly remembered voices. The thing about only ever knowing one parent, and then losing them, is that every piece of your history goes, too.

I belonged in that orphanage just as much as all those children. In a way, the castle had filled that role for me. A home where I was raised by those who were not my parents until someone else took charge of me. Only, instead of adoption into a loving family, my stay would end in marriage.

It might as well have been jail.

I sighed as I lumbered up the slight hill to the cemetery and felt the strain on my legs. They were tired, and so was I. Nightmares kept me awake most nights in this kingdom. Most of my life, too. The nightmares before my father passed away never stuck with me, only leaving behind the vague sensation of dread and a fear that radiated in my bones.

But the nightmares I'd had since being in Kembertus, since my father's death and the other frights that followed, were tangible. They tricked my mind into believing I was still there, caught in the dark. Like I'd never escaped and never survived. I could feel every swipe of my blade, and each blow. When I woke from those night terrors, I'd relive my pain and sorrow all over again. As if it was the first time I'd watched my father die.

I traipsed through the cemetery, weaving between the headstones, until I found my father's. It was granite and gray, a rectangle that stretched up higher than it was wide. I faced it and watched the glare of the setting sun glimmer over the surface. Sitting down into the cushion of grass, I ignored the way it poked me. I crossed my legs and again noticed I was holding the rose stems too tightly.

My hands unclenched and I looked down at them. I could see the indents the thorns made in my skin and watched as they rebounded.

I laid the roses against his headstone and tears welled.

"Hi." I whispered to the stone. "I'm sorry it's been so long since my last visit." My voice wavered. I bit my lip to stop it quivering.

I reached out my hand and traced the words carved into his headstone. *Wallace Manor. Soldier, husband, father.*

The friction from the ridged lettering caused a tingling sensation in the pads of my fingers. "But I made sure to carve out time today to come see you."

I knew the words were falling into empty air.

I was alone.

This wasn't even his true resting place. His bones remained where he died, beneath a century old oak tree somewhere in the forest between here and Neomaeros.

I didn't have the energy or strength back then to move him, or to even give him a real and sacred burial. He'd made me promise to flee as soon as he was gone, afraid more monsters would come.

The tears were free falling and I didn't bother wiping them as they landed on my wringing hands.

"I miss you. So much." I whispered against the pain in my throat. "Every day."

Despite this not being his resting place, and just an ornamental grave in his home-kingdom, I spoke to him. In hopes there was truly an afterlife. The Night. In hopes Mortitheos, God of Night, would allow my father to slip through the planes that separated us. Let him listen to the words I cried for him in the shadow of his grave, alone. Always alone.

I moved my elbows to rest on my thighs, chin on my fists.

"I can't believe it's been two years." I blinked hard and felt a few more tears break free. Felt the wind kiss the streaks they left behind. "I can't believe I've been stuck here, without you, for so long." I scanned the lower part of the headstone. Moss crawled over the glass casing that protected a locket that belonged to my father. It was opened to the picture inside, a painting of my mother with her soft smile and white-hued hair that matched mine. The only keepsake I had left from her. My fingers slipped over the glass as I tore the moss away.

"Is she there with you?" Alannah was her name. The love of his life taken by his own daughter. My birth was too much for her body, the physicians were too ill equipped to save her. "I hope so."

I jumped as a movement in my peripheral caught my eye. There was nothing there but the faint shadows forming from the setting sun.

I finished ripping the moss from the gravestone and flexed my hand, noting the green grime under my fingernails. I'd have to clean those before my aunt saw. I didn't need another lecture from her.

I took a deep breath.

"It hasn't gotten any better here." I began, picking up one rose and running my fingers over the soft petals. "Not for me, anyway. They are advancing in some ways, in some important ways. You might even be proud of your little brother." I said, referring to Elijah. "But I'm still forbidden to leave. They'd lock me in a cage if they could. Show me off to the men of this kingdom, and any others that were looking for a wife, and a dowry."

Another lump formed in my throat, and I wasn't sure if it was from anger or grief. I spoke through it.

"They refuse to let me leave. No matter how many times I assure them I'm able to do so. I want to go to Neomaeros or Correnti or Merwinan."

No matter how much I told myself, or my guardians, that I was ready to leave on my own, I knew I wasn't. I knew that even with proper supplies, weapons, and maps, I would never be ready to travel alone. Not in the woods where Vasi lurked.

But even if I didn't see a single one on my trek, I was bound to see men. And men were the real monsters.

I shivered at the memory that washed through me and gritted my teeth against the pain in my wrist. The sensation had my eyes snapping to the skies. Usually an ache in my poorly healed bones indicated there were storms on the way, but I knew this phantom pain was from the reminder of what broke it.

I let myself fall and landed on my back, spreading out to look at the sky. I could see the moon opposite the sun, one ready to dip away for the evening and the other ready to spring forward. The sky to the east was a dull blue. But toward the west, where the sun prepared to settle down, the blue melted into hues of pink and orange.

I wasn't ready to travel alone. My father's attack followed by my own just hours later told me that.

Memories of the men's hands on my wrists shifted through my mind and I tried to ignore them, to ignore the reminder that they were fully prepared to kill me back then.

"You know," I whispered toward the sky. "For one single moment that night, I wished they had killed me. I considered not fighting back for half a heartbeat. I had no concept of what life would look like without you." My voice quivered into the quickly chilling air above me. "And sometimes, even now, I have the same wish."

CHAPTER THREE

Maddox

"I'm so fucking sick of mortal food." Wyott grunted as he grimaced down toward his bowl, fork clattering onto the porcelain.

I laughed. "I'm surprised it took this long."

He pushed back from the table, crossed his arms over his broad chest, and leaned back in his chair.

"I tried, Maddox. I really tried. But I've hit my limit with this mush." He nodded his head down to the stew and the movement knocked a few strands of his sandy hair from the half-bun sloppily fastened on top of his head.

I didn't blame him. We'd been on the mortal continent for eight months and were homesick, for more than just our warmer climate; the mortals didn't make food like the Kova. Maybe it was that we were able to use fresher ingredients, maybe it was that we had a richer history and more knowledge on preparing food, or maybe it was just that we were used to the food from our land. Regardless, it was different.

"How much farther until Kembertus?" He asked.

I looked through the window beside us, as if a map would appear in the grimy panes of the glass. Only my gray, deep-set eyes, stared back at me.

"Not much longer. I'd say two days."

The relief was clear on his face. I almost felt guilty for allowing him to come along on this scouting trip, but I shrugged away the thought. Even though he had to leave his mate, Cora, back home, I knew he'd never skip travelling with me. Especially considering my father asked us personally to take this trip. And Wyott was nothing but loyal to him.

"Did Kovarrin give any special instructions on what to look for in Kembertus?" Wyott asked, mentioning my father as if he'd heard my thoughts.

I took another forkful of the bland, and now lukewarm, stew.

"He didn't say much of anything, just that he'd gotten some reports on odd occurrences near Kembertus and wanted us to check in. The only specific detail he mentioned was to take the direct route from Neomaeros to Kembertus and be on the lookout for anything out of the ordinary there."

Wyott nodded and reached forward, grabbed his wine, and took a deep swig. He wrinkled his nose before wiping a hand down his mouth and smoothing his scruffy beard.

"They don't even know how to make a good glass of wine."

I picked up my own glass and peered inside. "Wine gets better with time. Humans don't have very much of that."

Wyott and I were both Kova, immortal beings blessed by the Gods with this gift of endless time. All we had to do to maintain this state of being was to drink human blood. It wasn't too much to ask, especially considering our palettes craved it.

But the Gods didn't only create us, they created our twin species; the Vasi.

The Kova, who as a people were good and just, took our sustenance in moderation. Feeding only when necessary, about once a week, and never harming the humans we fed from. We'd use our Gods gifted power of compulsion – a mind manipulation – to take away their pain. And we healed them before they left. When they walked away, they were none the wiser to what had just occurred. And, once Kova found their mates they preferred to drink from each other, thus sparing humans altogether.

But that was only for those who'd found them.

The Vasi were our counterparts, equivalent in almost every way, besides the fact that they were monsters who fed even when not nutritionally necessary, and who took pleasure in the pain they caused their victims, before killing their victims.

Both species were stronger, faster, and had keener senses than humans. But we were parallels of each other. The only physical trait that differentiated us were the color of our eyes.

The Kova were taught that the Gods chose the color gray for ours because it was neutral and balanced. The humans could still know we weren't human, if they knew we existed at all, but wouldn't be alarmed. The Vasi were given the color of a deep maroon red. The color of the blood they drained from their victims as a warning sign to any humans who came across them. Evil.

"Ready to head out?" Wyott asked as he pushed his finished bowl away from him.

I smirked. I knew he'd still finish his meal. No amount of food or blood could ever satisfy him.

"Sure." I threw down a few coins, making sure to pull out the mortal currency and not the Kova, and grabbed the last roll off the table before standing to leave.

As soon as we walked out into the dying sunlight, a cool gust of wind hit us, and kept at our backs as we turned toward the path that would take us out of the Neomaeros walls toward Kembertus.

Wyott's gaze landed on mine. "Out of all the reasons to hate the Kromean Kingdoms, I think the highest on my list is their cold climate."

"At least it's spring." I offered.

The weather on the continent of Brassillion was cooler than the island we were from, Rominia. But the Kromean Kingdoms were some of the coldest. Just another reason we were grateful not to travel into them often. When my father asked us to take these scouting trips, we did so on foot instead of utilizing horses. He preferred we had no distractions while traveling between kingdoms.

We'd taken our time in the Madierian Kingdoms these last eight months. They were the three that had pledged an alliance with the Kova. Not that the townspeople knew, but in each kingdom the ruling family was aware of the existence of both the Kova and Vasi. Through their family's generations they passed on the knowledge of what we were, that when we were within their walls, it was to protect them. It wasn't Kova responsibility to shield humans from the Vasi, but we took it on.

The other three kingdoms on the continent of Brassillion were Arlomandrah, Kembertus, and Vestaria, the Kromean Kingdoms. Those three had not sworn an allegiance to Kova, and while Arlomandrah wasn't pledged to Kova, they weren't to the Vasi either. But Vestaria was. On these scouting trips, we never went further inland than Kembertus. If Vestaria had pledged allegiance to the Vasi then we would not set foot there. Doing so could start a war between the Kova and Vasi. The landscape of Widow Maker Plains had only just healed from the previous war. We wouldn't risk going to Vestaria.

But Kembertus was different. They originated as a state pledged to the Vasi in their early years. All three Kromean Kingdoms had. But over time Kembertus and Arlomandrah had strayed from that pledge.

In Arlomandrah, the most southern of the three, the ruling family had been slaughtered in a coup by their own people. Since the pledge to be sworn to Vasi or Kova was one that was done by word of mouth, that pledge died with the ruling family. The Vasi wouldn't dare reinitiate the partnership, either. If the wrong humans knew that they existed, and where they lived, they could easily build an army to take on the Vasi. And the Kova would join them.

While we wouldn't start a war against the Vasi ourselves, we'd aid the humans. If paired with humans, we'd likely win, with well over double the Vasi's forces. But thousands would die.

So, the Vasi allowed the Arlomandrah contract to dissolve, and only had Kembertus and Vestaria under their reign. Until, for the first time in five hundred years, the Vasi were rejected by a kingdom. The ruler that rejected the notion of being linked to the Vasi was a soldier who'd been told of the Kova and Vasi since he was young, set to be the ruler of Kembertus. But the older he became and the more he traveled, the more he learned. He befriended Kova along the way, myself and Wyott included.

We met on a battlefield, fighting for Neomaeros in a siege attempt by those same false rulers of Arlomandrah. Upon returning home to Kembertus, finally of age to take over after the passing of his father, he denied the partnership with the Vasi. And by the grace of the Gods, the leader of the Vasi did not retaliate. Likely because he knew it would start a war.

Then, that ruler left his kingdom of Kembertus, leaving it in the hands of his younger brother, whom he did not tell of the Kova nor the Vasi. He chose the safety of his family over the life of luxury he'd have if he'd stayed. But with a baby on the way, he and his wife had no choice. And they fled to Neomaeros.

"You know, he won't be there." I muttered.

Wyott glanced to me and nodded, his shoulders sagging. "I know." He said just as quiet.

When my father received the intel that prompted this trip, with it came the news that the Kembertus royal who rejected the Vasi alignment had been killed.

As Wyott and I walked out of the Neomaeros walls and into the shade of the forest, following the path that I knew that man must've taken when he returned back to his homeland, I couldn't help the feeling of disappointment that I would not get to see my old friend again. That I wouldn't be able to thank him for what he'd done.

I closed my eyes and sent a prayer to the Night.

May the Gods rest your soul, Wallace Manor.

CHAPTER FOUR

Evaline

The wind blew past my cheek, shaking the branches and rustling the leaves above us. It disturbed the white hair that framed my face, too short to fit back into my braid.

My father preferred traveling in the quiet, he thought it safer. Especially at this time of night.

"We're close to Kembertus." He'd said only hours earlier, after we'd crossed River Brawn. "If we keep at this pace, we can make it there before nightfall tomorrow."

While he wasn't keen on traveling in the dark, he was even less fond of spending any more time outside of a city's protection than necessary.

"If we make this push now, that's one less night out here." He said after making his decision, but I noted the way he looked over at me from his horse, pausing for my approval. I nodded.

We were a team, and I knew we always would be.

Now, as our horses made quick but careful steps over the forest floor, I took a deep breath. I enjoyed the night. It was peaceful and quiet and always carried a stillness with it that calmed me. The air was growing cooler the closer we got to Kembertus, and I suppressed a shiver in my long-sleeved tunic and cloak.

Knowing me better than he knew himself, my father's head tilted down toward me.

"Is everything okay?" Concern shone in his eyes.

"I'm okay, just a little cold."

He stopped his horse and I followed suit, but rolled my eyes when I saw him begin to unbutton his cloak.

"Absolutely not, I'm perfectly capable of a little chill for a few more hours." His hands didn't stop moving though, and he just shook his head. "I'm fine, I don't need it." I tried to argue again but closed my mouth at his pointed look.

He was halfway done with the line of buttons from his collar when he stilled.

The look in his wide blue eyes chilled my blood and terror wracked up my spine. Those were the eyes of a soldier, one that sensed danger. I ground my teeth to fight the chattering I knew I'd hear if I loosened my jaw. My entire body began to tremor as I strained my ears to listen, convinced I possessed the same instincts.

He held out one hand toward me, palm open, instructing me to stay still. The other moved silently down to his sword, resting on the hilt; ready to unsheathe it at a second's notice.

He cocked his head to the side, eyes still on me, narrowed with concentration. A heartbeat passed and the only sound was the wind in the trees and an owl so far away it was almost out of earshot.

Another beat passed and he did not waver, staying silent as he waited.

Finally, he straightened and I felt my heart unclench. "It must've just been the wind—"

I saw the blur before I heard it, before I felt the impact.

From behind him it flashed forward, hurtling toward me. Faster than I could blink, a pair of arms wrapped around me, my body was lifted from the horse's back, and I was whipped through the air. My scream mixed with my father's shouts and heavy hooves, before the world stopped and went silent.

I still faced my father, but there were suddenly several paces between us. He was on the forest floor, bucked from his horse. Both of the steeds had run off. My father's face had gone ashen, and even from where I was held, I could see the way his hands fisted into the dirt below him, see the worry in the tension of his locked jaw. I knew what caused it. I didn't need to see the eyes of the being behind me, I knew they were red.

The Vasi snickered in my hair, close to my ear. My heart pounded and his arms tightened around me. His face dropped so his mouth was on my flesh.

"What a fortunate find I've made tonight." He purred, lips moving against my skin. My body was still. I wasn't sure if it was from terror or instinct. "You're the first lot I've run into in days." One hand reached up and pulled my braid away from my neck, exposing it. "I have to say, I'm happy to see you're not asleep in some tent. I much prefer to engage with my food than slaughter it while it sleeps."

"There's no need for this." My father said across the way as he stood, his voice steady and stern and every bit that of the ruler he was supposed to be. "Let her go, no one needs to get hurt."

A chuckle sounded from the being behind me, and my father's face hardened in response.

"I think we both know you're not the one to give orders here."

My father nodded, straightening. He dropped the sword from his hand, letting it thud against the dirt. "You're right. Please, just let her go." He pulled the partially unbuttoned collar of his cloak down, exposing his neck. "You can have me."

"No!" I screamed and jolted toward my father. What was he doing?

The arms of the Vasi did not budge from my feeble movement. The immortal dropped his lips just below my ear. He moaned against me softly and my eyes widened, locked with my father's.

When the Vasi spoke again his voice had dropped an octave. "I'm wretchedly hungry." The words vibrated through my neck. "And she smells so," he paused and inhaled. "So delectable."

"Take me." My father begged. His voice was no longer level, no longer calm. "You can have me, and we can let her move on." He took a step toward us and the Vasi's head snapped at the movement.

"Again, with the giving of orders." He hissed.

My father shook his head. "Just a request, please. She's only twenty-two, she's barely lived."

The Vasi groaned and buried his face into my neck. My chin trembled as I tried desperately to hide the tears that surged up.

I should tell my father to run. To save himself. There was no use in both of us dying. But all I could do was stand in horror at the man wrapped around me, at the hunger in his voice, and the racing of blood through my veins.

"Please." My father croaked.

The Vasi grumbled low but then spoke, face never leaving the crevice of my neck. "I think you forget you're not speaking to a Kova. They may give mercy."

I took in a shaky breath.

"But the Vasi do not."

I felt his mouth open against my skin, felt his tongue poke out and feel at the artery that ran below it. My eyes strained to look down, to watch his teeth that were about to pierce me, to drain me of all my blood. I felt them graze my skin and a cry left my lips as I tried in vain to pull away.

Just as his teeth pressed, ready to cut, he froze, head snapping to my father.

I followed his gaze and saw my father standing there, blood spilling from a wound in his neck and a dagger in his hand, crimson covering the blade to match.

The Vasi let go of me and my legs gave out. The ground rushed up and I barely caught myself before my face smashed into the grass. I could only watch as the Vasi's face buried in my father's neck.

"Run!" He screamed at me, daggered hand raising and pointing toward Kembertus, his blood still falling from the tip.

I should. I should turn back and sprint and go to Kembertus. That's what a normal daughter would do. Obey the command and leave, flee for safety.

But I wasn't a normal daughter, I hadn't been since the first time he put a blade in my hand. The thought reminded me that I had them strapped all over me. I drew a dagger from my hip and shakily shoved myself back to my feet.

"Stop." My father shouted, wrestling against the Vasi. Not to get away, but leaning into the immortal, toward me. "Don't." His voice was desperate, a sound I'd never heard before leaking into it.

In the space of a breath my body lit into action, finally remembering the countless hours it had practiced for this exact scenario. I sprinted toward my father and jumped on the Vasi's back. My feet locked around his waist, and my hand clutched his shoulder, as I brought my dagger down into the side of his neck.

"Go, please Evaline, go." My father was yelling. He tried to shove me away.

"Stop pushing." I pleaded. It was enough to fight the immortal, I couldn't fight my father too.

I brought my dagger down, burying the blade deep into the neck of the Vasi. I felt his spine stiffen and heard the hiss released from his mouth.

"You little shit." The words dripped with venom and my body tensed, preparing for the onslaught I knew he'd unleash.

In a movement too fast for my vision he turned, one hand releasing my feet from his waist and the other throwing me away.

I flew before I slammed down onto my back.

Air.

I needed air.

It had all been knocked out of me and no number of breaths could refill my lungs.

I heard my father scream my name and I turned my head in time to watch as the Vasi launched him through the air, too.

But he didn't land on the forest floor.

A garbled cry fell from my mouth as my father landed against a tree. The Vasi had thrown him with such force that his back hit the trunk with a crash. I turned over on my side, still trying to catch my breath. His eyes were wide as he looked down, my own following and landing on the low hanging branch that'd plunged through his abdomen. Tears fell down my cheeks and the dark world blurred. The impalement was on the left side of his chest, directly below his heart.

I tried to scream, tried to speak, but no words came. I saw the Vasi approach and scrambled to my feet, back aching with the movement.

"Unfortunately, you've both just become more effort than you're worth." He said, his voice low. He grabbed the back of my neck and pulled me toward him roughly, the pain in my spine too much to handle. "Goodbye."

His mouth opened. The sharp canine teeth, that were normal a moment ago, elongated ever so slightly, and he drew closer.

I screamed. This time I finally had enough breath to. I pushed and kicked against him, but it was futile. His mouth moved toward the muscled flesh that sat between my neck and shoulder and he dug in.

The pain was unimaginable. White-hot and searing, but also deep and aching.

I felt him moan with pleasure through my flesh and heard my father screaming to stop, screaming for help, from somewhere far away. My eyes drifted up to him, stuck against the tree with the branch peeking through his chest. His eyes wide and tears streaming from them.

"No." He cried.

I continued to fight and push against the Vasi, but he did not budge.

"Evaline!" I heard my father scream and I looked back toward him. He squirmed and shouted in agony. He moved again, his eyes clamped shut and his teeth clenched against the pain.

What was he doing?

I watched as he planted his hands against the tree behind him, dug his feet into the ground, and pushed.

"Stop. No!" The words were falling from my lips, pleading, as my vision began to warp.

But he continued and I watched in horror as the branch disappeared inch by inch.

"You'll die!" I screamed, fighting harder against the Vasi.

If my father removed the branch from his body the bleeding would be too much, he'd have no chance at all.

I felt a stir within me, the sensation of something deep inside waking up. I heard a voice somewhere in my mind and swore the shadows around us all shifted. Was this what dying felt like?

But my father was free, sweat streaking down his face as he lumbered toward us, unsheathing a dagger from his hip, and sinking it into the back of the Vasi. I pushed against the being and this time there was give. I shoved again and he pulled away from me, stumbling back, my blood still wet on his lips. His eyes were wide with panic as they rose to meet mine.

"What...?" His hands moved up slowly, wiping my blood from his mouth. He stared at it shining off his fingers in the moonlight.

Now.

I couldn't tell if it was a voice or intuition whispering through my head. I didn't have time to question where it came from, this would be our only chance.

I pulled the dagger from my calf and jumped on the him once more, this time wrapped around his front. My body didn't hesitate and didn't shy away. I reached my free hand around the Vasi's head and grasped his hair so tight that my fingers ached. My daggered hand came around the back of his neck. I dug the edge of the blade into it, pulling it toward me as I wretched him by the hair into the dagger. He tried to pull me from him, but now it was his movements that were futile. My arms burned with the effort of pulling his head and the blade. When my dagger met resistance, I knew it was the spine. I cried out in effort and yanked.

I fell back off the Vasi and onto the ground, the momentum knocking me away from him as my blade rang free from its position. I looked up, and the headless Vasi fell sideways.

With the immortal no longer standing between us I saw my father once more, on the ground. I crawled toward him, and it was then I realized my hand was still grasping onto the Vasi's hair.

I shivered and released it, moving to my father.

"Pa?" I whispered as I met his side. His weak smile tore a hole in my chest that matched his own.

I held his head in my lap and tried to cover his wound with my other hand to staunch the blood. I looked for the horses, for a light in the distance, or anything that meant I could get him to safety, to a physician. There was nothing but trees.

"It's okay." His voice was even and small. I looked down to find him staring up at me. My tears landed in perfect droplets on his cheeks.

"No," I whispered, a sob working up my throat. I shook my head. "No, not yet." I looked up again and took in a breath, ready to scream for help until my throat bled.

"Don't." His command was quiet. I clutched my eyes shut, understanding his intention. "There's no reason to draw more attention to us, more harm to you. There is no saving me now, my darling."

"No. No." I repeated, head swiveling to find somewhere to rest. There, an old oak tree just down the path. Far enough away to be rid of the grotesque scene beside us. I stood and moved him slowly, dragging him as painlessly as I could the few paces away to the tree. I sat down at its base and pulled him onto my lap again, positioning my knee to cover the wound on his back.

"This is better. We'll wait here and someone will find us by morning, and everything will be okay." I affirmed, nodding my head, and ignoring the tears falling from my face. I covered the wound on his chest again and an unintentional sob released when I felt how slow the blood was moving.

My father held my hand in both of his, grasping my wrist and caressing it with his thumb.

"It's okay, Evaline. You're going to be okay." His eyes were clear and convincing as they looked up at me. No hint of fear or regret to be found.

My lip quivered as my vision blurred and I shook my head. "No, I won't." My breath shook as I used my other hand to pull his head against my chest. "Please, stay."

This time his voice wavered. "I would if the Gods would let me, you know that." He took a breath. "I'd give anything for one more day as your father, but we both know that can't happen." He shook his head slightly. "If the Gods were just, they never would've taken your mother."

At the mention of the other parent I'd lost my body shook with sorrow. "It's not fair." I cried.

"Life almost never is, darling." He took a deep breath, and I could hear the exertion it required. The blood against my hand barely trickled and I winced again at the pain I knew was coming for both of us. "You need to listen to me." His voice became serious, and I did my best to open my eyes and meet his.

"I thought I'd have a lifetime left to tell you everything you need to know." He scanned my face and looked as if he couldn't find the words. Now, real tears fell from them to match mine. "This world is bigger than the two of us. There's more at stake than I've told you." He raised his hand to catch a tear on my cheek. "When she was pregnant, your mother and I discussed how much we would tell you, and when." His breaths were coming in shorter increments. "She never wanted to tell you about the Vasi and Kova, to protect you, but tonight I'm thankful that I did." A small smile flashed on his face and his eyes lit with the dull pride he could muster in this state. "I've never been more proud of you than I am tonight, and that's how I know you will be okay without me."

A loud sob wracked through me. Of course that would make him proud.

But after a moment his eyes widened in fear and his grasp on me tightened. "When I'm gone, go to Kembertus. As fast as you can on foot."

I shook my head. "I'm not leaving you out here."

"Evaline." He cut me off, voice rough. "I will be gone. You must fight for yourself now, and you can't do that out here alone with no horses, no food, and hardly any weapons left."

"But—"

"Do not argue. This is a command. You will run to Kembertus as fast as you can. You know the way. Just follow the path. It'll be slower on foot but do not slow down and do not stop under any circumstances. Even if you have to crawl—do not stop moving. Do you understand me?" I nodded.

His eyes flashed between both of mine, and he shook his head, a fresh stream of tears falling from his eyes and his body shaking.

"What is it? Are you in pain?"

He let out a humorless chuckle and shook his head. "No, I just don't have enough time. I have so many things I have to tell you about your life and what the rest of it might look like, so many pieces of advice, but there's too many to put into words." He took a deep breath. "Go to Uncle Elijah. Tell him we were robbed, and you escaped with your life. Tell him I'm dead, if he has no fear that I'll resume the role as Lord he'll take care of you." He took another deep breath and this time I could hear the liquid in it. "Leave me here and run, do you understand that?" His eyes were trained on me.

I nodded against the tears. "Yes."

His hands tightened around me again. "Evaline, it has been an honor to be your father. I would relive this moment a thousand times over, if it meant I got to do it again."

I did my best to keep my eyes open, to maintain eye contact even if the only thing I wanted to do was to shut them and pretend that none of this was happening.

"Keep your head on your shoulders. Be smart. Train as much as you can in that Gods forsaken kingdom. Leave as soon as you're able with as much money as you can and head for the Madierian."

I nodded again and again as if my continued attention would keep him with me longer.

"Men can be evil. Vasi are evil. Dagger first and ask questions later." He took a breath and I sobbed at the wheeze in it. "But never tell anyone about the Vasi. Humans cannot handle this type of information and you will be hanged as a Sorceress." His eyes widened as if a thought struck him. "If you ever meet a Kova, be wary of them. Stay away if you can. But if you're in danger, and you feel you can trust them, do. Many a Kova were friends to your mother and I, they are overwhelmingly good, and they are reliable. But only trust them if you feel you can."

He shook his head and pulled my hand away from his wound, up over his heart, heaving a sigh.

"I've loved you since you were the first heartbeat in your mother's belly. And I will continue to love you from the Night. Go forward and be the strong woman I've raised you to be and that I know that you are." A pained sound fell from his lips. "Let me go. Let tonight go. And Evaline?" The small inflection in his voice commanded my attention again.

"Yes?" I said between breaths.

With one last squeeze of my wrist. "Please, be happy."

He held my gaze with that serious look, and I waited for him to speak again, but a heartbeat passed, and that last dull light behind his eyes faded, his body stilled, and he stopped breathing.

"No." I sobbed. I shook his body. "Pa, no." I said again, pushing my hand over his heart harder, begging a beat to thump against it.

Silent sobs wracked my body as I shook, his body held against my chest.

But the silence was short lived.

Rage, agony, despair all stampeded to the surface as I tilted my head back and screamed. I screamed into the night, into his hair, into the future I had as an orphan. And, as I did so, I felt something change within me. A turn of a key that both locked something inside and unleashed something forever.

I awoke to fresh tear tracks down my cheeks, and the pillow beneath my face soaked in them. The familiar throb in my chest ached from both the effort of weeping through the nightmare and the emptiness that sat there. The piece of my heart my father resided in, gone forever.

I sat up in the bed, slowly letting the daylight seep into my skin and remind me that it was all over. That I'd already lived the worst day of my life and anything beyond it was effortless. I angled my head to the side in an effort to crack my neck, the joints sluggish and cemented from my thrashing.

My eyes, that I already knew were red and puffed with tears, fell to the door. The door that led to the hallway where servants roamed day in and day out. The hallway that led to the wing where my guardians slept. The wing that held two people who had been notified of my night terrors countless times, who chose not to check on me.

I took a deep breath to quiet the anger that thought raised and slipped from the bed. I called for a bath that one of our kindest servants brought in. Her name was Natalia, and she was closer to my age than any of the others here in the castle. She was timid, but worked quickly, always fleeing my room as soon as she could. She didn't have to tell me why – I'd discovered the reason myself a year ago.

Natalia was one of the first people in Kembertus I met, she'd been working the night I was brought into the castle from my lonesome trek. My aunt had immediately handed me off to her, even as I tried to tell Therese what had happened to me.

Natalia had drawn me a bath then, much like she did now. While I'd washed, she ran to get me a warm meal with one glass of water and another of wine. I'd never been much for drinking but that night I welcomed the buzz that washed through me, after so many hours of feeling anguish, it was nice to feel something else.

We'd become friendly. I guessed she needed a friend just as badly as I did. But her visits became curt and quiet over the next year while I mourned. I'd struggled with loneliness after that until Aurora came to fit me for my first ballgown, the employee she'd tasked with it having to stay home sick.

We became fast friends since I'd grown used to Natalia's short visits. Then a year ago, right around the time I'd met Aurora, I'd caught my aunt chastising Natalia for spending too much time in my room and finally learned that Therese was the reason she was afraid to interact with me.

It didn't take much thought to discover Therese's motives. She wanted me off and married; spending all my time with a friend who worked in the same castle as I lived wouldn't aid in that.

The sound of the door closing behind Natalia pulled me from my reverie, and I stood. The joints and muscles that ached from the violence of my nightmare ebbed at the touch of the steaming water. I did my best to ease into the warmth and forget about the memories. I prayed, not for the first time, that I wouldn't be forced to relive them again.

CHAPTER FIVE

Evaline

The bells above the door to Aurora's boutique chimed as I walked in and I smiled at the welcoming air. As the diligent saleswoman Aurora was, her head popped out from behind the hip of the mannequin she was dressing.

"Evaline!" She dusted off the knee line of her skirt and stood, and her black protective twists swayed with the movement. "I wasn't expecting to see you today." She said as she enveloped me in a hug. I didn't miss the concern that wrinkled the brown skin of her forehead. She could always tell when something was wrong.

"I know, but with my father's anniversary yesterday I wanted to see a friendly face." Her embrace tightened at the mention of my father, and I felt her nod against my shoulder.

"That's understandable," she pulled away, her brows furrowing. "Do you need anything?"

I smiled and shook my head.

Aurora picked up the tea kettle from the checkout counter and poured me a cup of lemon tea. It was her favorite, so she always had it brewed for her customers. It was among the first things you noticed when you walked in, the smell brightened the store almost as much as the multicolored fabrics lining the walls.

I looked around the room as she handed me the cup.

"Is there anyone here?" She poured a mug for herself and shook her head.

"No, we've been slow today. I think people spent more than they anticipated yesterday splurging at the first temperate market of the year."

As she spoke, I drank, nodding along as the warmth coasted down my throat.

"I'm kind of surprised though, with the Ball coming up you'd think more women would be here ordering dresses." I remarked, looking around the empty store.

Her big, dark eyes grew larger at the words. "Evaline, you cannot say such things. Now the store will be packed to the windows."

I laughed at what I thought was a joke. "Oh, you're serious?"

She nodded vehemently and brushed a stray twist from her face. "Yes! You can't tempt the Gods that way." Her fingers wove through the air. "You can have fun explaining to Jacqueline why I won't be home for dinner tonight." She feigned angst but the smile in her eyes gave her away.

I laughed, bewildered. "You said it was slow! Doesn't that tempt the Gods?"

She narrowed her eyes and pursed her lips. "It's okay when I do it." She couldn't maintain her composure as she did so, and we laughed together.

She pulled a hanger down from the nearest wall and tugged on the skirt to show me the silhouette. I let out a breathy sound and raised my hand to my chest.

"Aurora, it's magnificent." My eyes scanned over the dress. It was a soft, dusty blue that reminded me of the sky on a winter day. The bodice was corseted with boning channels that cupped the breasts and that ran up the length of the top, giving the piece its structure. At the waist the bodice tightened and the skirt flared out below it. Tulle flowed over itself in layers down to the floor.

My favorite detail was the embroidery, because I knew Aurora would have spent meticulous hours stitching it. My favorite flower, roses, were splayed in white over the dress. They gathered around the waist and draped over the hips with loose petals dusting the tulle sporadically all the way to the hem, as if they were falling from the bloom.

Aurora could do everything an expert seamstress could, but what she did best was design and embroider. And the embroidery on this dress, the perfect white roses and free-falling petals, was breathtaking.

I saw her smile from my peripheral before she spoke. "I'm glad you think so, it's yours."

My head snapped back in surprise. "Really?"

Her grin widened. "Your aunt placed the order for your Spring Solstice Ball gown months ago. She wanted something extravagant."

That didn't surprise me. After giving me a modest amount of space to mourn the loss of my father, which happened to be through my first courting season in the city, they'd spent the last year and a half worth of social gatherings attempting to set me up with the stray businessman, or heir, or both. I was the furthest thing from interested in any marriage potential and the lifestyle it would require, and they knew that. But as with most of my preferences, they disregarded me.

Aurora's voice pulled me from my thoughts.

"She gave me artistic authority over the design. Which is the first time that's happened." Aurora moved to re-hang the dress and I realized it must be heavy after holding it up for so long. "Lady Therese is usually very…" she paused as she turned back to me, contemplating what word she should use. "Particular with her designs. I was thrilled when she let me pick." She turned her head to where the dress peeked out between the rest of its neighbors on the rack. Her fingers traced the roses that hung there. "I know how much you love roses, so I thought this would be the perfect addition for the Spring Solstice Ball."

I nodded. I was unable to look away from the embroidery. "It definitely is."

Aurora lowered her voice, and I could almost feel the excitement radiating off her. "And that's not even the best part." She whispered, knotting her fingers against her chest.

I turned. "Do I want to know?"

She nodded and went behind the boutique counter. She disappeared below it for a moment, before popping back up with a small box.

I cocked my head. "What is it?"

She said nothing as she slowly opened the box's top flap and revealed the small object resting atop a bed of silk.

"Oh my." Were the only words that I could muster. Sitting in front of me was the most elegant masquerade mask I'd ever seen. I shook my head slightly. "What is this for?"

Aurora furrowed her brow. "The Lord and Lady have given the Spring Solstice Ball a theme. You didn't know that?"

I shrugged, eyes glued to the mask. "I haven't paid much attention to the planning of it." I grimaced and met her gaze. "What's the theme?"

She gave me a bemused smile. "The Fresh Start Spring Solstice Ball."

I tilted my head. "And where in that theme is masquerade implied?"

She snickered. "It's not. They must've known that because the invitations were explicit."

She bent behind the counter once more and pulled out the invitation. Her voice changed as she tilted her head back and feigned a regal accent to read the cardstock, her beautiful wide nose raising with the movement. "You are cordially invited to the Fresh Start Spring Solstice Ball. Kembertus has had its fair share of change in the last few years.

"With this being the first event of the year, and occurring in the re-birthing months of spring, we thought it only necessary that this Ball have a theme to reflect that change. This event will be a Masquerade Ball. We encourage every citizen of Kembertus to attend to this event ready to mingle.

"In this time of fresh starts, some of the most important are the ones we have with each other. This will be a night of celebration, forgiveness, and kinship. Do not judge a person by who you think they are, or what they may have done to you in the past. Allow the masks to hide those misgivings and pay attention only to their heart."

By the time Aurora finished the lengthy invite my jaw was screaming in pain. They were trying to lighten the horrific history of the kingdom, and the behavior towards women that they allowed to happen within it, with a wave of a hand and the use of a mask.

No amount of coverage would hide their true selves, and never from me.

I tried to brush it off with a chuckle, but the insincerity echoed in the silence between us. I tucked a loose strand of hair that had fallen from my braid behind my ear.

"I think if you have to explain the theme of a party, it's not a great theme."

Aurora tried to stifle her laughter, and she glanced around to make sure we were alone, but she nodded in agreement. She never wanted a customer to hear her speak negatively about the kingdom or its leaders, it wasn't great optics for the business that sold dresses to be worn to parties in their castle.

I looked back down at the mask.

"This is beautiful and matches the dress perfectly."

I leaned forward for a closer look. There was small stitching spanning the length of the mask, which matched the dress, but the bell over the door startled me.

Aurora snatched the box and shoved it back under the counter. Before I could turn around fully, she was walking to the customer. She threw me a smile and led the woman through the store. Since they were going to the back, I knew she'd be busy for a while fitting a dress, so I moved to leave. I gave one last long look at my own dress that hung on the rack, and when I walked outside there was a small smile on my face.

"Evaline, how many times have I asked you not to come to dinner in your street clothes?" My aunt's insult floated down the dining table. The small shred of joy I'd held at Aurora's fled the moment Therese's shrill voice rang out.

I barely held back an eye roll. "I'm sorry. I went to the boutique and lost track of time. I would've been late for dinner if I'd changed."

At the mention of the boutique, she perked up. She gave a dismissive wave of her hand, her mood changing at once.

"Not a problem at all." She rested her elbows on the table and drew her hands together below her pointed chin. "Did you see your dress?"

"Yes." I reached for my glass of water and drank from it. When I realized she was waiting for further explanation, I made sure to take my time. I set it down gently, and her highly arched brow twitched with the effort of maintaining a sunny expression. "It is beautiful."

She clapped with a squeal and her blond hair bounced with the movement.

"It is, isn't it?" She peered at my uncle, who sat at the head of the table to my left. He didn't pay us any mind, only eating, and draining his second glass of wine. When she fixed her cold blue stare back to me, she had a smug smile on her face. "I love how Aurora can always make someone's vision come to life."

I nodded in agreement; she was an artist.

My aunt continued. "I knew she was the perfect person to give my design. When I told her I wanted there to be roses on it, because of how much you love them, I knew she'd execute it perfectly."

I clenched my fist around my fork as she took credit for Aurora's vision. I knew it wasn't worth arguing over, she never took accountability. But it still bothered me.

"I saw my mask too. I didn't realize there was a theme for the Ball."

Therese scoffed. "Of course you didn't. You reject every invitation to help plan events anytime I offer." She took a sip of wine and winced against the taste. "Raymond, could you get me a glass of that other red I love? This one is suited more to Elijah's taste."

Raymond, the salt and pepper haired servant came forward nodding and picked up her glass.

"No, I'll take it." My uncle said as Raymond moved to walk away with the wine. He nodded once more and crossed the table to Elijah.

He tried to set the glass on the table, but Elijah swept it out of his hand. Raymond's face remained unchanged at the behavior as he strode from the dining room to fetch Therese a different wine.

My aunt was rolling her eyes at my uncle when I turned back toward her. She didn't like how much the Lord drank. By the looks of his disheveled mousy hair and flushed cheeks that were normally ashen, he was well in his cup already.

She waved dismissively. "As I was saying, if you were more involved in the planning of events, you wouldn't find these things out secondhand. But yes, there is a theme." She straightened and pride beamed from her small mouth. "It was my idea for the Fresh Start theme. The masks will be a classic touch, but even more importantly it will give the citizens of Kembertus a chance to meet people they've previously ignored." She gave me a pointed look. "You could work on that, too."

I nodded vaguely and picked up a dinner roll to butter it.

"I think you haven't been fair to most of the eligible men in Kembertus. If you'd just give them a chance you may really fancy one of them." She pressed. In my peripheral I saw her, once again, turn to my uncle. No doubt looking for reinforcements.

My uncle cleared his throat.

"Yes, there's eligible men here, but there will also be travelers attending the party. Perhaps you'll take a liking to one of them." They were both nodding and looking at me expectantly, Therese more enthusiastically than Elijah, but he continued. "I have friends coming from all over, even Vestaria."

I almost cringed at the name of the only kingdom between us and the Kromean Sea. They were a cutthroat people. Only concerned with money and power, and willing to do whatever it took to secure it. They were another one of the cities the Madierian Kingdoms refused to work with until they began treating women better. Vestaria had not accepted the critique as Kembertus had, their society remained unchanged.

Of course, I knew more about Vestaria than most. It was rumored that Vasi lingered there. Working with those in power to maintain their friendship. There were countless stories of the high murder rates in Vestaria, but I knew better, thanks to my father. Vasi lurked those streets and killed their people, and their rulers let them. I didn't know what kind of deal they had, and I hoped I never found out.

Just then Raymond re-entered the dining room, another glass of red wine in his hand. My uncle was too focused on the lamb he was cutting through, oblivious to everyone around him. But with my head tilted down I was still able notice the way Therese's hand met Raymond's as he placed the glass, and their fingers lingered together on the stem for a moment.

I furrowed my brows and looked away, not missing the small genuine smile that now adorned her lips.

"That reminds me, Elijah, have you heard from Nathaniel? Does he have enough room at the inn?" She was referring to Aurora's father who, while having several employees to manage the inn, often did so himself.

My uncle shook his head. "I haven't talked to him, but you're right we should check in."

"I can go into town tomorrow and ask Nathaniel." I volunteered.

My aunt turned to me and squinted her eyes, as if trying to decipher why I was being helpful. It would be another task to get me out of the castle and away from potential talk of courtship.

I shrugged. "You said I don't participate enough in event planning. The least I could do is go down to see Nathaniel and ask if he's going to be booked up."

Therese smiled at that and I could already see the flush of victory spreading over her fair skin. "That is very thoughtful of you, Evaline. Thank you. That would be lovely."

I nodded, just thankful for another excuse to roam the streets, for another afternoon spent outside of these walls.

An odd sensation eased its way under the relief as I poked at my food. I tried to name it, digest what it could possibly be, but the only definition I could call up was a mix of anticipation and longing. I tried to push it away with thoughts of what I could do tomorrow after visiting Nathaniel.

CHAPTER SIX

Maddox

With each step toward Kembertus I felt an anxiety tighten inside of me, felt my heart beat out of rhythm every few pumps. I wasn't sure if it was the temperature cooling, the knowledge that Wallace wouldn't be there, or the ache for home that was starting to take over every thought along the way. But the closer we got to Kembertus, the more unsettled I felt.

It didn't help that it was the middle of the night and we moved silently, trying to listen for any Vasi. There'd been more and more reports in recent years of Vasi moving closer to the Madierian and no Kova liked the sound of that.

Wyott sighed beside me. I knew he must feel that ache for home too. Not just for home – for his mate. The further mates were from each other, the more a dull pain throbbed within them. A piece of their heart was missing, being pulled farther and farther away.

I didn't know the feeling; I'd never met mine.

All my friends, including Wyott, had found theirs when they were young. Most of them met as children, because we'd all grown up in Rominia together. That was how Cora and Wyott met. Equivalent to humans of about nine years old, but they'd already been alive twenty years by then. They started as the best of friends until they reached adolescence and felt more for each other. When the bond deepened and they fell into true and real love, I stood beside and pined for my own.

I loved Wyott like he was my own brother. He'd practically been raised to be, living with my parents and I after his father was killed. Just before Cora moved to Rominia and he met her. But the more I had to watch their love for each other bloom, the more my heart ached for the same connection.

In a culture where finding your mate is as divine as the Goddess who ties the bonds, not having one was difficult. Even more difficult after waiting nearly two hundred years.

It was rare to not find your mate within your first century. I knew my situation worried my parents. More my mother than my father, and I think it only worried her because she knew how badly I wanted it. How much I wanted to meet my counterpart, my other half. The person who would complete my world. Who I could love until I left this one.

Sometimes, after training, I would find myself alone. Wyott would be off with Cora, in the house they now shared together, and I'd pick one of the books off the shelves in my room. I'd sink into my bed, fall into a romance novel, and feel the weight of waiting on my chest. The fear that maybe I'd never find her. That maybe, the Goddess of Fate didn't think I deserved it.

I swallowed that same fear again, trying to erase the thoughts from my mind. My gaze drifted up to the stars, barely visible between the swaying tree canopies overhead.

A scream rang into the night, piercing my ears, and I'm sure Wyott's too, as our heads snapped toward it.

We didn't wait to see if it was a fluke, or a trick of the wind. Our ears were too keen to ever question what we heard.

Branches whipped past us and the forest floor beneath our feet crunched.

Another scream sounded clearer than before. A young girl.

"Stop, please don't hurt her! Take me instead!" An older man's voice begged. A chill ran down my spine as I recognized the plea only a father could make.

I pushed to run faster and broke through the thicket before Wyott, the scene clear in front of me.

A Vasi stood with his arms wrapped around an adolescent girl's body, mouth poised over her neck. Her father was on his knees, their belongings on the ground, his head bleeding from a blow that must've come from the Vasi.

Wyott appeared at my side and all three heads turned to us.

I heard the Vasi's sneer and watched as his eyes rolled.

"Just let me have my fun boys. Go on your way." His lips remained in the young girl's red hair. I watched as she shivered in his arms.

"How about you let her go, and we let you keep your life?" Wyott offered.

I hid my dissatisfaction for the words. I didn't want to leave this monster alive one more minute, but if it meant keeping this family intact, I'd have no choice.

"I'm getting pretty fucking sick of you Kova on your high horses. You're always looking down at us as if you're so much better. But you know? You're not. We're the same." His grip on the girl loosened, moving his head away from hers just a bit to lecture us. "You think you're better because you don't kill the humans you feed from? You're not. And you can't tell me there isn't an urge to kill every time your teeth sink into their flesh."

Wyott's hand flickered down to the blade at his side, small but sharp, a meager enough movement that I was the only one who saw it. With the Vasi prattling on, it was clear that he didn't notice Wyott move. But I knew what he was trying to tell me. I didn't bother nodding or making any other indication of acknowledgement. We'd worked together too long.

"You know the blood tastes sweeter when they're afraid, don't you? Like the richest cream you've ever tasted." He clicked his tongue. "Even sweeter than it smells." His eyes moved away from the girl's flesh and landed on us. "You really should try it sometime." He squinted his eyes and dropped his voice. "Join us, I promise it's more fun on this side of the—" Wyott's blade whispered through the air. The Vasi's hand flew up to stop it. But the blade still hit home, half in his hand and half in his face.

I was already moving, sprinting toward the pair. As soon as the blade made impact I grasped the girl and snatched her from his arms as gently as I could. I held her to my chest, hiding her face away from the scene, and ran in a flash back to her father. The entire exchange taking only a few seconds.

The Vasi's hiss cut through the forest.

"Stupid." He said as he pulled the dagger from his cheek. We watched as the cut healed in real time. He'd recently fed. "You stupid Kova."

Wyott stood in the space between us and the Vasi. I stepped in front of the humans, shielding the two with my body.

The father wrapped his arms around her as she whimpered from fear.

"It's okay, Marnie." I heard the father whisper, and the Vasi shook his head.

"You Kova can never mind your own, can you?" He took a step toward us and Wyott mirrored the movement.

"I don't know that this can be deemed as simply as not minding our own. But if it is, then no, we can't." Wyott seethed at the Vasi, whose red eyes lit with amusement.

"One day playing the hero will get you killed." The Vasi spat.

"But it won't be today." I said, and Wyott ran forward, sword drawn on the Vasi in a second. The Vasi pulled out his own sword, but his teeth were already bared, another weapon at his disposal.

I stayed with the family long enough to know that the Vasi wouldn't slip from Wyott's grasp and get to them. Then I joined Wyott. Their swords were clashing and when I came from behind the Vasi. He tried to slash out at me, but he was overpowered and overwhelmed. Wyott dug his blade into the Vasi's side; not lethal, but a nuisance. The Vasi shrieked.

I came up behind him, striking my fist through the flesh of his back. My knuckles broke the cage of his ribs in an instant, and I closed my fist over his heart.

He went still. He didn't drop his sword, but he didn't fight back.

Wyott stood in front of him, eyes still wild with the thrill of a fight, trying to even his breaths. I opened my mouth to speak, head right beside the Vasi's, but he cut me off. "Your First sent you looking for something here too, didn't he?" I stiffened at the mention of my father. He was the first Kova to be gifted immortality by the Gods.

"What do you mean?" I asked, eyes flicking to Wyott's.

"You thought you were the only ones who knew something happened here?"

My father had only mentioned that he was receiving odd reports from this area. Nothing specific. An uneasy feeling settled deep in my stomach.

"Why did he send you?" My fingers twitched against his heart.

The Vasi chuckled. "So Kovarrin still chooses to keep his people in the dark?" His head lolled back toward me. "Even his own son?"

I pursed my lips, wondering how he'd known I was the son of the First. But before I could say anything else, I heard the girl whimper again. She was still shaking with fear. I looked at Wyott, who nodded before turning back toward the family.

I lowered my voice to whisper in the Vasi's ear. "I don't know what you're looking for, or why Vasier sent you." I hated saying the name, and almost never did around Wyott out of respect for what Vasier had done to his father. "But I don't have time to find out. And you're lucky for that, otherwise every bone and organ would be pulled out until you were begging for him, and even then, he couldn't save you."

With the last word, I pulled my hand free. His heart gave one last phantom beat, then his body thumped dully against the forest floor.

Wyott knelt toward the father as I came up behind them.

"How are you doing?" He asked.

The father's eyes were still wide, his arms wrapped around his daughter. His hand was holding the back of her head tight against his chest, shielding her from what had just occurred.

He opened his mouth to speak, but no words came out. He closed it again and he simply stared between Wyott and I.

I took a knee beside Wyott, closest to the girl. "We can make you both forget."

The father's startled face swung to me. "What?"

I gave him a small smile, trying to calm him. "Among our powers of strength and speed, we're able to give humans commands that make their mind forget certain events."

His eyes widened even more, and he shook his head violently. "No! I don't want you messing with our minds!"

I shook my head gently. "Sir, I promise we won't do anything that harms you. We will only take away these painful memories." My eyes drifted to his daughter, her body still quivering. "She doesn't have to live with this for the rest of her life. She doesn't deserve that."

He looked down at her, the tension in his shoulders eased just a bit. He looked between Wyott and I again.

"You won't hurt her?"

I shook my head. "We will not hurt her, or you. If we wanted that, we never would've stopped your attack."

He frowned, and I could tell he was working it out in his head. I could just compel him to give us permission, but that was wrong. This was his decision to make, and I wouldn't take it from him.

Finally, he looked at me with misty eyes. "Do it, but only for her. I need to remember." He said, clenching his jaw. "For our safety."

That was the choice I was hoping he'd make. I wasn't a proponent of humans knowing we existed, but I wanted as many people to be protected from Vasi as possible.

"What do you need her to do?" He asked.

"I just need her to make eye contact with me. It'll only take a moment."

He nodded and I watched the fatigue churn behind his eyes, he had to digest so much information tonight.

"Marnie, I need you to look at this kind man for one second, okay? Then this will all go away, and everything will be okay again." He spoke into her hair.

I moved slightly, putting an extra foot of distance between myself and the girl. Just enough to offer them more comfort, but to keep me close enough that the compulsion would work.

A long breath passed before she moved. Timid, she eased her head from his chest, and looked at him.

"Do you promise?" Her voice was weak.

He nodded, his eyes filling with tears. "I promise."

She blinked hard, then turned to me. I smiled at her, and as soon as I had contact, I spoke.

"You are going to forget that you saw me, this man," I pointed to Wyott, "and the bad man with red eyes." She nodded, her look distant. "You and your father were on a walk, and he fell, hitting his head on a tree trunk. But you helped him up and he's going to be perfectly fine. You're going to continue on your journey and be just as happy as you were before this. Do you understand?"

Marnie nodded. "I understand." This time her voice was strong. Her spine straightened and all traces of stress were gone from her features. She turned to her father. "We need to get you home, father. We need to wrap your head and clean your wound."

His jaw dropped at her transformation. Gone was the traumatized girl. She spoke easily and calmly. Marnie stood and pulled him up with her.

We rose with them, but already she acted as if we weren't there.

"Are you positive you don't want us to take your memories too?" Wyott asked the father.

He nodded. "I'm sure. Thank you." He looked between us, toward the body of the Vasi dead on the ground. "Thank you so much."

"Of course." I offered. "May the Gods be kind."

Wyott and I watched them pick their way back to the path until they disappeared at a curve covered by the shadow of an ancient oak tree.

CHAPTER SEVEN

Evaline

My braid was heavy on my back, jostling as I walked. I was thankful to get out of the castle after spending a long night, and morning, in my bedroom.

I could typically sneak out whenever I wanted to by scaling the wall outside of my window, if it was dark enough not to be noticed, but I'd rarely done so.

The street was bustling around me as I walked toward the inn. There were women racing past me, heading to various shops, cold weather cloaks flapping at their calves. Some children were playing with a stray dog in an alley across the street, and a few men were taking up too much space in the walkway as I tried to move past them, oblivious to everything besides their own conversation. The warmth from the days before had been fleeting, and there was a painful chill in the air more characteristic of Kembertus spring. Everywhere I looked, I saw pink tipped noses and puffs of vapor as people spoke.

The freezing road hurt beneath the too thin slippers that my aunt forced me to wear. She thought boots, my preference because of their warmth and comfort, were unfitting for a young woman. She also disliked when I wore pants, like I was today. I didn't mind wearing skirts, but it was too cold for it.

I rubbed my hands together, warming them with friction as I approached the end of the road, where the inn sat, and gasped. There was a haphazard line queued at the door waiting for entry into Nathaniel's reservation lobby.

I'd expected there to be a handful of guests based on my aunts and uncles' discussion, but never imagined this many travelers were going to be at the Spring Solstice Ball.

I slowed to a stop at the end of the line and realized that in front of me sat a feast for a pickpocket. Everyone in the group was well to do, able to afford to travel, simply for a Ball. I began to push through the crowd as gently as possible, hoping no one would disrupt me from cutting through. No one would normally stop the niece of the Lord and Lady, but if these were travelers, they wouldn't know who I was.

I moved slowly and surveilled my surroundings, looking for anyone that seemed to be out of place, or unaware.

I was so caught up that I almost walked into the back of the man in front of me. I stumbled and looked up. He was tall, with loose black ringlets on top of his head. He was far taller than me, which was significant considering I was tall for a woman. His shoulders were broad, and I could tell even beneath the leather top he wore that he was muscular.

My eyes traveled down, from his strong arms to the dark skin stretched over veined hands, which were hooked into a belt holding an axe. My eyes widened as I stepped back and looked over what could only be described as a small arsenal strapped to his hips and back. Daggers, throwing knives, swords. Who traveled like this, and who traveled like this just to go to a measly Ball?

My father used to joke that the man who wore the most swords often knew how to use them the least.

I had to bite back my chuckle at what my father would think of this man. But just as quickly as the nostalgia came on a different feeling washed over me, faster, an urge shoved me forward, and my chest constricted with the feeling.

The hair on the back of my neck stood and I noticed the man begin to sway on his feet slightly, a show of discomfort. I took a deep breath and swallowed the unease. In his jostling I saw a small blade resting on the back of his left hip. Not a chance he'd feel me swipe that. I lifted a hand, then dropped it.

I'd been wanting a dagger for as long as I'd been in this damned kingdom. When I came to Kembertus my aunt and uncle stripped me of all my weapons and my father's sword. I didn't know where the rest of my weapons were – likely locked away somewhere – but knew my father's sword hung over the fireplace of my uncle's study.

I'd been saving all my money for a dagger and holster, but if I swiped this one, I'd be halfway there. It was small, but it would do for now. I breathed deeply and evaluated my options.

It was crowded around us. If I stood closer and removed the dagger, no one around me would see. And I doubted a man that carried this many weapons would notice the slight decrease in weight of the dagger I had my eye on.

Yes. I could take it and he would never know the difference.

My heartrate spiked and I noted that I was much more anxious than I usually was during a mark. I could feel the artery pulsing in my neck. My hand started shaking and I dropped them both down into fists.

Get it together, Evaline. There's no difference than any other time. I chastised myself.

But I knew there was more riding on this than simply stealing a purse from a rich man. In Kembertus women couldn't wield weapons, least of all me, the niece of the Lord and Lady. If I was found with it on my person before I could get it back to my room to hide it, I'd be in more trouble than ever before.

I took one last deep breath and convinced myself that it would be fine. I would nab it and slide past to go talk to Nathaniel quickly and leave.

But thinking of the innkeepers name reminded me that I had yet to speak to him. Scratch that plan, it was wiser to go see Nathaniel first. That way, when I walked back toward the mark I could take the knife and be on my way out the door in case anything went badly. That was the most important rule of pickpocketing that my father had taught me.

When in doubt, have a way out.

I clenched my fist again, trying to still the shaking, and shoved to the right. I gave the target a wide berth so he didn't notice me anymore than he had to. I ducked behind a pair of men between us, hoping they would hide me from his view. The less amount of time he saw me in his peripheral the better, my white hair wasn't the best for being discreet.

I pushed my way through to the desk. Nathaniel saw me and the small smile he gave me was bright, but I knew by the look in his hazel eyes, and by the thick rings under them, that he was tired.

"Hello, my dear! How nice of you to stop by." He stepped over to talk to me and the customer at the counter gave me a polite nod.

"Hi Nathaniel. My aunt and uncle just wanted me to stop by to see if you needed anything and to ask how the reservations were looking? They wanted to know if you'd be booked up."

He looked over the crowd. His normally rich onyx skin was pallid and slick with sweat, and his long fingers, the same thin ones that Aurora had, were shaking as he tapped his pen against the reservation book. He was busy, and I wondered why he didn't have any of his employees here helping him in the office, but just as the thought entered my mind, his assistant, Haekin, ran in from behind me and slid around the desk with Nathaniel.

Nathaniel's tension seemed to ease as he looked back to me and smiled. "We will be okay. It'll be tight but we will have a place for everyone. I never book more reservations than we can handle."

I tried to give him a reassuring smile. "Okay, well if you do need anything just let us know."

I knew this would likely be an unnecessary visit, Nathaniel had been running successful businesses for decades and knew what he was doing. My aunt and uncle likely also knew he wouldn't need anything, but they took every opportunity to appear helpful to their kingdom, without ever actually having to be.

He nodded and smiled. "Enjoy the rest of your day."

"You too, Nathaniel." I waved cheerily and made my way out of the lobby, aiming for the man with the dagger. I fixed my stare on the ground, not risking looking up at him or the man that was talking to him. That man stood on his right, better for me since the dagger was on the mark's left hip.

I would approach from the right angle, swipe it, hide it with my body, and be out the door with three steps. I raised my eyes, the men behind him were all looking up at the ceiling out of boredom or talking to each other.

The closer I got the more aware I was of his presence. It was like I could feel the heat of his body even though I was a few paces away. My heart sped up as I approached, and that odd pulling sensation in my gut tugged again.

As our paths met, my hand flashed out and closed around the hilt. But just as quickly, his own wrapped around the inside of my elbow, gentler than I deserved.

I stilled. He lowered his head until I could hear his deep voice in my ear, low and amused.

"I don't know whether I should be honored or agitated that you would pick me of all the men in this room to pickpocket." The mocking of his tone sent a wave of annoyance over my face, but I still didn't look up. If I was caught, my aunt and uncle... I didn't even know what they would do.

I ground my teeth and whispered back. "Surely you don't use all these weapons."

I felt the breath from his chuckle over my ear. "And you would?"

I tensed. He didn't know me, and he was already making assumptions just because I was a woman. I knew I shouldn't respond at all. I knew I should pull my hand off and walk away, but I couldn't. The energy passing between us was static and strong, and overwhelming.

"Better than you." My voice dripped with venom.

"I'd sincerely love to see that." He said and his grip on my elbow pulsed. Someone walked by and jostled me, pushing me closer to him. My shoulder touched the front of his and his other hand moved to catch me by the waist.

I felt his sharp intake of breath more than I heard it, but he cleared his throat to disguise it. "What's a woman in Kembertus wanting with a dagger?"

I'd had enough. Enough of his questions, enough of his snarky tone, and enough of the heat passing between us that made my heart race faster than anything I could remember. My head snapped up, eyes locking with his.

"What's a—"

But then I felt it. I saw it.

His hands tightened around me. His eyes widened and his throat bobbed, jaw opening as he looked at me. His head jerked back a fraction of an inch, knocking a stray black curl onto his forehead, half covering a fine scar through a thick eyebrow.

But what shook me to my core and sent ice freezing through my veins, were his dark gray eyes, like shining gems against the cool bronze of his skin. Everything about his face drew my attention back to his eyes. The broad planes of his cheeks and sharp jawline that were coated with a dusting of dark facial hair. Gray eyes. The bump in the bridge of his nose and his thick lower lip, where another scar sat proudly. Gray eyes. His soft chin. Narrow temples. Gray eyes, with dark smudges around them, and beautiful thick eyelashes further intensifying the steel color that only belonged to Kova.

I couldn't think, I couldn't move.

I should reply, but I should leave. I should flee before he realized who I was. I should run before someone else noticed our weird exchange. With all these scenarios running through my mind I was quite sure the one thing I should *not* do was voice to him that I knew exactly what he was.

But the words were out before I could stop them.

"What's a Kova doing in Kembertus?" My voice was so low even I almost missed it. For a moment I hoped I'd imagined saying them, or that perhaps I said them so softly he didn't hear.

But he did, based on the flicker in his hooded lids. Neither of us spoke and the world around us was unchanged. Everyone carried on their small conversations, the buzz of excitement was still sweeping the room. But now, the buzz between this man and I was almost painful. Yanking at my chest and taking my breath.

It seemed like he felt it too. But was this feeling just another one of the Kova's extra abilities? To lure their prey?

Prey.

I was prey once.

The thought of his twin species, the Vasi, and my horrific experience with them hit my mind for the first time in this entire exchange.

Stupid, I was so stupid.

I'd been so caught up in whatever this spell was that he had over me, that I somehow forgot that I was in the hands of a killer.

My father could tell me all he wanted that the Kova could be good, but the fact remained that my only experience with the immortals that drank blood, to date, had been the night that one had killed him.

The man beside my mark seemed to notice our interaction then, turning to look at us. I met his eyes briefly—gray. A few shades lighter than his friend, but gray all the same.

That put me over the edge. The thoughts of the last time I'd interacted with a being like this filled my mind. The Vasi. I could feel his teeth in my muscle, I could feel the way his head and spine felt against my blade.

It was too much. I pulled my arm away and he let me go. I rushed out of the inn.

I was embarrassed and scared and overwhelmed. I felt him move behind me, following, but as soon as I met the door I broke into a sprint and knew exactly where I was going. I sent a prayer up to the Gods to keep him from following me.

"Wait! Who are you?" His yell ricocheted off the stone buildings around us. I cringed at the words, hoping that no one standing there knew who I was either.

When I turned the corner that led to the cemetery, I ran faster, the slaps of my ill-fitting slippers loud against the slick cobblestones beneath me. Pain from the bricks bit my arches.

I nearly fell from exhaustion onto my father's grave. I landed on all fours, focusing on my breath, on sucking enough air back into my lungs.

When I looked up at his headstone I realized my eyes were full of tears.

What was wrong with me? Why did I ever try to take a dagger in plain sight? My arrogant thoughts flashed back. I couldn't believe that I'd assumed he was just a rich man who wore weapons for show.

I cursed at myself. I should've known better. I should've known by his muscular build that he very much did know how to use those weapons, and probably used them often. And then to tell him I knew exactly what he was? That seemed extremely dangerous. I sighed. This was just another reason why I needed a dagger.

I sat back hard, pulling my knees up to rest my elbows on them, and my head in my hands.

My father certainly never told me what to do if I was caught pick-pocketing a Kova. That seemed like an efficient way to make an enemy. I shook my head, what had I been doing pickpocketing in a room full of travelers? I was lucky he wasn't a Vasi.

The thought made my stomach quiver. It so easily could've been a Vasi. My hands started shaking. So, so dumb.

What was I thinking?

I took a breath, and tried to change my thoughts, to be kinder to myself.

I was thinking that I would do something I've done countless times in this kingdom safely. I was thinking that I was going to have a dagger to protect myself from immortals like him and the Vasi.

My hands stopped shaking and I released my hair, dragging my fingers down my face, scrubbing the tears. I rested my hands under my chin. There were two Kova in the city and now they knew that I was privy to their kind.

I fought the urge to go back to the inn to see his eyes again. To confirm what he was.

Heat flashed down my spine at the thought.

Was that the urge I was having? Or was it to see him again for another reason that had my chest fluttering?

I looked at my father's grave, reaching out and tracing his name as I'd done a thousand times since being in Kembertus.

"What do I do?" I asked the stone.

But just as it'd been since I'd lived here, and would be for the rest of my life, there was no response.

CHAPTER EIGHT

Maddox

I felt her presence as soon as she entered the lobby. The air changed and her scent hit me as hard as the rains of a summer storm.

I was talking to Wyott, quietly discussing the adventure from the night before, and we were speculating what the First Vasi could possibly want in this area when I felt her move closer. She was right behind me, and I could hear how her heart raced, smell the anticipation flooding her.

I didn't turn around. It was too crowded in here to do much of anything.

I felt her move away and then finally caught sight of her as she headed toward the front desk. Her hair was the color of an overcast sky. Somehow white and gray at the same time, and when sunlight from a nearby window caught it, it shined like polished silver.

All I could see was her long white braid, everything else was shielded by a black cloak.

I couldn't help the beat of my heart or the way everything inside of me screamed to get closer.

I shook it off, I was probably just hungry.

I heard her interact with the innkeeper. Nathaniel was his name, by the sound of their conversation. It was quick, but my ears strained to catch every word she uttered. It seemed as if she was someone of importance here. Her aunt and uncle were at least.

She came back my way and I turned back to Wyott. He'd been speaking to me the entire time and I'd only realized it after she moved. He was discussing how we could get word back to my father that we'd run into a Vasi. It was a good point, and I hadn't given it much thought yet, but I couldn't think of much of anything as she moved closer and closer.

Her head was tilted down, still not giving me the best look at her. I kept my eyes trained on Wyott, watching her in my peripheral. I was trying not to be too obvious but every nerve in my body was thrumming. I had to see her.

Please walk this way. Please. I begged internally as she neared. Finally, she was beside me.

I smelled the floral of her hair and felt the heat of her skin even through her cloak. I heard the tick of her heart and could've laughed when I felt her hand on the hilt of one of my daggers.

She was trying to steal from me.

For fucks sake. I needed to meet her more than I needed blood. I grasped her elbow lightly, to stop her and to see if what I was feeling was all in my head. But just one touch and I could feel the energy running between us.

I tried to hide the amusement from my voice as I spoke in her ear. "I don't know whether I should be honored or agitated that you would pick me of all the men in this room to pickpocket."

She tensed and her annoyance was palpable. It only stoked the race of my heart. "Surely you don't use all these weapons."

I chuckled and watched as a few strands of her hair moved with the breath. "And you would?" I loved a woman who could fight. It showed their strength and power, and above all it kept them safe.

"Better than you."

That almost made me laugh loudly before I remembered where we were. "I'd sincerely love to see that."

My hand on her arm tightened and I had to remind myself to be gentle. But everything about her was pulling me in, I'd never experienced anything like it. I tried to quench the hope that sprang free in my chest at what this could be. Who she could be.

A passerby bumped into her, pushing her further into me until we were almost chest to chest. I caught her by the waist and for the first time noticed how tall she was, the top of her head just grazing my chin. I took a sharp breath at our proximity and cleared my throat. I continued speaking, in hopes she'd stay longer.

"What's a woman in Kembertus wanting with a dagger?" I could feel her skin heat, annoyance boiling over.

Finally, she whipped her head up toward me, a few stray hairs around her face moving out of her eyes with the movement.

"What's a—"

And the world stopped.

Time lagged around us, the chatter of the room dulled, and all I could see were the wide, ocean colored eyes staring up at me. A mix of green and blue, almond shaped and bright against ivory skin. Rose tinged freckles dotted a pointed nose. My eyes skated over her downturned lips and a dimple in her chin, and as I turned my gaze to meet hers again, I realized her high arched eyebrows were the same silver color as her hair. I nearly smiled at that.

I almost missed her similar reaction to me. Almost. Her mouth dropped open, a distraction all on its own, before slamming shut. A slight pink blush rose to her full cheeks as we studied each other.

I knew what this was. I'd heard the stories a thousand times. Prayed for it more.

But as I stared at her, in the few seconds it had been since her bright eyes peered up at me, all I could hear were my mother's words in my head.

"When the time comes, you'll know. And it'll feel like something you've known all along."

I wanted to tell her. To remove that dagger from its holster and give it to her. Tell her that she'd never want for anything again. To wrap my arms fully around her and pull her close to me, something that I'm sure would've sent her running.

But before I could do much of anything she opened her mouth again, and this time, she spoke. "What's a Kova doing in Kembertus?"

My lungs compressed at the question, at hearing the name of my kind on her lips, in a town where no one was supposed to know we even existed. My brows knitted together and the need to know more about her swelled inside of me.

I couldn't form a word. Just stared at her in surprise. Gods, for an immortal being I was not acting the part. I guess that's what it does to you, though, when you find your mate.

Wyott turned to us and she looked up at him, eyes widening.

Before I could speak, she tore herself from my grasp and headed for the door. I stood in stunned silence, looking after her with my mouth agape, when Wyott pushed me.

"What the fuck are you doing? Go!" He demanded.

I nodded, coming to my senses, and ran after her. When I met the door of the inn I saw her break into a sprint, her cloak flapped around her legs and I caught a glimpse of wide calves.

"Wait! Who are you?" The words were all I could manage in the moment. I didn't chase her, I knew that wouldn't go over well, but I couldn't stay here.

My pulse quickened as panic overtook me. I'd finally found my mate and I let her walk right back out of my life, without even knowing her name.

A man in line just outside of the door of the inn leaned toward me, his shaggy hair falling into his eyes.

"That's Evaline Manor. She's the niece of the Lord and Lady of Kembertus."

I looked at him, my eyes wide, and nodded. "Thank you so much."

I turned toward one of the forests that surrounded the city, just inside the kingdom's walls, and didn't stop walking. Wyott was right behind me as the city street disappeared behind us.

"Are you okay?" He asked, his hand resting on my shoulder as we walked.

"She's my mate." I said, my voice even and dull as I worked to process all the information just given to me.

I saw Wyott nod from the corner of my eye.

"She certainly is. I thought the tension between you two would rip the place in half." He brushed down his beard and we walked in silence.

None of this made any sense. Or it made too much sense. I hadn't decided. "She's my mate and she knows what Kova are."

"Yes, that also seems to be true." We made it to a clearing and Wyott sat on an overturned log. I paced in front of him.

Evaline Manor.

It couldn't be. It was far too particular to be a coincidence, but it didn't make any sense. I turned on my heel and paced the opposite way.

Why would Goddess Rominiava do this? Not only cross my path with Evaline's, but his too.

I realized I'd gotten lost in my whirling thoughts and turned on Wyott. "Do you remember how Wallace denied the Vasi alliance?" I asked.

He cocked his head. "Yes, why?"

My brows furrowed as I continued to detangle the strings of every interaction I'd ever had with Wallace. "But he couldn't stay in Kembertus because he was afraid of retaliation from the Vasi." Wyott nodded along as I spoke, and I swallowed hard before uttering my next words. "He fled with his pregnant wife." I stared at him, waiting.

He blinked.

"Wallace Manor. Evaline Manor." I pressed.

Wyott's small eyes grew. "Oh, Gods."

I dragged my hands through my hair. "It doesn't make any Gods-damned sense." I whispered harshly. Why would the Goddess of Fate pair me with Evaline after introducing me to Wallace all those years ago?

"Maybe it makes perfect sense." Wyott offered. "Maybe the very reason Rominiava crossed your path with Wallace was because he knew what we were. What better human to pair with a Kova than one from a line that already knows we exist?"

I took a deep breath as the realization sunk in. "Maybe."

"I don't understand though. Does she rule Kembertus now?" Wyott asked as he leaned forward to rest his elbows on his knees.

I shook my head. "No, I listened in on her conversation with the innkeeper. It sounds like her aunt and uncle took over. Elijah, wasn't that his brother's name?"

Wyott's eyes narrowed. "Is that what you were doing when you were supposed to be listening to me discuss how we tell your father about the First Vasi?"

I began rolling my eyes but then stopped. The mention of that Vasi, of the First who was looking for something in this area, had fear rippling through me.

My heart couldn't handle anymore life altering information today, and the thought that the Vasi could have been heading here, where my destiny resided, was too chilling.

"What if the First Vasi was looking for Wallace?"

Wyott shook his head. "No, it's been a couple years since he died. By now he'd know that Wallace was dead, just like your father knew."

I nodded. That was true. But I'd hoped it was the case because the alternative was worse.

"What if that Vasi was sent looking for her?" The words came out slowly, so deep they fell unsettling on the ears.

Wyott shook his head, and I could see the leaps he was trying to make to reason away this likely reality.

"Why would he even want her?" Wyott started. "Wallace is the one who betrayed him, and he's already dead. What could he want with his daughter?"

I shrugged. "The First Vasi has done crueler things for less. Maybe he wants to make an example out of Kembertus, make sure Vestaria doesn't leave the alliance, too."

Wyott stood. "Vestarians are fucked in their own right, I doubt they need to be coaxed to remain in the partnership."

I ran a hand down my face. "But it's possible. Why else would a Vasi be sneaking around here?"

Wyott shrugged. "Maybe to convince Kembertus to re-align?"

I winced. "If that was the case he wouldn't have said he was looking for something. But those were the words he used. Looking for something. Just like we were."

Wyott nodded and took a deep breath.

"Okay, yeah. I think you're right." He shrugged. "I just hoped you weren't."

I nodded. "Me too."

CHAPTER NINE

Evaline

I'd spent the last three days in the castle since seeing those Kova at the inn. I knew I shouldn't hide out, and that I couldn't do it forever, but I was waiting until the day of the market. For now, I walked into the castle library and smiled at the beaming faces of Priscilla and Megin waiting for me. I stepped up to sit beside them, opening my mouth to ask how they were, when a loud bang filled the room.

Terror launched me into action, and I jumped in front of both girls, shielding them with my body.

"Sorry!" Natalia shouted from the other end of the library. "I dropped a few books I was putting back."

My heart hammered in my chest but both girls giggled. I released a shaky breath and smiled at them. They thought I was playing a prank on them. Thank the Gods for their innocence.

Please keep it that way.

"Alright, are we ready?" I asked them.

They nodded vigorously.

"What are we going to learn about today, Miss Evaline?" Megin asked.

Seeing their grins missing teeth, and the jelly from their breakfast still in the corners of their mouth, lightened me. The heavy weight lifted from my chest. I was safe in the castle where nothing could harm me. Not a Vasi, and not a Kova.

I opened the large book I'd laid on the table before they'd arrived and smiled at each of them. "I know how much you like learning about history and geography, so I thought today we could do both."

They clapped their hands frantically and I finally felt the last of my unease lift away.

This was what I needed. I smoothed my hands over the old canvas pages as I opened the book. Priscilla and Megin scooched closer to me, leaning in to see.

"It's a map!" Priscilla announced.

I nodded. "Good job, that's exactly what it is. Can either of you tell me what it's a map of?"

Megin jostled with excitement that shone in her green eyes. "It's a map of the whole world!"

I nodded. "Exactly. This is a map of our continent Brassillion, and all the oceans that surround it." My finger found the page and brushed up to where Kembertus sat. "And that's where we live."

Megin reached over and ran her pale little finger over the name of the kingdom.

"Kem-bear-tus." She pretended to read. I knew she didn't actually know the spelling, we hadn't gotten to three syllable words yet. She recited it from memory. Regardless, I clapped.

"Yes!" My fingers kept moving over the page. "And there's Vestaria, Arlomandrah, Neomaeros, Merwinan, and Correnti. Do you know what all our kingdoms are named after?"

"The Gods!" Priscilla said, raising her hand up as she did so.

I smiled and tucked one of her thin brown curls behind her ear, her russet cheeks dimpling at the gesture. "Exactly." I turned back to the page, circling Kembertus with my finger. "Kembertus is named after Kembertic, the God of Solar. Do you know what that means?"

"The sun!" They exclaimed together.

I laughed and nodded. "Yes, the sun. He is God of fire, light, and energy. They named our kingdom after him because we were one of the first vibrant and bustling kingdoms to be created in Brassillion."

We went on to name all the oceans and the landmasses and finished the day with writing practice.

By the time they left they were tired and ready for their mid-day nap. I was itching to get back to my room.

I hurried to my armoire and dropped to my knees. Under it was where I kept my stealing's from each pickpocket. I hadn't counted it in totality for a few weeks and I was anxious to see if I had enough money before market. I moved to my bed and dumped the coins out, ears straining for any footsteps outside my room.

I counted carefully. Once. Twice. I almost shrieked with excitement when I'd finished triple checking my count. If I picked a reasonable dagger, and a holster for it, I'd have just enough money. I ran my hands over the coins, feeling their cool metal slip past my fingers.

"Evaline." My aunt shouted from outside my door. My heart leapt into my throat. As she turned the handle, all I could do was reach behind me and grab my pillow. I dropped it over the coins and shoved my head on top of it just as she walked in.

"What are you doing laying like that?" She asked.

The lie was ready on my tongue. "Nothing, I was just thinking about what kind of hairstyle I'd like for the Ball."

Her face broke into a smile. "Oh, wonderful! We can discuss over lunch. It's almost ready. Wash up." She said and exited, closing the door behind her.

That type of lie always worked with her. If she thought I was fantasizing over meeting a man at the Ball, she'd be perfectly content. She'd do anything to get me out of this castle at this point, and I still didn't really know why.

With quick hands I put the coins back in the purse and hid it. I washed and headed out of my room, a smile on my face at the thought of finally owning my own dagger.

Chapter Ten

Maddox

Three days had never passed as torturously slow before. I'd waited a lifetime to find my mate. Many lifetimes over, had I been human. And here she was. In the same kingdom as I, but so unavailable to me. I might as well have been in Rominia and she here, that's how vast the distance felt.

Wyott and I walked the streets of Kembertus, as we had been all week. I knew where she was, I'd known since that first day we'd met.

After she'd fled and Wyott and I'd made our way out of the woods, I'd followed her scent. It was impossible to ignore, even though I'd tried to for a few minutes. It was sweet and rich and with every breath she took I felt it call to me.

When it led me to a cemetery, I felt the weight of the sorrow she must feel fall on my heart. She wasn't there when I arrived, but I walked to where I knew she'd been resting and looked down.

Seeing my old friend's name on a gravestone made the reality of his death all the more real. I was immortal, I'd mourned many friends. Death was a near constant presence in my life. But to see his name on that stone, in a kingdom that should be his, just having found out that his daughter was my mate, made the sorrow hit me harder than I would've expected.

"I'm sorry, Wallace." I'd said, shoving my hands into my pockets and staring down at his headstone. "I'm sorry that I'm the one here instead of you. I'm sorry that I didn't come back to check on you sooner." I shook my head, how easily I could've been here to prevent this from happening. For such a warrior to be taken out by a group of bandits, with his daughter in tow, no less, it was incorrigible. Unjust. "But I promise you, from now until my very last day, I will protect her with each and every breath I take."

I didn't know how he'd feel about his friend being destined for his daughter, even if I'd never known her until that day, but it didn't release the thought from my mind. Because I'd hoped he'd be happy. I'd hoped he'd be comforted in knowing that the soldier who stood beside him at the gate of Neomaeros, slicing through enemies to keep the innocent people of the kingdom safe, was now going to be doing the same for his daughter.

But as Wyott and I walked through the streets of Kembertus I found myself filled with unease. I didn't like the idea that the leader of the Vasi was looking for Evaline. I liked that I hadn't gotten to see her since we met even less. Keeping her safe would be far easier if she knew who I was. Not just a random Kova she ran into.

I knew telling her we were mates was the last thing I could do at the moment, or anytime soon. She fled after seeing me once – if she found out we were mates, who knows what she would do.

I knew she was in the castle, and each night Wyott and I did a sweep of the streets of Kembertus. If a Vasi ever got in we would know. I didn't like following her around without her knowledge, but I'd rather ensure her safety than her affinity for me. Even if we did get to know each other better and she disliked me, or chose someone else, I'd always be there for her. In whatever capacity she'd allow.

But for now, I hoped it wouldn't come to that.

"Do you think she spends all her time in the castle, or do you think she's avoiding us?" Wyott asked as we walked down the main street of the city.

"I think it's the latter. Seeing us in Kembertus, knowing what we were, that startled her. Rightly so, but I think she's avoiding us and just hopes we'll leave soon."

Wyott nodded. "Great. She's just as stubborn as you." Then rolled his eyes. "That's going to be really fun for me."

I chuckled and looked around. A few tables had been setup along the side of the street, even though it was nearing midnight and there was no one around.

"There must be an event here tomorrow." I observed.

Wyott slapped my shoulder. "Hopefully the blacksmith will come."

My eyes cut to him. "Why?"

He wagged his head, as if the answer was obvious. "So I can buy more weapons?" Okay, I guess the answer was obvious.

But it made me laugh regardless. "Wyott you absolutely do not need any more weapons."

He shook his head and pulled one of his daggers out. "You see? This blade has a chip in it. I knew I shouldn't have bought it from that little cart in Merwinan, it was probably off a pirating ship, and they always have the worst weapons."

I shook my head. "I'm not even going to argue, you just do what makes you happy."

He nodded. "That is the kind of support I was looking for." He re-sheathed his blade and then his face turned serious. "Can we talk about the First now?"

My chest tightened at the pain in his voice, and I turned to him. I knew he wasn't referring to my father, he'd just call him by his name.

"Yes, I'm sorry we haven't sooner. What did you want to discuss?"

We turned down a side street, staying close to the castle but still within the city below it.

"I think we should find a raven to send to the Lord of Neomaeros, and he'll send word to your father for us." I nodded; it was a good idea.

We could find a regular raven here, and the Lord of Neomaeros would have the proper raven to send to my father. Only white ravens were used to communicate with the Kova, it helped the birds not to be caught by humans because they disguised as gulls when flying.

"He needs to know. There has to be a reason that he'd send us here and once we arrive, we find that a Vasi was also sent by his First?"

"You're right. Tomorrow we'll go find one, it shouldn't be too hard." I said.

He nodded, but I knew his unease hadn't lifted.

"Is there anything else you wanted to discuss?"

I saw the muscle in his jaw twitch.

"I just don't like hearing about the First Vasi being involved in anything around me, I don't like the idea of him being on the continent and harming anyone else."

I nodded and clasped my hand over his shoulder. "I know. But we'll find him. One day, we'll get him."

He nodded, but his muscles didn't loosen.

In the entire time I'd known Wyott, he was not a person who hated. He was not someone who held onto anger at all. But if there was one being in this world whom he hated more than anything else, it was the First Vasi. And that was because of what he'd done to Wyott's father.

CHAPTER ELEVEN

Evaline

My legs ached below me. I'd started a quick pace when I'd left my father's body and hadn't let up, each step fueled by both anger and fear. Anger at what I'd just witnessed, anger that I couldn't save him, anger that he was gone. But fear infected all else; fear of the Vasi.

I was so afraid that I'd run into another that I'd walked straight through the night, all day, until the sun had fallen again. Based on my father's predictions I should've arrived in Kembertus during daylight, but without a horse I didn't know where that put me. We hadn't been moving much faster when we rode the horses, so I hoped that I was nearing the gates. That at any moment, at each turn in the path, there'd be an opening in the trees, and there it'd be, rising up from the foreground. But with each turn there was only more path.

I gritted my teeth and forced my legs to continue moving. The muscles strained, both underfed and dehydrated.

When the horses had run off they'd done so with all of our food and water. With everything we owned. The only items I carried were the clothes on my back, the couple of daggers still strapped to me, the locket on my neck, and the lone sword swaying from the holster on my belt.

After I'd torn myself away from my father and did the best that I could to give him a sacred burial – which had just been finding a few wildflowers nearby and sprinkling them over his chest with a prayer to Mortitheos – I'd grabbed his sword and the locket that he always wore around his neck.

I shuddered as the icy breath of night coasted up my legs, seeping into my skin, despite the thick clothes and cloak that clung to me. The dried blood from both myself and my father stiffened the fabric. The night was a veil of darkness around me, and I walked with my head down. My eyes adjusted to the shadows just enough to see the few feet of path in front of me.

I tried to force the thoughts of what I'd had to endure the night before from my mind, but it was impossible, and the longer I let them fill my mind, the more sorrowful I became. One moment I was tripping my way down a dark path with feet that were nearing numbness, and the next I was sobbing and almost falling on my face with each step.

I tried to quiet the sounds, but I couldn't. My body hurt too fiercely from the exertion and my chest felt as if it had been ripped open.

I flinched when I felt a stick snap beneath my weight. I hadn't seen it lying in the path, my tears blurring my already altered vision, but the sound it made reverberated through the quiet forest. I stopped moving, listening for any sound around me, hoping I hadn't just given away my position. An eerie feeling washed over me, and I straightened. I was not alone.

"It always astonishes me…" A voice floated toward me. I suppressed a shiver that began to rake through me and clenched my jaw. "How many young women I stumble upon in the middle of the forest, in the middle of the night." It was a man's voice, deep and frightening in the dark. He was somewhere in front of me, farther down the path. Standing between Kembertus and I. "Because what could they possibly be thinking? It's barely safe for a woman to travel alone in daylight, but at night? Almost never."

I swallowed and surveyed my surroundings, what little of them I could see. I could back away from him, but that would push me away from my destination. I could go to either side and sprint through the woods and hope I didn't fall, but it was so likely. The moon was covered by clouds tonight. The sky was as black as the shadows around me.

"So, what am I supposed to do?" His voice was closer this time. I needed to act quickly. "Help the women?" I heard his clothes jostle, as if he shrugged. "Get them to safety, just so they can repeat the same mistake again, on another moonless night?" Closer, still. Back – I'd just have to run back, for now. Running through the woods this close to him was a death sentence. But if I ran away, back down the path, and then ducked into the woods, there was a chance he wouldn't be able to see me.

I slowly pulled my cloak's hood over my head. If there was any light out here, I knew it'd reflect on the white tendrils and I'd be exposed.

"I could do that, but there's no lesson learnt." He was too close now, I had to move. I took a hesitant step back. "And it's far less enjoyable for me."

His chilling words sent a hardly veiled threat ringing through the abyss between us and I pivoted. My body was poised to sprint away, and I did, but that's what made the impact with the man behind me so painful.

I gasped at the contact.

"Thought he was alone, aye?" The man said, his arms already tightened around my body. Even being this close to him I couldn't see his face, but I could smell the liquor that doused his breath.

I wrestled in his grasp.

"Let me go." I gritted out, trying to keep my voice steady, and as menacing as possible, even though my heart was banging against my chest.

"But that would defeat the point of my whole lecture thus far, wouldn't it?" The man from before said.

Surrounded by them, the man with his grip on me let go. A circle of wolves around a single doe.

"Where are you from, kitten?" The man behind me cooed, his fingers reaching forward and sliding down the arm of my cloak.

I considered lying. I considered what I'd say instead, and what it would even mean if I told the truth. I decided that my energy was more valuable focusing on fighting my way out.

"Neomaeros." My tone was clipped.

I heard them chuckle around me, their breath coasting over my face. I had to fight the urge to gag.

"Damn. I was hoping you'd say somewhere more fun, like Arlomandrah."

I clenched my jaw. I knew exactly where these men were from.

"I'm sorry to disappoint." My hands were at my sides, but my weapons were veiled by my cloak. They couldn't see them, but I couldn't easily reach them without a noise.

"You, a disappointment? Never. Not when Lonix and I found ourselves bored out of our gourds here." The man behind me continued. "But now that you've graced us with your presence, I have a feeling we'll be entertained for hours."

Horror washed through me as comprehension finally flooded my mind. I was in the middle of a dark forest, fully surrounded by two men who clearly had nothing but bad intentions.

"Just let me go. I'll be out of your hair in a matter of minutes."

The man in front of me laughed. "You heard the man. You're our entertainment for the night." He took a step closer to me. The space I had between them was being eaten up. "If you survive that long."

I shrieked, damn the Vasi. Let them all hear me and come. I'd rather deal with the demons I knew than these monsters of men who'd torture and kill women just because they were bored.

I drew my dagger then, whipping it out in front of me and slashing haphazardly at the man in front. I didn't have the time or the room to make a great hit, but the blade skimmed around his chest, and he hissed.

"You bitch!"

Before I could swing the blade with more force, two strong arms looped around me and caged my forearms to my chest, the movement causing the dagger to fall from my hand. The man behind held me against him and I cursed.

"Things are going to be much more difficult if you keep putting up a fight." He snapped in my ear.

My heart pounded against my chest. I had only fractions of a second to consider my options. I couldn't fight off two men at once, no matter how much training my father had provided me. But I was close to the trees. If I could escape, as long as there wasn't a third to catch me, I'd make it into the woods around the path and hide. In this dark there was no way they'd find me if I was quiet this time. I re-evaluated.

Yes, the man behind me had a grip on both arms. But the grip was over my cloak. Hope blossomed in my chest as an idea struck.

"I don't suppose you men would like to negotiate?" I offered; my voice hoarse from screaming. The men didn't speak, and I took that as my cue. "I have jewelry I could offer you."

"Is that so?" The one in front of me said, recovering from his cut.

"Yes." I said when I realized they probably wouldn't be able to see a nod. "A necklace." My fingers crawled upward, I knew they could only see the vaguest of movements in the darkness. So when I eased the single button of my cloak undone, they wouldn't know.

Without warning I moved. Pulling left, away from the man behind me, and ducking under the arms of the man in front as my cloak slid over the sleeves of my tunic.

The man who held me was surprised, a sound of shock escaping him as I slipped from his grip and began to run down the path.

My braided hair thumped against my back as I ran, the cloak hood no longer in place to secure it. The forest debris threatened to trip me with every step, branches tore at my face and arms, but I refused to slow. *My heart stuttered in my chest, working to keep me moving, keep my legs pumping, keep me running so that I could escape the path and make it to a safe place in the woods.*

Pain suddenly seared through the back of my scalp as I was ripped to the ground by my braid. The wind knocked out of my chest as I made impact and a flash of pain lit up my arm from my wrist that had buckled beneath me.

No. I thought to myself. *Gods, no.*

The two men hauled me up and dragged me back in between them.

"That isn't a great negotiation tactic," one slurred over me until my back was pressed against the rough bark of a tree behind me.

One of them took hold of both my wrists, pinning them above me with one hand and pushing them into the bark until I heard another crack in my already broken wrist. I bit off my cry of pain and my mind raced to find a way to save myself.

"Let me go and I'll make you rich, just tell me what you want." I pleaded, my voice thick with pain.

The man beside me chuckled. "We already told you what we want, and it isn't jewelry or money, we have plenty of that already."

I started to scream, but the man beside me already had a hand moving over my mouth. Tears burned the backs of my eyes as my face grew hot from screaming into a void. I kicked my ankles and swung my wrists, even the one that throbbed. But nothing I did mattered.

The man in front of me tried to grab my ankles. "Do you have any rope?" He asked the other.

"No, it's all back at the tent." He hissed.

"Well then that's where we have to take her."

I thrashed my feet, not letting him get a hold on them. I didn't stop thrashing, even when they hissed at me to, even when the grip on my wrists grew tighter, even as the places where my skin met the bark behind me screamed for relief.

My eyes felt as if they'd burst out of the socket from the strain as I screamed against the dirty hand over my mouth. I could taste the salt of his sweat and bile rose in my throat.

I wished they would stop, wished that anyone would hear me. Wished that my father wasn't dead and that he'd come bounding down this path at any moment to save me.

Time slowed as my thoughts wandered to my father. A soldier, a protector, who wasn't here to do so now. I thought of all the days we'd spent together, sparring in the backyard of our home dozens of miles away. How he'd taught me to fight with a sword, a dagger, my fists. How he showed me how to counter offensive moves in battle and where to slice through a man's chest to pierce his heart.

I thought of the horror that would cross his face if he could see me, see what these men were trying to do.

The man in front of me finally got a hold of one foot but I refused to relent the other from kicking. Tears streamed out of the corners of my eyes, tickling my cheeks as they fell, getting lost into the hand of the man silencing me.

I had been taught to fight, something few women had any interest in, let alone the privilege of learning. I'd killed a Gods-damned Vasi the night before, and here I was, being overpowered by two vile men.

Even though I could feel the crack within me, the piece of my soul that was breaking away and hardening from this new trauma, the thought crossed my mind that nothing could be worse than watching my father die. These men could try whatever they pleased, but I was already broken, and as they struggled to get a grasp on me so that they could haul me away and into a night full of whatever horrors they were imagining, a single thought crossed my mind.

Maybe this is better.

Maybe dying now would be easier. Maybe Kembertus would be worse than I'd been told, maybe I couldn't survive in a world without my father.

Maybe being gone was better than being alone.

My muscles ached, my bones hurt, my head throbbed with a rising migraine.

The man grasped my other ankle and pulled my legs together. The one beside me didn't loosen his grip on my wrists but held them together. They pulled me from the tree and headed down the path toward Kembertus. I swung between them, one man holding my calves and the other my wrists.

But I could scream now, and I was. I was shouting and crying and pleading with them to let me go. To ease up on my wrist, that it was already broken. But all I heard was laughter and all I felt were the hands tightening over me.

As my weight swung above the dirt, I swallowed my previous thoughts of death.

No.

At any cost, I'd fight them. At any cost, I'd kill them. They would not get away with this, and I refused to allow them to continue walking this world to do it to other women who were far less prepared than me.

If anyone was going to stop them, I knew it was me. And with a newfound surge of blood through my veins, otherworldly in feeling as if the Goddess of Bloodshed herself was stepping into my body, I began thrashing again.

A heat surged within me, a feeling that was somehow familiar and foreign, but all I could concentrate on was wriggling my body around as much as I could to make the men drop me. They were pulling me closer and closer to Kembertus, and finally after a turn in the path I saw a dying campfire glow, mostly embers.

No. A voice filled my mind, and I couldn't tell whether it was mine. A constant drumming of the same word over and over, matching the rhythm of my heartbeat in my ears. *No. No. No. No.*

The shadows around us grew darker. My palms began to ache with heat, which would've puzzled me if the screaming in my head didn't cause my skull to feel as if it were splitting open.

My body started to thrum harder. As if a battle was being waged not only against my mind, but within my own blood.

I whimpered into the night as I saw the camp getting closer, time moving so slowly it was painful.

No!

Something screamed in my head as my palms burst open against their restraints, searing with pain and feeling as if wind swept past them.

But there was no wind, no air sweeping the hair that had fallen onto my forehead.

I was dropped suddenly, and the dirt beneath rushed up to meet me. But the impact did not deter the ringing in my ears or the buzz through my veins.

"What the fuck, Lonix?" The man who'd been holding my wrists said, rushing to his friend that had turned to look at me. The dull light from the embers wasn't enough to see their faces. He didn't speak back to the man, only made a gasping sound.

Were the Gods showing me mercy?

The man slowly fell onto his knees, his hands moving to clutch his shadowy throat. I couldn't see the expression on his face, but I could hear the sound of his desperate attempts to clear his airway. He clawed at his neck and the sound was chilling. The scrape of nails against soft skin, peeling it back as he gasped for air.

A warm buzz filled me with each wheeze of his lungs. The feeling started in my palms and quickly spread throughout the rest of my body, until it landed behind my eyes.

"Lonix, what's happening?"

The wind continued to soar past my palms even as they fell to my sides, although it felt weaker now, but the air around us remained still.

My body flushed with a foreign presence as I straightened, watching the man, Lonix, struggle. The foreign feeling changed, shifted, until it settled into every pore of my skin, every nook in my bones. Until it wasn't foreign at all, but familiar. A piece of me that had been silenced for years and was finally set free.

As I watched them, I noticed that the features of both men came into view. I tried not to wonder why as Lonix fell to the side and his last breath, that had so violently drawn out, left him.

The other man looked at me, his eyes widening, and I swore I saw a teal light reflecting at me. His mouth worked to form words, but nothing came. Instead, he fumbled to his feet and sprinted away, leaving me at his campsite.

I watched as he left and only when the shadows devoured him did I realize I was laughing, an uncharacteristic smile lighting my face as I stood up. Because as he stumbled away from me, back to the pit of Vestaria where I knew he hailed, I realized something that made the ache in my bones dull for a moment.

I had seen his face.

CHAPTER TWELVE

Evaline

I awoke with a jolt, sitting straight up in bed as the memory of that night two years ago slowly sifted away.

"It was a nightmare," I murmured to myself, trying to slow my heart's rattle against my chest. I released a shuddering breath, grounding my body in the present.

That nightmare haunted me far more often than I cared to admit.

I brought my hands up, smoothing the hair out of my own face as the man's flashed through my mind once more. His green eyes were deep set and rested below his large forehead. A scar fell over the bridge of his nose. I remembered the sharp edge of his jaw and thin, wide lips, and the sound of his voice as he spat at me.

I forced the memory away. I wanted to remember his face, I wanted to know exactly what he looked like so that the day I saw him again I'd know without a shadow of a doubt that I was getting revenge on the right man, but I didn't need the nightmares to remember it. I could do without those.

I swung my legs off the bed and moved to the armoire that sat across the room. I gathered my clothing; black pants, a grossly oversized long sleeved brown tunic and ill-fitting boots I'd found. I wanted to hide my physique as much as possible today.

As I dressed I felt the jolt of excitement flush through my body. Today, after two long years of waiting, I was going to the market and buying a dagger.

I'd known since my attacks that both Vasi and vile men wandered this world, and I refused to be weaponless the next time I met either one.

A smile formed on my face as I finished dressing and moved toward the vanity. As I held the ends of my hair, stroking the brush through to get the last of the knots out, I remembered how my father had always loved my hair. How he'd smile softly when he taught me to braid it and tell me that I looked exactly like my mother.

He'd sit me down on his lap when I was very young while he braided it for me, and when I'd grown, he'd reminisce about how awful he had been at controlling my hair before, while I would sit on the floor cross-legged. He said he never knew what was harder, finally getting all the knots out of my hair or trying to contain it all into a tie.

But he'd always remind me that it was just as soft as my mother's was, just as white. He'd assure me that everyone thought the color was beautiful even if the other kids mocked me for it.

"This is the hair color of Tremon women." He'd remark, referring not to his surname, but my mother's maiden name. "And Tremon women are fierce." He'd finish, always whispering the last part in my ear.

I would giggle and as soon as he finished securing the tie, playfully whip my head around so I'd whack him with the tail. Tears brimmed on the edges of my eyes as I thought of him, the ache in my heart swelling.

I set the brush down and ran my fingers through it. My hair color was unique. The only people I knew that had it were the elderly, and maybe that should've made me self-conscious, but my mother had this hair color, and that was something I would hold onto proudly.

I clasped the ivory handle of the drawer to my vanity and pulled it open. Under layers of junk that I kept in there to hide what I was looking for, I carefully pulled out a piece of stiff metal.

The silver barbed wire glinted in the morning light.

I laid the wire on the vanity and worked quickly, not wanting anyone to barge in and see what I was doing. I started braiding my hair, beginning at the crown of my head, as I did every time I left the castle. I worked to add small sections to the braid until it was at the nape of my neck with only three bunches left. With the skill of someone who had been doing this for two years, I pinched the wire between two barbs and added it to one of the three pieces I had left. I twisted the strands around each other then, forming a thick white and gray braid that nearly reached the small of my back.

I quickly fluffed my hair around the wire so that it was invisible. I pulled the braid around to rest on my shoulder and faced the mirror, meeting my own eyes.

I would never be jerked back by the hair again.

A deep breath filled my lungs as I slipped into the crowded market. I'd made it safely out of the castle without being seen through the back service entrance. The coin purse I'd looped about a hundred times around my wrist, under my cloak, felt as if it was burning through my hand. This had to work, after two years my heart could hardly stand the excitement and terror that my plan would fail.

The street was crowded with people shopping and knocking shoulders as they passed one another. I had to be constantly aware just to make sure I didn't trip. I couldn't afford to fall, or even a stumble, or any other move that would risk the hood falling off my head.

A small child cut in front of me, chasing a dog. I hissed, almost falling over him. He looked up at me in surprise, but I quickly recovered and smiled at him. He wasn't trying to trip me, it had been an accident.

He grinned back and continued on his chase.

Approaching the temporary tent of the blacksmith, I bit the inside of my cheek.

Please, Vestari. Please let this work. I threw a prayer up to the Goddess of Bloodshed, who in all the tapestries, statues, and paintings I'd ever seen of her had always been portrayed with a sword at her hip and a dagger on her thigh.

The immediate smell of leather overwhelmed my senses upon entering the tent. My eyes adjusted to the decrease in light quickly, and I noted that there were no other customers inside. I pursed my lips, unsure of how that would bode for me. I tried to calculate in my head whether it was better or worse to attempt this now, with no customers, or when there might be even more witnesses around. I set my jaw; I didn't have any other choice. I didn't know how many more times I could sneak out of the castle in this attire without being caught.

I scanned over the dozens of blades on display and tried not to get overly excited as I peered at all my options.

"Excuse me," a man said behind me. I tensed, praying I wasn't about to be thrown out.

I turned toward him, my head tilted to the ground so my hood wouldn't expose me.

It was the blacksmith. He didn't eject me, instead telling me about his stock and informing me the prices of the various items.

I nodded a thanks when he finished and began browsing again. As much as his interruption startled me, I was thankful for pricing information.

Walking to the back wall of the tent, I found the only items I could afford. I'd saved up enough money to buy a dagger and holster, but not a lavish set. I stopped in front of a table and heard new footsteps entering. I decided that wasn't alarming, the more customers to take up the blacksmith's attention the better. I noted a strange sensation prickle the hair on the back of my neck but attributed it to my anxiety and continued searching. I looked over the makeshift table, silently begging there to be a dagger. Then my eyes landed on it.

A beautiful silver knife. One similar to the color of my hair, in the right lighting. Medium sized, with a black handle that looked as if it was made of stone. It wasn't a work of art by any means, there were definitely more beautiful blades in this tent, but this was what I could afford, and it was beautiful to me.

I grabbed the dagger and its scabbard and stepped over to look for a holster. I'd considered what type I preferred for months. I couldn't wear it on my hip, or across my chest, it would be too obvious, and Therese would confiscate it before I could even practice with it.

I pined for a calf holster, but I knew that would be obvious, too.

My decision landed on one for my thigh. I could immediately access it when wearing a dress or skirt, while it was still hidden. When I wore pants, I would simply make sure the tunic or blouse fell low enough to cover it.

I heard a man start a discussion with the blacksmith behind me as I continued looking.

Finally, I found a thigh holster. It was a simple black leather, but that's all I needed. My hand stretched out and reached for it and my fingers closed around the deceivingly soft texture.

I turned toward the blacksmith, or where I thought he was at least. I kept my gaze cast down just looking for his boots.

I found him, but he was still speaking to the other man. I heard another customer move toward the back of the tent from which I'd just come, browsing a few paces behind me.

Please, hurry. I urged the man who was speaking to the blacksmith. They were discussing two different blades the customer had picked out.

"I'm sorry, give me one moment." I heard the blacksmith tell him, then his voice was closer. "Are you ready to pay?"

I nodded.

I held the items out, trying my best to hide my small hands, and he took them.

"Thank you." He said. He gave me the price and I nodded, frantically trying to pull the purse out of my sleeve and gather enough coin. I should've done this before I came up to pay, I could feel every eye in the tent on me.

"Are you…" The blacksmith started to say, and I froze. I knew his next words before they left his mouth. "Are you a woman?"

I didn't know what to do. In all my planning of this exchange I hadn't landed on a legitimate route of escape had I been caught, failing one of my father's most vital rules. I felt my face pale, and then burn with embarrassment. I clutched the purse to my chest, head still angled down, trying to evaluate what the quickest way out of the tent would be.

But before I could take a step a hand landed on the small of my back, and even though a touch like that would usually cause me to flinch away, I didn't.

"I'm sorry about that." The man's smooth voice said as he walked to my side.

Gods-dammit.

I knew exactly whose voice that was, and he was the last person I would want to interject into this situation right now.

"She was fetching this for me, I forgot about Kembertus' strict rules against women purchasing weapons." The Kova's voice was silk as he lied to the blacksmith.

"Oh, of course." The blacksmith said, and I swear I could hear his vigorous nodding. He must've been as intimidated by the Kova as I had been when I first saw him.

The jingling of coins slipping past each other sounded as the Kova pulled out the money to pay for my dagger and holster.

Was he going to keep it? Gods-dammit!

"Thank you for your purchase." I heard the blacksmith say, then he turned back to the original man he'd been speaking to. "Now this one here was made using…"

I tuned their conversation out as I ripped myself from the hands of the Kova and walked out of the tent. I needed to get lost in the crowd fast enough to get away from him.

CHAPTER THIRTEEN

Maddox

I'd never been so thankful for Wyott's inability to pass up a blacksmith's shop in my entire existence.

I had been looking for her as we walked through the market, but I hadn't spotted her bright hair anywhere, and there were too many people around for me to get a great trail on her scent. But Wyott had led me right to her, and I was thankful. The blacksmith seemed like a nice enough man, but who knows what he would've done, or been obligated to do, based on the Kembertus laws had I not been there to help her. Although it did not seem like she was the type of woman who wanted to be helped.

The moment he turned his attention from us she bolted. I followed her, but she was already weaving in and out of the crowd over the cobblestone.

I could hear her heart racing in her chest. Still reeling from nearly being caught, I was sure. But I wondered if it was something else. If she could feel me behind her, sliding past market-goers to catch up. Could she sense me the way I could sense her? Like the air was a coil between us waiting to snap that only tightened painfully the closer we were?

I fell in step beside her.

"Let's play a game." I said, my voice low.

I heard her scoff and watched as her shoulders moved with the sound.

"I..." She said, trailing off for a minute, despite her pace never faltering. "I don't even know what to say to that."

I smiled. "You could say yes."

One shake of her head. "I don't play games with men I don't know, let alone..." She didn't have to say it, I knew what she meant.

"But you don't even know the rules yet." I persisted.

I could hear the faint sound of her teeth grinding.

"Fine. What are the rules?" Her voice was deadpan as she tried to show me how disinterested she was, even though I could hear her heart's uptick in beat.

"The first rule is that you stop fleeing every time you see me."

She laughed, actually laughed, and I could feel the smallest bit of tension rise from her chest.

"Immediately I cannot abide by the rules of this game."

My lips quirked up into a smile. "The second rule," I said, ignoring her. "Is that you can ask me any question you want, and I'll answer honestly."

The crowd pushed us along with it and I watched as she tried to keep up while keeping her head low.

"That's a boring game. That's not even a game. There's no way to win."

I shrugged. "I'm winning as long as I'm talking to you." Her footing stuttered at the words and but she caught herself before she tripped. I heard her clear her throat and smiled at the small gesture of surprise she displayed. Had she never been flirted with before?

But she ignored me. "The other flaw in the game is that it's based off the assumption that I even want to ask you questions."

A man walked into her path and didn't move to let her by. His shoulder slammed into hers and she almost fell. I swiped my arm out, slipping it around her waist as the other hand clasped her hood, making sure it stayed in place.

"Thank you," she muttered as she righted herself.

"Of course."

We neared the gardens that surrounded the castle. Her head snapped around, as if looking for somewhere safe to hide.

We'd already exited the throng of people, and she stepped off to the edge of the road that butted up to the section of the gardens devoted to tulips, and swung to face me. She allowed the hood to slide back far enough that only I could see her eyes as she tilted her head up. They were breathtaking.

"I don't want to play your silly game. Leave me alone and leave Kembertus." She demanded.

I tried to hide the way those words ached deep in my chest. "I think you do want to play, you're just worried that you'll find yourself charmed by me."

She narrowed her eyes. "It's strange that this entire time you've been waiting for me to ask you questions, when you haven't asked the most important one."

I smiled at her. She was smart. I put my hands in the pockets of my pants. "And what question would that be?"

She pursed her lips before she answered, and the movement drew my eyes there. "You must be dying to know how I knew what you were."

I threw her a wink. "I've been told my eyes give it away."

She rolled her own, but I saw the blush that crept along her cheeks at my flirting. "You know what I mean."

Of course I did. She assumed I'd want to know how she knew what Kova were, and therefore how she knew what I was. But I already knew, and clearly she didn't realize that. "I already know."

Her eyes searched mine, gauging me. "There's no way. No one knows."

I shrugged. "Maybe that's because no one knew Wallace like I did."

Her face paled, her eyes glazed, and for a moment I thought I said the wrong thing. She deserved to know that I knew him, I didn't want another secret from her hanging over my head.

"Don't lie." She whispered.

My brows pulled together. "I'm not. We fought together. Him and I and my friend Wyott back there." I jerked a thumb behind us. "In Neomaeros."

"Why should I believe you?" I saw the desperation in her eyes that switched between mine, heard it in her voice. She wanted this to be true. She missed him that much.

Suddenly I regretted telling her. I never wanted to upset her.

"Because I'm telling the truth, Evaline." Her eyes widened at my use of her name, and I answered her next question before she asked it. "Someone outside of the inn told me, after you ran off."

She narrowed her eyes. "Of course, they did."

"My name is Maddox." I said, trying to catch her eye, but she spun again, looking around us. I tilted my head. "You seem to be in a rush."

She scoffed. "And you seem to be tempting fate with a woman who knows how to kill your kind."

I couldn't wipe the fucking smile off my face. She was everything.

"I can't tell if it's because you have to get back before you're in trouble or you just want to escape my presence." I teased.

"And somehow, it's both."

I took a small step closer, leaning in. "And somehow, I don't believe the latter."

The pace of her heart, the hitch in her breath when I drew near, the flush in her cheeks – she was attracted to me. Maybe she just didn't know it yet.

But her ocean eyes flashed with fear and I took a step back. I saw how scared she was. Scared to be talking to me, scared to be caught, scared at the pain of finding out new information about her father.

"Listen…" I started, rubbing a hand over the back of my neck. "I didn't mean to upset you by telling you I knew your father, I just wanted to be honest. He was a good friend during that time of my life, and when I heard of his passing, I was sorry for the loss. He was a good man, and he didn't deserve what happened to him."

But there were tears in her eyes. I was only making everything worse.

"Fuck, I'm sorry. Please don't cry, I was just... I don't know." I huffed. "I'm going to stop talking now." I finished and that last part caused a small laugh to bubble from her lips. The sound washed through me and I knew I needed to hear it every day for the rest of my life.

"I suppose I believe you. For now." She offered. I smiled, that's all I could ask for. "And I guess you're right. I do have questions, but I must go."

I nodded. That's okay. I had time. "I understand." I held the dagger and holster toward her, hiding it from the crowd with my body.

"Oh." She said, sounding surprised. Had she forgotten about it? She swiped them from my hand and swiftly hid them in her sleeve. Her gaze drifted up to meet mine again. "Thank you."

I nodded. "Of course."

She started to pull the purse from her other sleeve, but I shook my head, my hand covering hers. Heat passed between us, and I felt my heart rate increase to match hers.

"There's no need."

"But—"

"You're not going to change my mind."

She sighed and nodded. "Fine." She hesitated, not leaving, and not removing her eyes from me.

I shrugged. "I won't follow you." She narrowed her eyes at me again and started to leave. I didn't want her to. After a few steps I called after her. "But I do want to see you again."

She shook her head at the ground as she walked, and I hoped there was a smile on her face as she did so. Eventually she turned a corner and I lost sight of her.

A breath whistled past my lips. I knew Wyott was approaching before he spoke.

"Damn." He stood beside me.

"I know."

We both looked toward the spot she had disappeared for a moment, and then he turned toward me, a smirk on his face.

"I don't know whether that was a good interaction or not."

I rolled my eyes and turned to head back into town toward the mailing office.

"Cork it, Wyott."

We wove through the crowd effortlessly.

"Did you finally pick a blade to buy?" I asked him after a moment of silence.

He shook his head, a bemused laugh piercing the air. "Don't try to change the subject on me, we have bigger conversational material to cover than what blade I bought." He turned to look me in the eye. "But both. I bought both."

I laughed. Of course he did. Wyott couldn't make a decision to save his life. He was lucky he didn't have to pick his mate.

"But seriously, what are you going to do?" He continued.

I shrugged. "What am I supposed to do? You saw her, both times. She's hesitant around me. This isn't a normal Kova mating. Not even close."

He laughed. "I think this is as far from normal as you can possibly get. I've never heard of a Kova mating with a non-Kova, let alone a human."

I kicked a stone in my path once we left the swarm of people at the market. "I guess I just always thought it would be effortless. That we would meet and immediately come together, like everyone else traditionally does."

Wyott cast his eyes down. "Just because she's human, and this non-traditional, doesn't mean it's a bad thing, just new. And face it, you're the son of the First. You're going to be different than the rest of us."

I chewed my lip and said nothing.

I thought about her smooth skin, the dusting of freckles that coated her nose and faded out at her cheeks. Her bright eyes that looked through me. The pull of the bond was so severe I immediately found myself wishing I could be beside her again, if only to hear her voice.

We approached the mailing office and I was happy to see that they were open despite the market today. I opened the door for Wyott and he strode in, we'd already discussed what the parchment would say, so it was just a matter of writing and sealing it, and paying the mailer for the raven's travel.

"She's definitely not normal, but neither are you." He said as he passed me.

I rolled my eyes and remembered the dark thoughts I saw churning below the waters of her eyes.

"She has a fire in her."

Wyott scoffed. "Did you really think your mate wouldn't?"

CHAPTER FOURTEEN

Evaline

After tripping and catching myself on the chaise as I burst into my bedroom, I sank down onto the hearth. My bones were chilled from spending so much time outside in the frigid morning air. My heart shivered with excitement, and I convinced myself it was from finally owning a dagger.

Most definitely not from speaking with Maddox.

I pulled out the dagger, carefully holding it in both hands. It was sheathed in its plain black scabbard. It was beautiful.

And what if I was shaken by interacting with the Kova? It was entirely natural to feel as if I'd just touched a lightning bolt every time I spoke to an immortal being. I shook my head.

Carefully I pulled the blade out and examined it.

It felt cool in my hand, the way metal or stone usually does. But holding it, feeling the weight in my palm, sent a rush of warmth down my hand, up my arm, and through my chest.

It was a similar feeling to when Maddox caught me as we left the market.

My hand tightened around the handle. The mere possession of the weapon made me feel safer. Now I just had to remember how to use it.

I could almost hear my father's voice in my head, all thoughts of Maddox dissipated, as I stood and placed the knife on my bed and shed my cloak, throwing it to the side.

He'd remind me how to safely wield a weapon to ensure that I wouldn't accidentally hurt myself. To never aim the edge at myself, to always keep a firm grip on the hilt. But most importantly, to never let it go.

I chuckled as I thought of him shaking his head at the weapon's current location on my pink duvet. I could see the wrinkles that would form between his brows as if he stood right in front of me.

"A blade is either sheathed, in your hand, or in your enemy. There is no other way." He'd coach me, pounding into my head to never do what I'd just done.

Oops.

I was rusty, not only regarding the mechanics of owning a weapon, but with the responsibility that came with it as well.

Trying to ignore the itching feeling of my father's chastising stare that felt far closer than a memory, I folded at the waist. I had to widen my stance to attach my holster. When I stood comfortably, my thighs pressed together. I secured the belt-like fastener around my thigh and straightened, bouncing my weight from leg to leg, trying to gauge whether the binding felt too tight.

Nodding at the subtle squeeze, I turned on my heels and grabbed the scabbard off the bed. I fastened it to the holster, double and triple checking that it was secure with no chance of coming off on its own. Finally, I stood and grabbed my dagger.

I smiled at the thought. My dagger.

I played with the weight in my hand, allowing the handle of the knife to roll against my palm. I practiced switching the grip from a power hold – the typical way of wielding a dagger – to a reverse grip. The knife spun easily so my thumb sat closest to the pommel rather than the cross guard. This allowed me to tuck the blade against the length of my forearm, but gave me the flexibility to strike out at a moment's notice.

A wave of familiarity washed over me as I once again spun the dagger back into the power hold. It felt comfortable, as if my muscles had remembered every move my father had taught me, even through these last two years without him, and without practice. But there was something else. Something that had never been there before. A peculiar sensation deep within me that radiated through my veins and flushed through my entire entity. A confidence that hadn't been there when I sparred with my father.

I swung my arm out to strike an invisible assailant, and my legs naturally fell into the correct stance below me. Slightly crouched, weight on the balls of my feet so that I could react accordingly, and one foot forward and the other back, balancing my weight between the two.

A smile grew as I remembered a lesson with my father and the room around me seemed to dim as the memory filled my mind.

"Wielding a weapon puts you in more danger than not having one, unless you know how to use it." Repeating his words in a whisper, I slashed the air behind me, dagger to the throat of the nonexistent aggressor who was sneaking up on me.

It was one of his favorite anecdotes. He'd say it constantly, anytime he felt I was being irresponsible. When I was young, I asked him if he'd made it up. He chuckled and told me he'd picked it up from a friend on the battlefield.

My heart pounded as both the rush of adrenaline and the ache of sorrow collided in my chest.

"You're a woman, you must always be faster than those you fight, because you may not be stronger." The words left my lips before I could remember thinking them and I noticed a flick of light out of the corner of my eye. My head snapped, but I only saw some vague shadows around me. I shook my head as I straightened and flipped the dagger into reverse grip, tucking it against my forearm and folding my arms behind me, circling my absent prey.

I brought the dagger in front of myself, looking down at the light reflecting off the chrome.

For a moment I thought I saw a gleam of my father's eyes in the reflection.

The light would make his eyes sparkle with pride every time I swept his feet out from underneath him, or put a dagger to his heart, winning the spar.

I tried to swallow the lump in my throat as I tested my abilities. I flicked my wrist, the blade flipping in the air until I caught the dull, flat, edges of the tip in my fingers.

A whoosh of air left my lips, eyes widening, startled. I couldn't believe I could still do that.

"And what would you have done if you couldn't still do that trick? Lost a finger?" My father's voice rang so loudly through my head that for a moment I was unsure if that was where it originated.

Adrenaline coursed through my veins as I flipped it once more, higher this time so that the blade flipped once, twice, in the air before the hilt landed effortlessly in my palm.

A giggle escaped me; this was the happiest I'd been in years even if every minute holding the dagger was another reminder that he was gone. I spun to face the window.

Approaching the glass, I touched the edge of the dagger to it, looking past it and to the city below.

I felt free. Felt like no matter what happened, I would be okay. For the first time since his death, I felt my father's presence within me, around me, like he'd never left.

This time a grin stretched over my face as I turned away from the window, walking to the center of the room and tossing the blade into the air once more, far higher than my previous attempts.

It flipped once.

There were footsteps in the hall.

Flipped twice.

My aunt's voice followed them, snapping at a maid.

Three times.

The knob of the door began to turn, shadows around me rippled.

The hilt fell into my hand as the door cracked open, my heart pounding in my ears. Before I could panic my hand slid the blade into the sheath on my thigh, as if it was the most natural thing my body had ever done, and my tunic fell over it.

"Oh!" My aunt said as she saw me standing in the center of the room, the light around us somehow brighter. "I didn't expect you to be awake." I knew she was referring to my absence at breakfast.

I shrugged. "I wasn't hungry this morning." I lied.

My aunt's eyes dropped down my form as she shut the door behind her. "Evaline." She said with a sigh. "What in the name of the Gods are you wearing?"

I had to fight every instinct to roll my eyes.

"I was cold, so I thought I'd put these on." It was alarming how good I had gotten at lying in my time living here.

She clicked her tongue disapprovingly. "You can't dress like that any longer. You are a woman long past her coming of age, you need to dress every day as if you will be courted by a man." She strode closer to me and for a moment I froze in fear that she would suddenly lift my tunic or touch my braid.

But instead, Therese pinched my sleeve in disgust and lifted it only slightly, exposing how oversized it was on my arm. If she had her way, I would spend each and every day in a ballgown. It's not as if I never wore skirts or dresses, they were usually just not types she liked.

"I mean, how can you ever expect a man to want to wed you if you constantly look so haggard?" Therese said, waving a hand in the air.

I scoffed. "I don't live my life waiting for a man to want to wed me. I don't even plan on it." For one brief second, my thoughts drifted to Maddox. Luckily my aunt continued before I had any time to question it.

She tutted again and waved her hand. "Evaline, you will have to wed someday."

I met her gaze, tilting my head. "Why?"

I didn't pose the question because I didn't know the answer. Of course, I knew what my aunt was about to say; that I would have to find a husband to support me so that I may give him babies and carry on the family name.

And live the remainder of my life wasting away in another castle, Gods forbid, or another town where my worth was only measured by the weight of the purse my husband carried and how many sons I blessed him with.

No, I posed the question because I wanted her to hear herself when she said those words. To fully comprehend the kind of world she was asking me to be a part of. As if it was a pleasure to move from one prison to the next.

"What a silly little question, Evaline. You know why. You have to find a man who can support you so that you do not become some old hag who realizes too late that she should have done more to find a husband when she was still young and pretty." She pressed her lips in a thin line, accentuating the fine wrinkles on either side of her mouth.

A chill raised the hairs on the back of my neck. That was far worse than what I thought she would retort.

I was at a loss for words. How could the Lady hear herself make such a proclamation and then stand there and look as smug as she did?

I opened and closed my mouth, and she took that as her cue.

"There will come a day, soon, when a man courts you, or the Lord and I find an adequate match." She met my gaze as I absorbed the threat. "When that day comes, you will smile and allow yourself to be married, because time is running out. You will not be this beautiful forever. You're already twenty-four for Gods' sake." She lifted her chin, making her nose look beak-like as she looked down it at me.

My heart pounded and a beat of silence passed between us.

"Your father may have failed you in this department, but I refuse to watch you wither away in this castle." She finally said.

I took a step toward her as she degraded my father's name, the weight of the dagger feeling the heaviest it had since I strapped it on. Itching, begging, me to pull it out and show my aunt exactly how much he had "failed" me.

"Evaline!" My aunt hissed. I realize I had bared my teeth at her, my fingers twitching at my side as she took a step back.

She made a move for the door, trying to appear as if she wasn't retreating. When she reached for the handle, she turned. "I would tell you to wash-up for lunch, but I don't think we require such a negative presence. You will remain here for the rest of the day. I'll have someone bring your food up."

She slipped out of the room, slamming the door behind her.

A shaky breath passed my lips and I tried to keep myself from crying. I wasn't sure what brought the tears on. The threat of an arranged marriage, or the way my aunt spit out the insult of my father.

I tilted my head back, trying to dry the tears that had formed.

My father taught me to fight. He taught me to stand up for myself. He passed on his attitude and predilection for curse words. He showed me how to be brave and how to kill a man.

He did not teach me how to be a wife.

"People are going to underestimate you every day of your life." The memory hit me before I could sit down and I stumbled against the bed as his face became clear in front of me.

My father had just knocked me on my ass, he never held back. He stood over me as he spoke. "That's the way some places in this world are. Women are seen as less than men. I didn't think that way about your mother, and the same goes for you."

I tilted my head forward, looking to the floor as the memory washed over me.

"But what matters most is that no one's, especially no *man's*, opinion of you matters." The moon glowed behind his head, making him look like a saint. "Promise me that you will live your life without fear. Without a care for those who wish to demean you." He paused as he switched his dagger from his dominant hand and stuck it out to help me up. I took it, but before lifting me he leaned a bit closer.

"Promise me that you will live your life as men do, as if you own the very ground you walk on, and that you will never settle for a partner who doesn't worship that."

I'd stood, meeting his gaze, straightening to stick out my chest and tilt up my chin. "I promise."

CHAPTER FIFTEEN

Evaline

"Oh my Gods, Evaline." Aurora gasped, her hand flying to her chest. "Please tell me you're exaggerating. You can't really be confessing that you almost stabbed your aunt."

I rolled my eyes from where I sat across from Aurora at her dining table, a dress laid out upon it that she was hemming. "I didn't actually come close to doing it, it just crossed my mind." I mumbled.

"Regardless, that's not exactly a fine remark on your relationship." Aurora added. Her fingers moved back to work on the dress.

I scoffed. "Of course, it's not, we have a terrible relationship. I'm the niece by marriage that she never asked for." I traced the wood grain of the table.

My thoughts drifted to their son, Gabriehl, who was off living in some other city, apparently. I had never met him, but it felt as if I had from how much they droned on about him and how many of the castle's walls were adorned with paintings of him throughout his life.

"I can't wait to see you in your dress for the Spring Solstice Ball." Aurora tilted her head toward me but never broke her gaze from her project.

"Honestly, I wish that was my punishment. Not getting to go to the Ball." I settled into the back of the seat with crossed arms.

"I think it would be more likely that your punishment was to go to the Ball." She teased.

"You're probably right." I stood from the chair and pulled the dress further onto the table for Aurora, seeing that she was nearly done with her current section.

Aurora smiled at me. "Thank you, Evaline."

When Aurora became very engrossed in her work it was easier if I moved the fabric for her, so that she didn't have to break her focus. I'd asked her to teach me to sew so I could help her, but I was terrible at it. Her fingers flew over the fabric with such grace and ease that I questioned how she never pricked herself. I almost snorted at the thought. I supposed the same could be said of me braiding the barbed wire into my hair.

It was quiet for a moment and then Aurora spoke again. "Evaline, what is your plan if you do not wish to get married?" Her voice was low.

I sighed. "I don't know. I'd love to get a job and be able to live in town like you and Jacqueline."

I didn't bother confessing my true wish to Aurora, the desire that kept me up most nights; I wanted to flee this kingdom at my first opportunity. I was afraid to voice that to my friend.

I didn't want her to talk me out of it, or worse, to encourage me to go. Knowing I would someday leave Aurora and Jacqueline behind made the notion harder to swallow.

And even if I did stay, my guardians would never let me live out my life in peace – in town, in my own home, with a career I could be happy with. No matter what it took, they'd find a way to marry me off for their benefit. If that man stayed here, or traveled, I would never be happy forced into a marriage that I didn't want.

Aurora understood that, too. Some women in Kembertus got to live their own lives and be happy, like her family. I was thankful that Kembertus had progressed enough that Aurora's marriage to Jacqueline was accepted. While women from ruling families in Brassillion, or even wealthy ones like Aurora's, were forced to marry men to carry on their lineage, others were not. Fortunately, Aurora's and Jacqueline's had been just as happy the women had found each other, and were too well travelled to stick to Kembertus tradition.

It infuriated me that any woman could be viewed as a means to an end for a powerful family. People worshiped the Goddesses just as vehemently as the Gods. Shouldn't our society reflect that power dynamic? If the Goddesses were just as worthy as the Gods, shouldn't women be too?

But that was not the case, and here I sat, being threatened with arranged marriages, and forbidden to have a job or a life of my own. I wished I knew the moment in history when someone being born with a womb warranted their life not being their own, being treated as if they only lived to serve men.

I sighed, realizing the silence had stretched between us.

"I'm just glad I can open up to you about these things." I remarked, and Aurora met my eyes, breaking her concentration.

"I'm glad too, Evaline. You can always talk to me. And Jacquie."

And I had. I told them about my childhood, how I knew how to fight. Aurora knew that there was a dagger strapped to my leg just below the table, I'd told her as soon as I arrived.

I vented my frustrations about my aunt, as was evident from our conversation today. But maybe the most important piece of information I'd shared with the both of them, that I had never shared with anyone else, was my attack.

One night, in the very house I sat in now, I told them an edited version that reflected the story of bandits that I'd told my guardians regarding my father's death, and about my own attack. It wasn't until after the words stopped flowing that I realized how badly I needed to tell someone, needed for someone in the world to know what happened to me even if it did nothing to bring my father back or fight away the nightmares I struggled through almost every night.

They didn't judge me for crying or for taking up their time. They listened and held me on the chaise while I sobbed.

I told them how the Gods had protected me, how one of the men must have had a heart ailment of some sort and died in front of my eyes. I explained how I had felt at peace when that happened.

I was especially thankful they didn't judge me for that.

I had never felt squeamish when discussing death. My father would tell me stories of his friends who died in battle, how he'd drug them to safety and watched as they faded, heard their last breaths. His voice would choke when he described it, what it felt like to hold your friend's cooling body as the life drained from them and their soul went into the Night.

But in the next breath he'd tell me how he'd get up and tear through three enemies, avenging his comrade. He'd tell me how a sword vibrated when it connected with a man's head. He explained what it felt like when your fist broke a nose, crunching underneath your knuckles. And the sound of a man gurgling his own blood.

I had been raised around death – Mortitheos' vehicle to the Night. Hearing it, seeing it, delivering it. My mother's death, my father's, the Vasi's. Death had crept its way into my life and established itself, drawing an icy hand around my heart until it was almost as cold.

And in the span of hours from when my father died and I was attacked, it had blossomed within me.

Death was my greatest blessing, and my cruelest curse.

But Aurora and Jacqueline hadn't been raised that way. I was afraid to tell them that I enjoyed watching Lonix choke. I was worried that they would cringe if I shared the fact that joy expanded in my chest when I saw his eyes dim.

I didn't tell them that. I didn't tell anyone, because the only person in this world who would understand that notion was my father. And death had taken him, too.

The thoughts stirred the sorrow within, and I pushed them away, forcing my attention to my friend again. "How have you been this week? Busy with the Ball, I know."

Aurora nodded and broke her attention away from her work for a moment. "It's been good, I actually have exciting news I haven't gotten to tell you about yet." She said a smile on her face.

I perked up, leaning toward her over the table. "What is it?" I asked with a smile of my own.

She put her work down completely and leaned forward. "I've hardly told anyone about it yet because I've been worried it would fall through." She shrugged. "But my business inquiry was accepted and is pending review, so I feel like I can share."

I bounced in my seat. "Well don't keep me in suspense." I laughed, feeling my heart start to race as I waited for her good news.

She spoke carefully. "For the last few months, with the store so successful, I've been considering opening a store in Neomaeros."

My jaw dropped at the words but I immediately nodded my head. "Aurora, that sounds like an amazing plan." And it wasn't only because I desperately wanted her and Jacqueline out of Kembertus and somewhere safer, like Neomaeros, but because she was a successful business owner, and I did believe that she'd carry that into a store in Neomaeros as well.

She nodded with a flush of excitement reddening her face. "If I open in Neomaeros, I'm hoping in a few years having a store there will help me to breakout into the other Madierian Kingdoms, too."

"I definitely think it will. The Madierian Kingdoms are very communicative and people from all three travel between each frequently. If word got to the other kingdoms about your dress designs, they might reach out to you first."

She smiled. "That'd be a dream."

"You had to apply, then?" I wasn't sure how most business affairs worked, but Aurora had learned a lot from her father and they both were very business savvy.

"Yes, I submitted my business license request a month ago and received postage yesterday that my license has been accepted for review." She shrugged. "It's the first step to gaining approval. Now I just wait in the queue until they review it. I know I'll be approved, so it's just a matter of waiting."

"Did they say how long it would take?"

Her face fell at that. "They said they likely won't review it until winter because they're so backlogged." By the slight defeat in her voice, I could tell that wasn't ideal.

"You hoped it would be sooner?"

The corner of her mouth lifted. "I would love to open by next summer, that way I'd be running in time for Neomaeros's courting and ball season start. But if they don't approve me until the winter, I won't have enough time to hire employees or prepare the shop to open so quickly."

I lifted a brow. "That is a fast timeline, do you already have a building selected?"

She nodded. "Yes, my father was on business there last year and found the perfect storefront. He'd purchased it back then, knowing he could either start a gambling den there, or maybe a small café, but when I told him about my aspirations he told me he'd transfer the mortgage to me. I've already paid him all the money he's put into the building so far, so all that's left from beginning the rest of the preparations is the license approval."

"Doesn't your father have connections there? Could that kind of referral get you moved up the list?" I leaned forward. "You'd think they'd want a successful business in town."

She shook her head. "We've tried, the business owners that he's friends with there have all added a recommendation with my appeal, but they don't have enough sway to actually get me moved up the waitlist." Her thin shoulders folded in. "It's fine. I can wait until the summer after next to open the store."

I thought for a moment. There had to be a way I could help her. She'd done so much for me in our time as friends, and I'd never had anything to repay her kindness.

"What if Therese mailed Lady Margot and gave a referral?" I shrugged. "I don't know if it'll work to get you moved up, but it's worth a shot."

Aurora's eyes widened. "I could never ask Lady Therese to do that. If she said no, and was upset with me, it could impact sales here."

I chewed on my lip. I understood her concern, my aunt always wanted to appear benevolent, but rarely actually was. But that thought triggered another, and I straightened, knowing exactly how I could get my aunt to do this.

"What if I ask her? I'll frame it in a way that benefits her, that way she won't say no. And even if she does, she wouldn't know it was a favor to you. Just that it was a suggestion I made for her behalf."

Aurora thought about it, flattening her hands over the fabric in front of her.

"You don't think she'd be upset?"

I shook my head. "I don't think so, and I don't think she'll decline. She likes bragging about our kingdom, and if you open a store there, she can remind the other kingdoms who had your designs first; Kembertus."

Aurora nodded and smiled. "If you think it will work, I would really appreciate it."

I grinned conspiratorially. "It'll definitely work, and soon you'll get your approval." She twisted her fingers, and I could see that she was bursting with excitement at the potential of her plan being moved up. I couldn't help but beam at her happiness.

Aurora walked me to the door and as I stepped outside she spoke. "Are you sure you don't want to stay for dinner? Jacqueline should be home soon."

I squeezed her hand. "No thank you, I need to be heading back before it gets dark."

After saying goodbye, I left.

My thoughts wandered to Maddox as I walked down the same street we had strode together just the day before. I didn't dare tell Aurora about him. Not that a man had to save me from the blacksmith, and most definitely not that he was an immortal.

But here I was, thinking about a Kova on my walk home.

It was disturbing.

I wasn't positive that I was afraid of him, thus far, he seemed harmless enough, if not a little flirtatious. But what disturbed me was the way I felt around him.

But that was just one of their traits. They lured their prey in.

The castle loomed over the town and as I looked up at it my stomach felt uneasy at the thought of the gala. Why had my aunt brought up an arranged marriage? I couldn't count how many times she'd discussed marriage and how I should be trying harder to find a husband. But that was always a conversation involving my choice. Never had she threatened to arrange one.

The thought cast a shiver down my spine, and I knew my father would have the same reaction. He would've fallen on his sword before forcing me into a marriage with a stranger. I thought he would've liked the idea of his daughter getting married to someone she loved, but he had never really talked to me about what that would look like.

I'd read books about it, heard beautiful songs written about it, but never saw it growing up. I never got to see what my parents were like together, and he had never expressed interest in someone aside from my mother. Besides the late night trysts I'd had with a few men in Neomaeros, none of which could come close to being defined as love, the only examples of relationships I had were my aunt and uncle or Aurora and Jacqueline. My guardians were far from in love. They never showed each other affection, at least around me. They hardly ever talked.

Aurora and Jacqueline were in love, though, and it made me smile to see them together. But when I did see them embrace, or smile at each other with adoration, there was always a darkness that lurked within me.

You'll never have that.

CHAPTER SIXTEEN

Maddox

I truly tried to leave her alone.

Tried locking myself in my room at the inn, or occupying my time by training with Wyott or reading, but there was never a moment where she left my mind. I had so many questions that needed answers, even though she wouldn't be able to give them to me.

I wished I could talk to Goddess Rominiava, to ask her why she mated us. What was it about Evaline, or me, that made us two halves of one whole? Our souls were crafted for one another, and I was desperate to find out what that meant. To know what her hand felt like in mine. To feel her warmth next to me in bed at night.

I was desperate. Two centuries of pining did that to a man.

I tried to stay away. To bide my time until I found an appropriate way to get close to her. It had only been a few days since we met, after all.

But I was a man, a Kova, not a God. And I didn't have that kind of willpower.

I looked for her. I'd gone near the castle, hoping to find her sneaking about outside, but I hadn't. I'd traipsed through the main street as if I'd see her walking, but had no luck.

I could track her. But that seemed like it would not be the best way to gain her affection. So, I just waited, and as I neared the inn, ready to give up for the day, I heard her voice.

It was a street over and sounded like she was bidding a friend goodbye, that she had to get home before it was dark.

Good.

I knew she'd walk past the inn to get to the castle, so I waited inside the door frame, and fell in step behind her as she walked by.

She wore that same black cloak, fluttering in the breeze behind her. My breath caught at the sight of her long, white, braid that cascaded down her back. I could only imagine how long her hair was when it was free. I could see her neck, skin like creamy silk, saw the flutter of her artery below.

I almost didn't approach her. But again, with the willpower.

But before I could, she whipped around. Her braid landing around her shoulder and her eyes fierce as they pierced mine.

Breath evaded my lungs.

"It's poor manners to follow a woman down the street." She said low, eyes sliding to the couple that approached as she spoke.

A smile lifted my cheeks before I could help it. "I never said I had manners, Evaline." A ghost of a smile flashed in her eyes, but she hid it just as quickly.

"Well? Did you need something?"

You.

"Yes. A bite to eat at the tavern, would you care to join me?" Even the roll of her eyes was hypnotizing.

"I don't go to dinner with strangers who make a habit of following me."

My grin persisted as I cocked my head, sidestepping to make room for the passersby. "No, but you didn't run this time." I shrugged. "So, you're already following the rules of our game."

A blush crept up her cheeks. She crossed her arms and eyed me.

"Anyway," I started. "I was nearby and happened upon you. What are the odds of us continuously running into each other like this?"

"Probably very high considering Kembertus is a small city." She tried so hard to maintain a bored expression on her face.

I nodded. "Perhaps. But I'm choosing to believe it's because the Gods want us to become friends."

A humorless laugh erupted from her lips.

"I don't think the Gods bother themselves with trivial matters like the relationships of mortals." Then she shrugged. "Or...you." She said, instead of mentioning my species out in public.

One day, we'd laugh about this conversation. When we were tangled up in bed, perfectly happy together, she'd remember that the Gods very much bothered themselves with these matters.

"I think they do." My tone grew serious without meaning it to. I gauged her reaction.

"That seems like a waste of their energy." The wind blew past and the small hairs that framed her face blew with it. Her scent wafted over to me even stronger, and my grip on reality shook.

"The Gods created this world and the souls within it. I think it makes perfect sense that they watch over it and ensure those who were fated to meet, do."

She shook her head and looked down. "I think they should focus more on not taking good people to the Night too soon."

Something in my heart ached for her loss. I wished I could comfort her but knew I couldn't press her for that now.

"That's a good point." I said softly.

She looked up at me and I saw her eyes focus on something in the distance behind me.

"It's getting late, I have to get back before dark."

The sunset was behind me. I should've known that's what she was looking at. The way its light washed over her skin made it appear golden, as if she was a Goddess as well.

I nodded. "I understand." I wanted to walk with her, but I knew she didn't want me to.

She poked a finger toward me. "Don't follow me." The words were serious, but her tone was light.

"I won't." I smiled. But Gods I wanted to. "I want to see you again." I repeated my same line from our last encounter, as if the more times I voiced it the more it'd happen.

She rolled her eyes, almost playfully, as she turned, her arms slipped from her chest. "Like I said, in this small city it's bound to happen." She started walking away, throwing over her shoulder. "Especially if you keep following me."

I had to swallow my laugh. That sounded like a challenge.

I watched her off until she was lost in a slew of pedestrians on the street and turned back to the inn.

My heart felt light in my chest and my blood bubbled through my veins. I felt drunk off her, and we had only spoken for a few minutes.

But this feeling was addictive, she was addictive, and I needed more. I needed to know her favorite food, to see her hair down, to feel her laugh against my lips.

I sighed.

In time.

I'd lived nearly two centuries. I'd seen wars and famine. Droughts and long winters. I'd been tortured and wounded. And each of those experiences instilled a patience within me. But it dissipated when I looked at her. Any control I had vanished.

I had time for her to open up, to accept me. But I was struggling to find the patience.

I opened the door of the inn, the small bell in the top right corner signaling as I walked through it.

Nathaniel looked up from his task and shifted his glasses on his face.

"Mr. Vicor, I was just making a note to speak with you." Nathaniel still addressed me formally no matter how many times I encouraged him not to.

I turned and strode to the desk. "What can I do for you?"

"I wanted to confirm that you are still prepared to reserve your room indefinitely? There is a castle event tomorrow night and some out of town guests are staying here. Of course, I'm not trying to pressure you into leaving, but I just wanted to know whether I would have your room available for last minute reservations or not." His voice trembled at the end; he was afraid of me.

Maybe he should have been. Kova weren't evil like the Vasi were, I'd never killed anyone I drank from, but I'd killed. Hundreds of evil men, and Vasi. But I wouldn't kill someone who didn't deserve it.

I smiled. "Of course, I understand. I plan to have my room reserved indefinitely." But the castle event piqued my interest. "What is this event you're speaking of?"

He seemed relieved I wasn't angry. He shuffled his papers and filed them away in a folder.

"It's the Spring Solstice Ball. We have it every year to honor the God of Terra so he will bless our crops."

I nodded. "Can anyone go to this Ball?"

"Oh yes, the Lord and Lady welcome all citizens and visitors in their city to the event." He shuffled through some papers behind the desk before extending his hand toward me. "Here is the formal invitation, if you'd like to attend."

"Thank you, Nathaniel." I quipped.

When my back was turned and I headed up the stairs toward my room, a smile spread across my face.

Attending a Ball honoring Arlomandric in the castle where she lived wasn't following, merely proper etiquette. Of course, I had to help ensure a bountiful harvest this year.

Chapter Seventeen

Evaline

It'd been an hour since I spoke with Maddox on my walk home, but my body still hadn't recovered. I'd never experienced anything like it. When I was near him it felt like there was a string linking us. Some kind of pull that insisted I be around him, closer, and that I'd never be close enough. It was alarming, and I didn't understand how no one else around us seemed to feel the same.

When I left Aurora's, I got about halfway home when I knew he was following me.

I wish I could claim some kind of exceptional survival instinct that whispered in my ear that I was being followed, but it was more physical than that. I felt his presence behind me. Not like I'd felt anyone before.

Somehow my body knew it was Maddox before I could turn around and confirm it with my eyes.

But as I was seated at the dining room table of the castle with my aunt and uncle, the clink of our cutlery on the porcelain plates was the only sound filling the room, I thought about Maddox's fierce eyes. The way they pierced into me, dark and made of molten metal. The slight pout in his lips when he wasn't smiling, the scar that resided there. The way his voice lilted when he said my name.

It was just a name, and I heard it each day, but the word never mattered until it came across his lips.

And I didn't like how much it affected me.

"Evaline," my uncle said, and I started at the sound of his voice. "Are you excited for the Spring Solstice Ball?"

I shrugged. "I suppose."

The events had never really been something I was interested in, but it was better than being locked in this castle with no one to talk to.

"You should be excited. These Balls are something the citizens of Kembertus look forward to. They get to come into the castle and live like royalty. Eat our food and drink our wine. You should be indulging in those vices too; it'll make you more approachable at these parties."

I almost choked on my potato.

My aunt laughed nervously. "What he's trying to say is that perhaps if you opened yourself up more at the parties, you'd have more fun." Then her eyes cut to him. "But of course, you don't want to overindulge in the spirits, otherwise you'll run the risk of embarrassing yourself."

I stifled a laugh. My uncle was known for overindulging. If he was able to walk out of the events on his own, it was a tame night.

He waved his fork to dismiss the comment. "What I was actually trying to say," he broke his sentence to take a gulp of wine, the red staining his lips. "Was that the men from Kembertus, or even other cities, that come to these parties often are here for a chance to meet you. They're looking for a bride, and the niece of the Lord and Lady of Kembertus is highly coveted, even if you do not think so."

Fuck.

"Yes." My aunt said. "You are a highly desired partner, and after our talk the other day..." Her voice clipped. "I hope you had a chance to reconsider your attitude toward the idea of marriage."

It was easier if I didn't speak. Then I could finish my meal faster and leave.

My uncle nodded. "You're just like your father," I started to smile, but he cut me off. "That wasn't a compliment."

My smile disappeared as I pursed my lips.

"He was stubborn and naive. He chose to give up his claim to our family's money and status," his hands waved around the room. "This very castle. Just so he could go off and be a soldier."

My father did forgo his claim to this kingdom. He wanted to be more than a figurehead over a city. He wanted to live his life on the battlefield, not get sloppy at parties. And after, he wanted a family.

"And look where that got him." My uncle's voice pulled me from my thoughts. "Dead, too young, from a robber, trying to come back home. If he'd just stayed here, he would've been safe."

My jaw clenched. He had no right to speak of my father's death. He wasn't there, cradling my father's head as he took his last breath. He didn't hold the wound as his brother bled out before his chest went still.

"Don't be like your father, Evaline." He held my eyes then. "Be more tactful than that. Marry a man who can take care of you. Give him children to carry on his name. Accept help from your aunt when it is offered. We only want the best for you. And right now, that means finding you a husband before it's too late."

My eyes fell to focus on the slab of meat that I hadn't finished eating yet. It was easier to ignore them, but they made it so difficult. My father's death wouldn't be used as a lesson on how to be complacent. I bit back the words that rose to the tip of my tongue. The curses, the venom that was ready to be unleashed.

And instead muttered out my response. "Okay."

He seemed content with that, or maybe was more interested in his wine, so he dropped the subject.

He was done speaking to me, but he turned toward Therese just as she dropped her napkin onto the ground. Raymond came forward to pick it up for her while my uncle spoke. "Speaking of finding a spouse, have you heard from Gabriehl? He's not getting any younger, either. He needs to make more of an effort to find a marriage just as much as Evaline does."

At the mention of my cousin whom I'd never met, my eyes raised to the wall opposite the dining table. There, positioned above the fire place that heated the room was a grand portrait of Gabriehl. His skin was pale and it contrasted the bright red of his shaggy hair drastically. He appeared to be standing tall, even though the painting only portrayed his upper half. His broad chest was stuck out, and I wondered if he was trying to appear more confident, more Lord-like, than he felt.

My aunt nodded her head. "I know. Last time he mailed he said he was enjoying Arlomandrah. But I'll remind him in my next letter."

Elijah took another gulp of wine. "He's done plenty of traveling. He needs to come back home, learn how to run the kingdom. I'm not going to live forever." He hissed.

Thank the Gods for that.

The next morning, I couldn't get out of the castle fast enough. I had to move. I had to be around people who weren't my guardians or silent servants who weren't supposed to talk to me. By the grace of the Gods my aunt didn't request my help preparing for the Ball.

I didn't try to go to the boutique, I knew Aurora would be swamped with last minute alterations. Instead, I walked right past it. When I hit the dead end of the inn, I blushed at the thought that Maddox was inside. It wasn't really a thought but more of an understanding that he was there. That I could almost feel the rise and fall of his chest pulsing around me as I turned right to head to the orphanage.

I shook my head and took a deep breath.

The girls and I didn't have a lesson today, but I was lonely and needed a distraction. I decided to go to see all the children, and Jacqueline, and take my mind off the incessant threat of arranged marriage that my guardians were now not even bothering to hide anymore.

The metal gate creaked behind me, and I immediately heard the patter of feet from inside the house. The door burst open, and several children swarmed around me. Priscilla, Megin, Aliya, Simon, and others.

"Good morning, Evaline!" They shouted in unison.

The smile they forged on my face was bright and the warmth in my chest spread. I knew this would make me feel better.

"Good morning, everyone, where's Jacqueline?" I said as I walked up the steps of the porch. Just then she came into sight from another room.

"We're getting ready for breakfast." She said, smiling at me and bouncing a baby on her hip.

"Can I help?" I asked, looking down at all the kids.

Yeses rang through the air, and I laughed, shuffling them back into the house and closing the door behind me. Immediately hands were grasping for my own, and once those were taken others were fisting into my shirt, into my cloak, to escort me to the kitchen. For a moment I was concerned that the dagger was strapped to my thigh, hidden by my long skirt, but none of them ever came close to it.

"What's on the menu this morning?" I asked as we made it into the kitchen, Jacqueline sat the baby she'd been holding into its high-top chair and fastening the straps around it.

"I was thinking pancakes?" Jacqueline offered and the children screamed.

I raised my brows at the loud noise and smirked. "It seems that's the crowd favorite."

We gave the group supplies to draw while we cooked. They hummed with the constant noise that children do, and I turned to Jacqueline.

"Where's everyone else?" I asked, referring to the people who helped run the orphanage.

She shrugged. "Lillian was feeling ill last night so I made her leave, and she and Monte were the only ones supposed to be here this morning until the rest come this afternoon. But I told him to stay home and take care of her." Usually, they had two guardians there each night, cycling between the entire staff.

I nodded. "Hopefully she's feeling better today, and it was nothing serious." I said, washing my hands.

Jacqueline turned her wicked eye to me, her voice lowering. "I think she's pregnant."

My smile grew again. "Really?"

"Not that she even knows, but she just suddenly felt nauseous last night, and I know she and Monte have been trying." Jacqueline enthused. I smiled, I hoped she was, and I hoped she was feeling better this morning.

We continued chatting while we made breakfast. The children ate voraciously and I discovered soon after that the honey we'd used to cover the pancakes had made the wooden table quite sticky. I worked on scrubbing it away while Jacqueline leaned against the sink to wash dishes. The children had moved to the front living room to give us space to clean.

"So." She said, keeping her voice hushed so that only I could hear it over the slosh of the water. "Aurora told me what your aunt threatened the other day."

I looked up at her, quirking a brow.

"The arranged marriage."

"Yes." I sighed. I leaned my knee on a chair from the dining table and straightened from scrubbing. "They've made it pretty clear these last two years that I'm expected to marry soon." I wagged my head. "I guess, really, they would have already liked me to be married. But in the last week they've brought it up more so than in the past. And for the first time, they voiced that an arranged marriage was a possibility."

She continued to scrub but kept her gaze on me, nodding in understanding.

"I guess I never considered that they'd actually do it, but now with the Spring Solstice Ball I'm afraid they're going to be more persistent than ever. And when they do pick someone, how do I say no?" I continued.

Jacqueline's brows furrowed slightly, her eyes sympathetic. "It's your life Evaline, you have the right to live it as you wish."

I nodded. "I know, but they'd never let me. I'm not like you and Aurora, or Lillian and Monte. I'm one of them, a Manor, and they'll never stop until they've used me up in a marriage that suits them."

Jacqueline turned back to the dishes, but I heard her small voice. "Have you ever considered leaving?" She whispered.

I pursed my lips.

Every day.

CHAPTER EIGHTEEN

Evaline

I let my heavy lids fall as I sunk deeper into the tub. The water, that had once been almost scalding, was hardly lukewarm. My limbs searched it in an effort to find a warm spot hiding somewhere in the vessel.

I didn't want to get out.

But I needed to. My fingers and toes were pruned and the hair that curtained over the edge had long been dried from its wash.

Only the fading daylight seeped into the room.

I sat, trying to convince myself to get ready for the Ball. But no matter how hard I tried I couldn't find it within myself to rise. I was disturbed by my aunt's lecture regarding marriage, and the threat of an arranged marriage, but my uncle's comments at dinner yesterday only cemented those concerns. The dread that they were planning to marry me off to some stranger had grown the last few days, and if there was ever a time for them to hit me with the news it was tonight.

My head snapped as I heard the door to my bedroom shut. I jolted up from where I had been lying against the tub. My thoughts immediately shifted to the dagger that hid between the bedding and frame underneath. I was too far away to access it, and I was naked, for Gods' sake.

"Evaline, are you almost finished?" My aunt's voice called from the other side of the door.

My eye roll was so devastating my head fell back against the tub. Gods, did the woman know no semblance of privacy?

Swallowing the annoyance that soured my tongue, I stood from the bath. I didn't bother answering Therese, but I was sure she could hear the slosh of the water.

After drying I pulled on a strapless white slip and opened the door that entered my room, eyes falling to where my aunt sat on the bed.

She wore a robe, not yet ready for the Ball herself, but her hair was already pinned in tight ringlets on top of her head. It looked as if it might topple at any moment.

She smiled at me, sweeping her arm toward the vanity where several cosmetics sat. "I thought I could do your makeup?"

"I suppose so." I gave in. I didn't wear cosmetics often because I was too lazy to apply them. But I knew things like this made her happy, and if it got her off my back for a few days, I didn't see the harm.

I turned the vanity chair away from the table, facing the light of the burning fire. She stood from the bed and approached. For the first time I saw the dress that lay there in heaps of blue tulle. Therese must've sent someone to pick it up from the boutique.

I turned towards my aunt as she arranged the items on the vanity, sorting through what she planned to use and setting them in front of her.

"I feel so guilty over what I said the other day, Evaline." She looked me in the eyes and I was surprised that she seemed sincere. "I never should have said such a cruel thing about your father." She flashed a sad smile, picking up a horsehair brush that held some loose powder on its bristles. "He did the best he could after he lost your mother, and he did a great job, all things considered."

I closed my eyes as my aunt began dusting the brush over my face. I was thankful for the opportunity to do so because I knew the tears would be ready to fall at any moment if they were open.

I felt her pause with the brush and tilt my chin up slightly before continuing the task.

"He really loved her; you know." I heard a tap of the brush and felt a smaller one glide across my eyelid. "I hardly knew your father or your mother, only got to meet them a handful of times, but when they were together it was as if no one else existed."

The lump in my throat was painful when I swallowed. I had never heard someone talk about my parents this way and somehow felt as if I was getting some secret insight into who they were when they weren't simply parents, but when they were in love.

She continued while she worked on my other eye.

"Sometimes I'd have to remind myself not to stare at them, they were that in love." Her voice was melancholic. "I remember the way he looked at her, as if he breathed through her."

There were some more taps before she began on my eyes again.

"But it was reciprocated. Your mother loved your father so much that when they were separated in a room, her eyes would fall to him every chance she could. Like she had to remind herself that he was still there."

I wished I could've seen them that way. I yearned to be raised in a home with parents who were happy, hopelessly in love. My father would've been saved from so many years of heartache.

"Open your eyes." I did as I was told, and her brows furrowed as she examined them.

Then she turned back to the vanity and picked up a thin brush with so few bristles on the end I wondered if there was only a single hair there. She opened her tin of black powder and dipped her brush in a small oil cup, mixing it into the powder.

I tried to keep my eyes open as she delicately traced a line across the lash line of my top lid. Once dried, she repeated the process with the other eye, then moved to coat my lashes in black, too.

She stood back and took my chin in her hand, tilting it to each side to make sure both eyes matched.

Then she smiled. "Perfection."

I turned in the chair to look in the mirror. It was very pretty. She used neutral eyeshadow to brighten my blue-green eyes. I was usually self-conscious about how large they were, but even with the makeup only accentuating that, I thought they looked beautiful now.

"Can I help with your hair?" She asked as she stood behind me now, meeting my gaze in the reflection.

I hesitated for a moment before nodding and swiveling my chair back to sit straight against the vanity. I hardly ever allowed her to do my hair, but I didn't see the harm in it today. I wouldn't be wearing the barbed wire at the Ball since I'd be safe with plenty of guards around.

I handed her the comb and she worked the knots that had formed since my hair had dried. My hair was fine, which usually meant it was smooth, feeling like silk. But if I didn't get a chance to brush it while wet and then it dried, it was a nightmare to comb through.

We were silent for a while. It was calming to have someone else handle my hair. If I closed my eyes, I could almost pretend it was my mother.

"You look just like her." Therese said as she finished brushing out the ends. "I know you were barely born when she passed, so I know you don't remember."

She placed the brush on the table and patted my shoulder. "It is sometimes jarring how much you resemble her. I imagine that was both very hard on your father and the greatest blessing."

I grabbed my small jar of pins out of the drawer so that she wouldn't rifle through it and accidentally find the wire. She gathered some hair into her hands, deciding how to style it, I assumed, while I thought about everything she had shared with me tonight. We'd never had a conversation like this. I might've thought I was dreaming, but the painful tug of her fingers through my hair reminded me I was not.

But still, hope flared inside my chest. Perhaps she wouldn't try to force me into an arranged marriage like I'd been dreading. Maybe she just wanted to scare me straight. Maybe she wanted me to put myself out there more at the Ball, and that's why she'd brought it up.

I looked up at her as she worked, watching her eyes fall over my hair as she moved it this way and that, gauging what style she'd like. The more I watched her the more I considered that she could've been kind once.

Before she had the burden of a kingdom on her shoulders. Maybe we could've gotten along if she was just my aunt, and not Lady of Kembertus.

I smiled as I felt her begin to braid my hair.

Not the entire thing, just the hair that gathered on the crown of my head. She pulled the top half of my hair back and braided it, leaving the rest of my hair to fall in the natural loose curls. When the braid was secured she pulled on it so that it was thick, and then pulled some hairs around my face loose.

She backed away when she finished, and I turned to see the back. The braid stood out against my waves.

"Now for the most exciting part!" Therese's excitement startled me.

I turned in the chair as she gathered the mess of tulle in her arms and turned to show me the dress, holding it in front of her own body.

"Wow." I breathed, again struck by its beauty.

She beamed and helped me slide the dress over my slip. After she'd tightened and tied the corset, I crossed the room to the floor length mirror. I hadn't noticed until she put it on, but there were two long pieces of tulle on each shoulder. She came up behind me and tied them so that each made up a small bow with long pieces of tulle ribboning down my arms.

"You're exquisite, Evaline."

I smiled at her reflection, shocked at how much I agreed with her. I never much cared about my appearance. I knew others thought I was attractive, but I hadn't given it much thought. When you spent as much time as I did trying to be invisible, you didn't take much time to notice yourself.

But I couldn't tear my gaze from my reflection. The dusty blue of the dress suited my skin tone, and the white roses did the same for my hair. I even liked the way the corset cinched my waist and the contrast between it and my curves. I had never felt like such a woman before.

With her hands resting on my shoulders, she smiled at me in the mirror.

"Evaline, I was serious when I named this the Fresh Start Ball. It isn't just a new beginning for the kingdom and its people, it is for you, too." I tried my best not to let the scowl take over my features even though I knew she was attempting to manipulate me. "You never know what new adventures lay just around the corner, if you just open yourself to them."

I nodded. "I will do my best."

She smiled. "Thank you." She turned to walk out, but I spoke.

"Actually, Aunt Therese, I have a question." She turned back toward me. "This dress is beautiful." I said, running my hands over the fabric around my hips. "And Aurora is so talented, you've said so yourself." She smiled and nodded. "Well, when I went to the store the other day to try on my gown," I lied. "She told me she was trying to open a store in Neomaeros, too."

Her eyes widened. "That's a large step for any business, but I'm sure she'll do great there." She turned to leave again.

"Well," I said, moving back into her vision. "Her business license request is waiting in a queue to be approved, and who knows how long that could take. You understand, as a ruler."

"Yes, sometimes those things take a while. Did you have a question, Evaline? I have to get ready."

I nodded. "Yes, I was wondering if it would make sense for you to write a letter to Lady Margot in Neomaeros and recommend Aurora's shop, in hopes they'd move up her review?"

She winced. "Oh Evaline, you know how I hate speaking with the Madierian Kingdoms, especially Neomaeros."

I nodded. "I do. But you know Aurora will succeed there, just like she does here. And the sooner she opens, the sooner you can remind the Madierian Kingdoms who wore her original designs." I said, waving toward my own dress.

She pursed her lips.

"Plus, don't you think recommending a successful woman owned business to their kingdom would exemplify all the work you and Uncle

Elijah have put into meeting the Madierian Kingdom's progression demands?"

She looked away and I knew she was thinking, and after a moment a smile pulled on her face. "You're right. This will aid in our dealings with them, and help one of our own." She nodded. "I'll send it first thing tomorrow morning."

I smiled. "I think that's wise."

She clapped her hands. "We truly have to hurry now." She said and this time I let her walk to the door. "Oh, and don't forget your mask. It's on the bed."

My aunt rushed off to finish preparing herself for the Ball, after instructing me to meet her and my uncle at the internal entrance to the ballroom in fifteen minutes.

I picked up the small rectangular box and eased the top flap open, just as Aurora had done a few days ago, and was met with firelight sparkling off the silver strands woven into the mask. It wasn't a traditional silhouette. Instead of covering the whole face, or even both eyes, this mask was asymmetric. I crossed to my vanity and sat, placing it on my face and tying the pearly white ribbon behind my head to secure it.

On the right side the mask covered the cheekbone, around the eye, and up a few inches, until it ended at the hairline. It was cage-like with no backing, simply iridescent fabric covered wiring that swirled and stemmed in an elegant pattern. The mask covered the bridge of my nose before reaching for the other eye. But instead of curling underneath my eye as the right side did, the left side of the mask continued its pattern over my brow before ending at the ribbon that held the mask in place.

I tilted my head back and forth, testing how secure it was on my face, and after being satisfied with its staying power, I moved closer to the mirror.

Even in the dimmer lighting, facing away from the fire, I could see how the makeup Therese had crafted and the mask worked together to make my eyes truly remarkable. Partnered with the dusty blue color of the dress, it seemed as though the first thing people would see when looking at me were my eyes.

I smiled, I liked it. Although the mask hid my identity about as well as my white hair. If tonight was about fresh starts, shouldn't I be a bit more hidden?

But I knew the answer to that was a resounding no. Elijah and Therese very much wanted every man at the Ball to know exactly who I was, and how to find me.

I stood, my time alone was running out, and I wanted to slide my dagger on. Not for safety reasons, in such a public venue with guards I felt safe, but simply because it was mine, and I could.

I reveled in the soft touch of the leather kissing the sensitive skin of my thigh and the coolness of the sheathed dagger that sat there.

The dress fell over it and I looked at my reflection again, a smirk forming on my lips.

I relished having a secret hidden under all this feminine attire.

No one at the Ball would know that something so tasteful had something so sinister lurking below.

CHAPTER NINETEEN

Evaline

My uncle escorted my aunt and I through the grand doors of the ballroom. They opened to a short staircase atop a balcony, displaying the entire affair below us.

As was custom, the steward announced our arrival. It was an unnecessary gesture. We needed no more introduction than the Lord's bellowing laugh when he got ahold of his wine. But the crowd turned to face us as we stepped through the threshold and descended the steps.

At the base, the imperial staircase ended in another balcony with symmetrical flights diverting to the left and right. The landing was several paces deep, leaving space for the string quartet to play, along with the grand piano that remained a permanent fixture. The strings nestled to the left and the piano to the right, leaving a gap where the Lord would greet his guests.

I scanned the crowd as we made our way down, searching for Aurora and Jacqueline. I couldn't wait to compliment Aurora's work on the gown. I witnessed how much of herself she gave to her art each week and I wanted her to know how honored I felt to be wearing a special piece of hers.

The first sweep was unsuccessful, but I knew she'd be somewhere nearby.

I stood beside my uncle, who perched atop the landing, Therese my reflection.

"Every year, the Lady and I hold this gala to celebrate the Spring Solstice and honor Arlomandric." My uncle began.

I felt an odd heat flash over my skin. The kind of blush that crept up your neck when you were being watched. And of course I was, there were hundreds of eyes on me as my uncle welcomed his guests. But this was different.

"And each year turns out better than the previous as we get to meet more and more people of Kembertus, and our welcomed travelers."

I had been to dozens of these gatherings and felt many gazes upon my skin, but none that felt like this. Like it was tracking me, watching the rise and fall of my chest. I held my breath as I realized I'd only ever felt a gaze like this from one person, and the idea that he was here, that he'd see me in this dress, had my heart racing.

"Please, enjoy the food and wine as we honor the God of Terra!" Elijah finished with a flourish. The crowd laughed in the way they must during events like this, and my uncle beamed.

My guardians descended the right staircase, my uncle clapping a hand on the pianist's shoulder. I took the left, passing the strings who sat with their instruments between their legs or on their lap. I had to find Aurora and Jacqueline, their company was often my only motivation to attend these events, even if I had to hide it from Therese. She didn't want me socializing with women at courting events when there were plenty of men to get to know.

But I needed to shake this stare.

It was an alarming sensation to feel a gaze. Warm air whispered over my lips, down my neck, running over the way the dress hugged my waist and the tulle plumed off my hips.

I looked around, again searching for my friends. The dance floor sat in the middle of the room, sunken down a few steps. It was framed by a hallway held up by several large granite pillars that stood every few paces. They stretched dozens of yards up toward the cathedral ceiling. At these events you'd commonly find men and women flirting in the shadowed sections of the walkway, especially after they shook their chaperone. It's where I typically stayed if I could help it, as the shadows shielded me from my aunt's attempts to introduce me to more men, or mothers of those men. I leaned my hip against one of the pillars now and continued to scan the crowd.

My eyes caught another set, wide and hazel, but they flicked away from mine in an instant. I knew who it was even from across the room. Lydia turned completely away, putting her exposed back to me as she turned to face Clara and Brielle. The pale pink dress she wore didn't reach up to cover the tawny brown skin of the top half of her back. I pursed my lips as I met Brielle's eyes, and her already fair face paled further. She quickly snagged Clara's gloved hand and started speaking in a hushed whisper.

My stomach flipped with unease. I knew they were talking about me, even though we'd almost been friends once. Just as my aunt had done with Natalia, she encouraged the three daughters of prominent families in Kembertus to stay away from me. I didn't have any direct evidence, only knew that the three of them and I had become friendly, and a few weeks later they started ignoring me completely.

"They're your competition, Evaline." Therese had told me when I broached the subject. I hadn't accused her of meddling, even though I knew she must've, only mentioned that they didn't talk to me when we ran into each other anymore.

I couldn't be angry with them, they were only doing what the Lady of their city asked. But now, as I saw them thrive in this environment in a way I couldn't, noticed the way Clara swept some locs over her warm ochre shoulder as a man asked to dance with her, I found myself picturing what events like these could be like for me if I had been allowed to be friends with this group of high ranking women. If my aunt didn't keep me so isolated.

But the thought evaporated as thin hand slid into the crevice of my elbow, spinning me.

131 |

"Evaline, you look breathtaking!" Aurora gushed.

At once my unease lifted and whatever odd sensation I had been feeling was gone, but a tug on my heart stayed. And I knew what that meant. Who that meant.

I pulled her toward the beautiful granite pool under the balcony. A bench wrapped around its tub where I often sat to watch the fish that swam inside of it.

"Where's Jacqueline?" I asked, brows pulling together as we perched on the edge of the pool.

She shrugged, waving a hand toward the crowd. "She saw an old friend and wanted to catch up."

I nodded and remembered why I had been looking for her. "Aurora," I started, my hands running over the roses that lay on my waist. "This dress is divine."

Her smile met mine. "Thank you! But you compliment too much, you already said all of this at the boutique."

I laughed. "Seeing it on a rack is entirely different from seeing it on, especially in this lighting."

For a few minutes we talked about the dress she wore, which was a deep purple and sleek, running far closer to her body than mine, but landing so effortlessly beautiful against her brown skin. Her mask was gold, adorned with purple threading around her eyes to match her dress, and covered the top half of her face.

But Aurora's face changed then as if something dawned on her. Her jaw dropped open and she reached forward to grip my hands in hers.

"Evaline." She whispered, the words rushing out of her mouth. "I can't believe I nearly forgot." She shook her head incredulously. "The most handsome man is here." The words had my eyes widening. "I've never seen him before; he must be one of the travelers." My heart dropped; afraid I knew exactly who she was referring to. "He's so tall with the darkest hair, but oh," Aurora dramatically placed a hand over her heart. "His eyes."

I felt the gaze once more, fully aware that no amount of overhead chatter would stop a nosey Kova from eavesdropping this conversation.

And this time it wasn't just the feel of the gaze that startled me. Since Aurora had all but confirmed Maddox was around, a warmth grew in my chest – an otherworldly pull on my heart to go find him.

I cut my gaze to the side, an annoyed breath puffing out of my lips as I pushed the thought away. "Let me guess, they were gray."

The gaze moved from my eyes to my lips and a flutter flew through me.

Aurora cocked a brow. "How did you know?"

I looked down at the fish, trailing my finger over the water. "I already met him in town, at the inn, his name is Maddox." Aurora gasped, and I continued in a low voice. I knew she'd want more details. "I keep running into him, three times already, including last week at the market. He's agitating."

The gaze followed my arm, down to the water.

"He doesn't look agitating." Aurora countered and I laughed.

"Gods, woman, you're married!" I shook my head, laughing.

Aurora laughed too. "And I love my wife, dearly, but that doesn't mean I can't appreciate when the Gods bless this land with a work of art."

The gaze lifted to my face, falling back to my lips as my jaw dropped.

"He's truly not attractive up close." But I knew that was a lie. He was beautiful. He was every bit the specimen she described. Godly, even. All chiseled jaw and dark eyes, plump lips with a dusting of black facial hair. His hair that always seemed to wield a slight curl was the color of obsidian and his skin was olive toned. He was everything Aurora gushed about, but that didn't make him any less of a nuisance.

I ignored the nagging thought that perhaps he wasn't annoying, just my attraction to him was.

"Wait, he saw you at the market, the day you bought your," she lowered her voice even more. "Dagger?"

"Yes." I said, rolling my eyes. "He saved me, I was caught and he claimed I was buying it for him." Voicing that I'd been unsuccessful in my attempt to buy a dagger alone, and worse yet, that I needed a man's help, made me nauseous. Aurora's eyes softened at the remark, and I quickly followed it up. "But then he followed me and was quite annoying, so I stand by my categorization." I nodded firmly. "He's agitating."

Aurora ducked her head into my line of sight. "It sounds like he was flirting with you."

I let out such an audible laugh that several heads turned toward us. His gaze hadn't left my skin this entire conversation and only now did it peel away. It was unsettling, and for a moment I missed the warmth.

But before I could respond my aunt was snapping at me in a hushed tone.

"Evaline, what in the world are you doing? Get your hand away from those disgusting fish!" She pulled me up by the elbow while I flicked the water from my fingers. "Your uncle and I have someone we'd like you to meet."

I gulped. I was wrong earlier when I'd hoped my aunt wouldn't do this. But here it was. An introduction to some man they deemed fit to be my husband.

We walked through the pillared hallway toward the Lord.

Why did they even bother? I'd met nearly all the eligible bachelors in Kembertus. How were there more?

My breath caught as a connection formed in my mind.

Perhaps it was all too coincidental that I'd never seen Maddox in town before, and my aunt and uncle had never threatened an arranged marriage. Now, all of a sudden, those two events happened in the same week.

Not to mention the way Maddox regarded me. Teasing, mocking flirtatiously. As if he knew something about me that I didn't. Had I already met my betrothed? Or at least, whom my guardians would attempt to wed me to?

And if that was the case, if Maddox came here under the notion of marrying me, perhaps it was because he'd known I was Wallace's daughter before he ever arrived. Perhaps he wanted to get me out of this kingdom, if not only because he knew my father would hate my being here.

I found myself searching for my uncle, and waiting to catch my first look at the man they were introducing me to.

I tried very hard to ignore the way my heart raced, not from fear, but excitement. Hope for my future. Anticipation that perhaps he'd get me out of Kembertus and back to Neomaeros or another Madierian Kingdom.

But the more I thought about that potential, the more my heart fluttered for another reason. My skin buzzed with the thought of touching Maddox, kissing him. My eyes dilated with thoughts of his body against mine, what it might feel like to have those strong hands all over me.

Gods, what is happening to me?

Finally, my eyes landed on the Lord, his back turned as he was speaking with his guest.

My heart sped up. Maybe this didn't have to ruin my life. Yes, Maddox was annoying, but if he got me out of this city at least I'd be free. Maybe this was all a ploy, maybe he was a better man than I'd given him credit for. He was friends with my father, he couldn't be that bad, could he?

My uncle turned as we approached. My heart pounded in my ears.

"Evaline, we'd like to introduce you to an out-of-towner who is visiting our kingdom." I held my breath as I nodded, feeling the air prick my eyes with the effort to keep them open and catch my first glimpse, to confirm my newfound hope.

He turned and revealed the man. His head was tilted down, but his hair wasn't black. It was a light brown with the faintest hint of red undertones.

I tried to bite back my disappointment.

"This is Bassel." My uncle finished.

Bassel lifted his eyes to meet mine, a translucent red mask adorning his face, and the world stopped.

Because his eyes were green. Deep set. Separated by the scar that sat on the bridge of his nose.

And I hadn't seen them in two years.

CHAPTER TWENTY

Evaline

The music thrummed without melody and without pitch against my ears. The dancers slowed as if the floor were covered in molasses. The world halted around me.

All I could focus on were the green eyes that smiled at me. *Smiled* at me. As if he had no idea who I was. As if he hadn't looked into these exact same eyes just after Lonix died. The night he covered my mouth and further broke my fractured wrist. Even at the sight of him, I felt a pang of pain settle there.

My aunt and uncle were speaking but I couldn't hear them. Couldn't hear anything over the roar of my heart in my ears. I had to grind my teeth together to keep my lower lip from quivering. Had to curl my nails into the palm of my hand, pressing them against it to distract me from the memories raging through my head.

That feeling returned. The gaze coasting over my skin. Frantically searching my face as I was sure Maddox heard my heart beat out of my chest.

Bassel was speaking. His mouth moved with empty words. The mouth that once promised torture and pain.

I'd waited for this moment for two years. Waiting for the day I saw him again. I'd always hoped to have the right words to tell him what a monster he was. To tell him that he had no right to touch a woman against her will. To tell him that my wrist still ached when the weather changed, an unsolicited reminder. I wanted to ask how many other women had he attacked, how many hadn't been saved?

But I wanted more than that, too. I wanted to take my dagger, the one I bought for this exact moment and that ached so fiercely on my thigh, and slit his throat. Or pierce his heart. Anything to watch the light leave his eyes as Lonix's had.

But all I could do was focus on his eyes as he spoke, the edges of my vision muddled. Watch the way the corners of his eyes crinkled with wrinkles I never noticed the first time we'd met. Wrinkles of a man who'd spent a lot of time squinting or rubbing his temples. My eyes drifted to his scar, not big, just a slight notch over the top of his nose.

Who had given him that scar? A woman he attacked, one who tried to fight him off? I hoped she'd gotten away like I did.

That thought brought with it a chill that settled into my chest. That slunk through my entire body until I remembered who I was. That I was Evaline Manor, and I'd killed a Vasi. That I'd be damned before I ever let him touch another woman like that again. That if anyone in this world was going to take him out, it'd have to be me.

And then I came to.

I smiled, a different kind of mask than the one that was tied to me slid into place. "I'm sorry, I didn't hear that."

Bassel reciprocated the gesture, and a dimple adorned his left cheek, "I was saying what an honor it is to make your acquaintance. The Lord has been telling me about you all week." He shook his head as his eyes traveled down my dress. My smile faltered a beat as nausea crawled up my throat. "And I must say you are more than I could've imagined."

I curtsied before straightening – anything to draw his eyes back up. "Thank you, Bassel. It is a pleasure to meet you." I gauged his reaction. He didn't recognize me at all?

Was my attack such a commonplace occurrence for him that he did not recall, or was it so mundane he didn't harbor the memory of it? But maybe it was simpler than that. Perhaps it had been too dark that night for Bassel to see my features.

I pushed away those thoughts and fixed my eyes on his.

"Evaline," Therese said beside me. "Bassel is the son of Arthur Rydell, Ruler of Vestaria." I nodded, feigning interest, while the consequences of those words rested deep in my gut. "It's on the Kromean coast, maybe you can see it someday." I wasn't sure why she schooled me on the location, other than putting on a show for Bassel. There was no kingdom I was less interested in seeing than Vestaria, especially after my preview of the way they treated women.

The fake smile I gave my aunt was more like a grimace. "Maybe."

The music changed then. The lull of a ballad beginning on the piano.

Bassel angled toward me. "Perhaps we can converse more over a waltz?" He stretched his reach.

The Lady held her breath, no doubt expecting me to decline. Inside, I warred with myself for only a second. I never wanted to feel his hands on me again. But how else was I supposed to gather more information about him? How would I ever exact my revenge?

I swallowed my unease and placed my hand in his. "That sounds lovely."

I heard Therese's sigh of relief as he pulled me toward the ballroom floor, where he pulled me around gracelessly to face him.

Maddox's stare grew hotter by the moment, palpable anger suspended in the air. Odd.

I suppressed a shiver when Bassel's hand snaked around my waist, the other raising our already joined hands. He pulled me closer, and begrudgingly, I placed my hand on his shoulder.

Unnerved by the way he raked his eyes over me, I broke the silence. "What brings you to Kembertus?"

He shrugged against my palm. "I could say that I wanted to get away from Vestaria. That I've always found Kembertus a beautiful and accommodating kingdom. But the truth is that I came for the chance to meet you." I tried to ignore his final words, unable to deal with them at the moment. Instead, I focused on the fact that he'd confirmed that he had been here before. The thought of how many women in Kembertus he'd attacked fumbled through my mind. I could feel the anger burning the backs of my eyes and did everything I could to quell it. But the thoughts did not stop.

For all its faults, Kembertus was my home. I'd made a life here and made friends. What if he stayed, or came back here? What if the next victim was Aurora, or Jacqueline. Or in two decades, Priscilla or Megin?

I held my breath to stop it from shaking.

No. Never. He had to be stopped, and it didn't matter the cost.

I steadied my voice and asked. "Do you visit often?"

We followed the music with our movements. The song began to pick up slightly but was still slow and soft as the violins began.

He shook his head before he spoke. "No, I haven't been here in years."

My curiosity piqued. "That's a shame," the lie rolled off my lips. "What caused the delay?"

His face sobered. "I usually come to visit with a friend, he had family that moved here. But on our last trip here he passed away unexpectedly during the travel." He looked away as pain twisted his features.

"That is awful. I'm so sorry for your loss." The words felt like acid in my mouth.

Bassel pulled his gaze back to mine. He bought my fake sincerity. "Thank you," he inclined his head. "It was a devastating time."

I almost laughed. It was a minor miracle that I didn't, and I thanked the Gods for the willpower I was exhibiting, because no person in this room had less of a right to call that night devastating than Bassel.

It was comical, his delusion. But the memory hit me before I could stop it, and it took me under.

My body continued to waltz, but all I could see in my mind's eye were Lonix and Bassel over me. Smell their putrid breath and see the sheen of sweat on their foreheads. Recall the way their hands bound my wrists and legs as they hauled me up.

I forced the memory away, feeling ill. Bassel's touch was cold and sweaty. Unappealing as he gripped me.

I tried to focus on anything, everything, else to distract my mind from the memory that demanded my attention and his scaly hands on my skin.

The music. The colors. The dancers.

I let the world slow around me, allowing myself to dissociate.

The melody was beautiful. An enchanting lullaby that was soft and gentle but could grow wild and fierce. The surrounding dancers were a fog of silk and tulle, of purples and reds and pinks. And then a blur of black.

It skirted the edge of the crowd, between dancers, on the brim of my peripheral. I knew exactly where it was, even when I couldn't see it.

The music quickened, approaching its crescendo. A montage of heavy piano and quick strings, pulling together to form a beautiful melody that crashed towards its peak.

The room, the sounds, the colors, Bassel, drowned me. My chest heaved as breath flooded my throat.

Bassel moved, and I knew he'd spin me away. I relished the thought of a breath that wasn't tainted with his.

The coax of energy behind me kicked up as the dancers around us hastened, the music thrashed together, and Bassel spun me out.

The blurred lens veiling the world broke as a hand caught mine, tugging me into a new set of arms in one swift motion, pirouetting us away. I took a deep breath as I stared at the chest. It was jarring to be plucked from the air like that, but finally, I could breathe, and the only scent was a mixture of amber and leather. I looked up, although I knew who my partner was before I needed to see his face.

"Maddox."

CHAPTER TWENTY-ONE

Evaline

His smirk pulled up one side of his mouth.

"Evaline." He whispered my name and I tried to ignore the way my heart flipped at the sound.

His eyes danced in the light as he moved us across the ballroom, my dress sweeping over the granite floor. I'd prefer not to be dancing at all, but my body had already begun to relax.

"You wouldn't happen to be following me again, would you?" I asked as I looked over his shoulder. I could see Bassel leave the ballroom floor, shaking his head in annoyance. A wicked smile formed on my lips.

"Of course not." He said. I felt my heart rate uptick, his voice was so smooth that everything he said sounded like a flirt. It was getting to me.

"Because that would be a direct violation of the boundaries we set the last time we spoke," I tilted my head then. "Would it not?"

His smirk widened into a full smile. "It would. But I'm merely partaking in the festivities." He said before spinning me away. I looked back just in time to see his eyes moving over my dress and back up to my face, a gleam in his eye that didn't turn my stomach like Bassel's did.

When I landed back in his chest, it was closer than we'd been before. My hand rested on the thick muscle beside his neck, arm draped fully around his shoulder.

"You certainly don't make following our rules easy, though." Our eyes were locked, and it was overwhelming, but I couldn't look away. His mask was black, of course, as was the rest of his outfit. But the color did suit him, so I understood why he wore so much of it.

"And why's that?"

"Have you seen yourself tonight?" He shrugged. "Or ever, really?"

I rolled my eyes, but brought them back to his, my heart eager to hear the rest of what he had to say.

He chuckled and moved his head closer to mine. "And I don't think I'm the only one." His voice was low, his eyes moving to dart around the room. "Have you seen all of the men here tonight who have been following each of your actions, waiting for their turn to dance?"

I hadn't even thought about it until he said the words, but I followed his gaze around the room. He was right, I saw several of the single men from Kembertus here, along with others who must've traveled. They all stood on the periphery of the dancers, either looking at Maddox and I or attempting to look as if they hadn't just been watching us.

I clenched my jaw as I realized what happened. I turned back to Maddox, staring at his chest.

"That's why the inn is filled to capacity." I hissed. "My aunt invited all of these men here to court me."

I felt Maddox stiffen below my touch, but it went away almost as quickly as it came on. His hands tightening around me. "I don't mind a little competition."

I scoffed and narrowed my eyes up at his. "I'm not a prize to be won." I hissed.

"I'm sorry." His voice was light, his eyes kind behind the intricately designed mask that only further deepened the charcoal gray in them. "It was a joke, Evaline."

I pursed my lips and nodded. "Good." But my voice came out tighter than I expected it and I looked away from him, back over his shoulder. I chewed on my lip. I didn't like the thought that he could be just like all the men I'd dealt with before, here only to carry me as a trophy on their arm.

"You don't want to be followed, but you don't make staying away easy." He said, his voice gruff.

I looked back at him, confused, but his eyes were on my lips. I pulled my lower lip away from my teeth and elected not to respond.

The song stopped then, and as was custom all the dancers around us stopped to clap before the start of the next song. This was usually where couples would part from each other and swap for new dance mates, but Maddox did not let go. And neither did I.

He pulled away and lowered our joined hands. I let my hand fall from his shoulder but he caught that one in his too.

The dance floor around us became a tizzy of movement as everyone either left the floor or switched partners, but Maddox stood still. He met my gaze as he tightened his grip on my hands.

"May I have this dance?" The sound of his voice stirred something deep within me. It was gruff but soft, smooth but coarse. Full of something I couldn't describe as his eyes held mine. Heat flooded my cheeks. I didn't take the Kova as the type of men who were this polite, but maybe I didn't know nearly as much about them as I thought I did.

"Yes." It was breathless. "I guess." I added quickly, not appreciative of how wistful my voice sounded.

He smiled as the piano started a new song and pulled me back into position. I heard footsteps behind me and turned my head as Maddox looked to the suitor.

"Back off." He said and I could've laughed at how surprised Antony looked, his hand still held up in the air as he was about to ask to cut in.

He cleared his throat. "It's customary to switch each song."

"It's customary to allow the woman to choose, and she's already elected to dance with me." Maddox didn't wait for Antony to respond, simply moving us away and across the floor.

I couldn't hold it back anymore, I laughed. Maddox's eyes fell back to mine at the sound.

His eyes twinkled as he spoke. "What's so funny?"

I shrugged and noted the way his hand on my waist fell slightly at the movement. "I don't think the men here are as used to the idea of women getting a choice as you might think."

It was a joke, albeit a true one, but a joke nonetheless. Maddox's eyes hardened. "Yes. That's why I hate the Kromean Kingdoms."

I snorted. "Me too."

"Where would you go, if you could?" He asked, a rhetorical question but one that didn't sound like it off his lips.

I narrowed my eyes. "Is this part of your game?"

He winked at the mention. "You mean our game?"

I just shook my head, looking away. "Neomaeros, but only because it's the only other place I've ever been." I said, answering his first question instead of his second.

He smiled at me. "You know that isn't what I meant. If you could go anywhere, not just places you've been, where would you go?"

I looked away from him, toward the pool sitting at the base of the staircase. "Probably Merwinan." His hands tightened at the mention. "I've always wanted to see the ocean."

"Mmm." He mumbled. "The Madierian Sea."

I nodded. "Exactly."

"I think it would suit you." I met his eyes again. "Especially because when we met, my first thought was how your eyes matched the color of that ocean."

My brows furrowed. "Really?"

He nodded. "It's rumored that Merwinna herself had eyes the same shade, slightly blue, slightly green. And that's why she colored the oceans the way she did; an act of vanity." He shook his head, looking a little dazed as he looked between my eyes. "And tonight, yours rival them."

I tried to ignore the fact that he was comparing me to a Goddess, and instead changed the subject. "Where is your friend?"

He shrugged. "He's here somewhere." But he didn't look around, keeping his eyes trained on mine.

I nodded, all of a sudden unable to make conversation with the heat of his gaze. Maddox spoke so I didn't have to. "Have I told you how breathtaking you are tonight?"

Goosebumps rose in a wave over my neck, up past my ear, disappearing into my hair. I cleared my throat. "No."

He tutted and shook his head. "An oversight on my part. I should be reminding you every second of how truly gorgeous you are."

I tilted my head. "Do you tell all the women you stalk that?"

He chuckled. "I thought I already told you, I'm following the rules."

I rolled my eyes. "Somehow I don't believe you."

"Well, if I was following you, it worked in your favor tonight." I cocked a brow in question. His head nodded toward where Bassel and I had danced earlier. "I saved you from your suitor."

I scoffed. "You did no such thing."

He cocked his head. "Sure seemed like it to me, you looked mighty uncomfortable."

I pursed my lips. Maybe I wasn't doing as good of a job at hiding my distaste for Bassel as I thought. "I had it covered. I don't need your saving."

His smirk stretched into a grin. "I don't doubt you can handle yourself." He regarded me, a glint in his eye, as if he knew far more about me than he did.

"And what if I'm uncomfortable now, dancing with you?" I posed.

A deep throated laugh left his lips, the breath dancing over my lashes. "You're not."

The sheer arrogance in that remark had my chin tilting up to level him. "But I am."

His eyes sobered as he leaned his head down so we were inches apart. "You're lying." It was soft, a secret he shared for only me to hear.

But I didn't waver. "No, I'm not."

He smiled, his face still so, so, close. "Evaline," my name on his lips threw a shiver down my spine. "You forget what I am." He tilted his head. "I can hear the rise in your heartbeat when you lie."

I cut my eyes to the side, observing the couples who danced around us, trying to dispel the way my heart was racing.

"Have I told you how maddening I find you and your extra abilities?" I muttered.

"I can't recall." His voice was low in my ear.

I scoffed. "Well, I think that goes on the list. No more using those on me, either." But the blush that crept onto my cheeks gave me away. I wasn't uncomfortable, it was quite the opposite. I was enjoying my time with Maddox, and that was the problem.

He just laughed and took in my blush, bending to whisper in my ear, voice low. "Are you wearing it right now?"

My blush doubled down, if that was even possible, and I pulled my head back to look up at him in surprise. He straightened to avoid the collision, but amusement played on his features.

"Pardon me?" I sputtered. His question sounded so inappropriate.

His eyes were alight. "Your dagger."

A breath of relief coasted out of my mouth. "Oh." I shook my head to clear the muddled thoughts away, what had I expected him to mean? I rolled my eyes, attempting nonchalance. "Wouldn't you like to know?"

The hand on my waist moved, lifting onto my back and flattening against the fabric, fingertips stretching up and brushing the bare skin there. Hot and cold all at the same time. He pulled me closer to him until our chests nearly met, and lowered his voice, as his dark eyes devoured mine.

"I think it's fairly clear that I would very much love to know what you've got on under that dress." His eyes drifted down to my lips. "Regardless of the dagger."

I looked over his shoulder as we danced, finding myself overwhelmed. Not by horrid memories or repulsion as I had been with Bassel. But by Maddox's scent filling my senses, the warmth of his touch enveloping me. The molten eyes that looked at me as if I was the only person in the room.

I cleared my throat. "Yes, I have it on."

His hand on my waist tightened, ever so slightly. "I'm torn."

I looked back at him, confused. "What?"

He met my eyes, teeth grazing his lower lip before speaking. "I'm torn because part of me finds that exceedingly attractive. But another part is concerned. Wielding a weapon puts you in more danger than not having one—"

"Unless you know how to use it." I finished, tears threatening to sting the backs of my eyes. I blinked them away. I hadn't heard that line since the last time my father said it to me.

Maddox smiled at me, "I take it you know how to use it, then?"

"I do." I stared at the dusting of dark facial hair that faded down toward his neck until it was smooth, bare skin. "I take it you were the old friend my father picked that phrase up from?"

I heard his soft chuckle. "It would seem so."

I nodded.

"What did he teach you? How to use daggers, swords, hand-to-hand?" Maddox asked.

"Now, why would I give all my secrets away?" I whispered back, my voice low.

"Because I doubt you have anyone else to discuss these things with."

I didn't respond, but my pursed lips were confirmation enough.

When he spoke this time, his tone was serious. "Your father has been gone for years, Evaline. You need to be training with someone to maintain your skills. It's been too long."

I sucked in a harsh breath. "I've started training on my own. You don't know anything about me."

I looked away, eyes landing on Bassel across the room, glaring at Maddox and I dancing. I looked away with haste and felt Maddox follow my gaze. I heard a low growl from his chest and he turned us so that I could no longer see Bassel.

"I know your father wouldn't want you to be unprepared, and neither do I. Training on your own is not enough, and you know that." His eyes softened slightly. "I can train with you."

I clenched my jaw, why did he care?

"I don't need your help." I said, my voice stern and my jaw set.

"While I find it charming that you are clearly independent, I must insist you train with someone."

I shook my head in disbelief. "Why are you concerning yourself with the choices of a stranger? You don't know me, Maddox."

His jaw clenched, eyes reeling as if he was holding himself back from speaking the words he truly wanted to say. His hand dropped from my back, down to my waist again, and he pulled me in against his chest.

"I have a feeling we know each other better than we think." His voice was thick. His eyes drifted down to my lips, and back to my eyes. Soft. Slow.

I shook my head. This was too much. His scent, his eyes, his lips. I backed away from him. "I need to go." The music switched then, signaling the end of the song we were dancing to, and he fully released me.

As I turned to walk away, the clapping sounded throughout the room, but the roaring applause didn't shield his words.

"When you decide you need me, I'll be at the inn."

CHAPTER TWENTY-TWO

Maddox

How many times would I have to watch her walk away from me, wishing I had more time with her?

I had a feeling it was going to be far more than I cared for.

Evaline's dress rippled behind her, kissing the floor with every step. Her white waves bouncing against her back. She disappeared into the crowd, into the mass of pastel fabric and tulle.

I clenched my jaw and turned, allowing my gaze to sweep across the crowd.

I'd touched her. Held her. And knew no amount of such would ever be enough. And now that I'd had a taste of it – of her body held against mine, of her breath flitting across my face, of hearing her heart quicken when I looked at her – I needed more. Endlessly, more.

I knew Wyott was making his way to me but I wasn't concerned with that.

When I'd made the comment that I wasn't the only one that noticed her beauty, of course I'd already witnessed how many men were following her every move the entire evening. But I didn't really consider that it would've been abnormal. I only realized just how deeply the thought bothered me after she walked away, when the air was almost clear of her scent and the tingling in my fingertips had begun to dissipate.

She'd said the men came to court her. I didn't like that. I didn't like that one fucking bit.

My eyes scattered through the crowd, roving over the faces of the men who still watched her off the ballroom floor. I sighed at seeing the familiar look of desperation on their faces.

Gods, please let her choose me.

What bothered me more than the idea that so many men were invited to see her, was the thought of who invited them. Undoubtedly it was her guardians, the Lord and Lady of Kembertus. That much was evident by the way her aunt dragged Evaline over to meet the man she danced with.

I swallowed my fear that I'd lose my chance with her before I ever was truly given one, afraid she'd find some man here in the kingdom and fall in love before she got to know me.

If all of Evaline's interactions with other men followed the one I'd witnessed with the man her guardians introduced her to, I'd be fine. Before she'd even taken one full breath after seeing the man, I felt the wave of discomfort rolling through the ballroom, coming straight from her.

The bond was a living being, a tether between the two of us. And even though she didn't know it existed yet, she'd still sense it. And even now, before the bond was totally fused, we could sense strong emotions from each other. Know when the other was in the same room. Feel each other's gaze as if it were fingertips grazing over our features instead of a look.

So, when she'd seen the man, the color that drained from her face wasn't my giveaway that she was deep in fear. It was the feeling that swept toward me and almost knocked me on my ass.

What the fuck did he do to her?

It was the first thought I'd had when I witnessed the interaction, and it knocked around in my head again as it jogged my body into motion, finally taking a step away from the ballroom floor.

Bassel Rydell. Gods-dammit.

"Are you ready to leave?" Wyott's voice pulled me from my thoughts as he came to stride beside me.

I shook my head. "Not quite."

He seemed to sense my unease and fell in step behind me. I heard Bassel's chuckle across the room and followed it. I didn't approach, I just wanted to observe how he interacted with other women.

I knew that name just as I knew the name of all the ruling families in Brassillion. I didn't like the idea of Evaline dancing, or being courted, by any man besides me. But I'd take any other man a thousand-fold over the idea that she'd be courted by the eventual ruler of Vestaria.

He was talking to a woman around Evaline's age, her hair raven black and straightened. Her dress was a bright orange that didn't quite suit her white skin.

From what I could tell he didn't seem to make her uncomfortable, but quite the opposite. I couldn't understand what it was about him that upset Evaline so violently. But I had to keep him away from her.

I watched him pull the woman to the dance floor, never stopping to ask her to join him and just tugging her along, but she followed happily. He curled his arms around her as she did him, and they both looked perfectly content.

I was about to turn around, convinced I wouldn't be able to uncover any information on him, or Evaline, tonight and ready to leave.

But, as I began to turn, I watched his eyes skate over the figure of a different woman dancing in a pairing nearby, his own partner's eyes cast down in flirtation.

I scoffed. He leered at another, when he had a perfectly pretty woman in his arms.

That wouldn't do. Even if Evaline didn't choose me, even if she chose someone else in this room or in this kingdom, even if it was him, that wouldn't do. If I couldn't be with her, then she must be with someone who would worship her just as much as I.

I gritted my teeth and turned toward the door. Evaline had left the Ball as soon as she departed from my arms. There was no point in staying.

"What were you looking for?" Wyott asked me as we entered the cool night and began our walk home.

I shrugged. "When her aunt and uncle introduced her to that man, the bond shivered. Like she was shaking in her own skin, begging to get away from him."

Wyott considered that. "Yet she agreed to dance with him." His brow furrowed. "She strikes me as the type of person who doesn't do anything just because she's instructed to, and that includes being polite to men who make her feel uncomfortable."

"I agree." A beat of silence passed between us as we both pondered that.

"How was the dance?" He asked no doubt referring to the fact that I'd just held her in my arms for the first time.

A smile immediately made its way to my face, a warmth filling my chest. In one sweep of the wind all thoughts of the suitor and Evaline with another man were gone, replaced with the memories of our dances together. The way she'd giggled when I'd spun her away from the man who asked to dance with her between songs.

"It was everything." The soft spring breeze blew the trees around us as we walked. "She can fight, Wallace taught her." I turned to look at Wyott and continued giving him details, although on some level I knew he likely heard the entire exchange. "She has the most beautiful laugh and a surprisingly strong grip." He laughed at that and I looked forward again. "She has a quick tongue and isn't afraid to bite back."

I had so much to learn about her and the questions were already piling up in my mind. I wanted to know why her aunt and uncle were taking caring for her instead of her mother. I wanted to know if someone had been with her when her father died, or if she had to grieve alone. I wanted to know how she swiped a blade through the air and if she could land a blow.

But more than that I just wanted to be around her more. I wanted to train with her. I wanted to comfort her when the thought of her father's death, that so clearly haunted her, wracked her brain.

I smiled again as I thought of her conversation with her friend by the pool. She had tried so fiercely then, and again in my arms during the dance, to fight her physical attraction to me.

I'd give her time. I didn't want to, necessarily, but I'd do whatever she needed.

Finding your mate is something that ignites a piece deep inside you and changes the way we see the world. I'd give her time to explore that.

CHAPTER TWENTY-THREE

Evaline

I couldn't race out of the ballroom fast enough. My feet tripped over the skirt of my dress no matter how hard I tried to lift it out of the way, and my fists ached from how tightly I clenched the fabric.

By the time I got to my room, and shut the door behind me, my skin was flushed and my heart was pounding. I sat on the side of my bed, placed my hand over my heart, and begged it and my lungs to calm.

I couldn't tell what caused this reaction. If it was seeing Bassel for the first time since the night of the attack and having to be so close to him, the memories of that night ravaging my mind. Or if it was from dancing with Maddox. Being in his arms, feeling his hand in mine, the way his whispers in my ear made the goosebumps scroll over my flesh.

My breathing refused to slow as I began to hyperventilate. I fell back, lying down on my bed to open my airways as much as I could, hands ripping at my corset. My absolute worst nightmare was coming true, as it appeared my aunt and uncle were planning to arrange my marriage to the one person in this world I'd rather die than marry.

I cursed myself for every time that I dreaded being arranged to some boring man in a boring city. Now, I yearned for that life. Because anything was better than the thought that I would likely be marrying Bassel.

My gaze landed on the ceiling, the mosaic of tiles a whirlwind of colors and patterns, and tried to calm myself. I always thought that I would be up for it, that someday when I met Bassel, finally put that name to that face, that I would be able to wield a dagger and punish him for everything he'd done to me and likely to other women.

But the shock of seeing him was too much and I pushed myself too far.

I thought of how Maddox swept me away from Bassel, sensing my discomfort and saving me as I fell deeper into the hole that was my despair. How his soft voice and strong embrace almost immediately eased the tension that had been coiling in my shoulders, how it pushed back the nausea that was roiling up to the surface. He'd helped me, and all I'd done in return was told him that I didn't need saving. But if I was being honest with myself, I had, in that moment, because I had slipped too far away to save myself, and I had appreciated it. Because one more second in Bassel's arms and I would've fallen to the floor.

Tears sprang in the backs of my eyes as I realized that I wouldn't be able to go through with my original plan of killing Bassel, not when I couldn't keep my emotions in check around him.

I tried to tell myself that it was okay if I didn't kill him, and that I wasn't letting down my father, or myself, by forgoing that plan.

There was no way that I could pull it off.

But what could I do? Tell my aunt and uncle that I refused to marry Bassel? They would only think I was being difficult. Even if I told them about the attack, would they take my side? Would they even believe me?

The panic started to rise in my chest and my breathing wouldn't calm. I let my arms fall above my head to stretch my ribs further. Hysteria began to swell my throat, closing it to cut off my breathing completely. I was gasping for air and a migraine started to hammer in my head. I was crying and having a panic attack but all I could focus on was how hopeless I felt. Alone in this room, in this castle, in this kingdom, in this world where the only people who cared about me were Aurora and Jacqueline, and they couldn't help me with this.

Tears puddled in my eyes before cresting and falling down my temples and disappeared into my hairline. In this moment, for the first time since my father died, I hoped that there was no Night, no afterlife, simply because I didn't want my father to see me. To see that I was too scared to go through with my plan, to do the very thing he raised me to do.

But before another thought could enter my mind, the pain took over, my throat seeming to shut, and my breathing ceased. I gasped for breath as I noticed a haze falling over the room, a dull glow before me.

Calm down, I instructed myself.

A sob slipped past my lips, and I pressed my fingers against my forehead, willing the migraine to go away. I knew I needed to control my breathing, but I couldn't. And then I was enveloped in the blue haze of the room.

I awoke to the chirping of birds outside my window.

My head was sore and I could feel the dried tears on my cheeks. I sat up in bed and realized I was still in my dress from the night before. I eased myself out of it, no easy feat with the corset. I laid it gently on the chaise near my fireplace and requested water for a bath. I spent the day that way, trying to forget about the night before. Trying to repress how Bassel's eyes felt on my skin, trying to forget the way Maddox's made me flush.

I practiced with my dagger and spent the rest of the day reading. My aunt sent up the first and second meals of the day, something I usually had to attend the dining room to receive. I understood the small gesture as a show of appreciation for my dancing with Bassel last night. She must not have seen Maddox whisk me away.

But after sunset had fallen there were steps outside of my door and I knew who was behind it. I was brushing my hair at my vanity and turned to face my aunt. She cast me a look as she crossed the room and sat on my bed. I turned to face her.

"Evaline you looked absolutely marvelous last night, and I was quite impressed with how well you and Bassel got along." She smiled and then waved her hand. "Also, this morning I sent the parchment to Lady Margot. Hopefully we hear back soon."

It made me happy that she'd already sent the postage, but her comment on Bassel turned my stomach. If she saw my dance with Bassel get cut off by Maddox, she didn't let on. I opened my mouth tell her that there was no way I could marry Bassel, to not waste her energy in an attempt to negotiate because it would never happen. That the dance with him was all I could give them. That even that had been too much.

But before I could, she spoke. "As I'm sure you're aware from the talks your uncle and I have had with you these past couple years, and this last week, we feel it is time for you to marry. And after seeing how well you got off with Bassel last night, and his membership to one of the other ruling families, it seems obvious that he be your groom."

The world dimmed around me as the words, confirmation of what I feared most, sank in, swirling through my mind until they didn't sound like words anymore. Until all I heard was the scrape of my skin against the bark of the tree Bassel pushed me into and my stifled screams.

A piece of me knew the moment I saw Bassel that this was inevitable, that of course this would happen to me. But the reality was too cruel and unforgiving, and I wasn't nearly as prepared for it as I thought I would be.

"Aunt Therese," I started to shake my head at her, but she interrupted me.

"Lord Elijah and I have already coordinated it with Bassel's parents, weeks ago before his arrival. He traveled here under the notion that if he met and fancied you, he would have your hand." She waved hers. "He fancied you."

My mouth snapped shut, which must've been her goal. I fully shook my head this time. "I will not."

She stood, rolling her eyes and then cutting them back to me. "It is already done."

I stood and moved in front of her so we were eye to eye. "Please understand, I cannot marry Bassel…" I trailed off; I didn't know how to tell her. I didn't know how to tell someone who barely seemed to care about me at all about one of the worst nights of my life.

My thoughts tipped back to two years prior, the night I'd come here, when I'd tried to tell her. When she took me to my new room and just before she handed me off to Natalia. I'd tried to discuss it with her, to tell her what had happened to me. I'd already told the both of them the bandit story my father had instructed me, but he hadn't prepared me for how to tell a stranger that I'd been attacked.

And when I finally had spoke, raising my chin toward her, eyes glassy with tears, she'd only interrupted me. Told me that Manor women didn't discuss such things. That it was our duty to be strong for our kingdoms and our husbands. That we didn't get to break down.

And now, standing in front of her again, the same words ready on my lips, died. Because I knew she'd never care, even if she believed me.

But she stomped her foot out of annoyance and snapped at me. "Evaline this is no debate, you will marry Bassel. And you will do so in a month."

Tears began streaming down my face and I knew that this was the first time I'd cried in front of her. "You can't make me." I whispered as I felt my face contorting into that of anger.

"That is exactly what I can do, I am your guardian. You will marry him and then will move to Vestaria when he deems fit."

I stood strong, or as strong as I could with tears streaming down my face. "I will not." I repeated.

I heard the slap before I felt the sting on my cheek.

My mouth dropped open as I looked at the floor, and my hand instinctively moved to my thigh where my holster did not sit. She didn't notice that move, because she was too busy fleeing the room.

"It is done." Was thrown over her shoulder before she left. Coward.

I was rooted in place after the slap, but kept my eyes cast down. The rage inside me caused by that strike echoed through my body. Echoed back in time two years to my attack. Echoed in my improperly healed wrist that Bassel had crushed.

And then a calm realization fell over me.

I wasn't sure if it was the shock of the slap, or if the news had shook me straight, but I had a confidence now that I did not have twenty-four hours ago. I would kill Bassel. And I would do so on my wedding night, in the only instance I'd be granted any time alone with him long enough to pull off such a feat.

Before I could give a second thought, I was dressing in a long sleeve tunic, throwing on my dagger holster and my cloak, and scaling down my wall as night fell.

CHAPTER TWENTY-FOUR

Maddox

I could hear her voice through the floor below my room. She was asking Haekin for my room number, and I could only imagine the things that must be running through his head at the sight of the niece of the Lord and Lady of Kembertus searching for me at this hour.

I was shocked. Of course, this is what I wanted, her to come searching me out, and I knew it would happen eventually. The pull of the bond was too strong to avoid forever, even if you didn't know it existed. Although I admit, I didn't think it would be so soon. But I wasn't going to complain about a white-haired beauty with an urge to see me after the town had gone to sleep.

I crossed the room to the door as I heard her approach. A smirk sliding into place as I pulled the door open. She was on the other side, hand raised and ready to knock.

She rolled her eyes and dropped her hand.

"I knew you wouldn't be able to stay away." Her scent filled my senses.

Her gaze met mine and her demeanor changed. No longer jovial or mocking. "Can I come in?"

The desperation in her tone wiped the smile from my face and my mood grew somber in an instant. I moved away from the door so she could enter, my heart picking up pace, and followed her quietly as she crossed to stand near the fireplace, too proud to extend her hands to the flame, even though I knew she was cold from her late-night trek.

When she turned and opened her mouth to speak, I could see the fire dancing in her eyes, but something else caught my attention.

The bright red mark of a hand on her cheek.

I took a step toward her, my hand raising to graze a thumb lightly over the welt. My blood heated and I could feel my heart pounding in my ears. She winced away from my touch, but not before she felt it for a moment.

"Who did this to you?" My voice was rough, anger roiling inside of me, barely controlled.

Her voice was small. "It's none of your business."

I clenched my jaw. Everything about her was my business, as I was hers. Gods, it had been just over a week since I'd met her and already I was warring with impatience, needing her to know what we were to each other.

But I swallowed the rage that sat in my throat and bit back the impatience in my heart. If I reacted too extremely, she'd run. I could smell it on her. The refusal to be kept.

"If you won't tell me who did that to you then why are you here?" I tried to keep my own voice even.

She raised her chin and I wished she'd let me hold it, tilt her head to examine her wound. Tell me who did it and excuse me to go gut them. The mere thought of her experiencing an ounce of pain felt like pouring liquid metal, so hot and thick, through my veins.

"I've decided to take you up on your offer." She looked away then. "If it still stands."

"Of course, it still stands." My voice came out hoarse, and I knew she could hear the rage in it.

She met my eyes again. "Okay."

I nodded. "Okay."

She seemed uneasy, she thought it would take more convincing.

I'd do anything for her, least of all train her to keep herself safe when I wasn't around to do it.

"Why the sudden change?" She was quiet and I continued. "Because I don't think it's a coincidence that you were adamant about not needing training a day ago, and now you show up here with a welt of someone's hand on your cheek."

She crossed her arms over her chest in the cloak that swallowed her. "I don't need to have a reason, Maddox."

I sighed. Nothing would ever come easy with her, would it? But all I could hear were Wyott's words repeating in my head. Did I really think my mate would be simple? I wasn't. I needed to stop expecting my partner to be without flaws, without walls.

"Fine." Was the only response I could come up with that wouldn't piss her off even more.

"I need a lot of training right away." She pressed.

I nodded. "Okay. How often can you get away from the castle?"

She shrugged. "I can meet most nights, it'll be the easiest time to train in hiding." The conversation was another reminder of how much I hated the Kromean Kingdoms. Back home in Rominia women were treated as equals. They were taught to fight, to protect themselves. In Kembertus, a woman learning to wield a blade was as forbidden as sorcery.

"You'll need to bring your dagger, obviously. And you'll need new boots."

Her eyes widened, surprised. "Why?"

I motioned down to the things that were oversized. "You're just going to end up hurting yourself in shoes too big. You need a proper pair to practice footwork in."

I could feel her skin pale. "I'll have to buy them in disguise again, my aunt will know something is going on if I buy a pair in public."

I shrugged. "I'll get them. Just tell me what size you are." She started to protest, and I put my hand up. "Do you think I'm going to let you break an ankle while sparring with me? No. It's better on my conscience if you have a pair that fits properly."

She was quiet for a moment before telling me her size. I'd pick them up tomorrow.

"Thank you." It was quiet, and she looked toward the fire when she said it.

"Of course." How do you tell someone you've only just met that you would throw yourself into an inferno for them, so the task of buying them a pair of shoes was quite menial?

I explained to her where we could meet. At the clearing in the woods just inside the west wall of the city an hour after sunset.

"One last thing." She said, wringing her hands slightly beneath her cloak. I didn't like the nerves she was showing around me.

"Anything." I said softly.

She nodded. "Haekin saw my face, and no one can know that I came looking for you this late or I'll be locked in the castle for a month. Can you compel him to forget I was here?"

My brows furrowed. I didn't recall Wyott or myself ever telling Wallace about our ability to compel, or ever doing it in front of him. How had he known?

"Of course, I'll compel Haekin. Your secret is safe with me." I tilted my head. "And Wyott." Her eyebrow cocked. "You can trust him."

She nodded as her shoulders sagged and moved to leave. She approached the door, hand closing on the knob and ready to pull it open.

But as my eyes drifted to the space she'd just vacated, darkness filling the light she embodied, rage slithered through me again at the wound she bore. I couldn't let her leave without the full comprehension of just how infuriated I was at the red that stained her cheek, she couldn't go to sleep one more night unaware that any violence against her would not stand. I moved across the room in a blur of her vision, one hand pushing the door closed that she had begun to open. She stood there, in a shield of my body, and the florals in her hair intoxicated me as much as my rage.

"You don't want to talk about that print on your cheek? Fine." My voice was low and deadly. She swallowed and I could hear the way her heart raced. Being here, being this close to her with a heartrate that rivaled the speed of her own, there was nothing I wanted to do more than to push her against this door. To kiss away her nerves, her fear. To hold her close to me so that she felt just as safe as she tried so desperately to appear unperturbed. But I couldn't, and I didn't know if I ever would. "I'd very much like to kill the person who put it there, but you obviously don't want anyone to fight your battles." I cleared my throat, a low growl sneaking through, and spoke my vow. "I'll make sure you can do it yourself."

Her body straightened and I could feel the heat radiating off her, noticed the way she squeezed her thighs together and had to wrangle my self control by the thin shreds of yarn that held it.

But she just nodded, and I let her leave when she opened the door again.

CHAPTER TWENTY-FIVE

Evaline

"It was that easy?" Aurora asked from her seat beside her wife, near the fireplace while I paced the room in front of them. Three days had passed since I'd seen her at the Ball, and so much had changed.

I nodded. "I told you it would be. Therese said she sent it first thing the morning after the Ball, so you should have news within the month."

She smiled and Jacqueline wrapped an arm around her.

"This is so exciting!" Jacqueline enthused and Aurora nodded.

"I didn't think it'd be so simple. Thank you Evaline." She said looking at me.

I waved my hand. "Please, Therese and I did nothing. When they approve your license it'll be because you deserve it." I said, stepping forward and squeezing her hand.

"A month isn't much time to wait at all." She said and my smile faltered.

I shook my head. "It's not." I sighed. "I should probably tell you both something before you hear it from everyone else."

I explained everything that had happened. The dance with Bassel, my aunt's revelation that I was to marry him, that it'd been setup for weeks.

"I'm so sorry, Evaline." Aurora said.

SAMANTHA R. GOODE

"I don't even know why I was surprised, I knew this was going to happen. They couldn't have been more obvious about it all week." I sighed and drug a hand over my face.

I did tell them about the arranged marriage, but left out that I knew Bassel's true identity. It was agonizing not to tell them, considering they were the only people in the world that knew what happened to me, but I knew I couldn't. If I did kill Bassel, and right now that's all I could stand to think about without being overwhelmed by dread, then I surely couldn't give my friends any information that could harm them. I'd have to leave the city after killing him, but I was also trying not to focus on that fact too much because I had absolutely no idea how I'd pull it off.

"Perhaps it won't be as bad as you think." Jacqueline said, pulling me out of my thoughts.

My eyes cut to her. "Jacqui, I love you and I know you're just trying to be positive, but if you try to tell me that maybe I'll fall in love with him one day, please don't."

"Duly noted." She said with a small smile.

I slammed down into a chair. "Let's talk about something else, I can't stand thinking about it anymore today."

A wicked look lit Aurora's eyes. "Okay." A look passed between the two "I saw you dancing with Maddox."

I gave a curt nod. "On second thought maybe, we should circle back and start talking about how I want my wedding dress designed."

They laughed, and pulled a chuckle out of me as well.

Aurora grew serious. "Okay, let me grab my sketchbook." She stood to grab it, calling my bluff.

"No!" She sat back down. "Fine, yes I danced with Maddox."

Her smile grew. "And…?"

I shrugged. "And it was…intense." I met her eyes and she nodded, encouraging me to elaborate. I didn't.

"Oh, come on, Evaline. You can't tell me you didn't feel anything." Jacqueline chimed in.

I scoffed. "Don't tell me you're on her side too."

Jacqueline seemed unable to help the giggle that evaded her lips. "All I'm saying is that no woman at that event could take their eyes off Maddox, and none of the men from you." She said with a flick of her hand. "Some cases, vice versa."

I rolled my eyes. "He is an attractive man; I will allow you that. But his arrogance lessens his appeal."

Aurora's face dropped into a look of mock annoyance and her eyes leveled with mine. "Is it that he's arrogant or that he's strong willed? Something that you are quite prone to being as well."

I opened my mouth to respond and then realized I didn't have an answer to that. I could be quite stubborn, and at times snippy. But could those same traits in Maddox be what's building this wall I've made against him?

I shook my head. "No, it's his arrogance."

Aurora smirked and by the gleam in her eyes I knew my convincing didn't work. "I saw the way you two danced together, the chemistry between you. You felt something."

Jacqueline stood to add more wood to the fire, and I followed to help.

I'd spent most of my life wondering what love felt like, when I would feel it. But surely I wouldn't feel such a thing with Maddox.

The immortal's gray eyes filled my mind before I could help myself and I shook my head, as if that would toss the image out of my ears.

I brushed off my hands. "It doesn't even matter, I'm being married to Bassel."

I knew that wasn't true, I knew I wouldn't be with Bassel come the day after the wedding, but they didn't need to know that.

Jacqueline gave a sad smile and didn't say anything in response, and I was happy for that. I helped them make dinner before I headed home just before sunset, and we didn't talk about either man again.

My walk home was quick, I'd hustled, not wanting to jeopardize the dark.

But that thought had me recalling the night when I'd gone to Maddox's inn.

The entire walk was a blur, filled with hatred for my aunt, fear squeezing my throat and desperation fueling each hurried step. I slipped into my room without a sound as I thought about that conversation with Maddox in front of his fire.

His eyes, so dark in their normal shade of gray, turned nearly obsidian when they beheld the mark on my face. I wasn't sure if he disagreed with the abuse of women period, or if it was because it was my cheek splotched with red. I settled on the former. But something inside of me melted at his reaction. A small piece, deep in the depths of my soul seemed to thaw when his hand reached to caress my face, and I allowed myself a mere second of it before pulling away.

I laid my cloak over the chaise near the fireplace and added some logs to warm the room from my cold walk. The flames began rising to consume the wood and I watched them.

His reaction had been almost feral and I couldn't understand why. I was thankful he accepted my plea to train me. I honestly wasn't sure what he would say, and when he agreed, I'd breathed a silent sigh of relief. Then his kind offer to buy me boots that actually fit me. My heart did an odd thud inside my chest at the thought. Besides my father and my friends, no one had ever made such a kind gesture with no requirement of anything in return. Sure, my aunt and uncle provided a roof over my head, but I think that was more out of politics than kindness. A public obligation to the daughter of the true ruler of Kembertus.

The blaze grew until my cheeks were so warm from the flames that I had to move away. A knock on my door startled me as I stood away from the fireplace.

A servant who's name I didn't know entered the room. "Evaline, would you like me to prepare you a bath?"

Soaking in the heat sounded like exactly what I needed, so I nodded and let her work as I undid my braid, waiting for her to disappear into the bathing chamber as I expertly removed the wire and slipped it into my drawer.

After she left, I undressed and slipped into the warm water, trying to think of anything besides Maddox. But my traitorous thoughts floated to him. The way he'd stormed toward me as I opened the door at the inn, slamming it shut with one arm, his entire body covering me as if to keep me from further harm. His words, so protective with a spear of malice stuck through them for whoever had hurt me. My aunt. But he didn't know that, and when he stood over me saying those words it felt like lightning sparked between our bodies. Every instinct inside me screaming *close, close, closer.* Demanding I back up, into his waiting embrace.

For half a moment I had considered it, after everything I'd been through that night, and the day prior. After my aunt's demand that I marry a monster, wouldn't it just be lovely to spend a night with Maddox? To stroll into the castle the next morning, hair a mess and in a day old pair of clothes. For not only my aunt, but everyone else in the castle to see me, to know where I'd been. What I'd been doing. Perhaps it'd be a quick end to this farce of an arranged marriage.

But the more I thought about what it would be like to be with Maddox, my cheeks heated, and I didn't fool myself into thinking that it was from the warmth of the bathwater. I touched my cheek where Maddox had, even if it had been brief, and thought about that touch again. Then thought about our dance, his hand fanned on my back, holding our bodies close together. His lips at my ear speaking words that sounded like they came from a lover and not someone you'd just met. As if he'd known me his whole life instead of just a few days. I thought about that hand moving to touch me elsewhere, how it would feel raking against my skin, or pushing me against the door he'd shut in front of me.

I might not have been a virgin, but none of the men I'd been with had ever touched me like Maddox did. No man's touch ever made my breath falter or my heart quicken. I felt a wetness and closed my thighs, and for the second time in a night, I knew I couldn't blame the bathwater.

CHAPTER TWENTY-SIX

Maddox

If I'd thought life before finding my mate was slow and monotonous, it was nothing compared to meeting her and being unable to be around her every minute of every day. It had been a few days since I'd seen her, and after getting a taste of what life could be like with her in my arms, I couldn't wait any longer. I knew we had a training tomorrow evening, but it didn't matter. But I also knew she didn't want me following her, and while Wyott and I still took turns guarding the castle at night to make sure she was safe, I didn't go searching for her throughout the day.

I was antsy in my room and couldn't handle sitting around again, so I got up to leave. I'd lapped around the kingdom multiple times in our couple weeks since arriving, but one place I hadn't yet gone was to the horse stables.

Wyott and I didn't have horses with us, but riding had calmed me since I was a child.

I didn't bother to let Wyott know I was leaving. After breakfast, I'd sensed his mood and knew he wouldn't want to attend. He was homesick.

A pang of guilt hit me as I jogged down the steps. I knew it was hard for him to be away from Cora, and for Gods' sake, look at me. I'd only been away from Evaline for three days, only known her just under two weeks, and I already couldn't get enough. I couldn't imagine what he must feel being away from Cora for months, after knowing her for a century and a half.

I swallowed, I'd get him back to her as soon as I could. The thought had unease crawling up my skin, but I continued and walked through the door and out into the mid-day light. I didn't know how I'd get him back to her with Evaline by my side. It would take time for her to feel comfortable enough to leave with me, if she ever wanted to at all, and Wyott was deteriorating.

He tried to hide it from me, but I heard the way he turned in bed at night. I saw the slight dim in his eyes grow darker every day away from her. He valued my father and I, and even though he'd grown up with me like a brother he still acted as if he owed us something. But he didn't, and I hated that he felt that way. But I knew it was the reason he'd agreed to come on this trip with me, along with his urge to get justice for his father, if he ever had the chance.

I took one last deep breath, making a mental note to talk to him later about it, if he wanted to head back, he could, and I would never be upset with him about it. It would take far less time to head straight back to Rominia than the eight months we'd spent coming out here. It would only take a week and a half by horse, a few days if he ran the whole way. But I understood now a fraction of what he'd felt in our time away, and I did my best to swallow that thought as I approached the stables.

As I introduced myself to the owner I sensed her nearby.

I half listened as the owner informed me that he had only three horses available, and they were being used for riding lessons. I nodded, ready to turn back, when I heard her heartbeat.

I turned, watching her walk up the short dirt road to the barn, two young girls on each side of her, their hands in hers.

My cheeks heated at the sight. I'd never considered that she had children, but with the girls standing in front of me I realized it was a possibility. I smiled at them before meeting Evaline's gaze. The look in her eyes was telltale, and she was angry.

"Oh, there's one of my lessons now." The owner said beside me, moving toward her.

Her eyes were narrowed on me, she turned to him for only a moment, handing him both young girl's hands and instructing them to stay with him.

When she stomped over to me, grasping my elbow to pull me out of earshot, I had to remind myself to wipe the smile off my face. She was angry, but Gods was she beautiful.

"What are you doing?" She hissed, whipping around to face me.

I raised my hands in innocence. "I swear to the Gods, I was just coming here to ride myself. I had no idea you would be here."

Her eyes narrowed further, somehow, and she evaluated me. "I don't believe you." She said finally.

I shrugged. "There's nothing more I can do than tell you the truth." I said and saw a small wave of shock roll through her eyes. She'd been expecting me to have an excuse, I guessed. "I wasn't following you, but I will leave."

I turned before she spoke. My emotions were going through the ringer. I felt guilty that I upset her, but upset myself that she so clearly didn't want to be around me. Logically I knew it was only natural. I was glad she was this wary of immortals she'd just met because it leant to her survival skills. But when it was with me, logic was hard to manage.

I swallowed my disappointment and the sinking feeling in my gut that had been soaring only moments ago from seeing her, when I felt her hand catch my elbow again. I stopped, half turning.

Her face, while still guarded, softened. "Stop." She sighed. "You don't have to leave, I'm sorry. I just thought…" But she trailed off and shook her head. "It doesn't matter." Evaline let go of me and headed back toward the girls she'd arrived with. "The point is you can stay."

I fell in step beside her. "I don't think I can though, he only has three horses available, and it appears he'll be using two of them for your lesson and one for theirs." I said nodding to a mother and son who strode toward the owner. "But I appreciate your offer."

She threw a look up to me and then to the girls, chewing her lip. I cleared my throat like it would silence the dirty thoughts running through my mind at the move, and looked away. When we rejoined the group, the owner had just finished talking with his second lesson and turned to Evaline and I with grateful eyes.

"Thank goodness you're friends," he said nodding toward Evaline and I. "It looks like Mr. Scott wasn't able to attend today so I will have to work with Mrs. Scott and their son." I noted the way Evaline straightened beside me. "But since you brought a helper, you both can handle the lesson with the girls, right?" He said, eyeing Evaline.

She pursed her lips and looked down at the children, their eyes eager and expectant. Evaline sighed and looked up at me.

"Would you mind?" She asked.

I smiled and shook my head. "Not at all."

The owner walked away with the mother and her son, grabbing one of the horses reins and leading it to the other end of the stables. He moved to the smaller riding ring, giving us the larger one.

I stood quietly, waiting for Evaline's lead, but instead just saw her fidgeting with her hands looking over her shoulder for where the horses were.

I bent down, keeping my distance from the girls so as not to alarm Evaline. I don't think she thought I would harm them, but I was still an immortal being she hardly knew and didn't want to push my luck.

I looked between the girls and smiled. "Hi, my name is Maddox. I'm your mom's friend."

Immediate giggles wrapped the air around me as the two girls covered their faces with their hands. I looked up at Evaline who also had a smile on her face and blush surrounding it.

"She's not our mom!" Said one of the girls, the one with blond hair.

I looked back up at Evaline as I rose, and she nodded.

"This is Priscilla," she said nodding toward the young girl with brown hair. "And this is Megin." She said, her hand moving over the head of the blond. "They both live at the orphanage, and I visit with them."

I nodded, a blush perking up my own face now at my misinterpretation. I couldn't help but notice the slight disappointment that settled on my heart at the thought that I wasn't getting to meet her children, though I should be happy she allowed me to meet the girls at all, considering they were clearly important to her.

"More than that!" Priscilla said, throwing her hands up to grab my attention. "Evaline teaches us how to read and how to write."

I cast an eyebrow to Evaline, I didn't want to say the thought aloud, the girls didn't need to hear it. But I knew Evaline understood my question.

Young girls were allowed to read in Kembertus now?

She just nodded. "It's been a recent update but one they're only doing because of the Madierian Kingdoms."

I nodded, immediately understanding what she meant. There'd been whispers for years now that the Madierian Kingdoms were working to extort the Kromean Kingdoms into progression. It made me happy to hear that things were changing, even though I still wanted to get Evaline out of here as soon as I possibly could.

Just as the thought passed through my mind another one followed.

Would she ever want to leave, if it meant leaving behind so many people she loved?

I pushed the thought away, not wanting to deal with it at the moment, and put a smile on my face. "Are you ready to get started?"

She took a deep breath and nodded, reaching both hands out to the girls. They started walking toward the large pen which had two saddled horses in it, strung up to a post and waiting for us.

"What do you want to do first?" I asked Evaline.

She shrugged. "I hadn't really thought about it, I assumed that the owner would kind of lead the lesson. I didn't realize that I'd be doing it by myself." She looked up at me as if remembering I was there. "Any suggestions? I've never taught anyone how to ride before."

I had, but this was her lesson with her friends, I didn't want to step on her toes. I looked down at her. "How did your father teach you?" I didn't need to question who taught her, it seemed Wallace skillfully prepared her for a world without him.

I didn't miss the slight smile across her face as she turned back toward the horses. "First we have to focus on getting on the horse." She said, putting a hand gently on the horse's snout. Evaline looked between the height of the horses and that of the children. "Which doesn't seem very possible today." She laughed.

I turned back toward the stables, looking for anything to help elevate the girls, and saw a few large wooden boxes.

"We could stack those boxes," I said, pointing to them. Her eyes followed. "Then it would just be a matter of making sure they don't fall off."

Evaline smiled and nodded. "That's a great idea."

She pulled the leather helmets that were waiting for us off the post and started fastening them to Megin and Priscilla's heads while I went back to get the boxes. I moved to pick up both but reconsidered, walking back to drop just one off at her feet. Normally remembering to portray my strength as that closer to a human man's was second nature, I'd been doing it for centuries, especially since we'd been traveling in the mortal lands for the past eight months. But when I was around Evaline, all my thoughts were muddled, all my intuitions scattered. I clenched my jaw and moved back to get the second box, if I was going to keep her safe, I needed to be mindful.

When I came back to drop off the second box Evaline was guiding the white horse with brown patches.

Again, letting her take a lead, I stepped back, stuffing my hands into my pockets, waiting to be useful.

She looked at the girls, a smile spreading on her face. "Are you ready?"

They nodded furiously, their helmets bobbing one second behind each movement. Evaline straightened and held a hand out to Priscilla. "Do you want to go first?"

The girl almost jumped into Evaline's arms as she bounded forward and climbed up onto the boxes, Evaline's hands reaching out just in time to guide her.

Without instruction, Megin quietly came to stand beside me, and I smiled softly. I enjoyed watching children experience the world, always loved the way they saw it in only colors of joy and fun. It was refreshing after so many decades of unhappiness, waiting for Evaline.

She turned toward Megin and I, eyeing us and casting an uneasy glance toward me. I just smiled, there wasn't much more I could do.

I won't kill a child. Is that what she wanted to hear? She knew Kova didn't murder people to feed.

She just looked away and turned back to Priscilla. I watched as Evaline instructed her on how to put her foot in the stirrup and swing one leg over of horse. Priscilla put her foot in and was able to stand, small hands gripping the pommel, but that's where Evaline came in. She stood on the boxes as well, reaching both hands under Priscilla's arms and lifting her so Priscilla could swing her leg over.

Priscilla squealed as she settled into the seat. She looked down at Megin, her russet cheeks deepening with a red flush of excitement. "I did it!"

Megin jumped and tugged on my sleeve. "My turn, my turn!"

Evaline's eyes once again fell to us at the movement, and they zeroed in on Megin's hand on my sleeve.

"Maddox." Evaline said. "Will you hold the reins of Priscilla's horse while I help Megin on hers?"

I nodded. "Of course."

Megin ran over to Evaline while I strode to gather the rope of Priscilla's horse's rein. I guided the horse gently, moving a few feet away.

Priscilla's smile hadn't left her face and she couldn't stop looking over the side of the horse at how tall she was. "I'm as tall as a tree!"

I laughed and smiled at her. "Taller, I think." I agreed, even though we were at eye level.

Evaline instructed Megin on the same procedure, and she had a similar reaction as Priscilla when she landed in the saddle.

We spent the next few hours teaching them how to use their lower legs to control the speed of the horse, how to tug on the reins to steer them all while either Evaline or I had our hands on the guiding rope to keep control of them. We switched between who we were working with, and the entire day was enjoyable. I couldn't remember the last time I'd had so much fun with someone other than Wyott, and usually when he and I had fun it involved alcohol or knives.

When our time with the horses ended Evaline helped both girls out of the saddle while I put everything, including the horses, back as we'd found them.

Evaline shouted her thanks over to the owner, and he waved back at her.

As we walked back through the barn toward town I knew I should depart from them. We were walking the same direction, I'd passed the orphanage on my way here this morning. But I moved to divert my path anyway so as not to intrude.

"It's been a great day with you girls, thank you so much for letting me be a part of your lesson." I said smiling at them. I nodded at all three as I said my goodbyes. "Megin, Priscilla, Evaline. Have a good day."

I turned to leave but a hand reached out and grabbed mine. I turned back to see that it was Priscilla.

She turned to Evaline. "Evaline, please, can Mr. Maddox walk us back home?"

For the first time today, there wasn't a pause or any contemplation behind Evaline's eyes. "Yes, of course he can." She said, looking at me briefly.

I bit back my smile and continued to hold Priscilla's hand as we made our way down the street.

The walk to the orphanage was short but I appreciated it nonetheless.

After dropping the girls off we strode down the main street in silence and I bit my lip. It wouldn't be long before I had to depart from her, the inn was close. I should talk to her, offer to walk her home, but I knew she'd decline. And probably be insulted. But as I turned, my mouth opened to speak, she did the same, and we spoke over each other for a second. We smiled at the coincidence, and I nodded. "Go ahead."

She smiled briefly, casting her eyes forward again. "I was just going to say, thank you for helping today. If you hadn't shown up, I think I would've had to cancel."

A swipe of heat went over my heart. I looked down at her even though she didn't meet my gaze. "You never have to thank me, Evaline. I'm always happy to help you."

I saw a flash of pink creep up the back of her neck and looked away before I could find myself anymore in awe of her. Everything about her was beautiful, even the blush over her skin. "Well, anyway." She started. "Thanks."

I just nodded. We walked a few more paces, closer to the inn, and I noted that her stride slowed down. I smiled.

"I'd ask if you'd like me to walk you home, but I think I might end up with that dagger in my eye."

A smile flashed on her lips before she forced it away, eyes still forward. "With instincts like that it's no wonder you're immortal."

I laughed, not for the first time today, and nodded. "They've gotten me by this far."

That got her attention, and her head tilted up toward me. "And how far is that?" She asked, shrugging. "Or how long, I mean."

I raised my eyebrows, feigning insult. "I don't know about Kembertus, but where I come from it's rude to ask someone their age."

She just rolled her eyes again, a smile quickly following. "I don't think that applies to Kova."

I shrugged. "I know, I don't care. I'm almost two hundred years old. One hundred eighty-nine."

I watched as her eyes widened and she pursed her lips.

"Older than you expected?" I asked.

She took a deep breath and turned back to watch where she walked. "I don't know what I expected, I guess I'm not even sure how long Kova live." She waved her hand quickly. "Well forever, obviously, but I mean I don't know how long it takes for them to mature into..." She waved her hand up and down the length of my body, her eyes following, sticking on a few places. My chest, my hands, my eyes.

I smiled. "Kova are what you would consider children, human ages from infancy to nine years old for about fifteen to twenty years. Adolescents for fifteen more, and usually mature like me by forty years."

She nodded. "I see." But her voice was meek, and I didn't know if it was from surprise at my age, or fear.

She'd acted more restricted around me throughout the riding lesson than the entire time I've known her, and I knew it was likely because she had the girls to take care of. I'd be wary too. But she'd been more shut down around me, more hesitant, than the last time we spoke. And I wasn't sure what changed.

I stopped walking and was only slightly surprised when she did the same. I turned to face her.

"Are you afraid of me, Evaline?" I asked and could've grimaced at how heartbroken my voice sounded even to my own ears. A part of me was angry that I'd asked her, because I was afraid of the answer. I hadn't given her any reason to be, apart from how I was born.

Something flashed behind her eyes and she opened her mouth to speak. My eyes dropped there, but she didn't say anything and instead closed it again. She took a breath.

"I'm not supposed to be." She started and looked sidelong. "My father told me that Kova were generally good, to trust them if I felt I could." She shrugged. "But it's not that easy to do after watching…" She stopped herself and I waited for her to continue. She moved her eyes back up to mine, a sheen of fresh tears in them. "After watching him die because of a Vasi."

Without thinking I moved forward, grasping her hand gently in mine and swiping my thumb over it.

"Wallace was killed by a Vasi?" I asked softly, then shook my head. "I don't know how I never heard about that."

She just stared at me. "You didn't hear about it because I've never told anyone."

My eyes searched her face, seeing all the pain that had lived there for so long, so alone. "Evaline, I'm so sorry." Was all I could say, all I could do for her.

The tears swelled for a moment before I watched her will them away. "It is what it is."

I wanted to ask so much more. Why did the Vasi choose them, what did the Vasi look like, how had they gotten away. I knew I couldn't ask them all right now, but as the last question entered my mind it was out of my mouth before I could stop it.

"Did it bite you?" It was rare for a human to survive a Vasi attack, even rarer to do so unscathed and without an attempted feeding. The thought of her being bitten, of a Vasi putting their teeth on this woman who didn't deserve any of the trauma she bore, infuriated me.

Her face dropped and I knew I'd asked the wrong question. I steeled myself, ready for her to pull away, to storm off. But instead, she swallowed and brought up her left hand, the opposite of which I was still holding, and tugged slightly at the collar of her tunic. She pulled it so that the muscle connecting her neck and shoulder showed, and I saw it.

"Oh, Eva." My free hand was already moving over the two small circular shaped scars that reflected each other on her skin. I heard her soft gasp and felt the goosebumps that formed beneath my fingers. But I didn't move, and she didn't pull away. Instead, I met her eyes.

"How did you survive?" My voice was choked, the words hardly passing through the lump that lodged itself in my throat. She'd almost been taken from this world years before I ever got the chance to meet her.

Thanks be to the Gods for protecting her. I prayed.

Her eyes searched mine, as if she could see the words I thought. Could see the prayer I'd whispered in my head, like she could pluck them right from the sky as they drifted toward the heavens. Or perhaps she heard that? I'd spoken them in a similar fashion as I would if I was trying to speak to her through our bond, but I hadn't sent it down the tether. I'd felt around countless times since we'd met each other, it was closed.

She reached up and pushed the pads of her fingers between my furrowed brows, smoothing the skin there. "You don't need to worry about me all the time, Maddox. I can take care of myself." She whispered.

My heart ravaged in my chest, full of hatred for the Vasi who hurt her, pain for which she felt, and joy at how vulnerable she was being with me. I swiped my thumb over the scars on her shoulder. "That doesn't mean you should have to."

We stayed that way for a moment, and if it was any other time or any other conversation, I would've kissed her. But she was vulnerable right now and I'd never want her to think that I was only interested in her for physical affection.

But the chime of the bell in the castle boomed around us and she jumped out of my grasp. Eyes flashing up and down the street to see if anyone was around. We were alone, everyone was inside eating dinner at this time, but she checked nonetheless.

"I have to go." She said, her voice curt. She didn't meet my eyes and I knew the moment we'd shared was gone.

"I understand." I turned toward the inn and we began walking again. When we made it to the corner beside the building we stopped again. I turned to her and once again her eyes were cast down. "Are we still on for tomorrow night?" I said softly.

She nodded. "Yes." Her eyes flashed up to mine. "If that's still okay with you?"

I nodded back. "I don't break my vows."

She nodded as she started backing away. "By the way, Eva is not my name."

A smile lifted my lips. "Of course, Evaline." I said and watched as her eyes fell to my lips as I said it. She whirled around and headed up the street toward the castle.

Unease tugged at my gut. She'd gotten lost in the pull when we'd been in an embrace, and again when we'd said goodbye. She was drawn to me because of the bond, as I was her, I just hoped that it wasn't the only reason she was drawn to me.

CHAPTER TWENTY-SEVEN

Evaline

I nearly tripped over a root as I made my way to the clearing where Maddox had instructed I meet them, and I knew that it was a good idea that he'd bought me new boots. The pair I'd found by happenstance were far too big, and were a broken ankle waiting to happen; I was lucky they hadn't already injured me.

It was dark, the town had already gone to bed, and all I had to guide me was the moonlight. I knew I was nearing the clearing when I saw firelight through the trees, lighting my way to him.

When I entered the clearing I saw Maddox and his friend sitting beside the fire on the far end of the space. Maddox turned to smile at me, his eyes doing a quick sweep over my body that he tried to hide, and then meeting mine. I wore black trousers, snug to my form, and my oversized boots, a warm tunic and my cloak. My dagger strapped to my right thigh.

He stood and greeted me as I made my way over to them.

"Evaline, this is Wyott." He gestured to his companion. I gave him a small smile and waved. "I hope it's okay he came; he'd be lost without me if he stayed back at the inn."

Wyott scoffed and stood, offering me his hand. "I've heard far too much about you." I shook it and he gave me a wicked smile. He was just as tall as Maddox, but had broader shoulders and a thicker chest. His honey blond hair fell past his chin, to a rough beard, and he had half of the waves pulled into a bun on top of his head.

Maddox rolled his eyes, but I smiled at the interaction.

"Take a seat to put on your boots." He turned and handed me the new shoes and I smiled. They were plain and black, but they were my size.

"Thank you." I looked away quickly, not wanting to retain his gaze for too long for fear it might swallow me.

I sat and started strapping them up my leg. They reached up high, falling just below my knee. While it was still unfortunate that my guardians had taken away the pair I'd had when I came to Kembertus, I knew as soon as Maddox had handed me this set that they were far higher quality than the pair I'd had for so many years. These felt more cushioned, as if I could walk for miles and miles, and the leather around my legs was soft and pliable while also being protective of my ankles when laced.

As I changed boots, Maddox explained the plan. "We can meet here as often as you'd like, although I think you're going to be sore the first few times since it's been so long since you've trained with a partner. If you'd like some rest between sessions just let me know."

I almost scoffed. Not because he was wrong, he was likely right. My muscles had been mostly out of commission for years, and there was nothing like that first training session to reactivate what you forgot you had. I scoffed because I didn't have time to take rest days, the wedding was just under a month away.

I bit my lip and he continued.

"You should be making sure you're getting plenty of sleep, even though that might be hard because we train at night. And you need to make sure you're eating enough, you'll want to build muscle and we're going to be training hard, I don't want you losing weight."

I nodded, tying my second boot.

"Today we're just going to focus on the basics, hand to hand combat, no weapons."

I finished tying it and looked up at him, aghast. "What? I bought a dagger for a reason, I—" He shot me a look and I could almost hear the next words out of his mouth. What happens if you're disarmed? I held up a hand before he could protest. "Okay I get it, save me the lecture."

He shot Wyott a smirk.

"I like her." Wyott remarked.

I snorted as I stood. "Then clearly your threshold for liking people is rather low."

He cocked his head. "The lowest."

I smiled and looked between them. Interacting with them felt natural, and that fact startled me. I swallowed and again looked at them both, this time unease crawled up my spine, the reality of where I was dawning on me.

"It has only just now occurred to me that I agreed to spend my nights in the middle of the woods, alone, with two Kova."

The two bellowed laughs.

"Yeah, I definitely like her." Wyott responded.

Maddox smiled at me. "You don't need to be afraid of us. We don't make a habit of harming women, especially not –" he paused. "Women we agree to train for their own safety."

I nodded. What did I have to lose? It was either be killed by them, or marry a monster. I didn't know which was worse. I took off my cloak to have a better range of motion, and because Maddox didn't have one on. Did Kova get cold? He started disarming himself, so I did the same. But where I just unsheathed my one measly dagger, Maddox had an arsenal.

He pulled a dagger from his ankle, his thigh, had a few strapped to his chest. The swords on his back.

Lastly, he removed the weapon on his hip.

And I laughed. "Why do you have a hatchet?"

Wyott's immediate laughter burst beside me. "I *told* you it was a hatchet."

Maddox rolled his eyes. "It's nothing, just an inside joke from back home." He tossed the hatchet on the ground beside all his other weapons, but Wyott was on his feet in an instant.

"Oh, it's not nothing." He said, spreading his hands for dramatic effect. "It's quite an amusing story. Evaline, would you like to hear it?"

I felt the way Maddox tensed, saw the roll of his eyes out of the corner of my own.

"I would've said no, but considering how much this is clearly annoying Maddox…" I said, turning to look at him briefly, then whipping back to Wyott. "I must know."

Wyott's smile was wide as he dropped to grab the hatchet from the pile of weapons. He held it up so I could see its size. "When we were young and first allowed to start training with weapons, Maddox was terrible with them." Wyott said, nodding the blade toward his friend. "He was smaller than all of us, he didn't get his growth spurt until a decade later, so he was slower and weaker."

I allowed myself to peek at Maddox for a breath. He was so tall, easily over half a foot taller than me, and so wide. It was hard to ever imagine a time when he was weak.

"So when it came time to start training with weapons, they were hard for him because they were heavy." Wyott shrugged. "We'd train with heavier weapons than we'd normally carry, to condition, but he had trouble with them, so he'd throw fits."

A small laugh left my lips. Maddox, who had been pretending not to listen and instead opting to look anywhere else besides at Wyott and I, looked down at me for a second.

"What kind of fits?" I asked, turning my attention back to Wyott.

"He'd curse, he'd grab whatever weapon he could hold and throw them across the room. He'd storm off, and sometimes he'd just cry."

Maddox groaned. "What is happening?" He muttered to himself, his head falling back.

"But when he would regain his composure, or get yelled at by our trainers or his father, the leader of our people, by the way." He whispered the second part and I smiled at how dramatically Wyott told stories. But that was interesting, I guess it had never dawned on me that of course the Kova would have a leader. It was only natural for beings to seek leadership in some fashion. And with his confidence, and the air of authority he had, it wasn't shocking to consider Maddox a member of their ruling family. "He'd grab an axe. We only had them in the barn for cutting logs, but he'd pick it up because it was the lightest bladed weapon we had, and he'd train with that."

I looked up at Maddox as Wyott spoke, and he tilted his head down to look at me, too. I smiled at the small hint of blush that tinted his cheeks.

"Because of his fits, and the weapon he chose, we made a nickname for him, which fit from his actual name." My attention turned back to Wyott now.

My smile widened. "What is it?"

"Mad Axe." Wyott beamed. "It's not perfect, his actual name isn't pronounced with the 'axe' sound, but you get the sentiment."

I chuckle and turned to Maddox. "If your name is Mad Axe, then why do you carry a hatchet?"

He rolled his eyes and snatched the weapon from Wyott, lifting it up as if to show me better. "This is an axe."

The laugh that erupted out of my mouth might've been too loud for three people in the woods doing something they were definitely not allowed to do, but I couldn't help myself. The serious look on his face was hilarious, and I couldn't stop laughing. And even though I was laughing at him, Maddox's lips lifted into a smile.

I wiped a tear that had begun to fall from my eye at the effort of laughing, and when I was done, I looked at Maddox. "That's a hatchet."

He threw the thing onto the ground near all his other weapons. "Listen, I can't carry a full axe on my belt that's insanely impractical."

Wyott and I shared another look, and I could tell they'd had this argument hundreds of times. He turned to Wyott now. "Thank you, friend, for embarrassing me. Can we get started with the lesson now?" Maddox asked, waving toward the log where Wyott had previously been sitting.

Wyott just nodded and turned to go back to the log, but not before bending down toward me and whispering in my ear. "See what I mean? A fit."

I snorted and turned back to Maddox, who was doing his best to look bored of Wyott and I, and I swallowed back my smile.

Maddox moved to the center of the clearing, away from the fire and where Wyott sat down next to it, and I followed.

"I'm sure you practiced without weapons with your father."

I nodded.

"So you probably already know most of this –"

I cut him off. "Feet wide, balancing your weight. Knees bent. Punch with your whole body, thumb out of the fist, obviously. And fists up to protect yourself."

Maddox smiled at me. "Well then, clearly I'm just here as a sparring dummy."

"You're definitely one of those things." He shot me a smile, but then I nodded. "I told you, I've been trained before."

He started to circle me, and I fell into my fighting stance, keeping an even distance between us. "We'll just work on building your strength and reflexes then."

But as he finished his sentence, he shot out a punch, and it was slow. I easily dodged it, a smile widening on my face. "You're telling me that's as fast as a Kova can move? Or are you trying to go easy on me?"

Wyott's laugh rang from the fire. A gleam lit Maddox's eyes. "Of course not, but I must gauge your skills first. I don't want to accidentally hurt you."

I would've rolled my eyes, but it would've taken them off of him. He threw another punch, faster this time, but I ducked and swung one of my own for his stomach, which he dodged.

"Good, using the height difference to your advantage." He remarked as we circled each other and I tried to ignore the flutter in my belly from his praise.

We continued like that for what seemed like ages, but probably was only an hour. Sweat pooled on my back and forehead. My breathing became labored, I couldn't even remember the last time I'd been active for so long.

But it felt good.

Maddox noticed my fatigue. "Just a few more minutes and we'll call it a night."

I nodded, knowing if I was going to try anything risky it'd have to be now that we were about to finish for the night, and considering Maddox probably thought I was too tired to do so. I had no clue if I could still do it. For Gods' sake I hadn't even been stretching lately, but I wanted to try.

Maddox shot a fist out and I ducked it, using the momentum of my kneel to spring up, twisting on one foot as the other straightened in a kick heading straight for his head.

He caught my leg, one hand holding my calf and the other on my thigh. The inside of my thigh.

His brows rose. "That was impressive." He looked to where it landed, mere inches from his face. "A human wouldn't have been able to dodge that."

I smiled, pride swelling inside of me. I guess my skills weren't as rusty as I thought they were. His eyes focused on my lips, and I swear his hands squeezed my leg. But I was losing my balance. I made a move to take my leg back and he let me, but not before letting his hands run down it as I pulled it away. My cheeks might've heated, but it was hard to tell whether it was his touch or the physical exertion.

We said nothing as we sat and Wyott handed me a canteen of water.

I smiled at him. "Thank you."

It meant a lot, especially considering Kova didn't really need to drink water, not to survive. Did they bring it just for me?

"I can't tell if you're a natural, or if your father was just a very good teacher." Maddox said across the fire as he started strapping all his weapons back on. He strapped the hatchet back onto his hip and I watched his hand's movement across his body as he continued attaching daggers to his chest, and the sword to his back. His muscles were clearly defined through the tunic he wore. When he looked up and caught me staring, I pretended to be looking at the flames between us.

I shrugged and looked down at the canteen in my hands. "I like to think it's a bit of both."

He rounded the fire to hand me my dagger, but as he did, he frowned at the blade. "This isn't very big."

I sneered at him as I snatched it from his hand. "It was all I could afford, that's why I picked it."

His jaw clenched, but I ignored it and slid the knife back into its sheath.

"You're the niece of the Lord and Lady of this city, aren't you wealthy?" Wyott asked beside me.

I shrugged. "They're wealthy. But they don't allot me any money and I'm not allowed to work for it, so I —" But I caught myself before I continued speaking.

Maddox's lips quirked up into a smile. "You pickpocket."

I pursed my own but nodded. What was the point in keeping it from them? They'd already caught me once. "I did. But only from the rich, and I always gave a majority of the money to the orphanage. It's why it took me so long to save up."

Wyott spoke while Maddox evaluated me. "You're a good pickpocket. If we hadn't been Kova, Maddox wouldn't have caught you that day in the inn."

I smiled at him. "Thank you. But I had to be. If I was caught, and they told my guardians," I sighed, looking down at the ground in front of me. "Who knows what they would've done."

Maddox tensed in front of me, and I didn't need to see it to know. I felt the air ripple off him just as hot and angry as that which came from the fire.

He opened his mouth to speak, but Wyott cut him off. "We should probably get you back so you can get some rest."

The conversation ended there, and after we put out the fire and gathered our belongings, we left. They walked me back to the castle, stopping before we entered the gardens and risked being spotted by guards.

"It was nice to meet you, Evaline." Wyott waved, heading toward the inn.

My returned wave was mostly to his turned back. I looked at Maddox, quirking a brow at him. Why was he still standing here?

His eyes roamed my face as if searching for something. "You're very skilled." His tone was soft, and there wasn't a hint of mockery in it. I believed him.

"Thank you." My heart sputtered against my chest. Could he hear that?

"Seeing you fight, it makes me feel better. To know that when you're roaming the city alone, you're able to protect yourself."

I nodded. "Well, I've been doing a good job of it for two years, except —" I stopped myself before I could finish my sentence. *Except for when it mattered most.* Why had I come so close to sharing that information?

His eyes cut to mine. "Except for what?" And surely the darkness of the night was impacting my vision, because I almost thought I saw a flicker of fear in his gray eyes.

"Nothing, goodnight. Thank you." And I turned before he could respond.

When I got into bed that night, I didn't miss the way my skin sang in only the spaces where he'd touched.

CHAPTER TWENTY-EIGHT

Maddox

I caught up to Wyott easily. He looked at me when I joined his side and I nodded at him, a silent thank you for giving me time alone with Evaline, even if it was brief.

"She can fight." He observed.

A smile tugged at the corners of my lips. "Yes, she can." My mate, a fighter.

"Thank the Gods for that." He continued. "Because knowing you she'll probably need to knock you on your ass for all the stupid shit you say."

I couldn't even argue. We rounded the corner in town, nearing the inn. I felt him peering at me, even though he tried to hide it.

"What?"

He shrugged. "When was the last time you ate?" His eyes moved to the entry of the tavern as we passed it.

I stayed silent and allowed us to pass the establishment, knowing he wanted me to walk inside and pick someone, man or woman, to feed from.

"Maddox," he hissed and I knew he was angry.

He very well knew the last time I ate, because he was there. A day before I met Evaline. "If you already knew the answer why bother asking the question?" I mumbled.

A low growl rolled through him. "You know that I understand better than anyone how difficult it is to drink from someone else after meeting your mate. But you need to eat. No matter how unpleasant it seems. You'll only become weaker and slower, and you and I both know what will happen if you let yourself become too far gone."

We entered the inn, Nathaniel jolting awake from where he'd dozed at the desk.

"I know this." I waited until we were in the hallway, where our rooms resided beside each other, to hiss the words at him.

He stopped at his door, hand on the knob. "Then act like it." And pushed inside, leaving me standing alone.

I clenched my jaw and went into my own room, struggling to not slam the door. I tried to ignore his words as I cleaned and prepared to lie down for the night. I'd have thought my body would relax as I slumped into the sheets, the cushion of the mattress seeming to hug me everywhere it touched, but my bones felt heavy and my muscles rigid.

Wyott's words ran through my mind. *No matter how unpleasant it seems.* But that was the issue. It's not that it seemed unpleasant, it seemed impossible. It was impossible. I'd already tried, without telling him. The night Evaline came to my room with that welt on her face. After she'd left, a wild rage had begun boiling inside of me over the thought of someone striking her, hurting her. I needed to feed, if not only to quell the fire in my own blood.

But it hadn't worked then.

I swallowed the anger racing up my throat and walked back out my door. If Wyott wanted me to try again, I would. Maybe it was a fluke.

I walked out of my room and passed a few men in the hallway. Through my rage it took a moment to realize the one who was speaking was Bassel, the man who'd danced with Evaline at the Ball. I turned my eyes away from him, knowing he'd likely know what I was if he saw them. As the future ruler of Vestaria he would be told of the Vasi and Kova.

"It's done, all I had to do was say the word and he shook on it." His words drifted down the hall as I turned the corner. "It won't be long before it's final and I'm back in Vestaria."

I went to the tavern and found a man brooding in the corner. He was the only person in the room who was alone.

And as usual, I compelled him to follow me out into the alley back behind the tavern. "Don't scream, don't move. You will not feel any pain, this does not hurt." His eyes glazed as I looked into them, altering his mind to do what I wanted with. But the moment my teeth sunk in, I pulled back, gagging and spitting.

It burned, just like the last time I'd tried. I looked up at the man who looked dully at the stars.

When the horrific feeling faded, I straightened, swiping a quick tongue over the bite marks so that he'd heal, even though the blood that resided there burned once more, and compelled him to forget.

I shoved my hands in my pockets and walked out of the alley.

I shook my head. "What is wrong with me?" I quietly questioned aloud.

It was as if I'd taken a mouthful of red, molten metal into my mouth and tried to drink it. Not causing any actual physical damage, but feeling as if it tore a hole through my esophagus. Having that experience with one human was a fluke, two was an issue. I turned back for home. Or the inn, anyway.

As I laid in bed again, I raised a hand to my throat, stroking over it as if to see if a hole really had emerged. Unpleasant. It surely was. But it was more, it was horrifying. To feel like I was choking on fire. Wyott never experienced that. He claimed blood from someone other than your mate simply tasted gross, like the blood had gone rotten. But this was worse. This was poison.

I hadn't fed since I'd met Evaline, and wouldn't until it was from her. If she'd ever let me. I swallowed the fear that thought induced.

Instead, I tried to think of the way Evaline's body moved when she fought. The smoothness of her skin when I caught a fist she threw, the movement of her thick braid as it flung around her back when she'd twist. The feel of my hand on her leg – how close the one on her thigh had been to, no doubt, the sweetest part of her.

I dragged a hand over my face.

She was going to be the death of me.

CHAPTER TWENTY-NINE

Evaline

I couldn't remember a time when I'd felt more beaten down before.

The night's training had taken its toll and I hissed a curse as I sat up in bed. My body was wrecked. My bones felt like lead and my muscles like they were coiled into tight balls, and every movement was shredding them apart. I bit my lip as I got up, a gasp escaping me as I stood and felt the resistance from my legs.

It was painful, but I felt amazing. After two years of sitting in my room, walking my only form of exercise, this pain was the cost of becoming myself again, of feeling like myself again.

One of the servants drew me a bath and I soaked in it long after the water had gone cold, because in an odd way the chill helped my muscles, too. I had just finished dressing in trousers and a blouse when my aunt burst through my room.

I bit back a yelp of surprise and then narrowed my eyes at the fabric in her arms.

"You've been quite the homebody today." She said, and I shrugged. I hadn't talked to her since she confirmed that I'd be married off.

She moved further into the room. "I hope you're feeling rested because we have a special guest for dinner tonight." She set the dress on the bed. It was a pale pink.

"You don't mean…" I silently pleaded her not to say his name.

"Yes, Bassel will be joining us for dinner. He will be your husband in only a few weeks' time, we need to start treating him like family now."

I bit my tongue. There was no use in arguing. I'd have to start getting used to spending more time with him as the wedding drew near. My mind flashed to the dagger stowed below my bed. I didn't normally wear it around the castle, I felt safe here. But if he'd be lurking these walls more and more then I wouldn't be caught without it.

I wouldn't kill him, yet, but I wouldn't hesitate if he touched me again.

"I can get myself ready." I told her as she moved toward my vanity.

She turned, ready to argue, but the look of my sad eyes must've changed her mind. Pick your battles.

She tried to hide the sigh that released from her chest and nodded. "Be ready in one hour and meet us in the dining room." Then turned to leave. I turned toward the dress, it looked pretty enough. "Evaline?" She turned halfway to the door.

"Yes."

"Please look nice. I know he's already agreed to marry you, but it never hurts to make him *want* to marry you."

My teeth ground together as she left the room. She was a master of continuously lowering the amount of respect I had for her. I moved to the vanity and prepared to put makeup on, knowing if I didn't, she would complain, and I didn't want to give her any extra reasons to come to my room any more than she already did.

But when I caught sight of myself in the mirror, for the first time in what felt like ages, I looked at myself. Truly looked at myself. Looked at the bags beneath my eyes that had been there for months, symptoms of never getting a wholly good night's sleep. Looked at the red ring around my eyes from waking up crying as I did every morning. Into my eyes that had seen too much sorrow and not enough joy.

But most of all, I looked at the reflection of a tired girl. A woman exhausted with putting on a happy face for appearances. Who had smiled one fake smile too many. Who had lost pieces of her in the show. And not just since Bassel had been here, but my entire time in Kembertus.

The prospect of having to deal with his presence only worsened my fatigue, only made the nightmares worse and awoke the trauma inside of me. I watched as those eyes filled with tears and brought my fists forward pressing them against the wood of the vanity's tabletop in front of me.

I didn't have time to cry about him anymore. I didn't have the luxury of shutting down, even when it was the only thing I wanted to do. I had to protect myself and others from him. I had to end his plague on this world.

And I had to do it with another smile on my face.

I did my makeup, lining my eyes just as Therese had done for the Ball, and then coating my lashes. I pulled my hair into a braid, naturally, and made sure to weave the wire in. If Bassel would be at this dinner tonight, I refused to be unprotected in any way.

I lifted the dress before realizing it had a corset built in. I huffed. I poked my head into the hall, needing a second pair of hands to help me with the task. Natalia saw me and came to help. I stepped into the dress and held the top in place as she began to tighten the corset. I didn't bother wearing a breast undergarment beneath it, there was no room. The cups of the bosom hardly covered anything. I gritted my teeth again.

In the Kromean Kingdoms a woman had to be a virgin to be alluring for marriage, yet this was the dress my aunt chose for me. I rolled my eyes, even though she didn't know my sexual history, her hypocrisy never ceased to amaze me.

As Natalia tightened the corset, I dropped my arms, no longer needing to hold it in place.

I looked in the mirror as she worked. The skirt was long, to the floor, but wasn't full of tulle beneath it to give structure, like my ballgown had been. No, the silk this dress was made of simply hung down my hips, a long slit starting halfway up my right thigh and exposing my leg, wide with remnants of old muscle, the further it fell to the floor. The bottom of the corset tucked into my waist, accentuating the outline of an hourglass. The corset was made of the same silk, but had strong panels

195 |

that maintained its structure. A hard tug from Natalia had a gust of air coughing through my lips.

A thought on my distaste for the uncomfortable garment was entering my mind, but the more I stared at the thing, I considered how if it were made of metal instead of silk, it would be useful as armor in battle. For a moment I considered what Maddox would say to that and a smile formed on my lips. He'd laugh.

Natalia finished and I breathed a sigh of relief, shocked I still had breath to sigh.

I saw the two pale puncture scars that rested near my shoulder, the gift the Vasi had left behind, and thought of Maddox's reaction to it. He'd seemed devastated, the sight of my scars paining him as if they were his own. Most people couldn't see them. With the freckles that dusted my shoulders, the small scars that were just barely paler than my own skin blended in. But I knew he'd see them with his keen sight, and his knowledge of what the marks would look like.

After that interaction, his hands on my skin, and the nickname he'd given me, I'd tried to think of a logical reason that he'd be so invested in me. I couldn't think of any that didn't cause my heart to falter out of beat.

It took every ounce of willpower not to snarl at Bassel when I walked into the dining room. My aunt, uncle, and groom-to-be already sitting.

His eyes raked over every single inch of my body and the feeling sent ripples of nausea through me. I made my way to sit at the last table setting, directly across from Bassel. My uncle and aunt sat at their usual positions at each end.

Before I could sit, Bassel jumped up, coming around the table and pulling the chair out for me, helping me to sit. I forced the mask to slip over my face and allowed a smile to form, thanking him.

"Of course, Evaline."

When he sat back down across from me, I became very aware of his eyes on me. Not in the same way I'd felt Maddox's heated gaze. This was unnerving, and my gut screamed at me to flee. All instincts informing me of a predator.

I grinned and beared most of the dinner, only half listening as the others discussed all matters. Bassel's home, and what it's like there in Vestaria. Bassel's thoughts on Kembertus. Bassel complimenting my uncle on the Ball's success.

I almost laughed at the glare I caught my aunt throwing towards my uncle at the mention of the Ball. As predicted, he'd gotten belligerent off the wine. But mostly I ignored their talk. I shoveled food into my mouth. Maddox had warned me to stay nourished and this was my first meal today – due to sleeping in and my long bath, I'd missed both breakfast and lunch. But I knew my muscles would need the nutrients this meal provided so I continued adding to my plate from the dishes on the table.

I watched Bassel from across the table. It was the first time I'd truly looked at Bassel since the Ball, and I only dared to do so because he was in a heated debate with my uncle over what area of the world the best grapes grew for wine, and I did it through my lashes, hoping he couldn't tell I was staring. He'd pushed his chair slightly away from the table and sat back, done with dinner and here for the chat, I supposed. His hair was like I remembered, just more put together than it had been that night two years ago.

My eyes traveled down. He was wearing a white long-sleeved shirt, the arms slightly puffed and poking out of the leather vest that covered the torso.

In the time I'd been looking, only a few seconds, his hand kept reaching to move over his left pocket, like something important was lying there. When his hand moved, I noticed the slight bulge in the fabric.

My eyes cast down, panic rising in my throat. I knew what that bulge was. It had to be a small box with a small piece of metal inside it. I tried to swallow the fear rising in my throat, I knew this was coming. I'd heard too many stories. I took a breath.

It won't be forever. Breathe. Calm down. I clamped down on the fear, made it dissolve away into hard, stone like, will.

It was then I noticed the wine glass sitting there. I'd been drinking water throughout the meal and hadn't noticed I'd been served wine. I hardly drank, but if any situation called for it, it was this one. I reached for the glass. I tried not to look like I was gulping the wine down, but my aunt frowned at me anyway. I decided I didn't care. And as the warmth spread through my veins, feeling fuzzy down my legs and in my lips, I was glad I drank it, because Bassel stood and made his way over to me, offering his hand.

"Would you do me the honor of joining me for a walk in the garden?"

My eyes shot to my aunt, and I know she took the look as asking for permission, or maybe she saw the raw panic there. But she nodded.

In the fraction of seconds I had before it was obvious I was stalling I ran through scenarios in my head. I couldn't go out into the garden, not alone with him. Not at dark. The guards were likely patrolling by now, but who's to say Bassel wouldn't cart me down the street or into the woods, somewhere hidden?

An idea struck and I took his hand, trying my best to sound nonchalant, I proposed as I stood. "Surely, you've already seen the castle's gardens, how about we take a walk through the courtyard?"

He nodded and smiled at me.

We'd still be alone, something I most definitely did not want to be with him. But the courtyard was the better option. It was not overly large, and was lit on every side where the castle swallowed it. The light reached nearly the entire area. And perhaps the most important aspect was that one of the walls that made the border of the greenery was the kitchen, where I knew the staff would be cleaning after dinner. If I screamed, I'd have a better chance of someone hearing.

I tried to ignore the fact that I resented having to think about these precautions at all.

We entered the courtyard and Bassel mused. "I see why you suggested this over the gardens. The landscaping outside the castle is beautiful, but this," he looked around at the dozens of flowers lining the path through the courtyard, leading straight for a water fixture. "Is much more intimate."

I silenced my gulp. He crooked his elbow and nudged it toward me, I placed my hand gingerly inside as he walked us down the stone path. I tried my best to hold onto the fabric of his sleeve rather than the flesh that lay below. Anything to stay as far away from him as I could throughout my ruse.

The only sounds were the crickets in the distance and our footfalls against the path. The courtyard was lined in greenery. Bushes, small decorative trees, and ivy that climbed up the brick perimeter. But the most beautiful detail was the large reflective pool that sat in the middle of it. At this time, in the dark, it was black as night, mirroring only the faintest light from the lanterns hanging against the walls that framed us in. On the other side sat a beautiful statue of Kembertic himself. It was marble and intricately crafted, showing the sun God with his sunburst crown sitting on his head.

"In all my travels I've never seen a city with such simple beauty as Kembertus."

I contemplated whether that was his way of calling our city poor.

We were less endowed than other cities, from what I'd heard. But Bassel's city, Vestaria, was founded on top of a diamond mine. They were one of the richest kingdoms in the world.

I realized I should probably respond. "I wouldn't know, I've only ever lived here and Neomaeros."

He looked down at me, smiling. "Do you want to travel?"

"Yes." I kept my answer clipped. I didn't like sharing pieces of myself with him. We stopped in front of the pool, and he turned to face me.

"Well maybe I can do something about that." He reached forward and took my hands in his. "Evaline, I'll never forget the moment I met you at the Spring Solstice Ball, because you were the most beautiful woman I'd ever seen." The dread rippled inside me, clawing up my throat and begging to be released. "I knew then that I had to ask your uncle for your hand." I almost scoffed. He didn't even pretend to act as if he wanted to know me, or love me, or do anything with me other than parade me around on his arm. Or worse.

He broke the contact of our hands, and I thanked the Gods. He lowered himself onto one knee, reaching to grab the box out of his pocket that I'd spotted earlier.

"Evaline Manor," he started, bringing the box forward. "Will you marry me?" He opened it and revealed the largest diamond I'd ever seen perched atop a ring. My jaw dropped open. I couldn't stop the reaction. The diamond's shape resembled that of an emerald; it was rectangular and elegant.

And the size of my fucking thumb nail.

The band was thin and gold, and for a moment I pondered how such a frail thing could possibly hold the weight of the rock.

I closed my mouth when I realized it'd been open too long, and I hadn't given a response yet.

A war raged inside of me. One side begging me to say no. To pull my dagger out and kill him here. The other instructed me to follow the plan, even if it wasn't fully conceived yet. I wanted nothing more than to end Bassel every time he laid eyes on me, but if I did it now I'd be caught without question, and I'd be executed. There had to be a better option.

In the end, the latter side won. The side of survival. For the time being, I had to follow my guardian's plan. I forced myself to look into his eyes, feeling my own glaze over from my mask.

I smiled. "Of course."

As if I had a choice.

As if he didn't know I didn't have a choice.

As if this entire moment hadn't been meticulously planned and executed.

As if he hadn't attacked me in the middle of the night in the middle of the woods.

He rose and time slowed as he slipped the ring over my finger. It felt cold and heavy there, and deep in my chest I felt the heavy thud of an hourglass turn over as it settled into place.

Chapter Thirty

Maddox

I sat on Evaline's bed, waiting for her return.

It'd been easy enough to break in, the climb up to her window was steep, but fast. I knew when she arrived she'd make a comment about how I was following her. And to be fair, this time I was. But only because I was concerned about how she was feeling after our first training session last night. If when she walked in she was angry and demanded I leave, I would.

I heard footsteps in the hall and knew they were hers. Heard her heart raging in her chest. I frowned, afraid something was wrong. She slipped into the dimly lit room, the only light emanating from the dying fire. She closed the door behind her, facing it and resting her forehead there. I heard her breathe deep.

"Rough day?"

With speed I'd never seen from a mortal, she spun, planting her back against the door, and my breath escaped at the sight. Her braid fell over her shoulder, the skirt of her pale pink dress swaying around her legs.

I didn't know where to look first, every inch of her was tantalizing, but my gaze landed on her right hand. In pure instinct it had slipped through the slit in her dress, up to the dagger that sat there. Her hand gripping the hilt.

I forced my eyes to raise and meet hers and smiled. "Excellent reaction time."

A loud huff escaped those pink lips.

"Maddox." She breathed, and I was surprised to hear relief instead of annoyance.

I stood and walked toward her. Her body didn't relax as I approached, but her hand did fall away from the blade.

My heart fluttered at the show of trust.

I took in the sight of her. How the pink of her dress complimented her lips, her hair. The contrast between the cinching of her waist and the curve of her hips, the pink fabric hardly covering her chest. My blood heated and I felt a stir low within me.

"What are you doing here?" She asked.

I stopped in front of her, close. "I came to check on you."

Her cheeks heated as she gazed up at me, scanning my face. "Check on what? That I wasn't broken after one training session?"

I smiled and ignored her question. Her scent, her eyes, the way her chest heaved slightly toward me as she breathed. It was all suffocating, and I needed more. I allowed my hand to fall forward, spanning the distance between us and landing on her exposed thigh. The back of my hand rested there for a moment, giving her time to stop me if she chose.

Her body tensed and her gaze didn't leave mine, but she didn't bat me away. I slowly slid the hand up until I felt the sheathed blade. Sliding further until I pulled it out and stepped away from her, turning to face the fire and acting as if I was inspecting the knife.

I heard her release the breath she'd been holding the moment my hand touched her.

"I had to see how sore you were."

I could almost hear the eye roll. "What, it's impossible for me to not fall apart after one session?" She pushed off the door and strode toward me.

I whirled, and she stopped in her tracks. "So, you aren't sore?" I challenged.

She crossed her arms and I tried not to look. "I didn't say that. I just think it's a bit presumptuous to think you're allowed to come here for something as menial as seeing if my muscles ache."

I shot her a wicked smile. "So, I should come up with a better excuse next time I want to see you?"

She tried and failed to cover a small upward tug of her lips. "Maddox." Then as if something dawned on her. "Wait, how'd you even get in here? And know which room was mine?"

I shrugged. "I compelled a guard to tell me which window was yours and just scaled the wall." I handed her back the blade. "Not that hard."

She took it and replaced it, exposing so much sweet thick thigh to do so, and nodded. "I know it's not." She said in a knowing tone.

My eyebrow quirked. "Miss Evaline, do you make it a habit of scaling castle walls?"

She met my gaze and let the dress fall back into place. "How do you think I leave at night?" She tilted her head, challenging me to underestimate her again.

Heat, thick and slow, surged through my veins.

I shook my head as I examined her. "You're unlike any other woman I've ever met."

She shrugged. "Not sure if that's a compliment or not."

I smirked. "You are sore, then?"

She nodded at me, wincing as she sat down on the chaise in front of me. "Extremely."

Her hands ran over her thighs, massaging the flesh there and I felt myself start to get hard. What was she trying to do to me?

"I can help with the pain." I didn't have a moment to reconsider saying the words, they were already out of my mouth. My voice far deeper than I intended.

She looked up. "You have healing powers? I didn't know Kova were magic."

I smirked and flexed my hand toward her. "No magic powers, just a magic touch. I've been told I give divine massages."

She scoffed. "No."

I shrugged and let my hands fall and pretended like internally I wasn't begging her to say yes. "Fine, but it'll make them feel better, and recover faster."

She mulled it over for a second. "Fine." She hissed. "But only my back, because that's the only spot I can't reach."

I didn't dare press my luck as I strode behind her on the lounge.

She reached up and swept her braid away from her neck, and then I was looking at her exposed upper back, neck and shoulders. Evaline was strong, but her muscles weren't obvious, they didn't protrude like someone who worked to keep themselves toned. She was thick with the curves that came with genetics and a healthy diet.

I lowered my hands onto her soft skin, over the muscles between her neck and shoulders, and pressed my thumbs into the flesh that I knew ached.

Her head immediately rolled forward as she stifled a gasp.

"Tell me something about you." I whispered, moving my hands slowly to press my thumbs deeper into her back.

Her voice was soft. "Like what?"

I shrugged, and then realized that she couldn't see me. "Anything."

She was quiet for a moment. "I hate living here."

My hands moved to her shoulders as I kneaded. "Why?"

I moved down toward her back as I continued. She gave a soft sigh.

"Besides the obvious, I'm an outsider, daughter of Wallace Manor or not. I don't fit into the mold my aunt tries so desperately to cram me into."

My heart panged for her. Another pause.

"Tell me something about you." She said this time.

"I hate living here, too."

She snorted. "So why don't you leave?"

My hands grazed down to where her dress started, just below her shoulder blades. "I found a reason to stay." I said softly.

Goosebumps rose over her skin. "Why do you hate it here?"

"I don't like anywhere on this side of River Brawn." I started. "The Kromean Kingdoms treat women like they're something to be had, instead of worshiped. Something to be used, instead of cherished."

She tensed for a moment and my hands drifted back up to either side of her neck.

"What?" I asked at her reaction.

She relaxed. "Nothing." She paused. "I rarely hear men speak about women that way." A sigh. "It's nice."

I rested my left knee on the chaise as I half-stood behind her. I moved my hands up her neck, massaging the base. A sigh escaped her lips as her head rolled forward again. The sound clenched a fist around my heart and had my hands digging deeper into the aching muscles. A soft moan this time and she rolled her head back, exposing her face, neck and chest to me, eyes closed.

"Are you sure I can't help massage anywhere else?" I murmured, staring at her chest.

She smiled again, snorting. "I'm positive." She said softly as I continued working on her neck.

"I wouldn't want you to show up to our next session still all coiled up."

I could already feel the muscles loosening under my touch as I roved them. Her eyes were closed as she bit her lip. I clenched my jaw, willing the fast-growing erection to stop.

"I've got it covered, Maddox."

Everything hit me at once as she murmured my name. Her flushed skin, her soft breaths, the way she bit her lip. She was aroused, and that knowledge drove me forward slowly, face nearing her exposed neck as my fingers massaged it. Just one kiss, just one graze of my lips. I could survive the next month on it alone. I clamped one hand around the base of her neck, just below her hairline, and squeezed, knowing tension would be built there.

A louder moan this time and my lips neared her neck, a breath away.

She nearly fell back against me, but caught herself. Throwing her hands out to the side and planting them onto the chaise.

The fire glinted off her left hand.

CHAPTER THIRTY-ONE

Evaline

Maddox's hands stilled, even the breath on my neck stopped and I knew it wasn't because he'd pulled away. I could feel heat roiling off of him.

And then his voice in my ear. Rough, every word clipped and hardly controlled as he grit out. "What the *fuck* is that?"

My eyes shot open, and I straightened, still in his reach. Fuck.

I'd hidden my left hand the entire time he'd been here, not wanting to tell him the news. Not really sure why, either.

His left hand slid off my shoulder and down my arm, picking up my hand gently and examining it. "Evaline." It was choked.

I sighed and pulled my hand from him, dropping it into my lap and covering it with my right. I looked down. "It's nothing."

He scoffed behind me before he rounded the chaise. "It doesn't fucking look like nothing." The tension in him seemed to build as I stayed silent. Really, this was none of his business. He stopped in front of me, and his fingers caught my chin. Lifting it up until I looked at him, maintaining a soft touch even though he was clearly upset, his height staggering over me.

"Tell me that's not what I think it is." His eyes seemed to plead, beg, me to counter what I knew already filled his mind.

"It's not." Where I thought I'd see relief, doubt loomed.

"It's not an engagement ring?" A beat passed and I didn't answer. "*Evaline*." He growled.

"Yes." I hissed. "It is an engagement ring."

He fell to his knees in front of me and for reasons I wasn't sure, my legs opened to allow him to fill the space there. The skirt swept open just enough to reveal a leg.

Rage showed in his features as he snapped. "Well, then it's exactly what I thought it was." His eyes scanned mine, searching for something and right before me I saw a wall build behind them, brick by brick, until his expression almost seemed uncaring. "You love this man?"

The reaction that my traitorous body displayed was faster than I could've stopped it. "Absolutely not." The sneer on my face and snarl in my voice seemed to break the wall, and this time, he did look relieved.

"An arranged marriage?" His hand reached out to pull mine from my lap, examining the ring. I allowed him to.

I swallowed and looked sidelong. "Yes."

His thumb swept over the rock, and he looked back up to me. From his kneel on the ground I looked directly into his eyes. "Let me take you away."

My mouth dropped open slightly at the sentiment, the offer. But not only at the words, everything. At his eyes, that begged me. His tone, small and vulnerable, shaking. The grip on my hand, and the touch that I now felt on my exposed knee. His eyes dropped to my lips and the action had me closing them.

I straightened. "You would do that?"

Some sensation washed over his features, and he spoke quickly. "Yes." But I had a feeling there were other words he would have preferred to say.

I shook my head slowly and looked down at where he touched my knee.

This was the part of my plan I had absolutely no inkling of. I'd barely been on my own outside of these walls, or any walls, and when I had, Bassel and Lonix had found me. It was this part of my plan that frightened me, because while I knew I couldn't stay, couldn't truly marry Bassel, and that I absolutely had to kill him, I knew going out on my own was a deathtrap.

But Maddox, this offer, it felt as if the Gods had placed him in my life for just this reason and I thought back to his words from days ago.

"I think it makes perfect sense that they watch over and encourage those who were fated to meet, do." He'd said.

I raised my head again to meet his eyes. "Yes. Please." I whispered.

The smile that lit his face was almost contagious, and everywhere he touched me, his hands tightened.

He stood, breaking the contact and strode toward the window, thinking.

He turned around.

"We'll leave tonight. I'll go back to the inn and get Wyott, send him off to scrounge up food and supplies—" I stood up, cutting him off before he could continue.

"No." He whirled to face me, but I continued before he could voice the question in his stare. "Not yet."

"Then when?"

"The wedding day." And it was at that moment my full plan formed in my mind's eye.

His head cocked. "And when is that?"

"Three and a half weeks."

His body went rigid. "You expect me to allow a month to pass before we leave? To put you in the position of having to be around him, every day?" The words dripped like venom from his lips, like each one pained him more than the previous.

It was my turn to scoff. "Well considering you're the one who offered to help, I would hope you'd allow me the time to prepare for departure."

His jaw muscles strained below the force of his clench. He released a ragged breath. "Fine." But he was agitated.

"Fine." I responded, crossing my arms.

There was a long pause as we stared at each other, each challenging the other to break the gaze.

"He proposed tonight, then?" His words were soft.

I nodded.

"Where?"

"In the courtyard of the castle."

He nodded and looked down; I didn't understand why he was asking such things.

"We will continue our lessons as often as you're able," raising his gaze to mine. "I won't let you go unprotected if you insist on waiting the month." My heart did a painful clench. If only he knew. "Plus, you'll need to be prepared to protect yourself on our journey."

I, again, said nothing in response.

We didn't discuss where we'd go, or what we'd do when we got there. But the weight of the day hit me then and I was exhausted.

His words from earlier entered my mind. "What about your reason to stay?"

He cocked his head as he looked at me, and I could see the exhaustion in him too. "It just became a reason to leave."

I pursed my lips and didn't try to pretend like I knew what that meant.

His eyes widened as if something dawned on him, too. His body rigid. "Was he the one who put that mark on your face?"

I paused. Not because I didn't want to tell him, but because I wished I could tell him the whole truth. The whole history of what Bassel had done. Because he hadn't slapped me, but he'd done far worse.

"No."

He examined me. "Good. Will you tell me who, yet?"

A small smile formed on my face. "No."

He nodded. "Fine." He looked over his shoulder at the window. "I should go."

"Okay." I said softly.

He turned back to face me. "Okay."

Another long look, and then he was turning to leave. Before I knew what I was doing I'd crossed the room and caught his hand, pulling him to turn back to me. I miscalculated how hard I pulled, considering his strength, and accidentally pulled myself right into his chest.

His free hand caught my waist and steadied me, my hand flying to his chest to do the same. An awkward chuckle left my lips and I pulled back. I let my hands fall from where I touched him but noticed his hand on my waist did not move.

"Sorry, I didn't mean to…" But his eyes devoured the words I'd been planning to say as he stared down at me. The gray seemed to shift a shade darker. I cleared my throat. "I just wanted to say thank you."

"No need." His voice low.

"Still, it's an extremely generous gesture."

His head cocked. "You're not used to those are you?"

Suddenly the room felt too small, the heat between us becoming too much. I just shook my head.

"Eva." My nickname on his lips filled something inside me, heated something below. "I think you'll find there isn't much I wouldn't do for you."

And then he was gone.

CHAPTER THIRTY-TWO

Maddox

By the time my feet hit the ground below Evaline's room my breathing was already erratic, and it wasn't from the exertion of climbing out of her window. I'd done my best to keep as calm as possible in front of her but the moment I stepped away and out of her grasp the despair had set in. I stalked away from the castle and disappeared into the gardens and bent over. I placed my hand over my heart, feeling the way it beat out of tune and rhythm.

What was wrong with me?

Before the thought was even finished I knew what it was.

Rage. Pure, unadulterated, rage slid through my body, over my eyes until my vision blurred.

She was engaged to be married.

My mate.

I walked toward the town as I tried to swallow the fire in my throat.

The anger threatened to consume me, but I hardly tried to stop it, because of course out of all the kingdoms in this world where arranged marriages were considered archaic or were illegal, of course my mate happened to be forced into one.

But anger wasn't the only emotion flooding my senses.

There was fear. Fear that I'd lose Evaline before I ever truly got to know her. That I'd have to watch her fall in love with this man. Fear that

I'd have to do the thing that I was most afraid of. Letting her go if she didn't choose me.

Words would never be able to describe the fear that had lingered in the depths of my soul as I'd waited for her response to whether she loved this man or not.

I didn't even need to consider what I would have done had she said yes, because I already knew.

I'd let her live however, love whomever, she wanted to. Even though it'd tear a gaping hole in my chest. Even though I'd have to discover some way to feed again, fight through the pain of the searing blood, I'd do it. For her.

I forced myself to take a breath.

I didn't have to think about that right now, because she didn't love him, and she was coming with me.

I realized we didn't discuss the particulars of where she wanted to go yet, but it didn't matter. I'd trek or sail anywhere she wanted to go. I'd search the world until she found the perfect spot for herself and pray to the Gods that she'd invite me to stay. I ran my hands through my hair, I could only imagine how disheveled it looked. But I didn't care, my feet were moving, and I had to stop myself from running at my fullest potential.

It took every fiber of my being not to turn around, go back up to her room and ask her who her groom was. That word alone made chill crawl up my spine.

She would not be getting married.

Not if she didn't want it.

I considered what I would do if I knew who the man was. I could get rid of a mortal extremely easily. It would hardly take any effort. I wouldn't even need Wyott, but I knew he'd come along.

And if this man was okay with bartering for a woman's life, clearly the world would be better off without him.

I swallowed a lump that was beginning to form in my throat, made up of frustration and fear and anger.

I had to calm down, and normally I'd feed to do so but I knew I couldn't. And I couldn't run, there wasn't enough space in this kingdom to do so effectively without being seen, but I needed to exert some kind of energy before I exploded.

My fists were clenched so tightly that I could smell the prick of my blood hit the air as my nails broke through the skin. I sighed, opening my hands, looking down, watching the wounds heal. I closed my fist again.

I wanted to hit something.

Preferably someone, but even if I knew the name of the man who was to wed the love of my life, I knew I couldn't harm him. It wouldn't look great for her guardians, which in turn would harm her.

I needed to calm the fuck down.

But I couldn't. As I made it to the main street of the town, I recalled what she'd said about the proposal.

It had been tonight.

He'd seen her in that dress. In that revealing dress that I couldn't get out of my mind.

She looked ravishing in it, but I didn't like the idea of other men looking at the way it fell over her body.

Not because I was jealous, but because I knew the vile thoughts some men considered when evaluating a beautiful woman. Even more so of a beautiful woman who'd give them a tongue lashing for even glancing at her. I thought of the man's hands on her skin, slipping the ring on her finger. The things he must have pictured himself doing to her on their wedding night.

My self-control snapped as I recalled the other piece of information she'd given me about the proposal.

It had been in the courtyard.

CHAPTER THIRTY-THREE

Evaline

After Maddox left, all I could do was walk to the base of my bed and fall back onto it.

I stared at the ceiling of my bed chamber, the tiles a work of art as the designs swirled around the room. Blues and pinks and ivories.

The weight of everything that had just occurred hit me at once. Not the dinner, not Bassel, not the proposal. Maddox.

I closed my eyes and could still feel the way his hands roamed my body. Squeezing here, kneading there. Goosebumps spiked on my flesh at the thought of it. No man had touched me like that before. Not as if he needed the touch just as badly as I did. I sighed and brought my hand up to my face, pushing back the hairs that lay around it.

As I did so I felt the weight of the ring on my hand. I pulled it back to look at it, huffed, and let the hand fall onto the bed. That dammed ring. Unless I'd been mistaken, I swore Maddox's lips had been mere inches from my skin before he'd seen my hand. What had he planned to do? Kiss me?

Would I have let him?

Would I have liked it?

I bit my lip as I knew the answer to those questions was a resounding yes.

I was awoken by a scream that pierced through the halls of the castle.

I jolted up, my hand finding my dagger hidden beneath my pillow, ready for an attack, but before I could get up my aunt swung open the door to my bedchamber. I hardly had enough time to stash the blade back under the pillow.

"Evaline!" She hissed and walked over, grabbing me by the upper arm and using the grip to drag me from the room.

I stumbled behind her through the halls, half in shock at the rude awakening and half in awe of the grip this woman had on her. I furrowed my brows as my aunt swung me around the door and the full view of the courtyard came into frame. My lips parted involuntarily as I took in the scene. The damage.

The courtyard where Bassel and I had been just the night before was not the way we'd left it. I walked around, assessing the damage near the far end of the reflection pool. Once large and beautiful, the marble statue was shattered stone. The God of Solar that once stood proud over this space was knocked on his side, like someone had kicked it, and the lip of the pool was shattered under the weight. The water level was low as it had slowly leeched out into the grounds around.

I looked back at my aunt, her face twisted in fury, as she stared at me.

"How did this happen?" I asked.

She laughed. "You tell me, Evaline."

I furrowed my brows and winced. "You think I did this?" My tone incredulous.

"Who else would have done it? You and Bassel were the last people here, and I know Bassel would never do such a thing."

I laughed. "Aunt Therese, I didn't do this. I don't even know if it is possible any one person could cause this damage." I looked around me, the raw power that would be required to pull something like this off, unheard and unseen, was impossible –

I didn't even need to finish the thought as my mouth clasped shut, because I knew exactly who did this. And for some reason it wasn't anger that ran rampant in my mind, through my heart. I looked back up at her. "Surely there must be another explanation."

She regarded me and then must have allowed herself to accept that it was impossible I'd done such a thing. But her glare didn't soften and I knew I'd be punished anyway.

She instructed me to go change and come back to clean up the mess. I rolled my eyes but did as she said, reminding myself that at least this was an opportunity to stretch out the muscles coiled up in my body.

I started at the base of the stone structure, picking up all of the pieces of rock that shattered away from their home and threw them into a wheelbarrow.

Shortly after, Bassel strode into the courtyard, his brows raised as he took in the scene.

"What happened here?" He asked, but I was questioning why he was left unattended in the castle.

I shrugged. "I'm not sure. Maybe it was struck by lightning?" I suggested, hoping he'd deem it plausible.

I heard my aunt down the hall, yelling at a servant, and realized she must've been giving Bassel a tour of the castle, or having him for lunch. Who knew?

I was on my knees at the base of the pool now. It hurt too badly to keep bending over, I decided to kneel and pile the bigger rocks up and then move them into the wheelbarrow.

I expected Bassel to leave and continue on with my aunt, but we could both still hear her voice in the hallway, and instead he just stared at me. I kept a piece of the broken sculpture in my hand, hiding it from his view. It had once been a piece of Kembertic's sunburst crown, but now it was sharp and ready to be wielded against Bassel, if he made a move.

"You look like you have something to say, Bassel." I said as I caught his lingering stare, his expression speculative.

He shrugged. "I'm just trying to figure out what could've caused all this damage. I think it's a bit coincidental that the night I propose to you in front of this pool, it gets destroyed."

I nodded from where I sat on my knees, piling the rubble with one hand. "Yes, it is very coincidental."

What did he expect me to say to that?

He was quiet for a few heartbeats. "I just can't help but wonder if someone did this on your behalf."

I didn't look up from the ground, not wanting him to see that I was questioning the same notion. "It would've surely taken more than one person."

I heard him move and knew he was walking over to me. I tensed. He stopped directly before me and grabbed my chin, harshly angling my head up to look at him, my neck screaming in protest. I gritted my teeth against the move and pushed the sharp rock in my hand out of his view, fingers tightening around it painfully.

"Is there another man in your life I should be worried about, kitten?"

A laugh bubbled from my mouth before I could stop it at the absurdity of his question, and his eyes narrowed. "No, there's not."

He regarded me, eyes sweeping over my face.

"There better not be." His harsh tone shocked me. I knew he was evil, I'd known that for two years, but he'd been doing an adequate job at portraying a good man since he'd been here. I was surprised he'd let this side slip so early into this visit. But in his eyes, where I expected ego or rage, sat fear. It was something I'd never thought I'd recognize so easily in someone's expression, but it was plain as day before me. He was afraid of something, of someone, and the thought curled the edges of my lips up into a smile.

He dropped my chin and left, not so subtly kicking over the pile of rocks beside me.

The walk to the meadow was quiet, as it should be this time of night. But I made haste as I tripped my way through the woods. I didn't want to risk getting caught considering the thin ice I strode on with my aunt after the courtyard disaster.

When I finally made it, I once again saw Wyott and Maddox sitting beside each other near a fire on the opposite side of the clearing.

Wyott worked on stoking the flames, no doubt for my benefit, as Maddox sharpened a blade against a stone. My lips tugged into a smile without my realizing it as I saw the blade, and they noticed before I could hide it.

"Aw, Maddox." Wyott started with a mocking tone. "Our little sadist is here."

I rolled my eyes, "I'm not a sadist." I joined them near the fire, sitting across from Wyott.

"Right," Wyott continued. "You're just a girl who gets a sick look of pleasure when she sees a blade."

Maddox's laugh thundered through my ears, almost like I heard the sound not only in the air but in my mind.

I narrowed my eyes. "Oh, you've got jokes now, Wyott?"

He shrugged. "Always had 'em, babe."

I rolled my eyes, but a smile met my lips anyway. My gaze landed on Maddox's blade. Not the hatchet this time, but a beautiful dagger made of a deep obsidian material. Its color made it appear stone-like, but as he swept the blade down the edge of the rock, the fire glinted off its edge in a way only metal could.

I cocked my head. "What kind of metal is that?"

Maddox looked up, acknowledging me for the first time since I'd arrived. He seemed hesitant, and I could spot the guilty conscious a mile away. He flicked his wrist and the blade twirled in the air before he caught the tip in his fingers, reaching his arm around the fire to hand it to me.

I grabbed it and turned it over in my hands. The metal was obscenely cold, almost other worldly. It was a simple black blade with standard, straight cross-guards, and a plain handle. I wasn't sure why I expected him to have something fancier. But I suppose when you constantly carry the arsenal he did, it was function over fashion.

I laid the blade against my hand and watched the light gleam over it.

"It's a Rominium dagger." Maddox answered my question from minutes before, the sound startled me out of my trance and I looked up at him to find his eyes focused on me.

I handed it back to him, uncomfortable from his gaze and how it consumed me. "It's what?"

He holstered it on his thigh. "It's from our home." He gestured to Wyott. "Rominium is a compound found deep in the mines of our island, near the volcano."

I cocked an eyebrow. "What's a volcano?"

Maddox smiled at me. "Think of it like a huge mountain that has liquid metal under its surface slowly churning beneath. Every once in a while the pressure becomes too much, and it spews out."

My eyes widened. "That sounds horrifying."

He and Wyott laughed. "It is." They said in unison.

Maddox strode toward the area where we sparred last time and gestured for me to follow him. "But mostly it's harmless. It's erupted a few times in my lifetime, but we just evacuate the homes around it and rebuild them if they're damaged." He stopped in the center of the clearing and turned to face me.

"Why wouldn't the people near it just move?"

Maddox's eyes shined with amusement. "Evaline," he breathed my name. "You don't seem like the kind of woman to avoid something just because it might be dangerous."

I stayed silent as the connotation of his comment settled into me. He wasn't talking about the volcano anymore. I changed the subject.

"Our blades are still on."

"Yeah, she's a genius that one." Wyott called from the fire. I threw a glare at him, then turned my eyes back to Maddox.

"What I meant to say was, are we using blades today?" I tried to hide the hope in my voice.

Wyott scoffed. "And you claim you're not a sadist?"

I whirled around to face him. "Wyott shut your mouth." I hissed at him and saw the smirk peek out from behind his curtain of hair that was hanging loose.

"Okay children, it's time to pay attention." Maddox cooed at us.

My head whipped to him. "Oh, and now you have jokes?"

His smirk lit his eyes. "Always had 'em..." He paused, his eyes flickering to my mouth for less than a heartbeat. "Babe."

I rolled my eyes at the echo of Wyott's words, and instead of justifying them with a response, I drew my dagger and fell into stance. That light flickered through his eyes again as he did the same, pulling out a wooden dagger.

I straightened and scoffed. "Fuck no." I gestured to his fake knife with my own. "You aren't going to fake fight me. Get a real blade."

His eyebrow quirked as he straightened as well, one of his loose black curls falling onto his forehead. "I don't want to accidentally injure you."

I crossed my arms, my blade angling out over them. "How are we supposed to train for real fights if you won't really fight me?"

He tilted his head as he examined me. One...two...three heartbeats. "I'm immortal, Evaline. I'm stronger, faster than a mortal man."

I shrugged. "My father never used a fake knife with me."

A ghost of a smile swept his lips. "Your father wasn't a Kova."

"No, he was a soldier." I said, as if the two were equal in capabilities.

He just laughed and shook his head, running his hand over it to clear his hair out of his face, and dropping back down into his stance. "Just remember that you asked for this."

I didn't respond as I matched his pose. We circled each other for a moment before he struck out his blade, aiming for my midsection.

I jumped, my body arcing, as I jolted my stomach away from the sharp edge.

"I'm going to try not to really cut you. But I can't promise I won't nick you." He warned as we circled each other again, the light of the fire playing in his dark eyes.

"I can't promise I won't nick you." I warned back and knew Wyott's laugh would ring across the grass before I heard it.

Maddox smirked.

I swung my free fist toward his face, and when he blocked it with his daggered hand, I swung mine towards his gut, where his free hand caught my wrist.

He tsked. "Going to have to be more clever than that." Maddox taunted as he released me.

I narrowed my eyes as I fell back. I could feel my heartbeat in my throat, hear it in my ears. I missed this. I loved this. I needed this.

"You're going to be eating those words when I draw your blood before you ever draw mine." I retorted, not recognizing my own voice. So light, so playful. So happy.

Wyott called. "Now who has jokes?"

I chuckled as Maddox and I circled each other slowly, each scanning the other for any potential offensive moves.

"I have another one for you." I called to Wyott, never taking my eyes off my opponent.

Maddox's eyebrow quirked.

"Let me hear it." Wyott said again, having to raise his voice for me to hear over the fire.

"It's more of a riddle." I started, eyes locked on Maddox. "Who is 6'5"," another rotation around each other. "Thinks a hatchet is an axe," his wild eyes were so focused on mine. "And trashed the castle courtyard last night?"

All I needed was the fraction of a second when his eyes widened, and his attention shook.

I pounced forward, tackling him to the ground as I gripped his daggered hand by the wrist and shoved it away from me. When we landed he gave a huff, as if surprised by my strength, and I sat atop him. In the straddle around his hips, with one hand pinning his arm overhead and my other holding the dagger to his jugular, I'd never felt more powerful.

Something buzzed through my veins, stirring.

When the dust settled, Maddox was staring up at me and the look in his eyes... it could only be described as awe. They devoured mine, growing almost black, as I looked down at him, my body covering his and our faces inches apart. The feeling of him beneath me... well I tried to block the feelings that stirred where my hips met his.

Wyott cleared his throat, but I didn't move my eyes from Maddox. "I think a safe assumption would be... Maddox?"

I smirked. "I also would have accepted 'A fucking idiot.'"

It was then that I noticed Maddox's free hand had latched onto my hip the moment I landed on him, and I only noticed it now because it squeezed me.

His brows furrowed as he looked up at me.

I broke our gaze for the first time and looked down at where my dagger pierced his skin ever so slightly. I lifted the blade into his eyesight. A single drop of blood hung there, and as his eyes adjusted away from me and to the blade, it fell onto his slightly parted lips.

Maybe it was the adrenaline. Maybe it was the validation from his expression. Gods, maybe it was the fall. But without consciously deciding to, I flipped the dagger away and lowered my hand over his face. I wiped the blood across his lip with my thumb so slowly that I could feel the smoothness of them, the breath that coasted onto my flesh between them. And, Gods, if I didn't feel those lips pucker against me.

With my thumb still resting there I leaned even closer and whispered. "That clever enough for you?"

CHAPTER THIRTY-FOUR

Maddox

If last night I had felt pure, unadulterated rage, then this was pure, unadulterated awe.

The feel of her against me, of that place between her legs that rested against my hips, where I could feel the heat radiating. The image of her above me, braid tossed over her shoulder, almost touching my face from where it hung between us. The pain from the prick of her blade dulled by the Goddess above me.

And, Gods, when she swept her thumb over the blood on my lips. If Wyott hadn't been there...

All I could think about was what it would be like if we'd been naked.

"That clever enough for you?" She whispered, her head lowered even closer to mine.

All words escaped me as I nodded. As the smirk lit her face, I further opened my lips and nipped her thumb lightly. My eyes locked on her as her expression changed from smug to shocked, and she pulled her thumb down my lips, her eyes caught there for a moment.

"Should I leave?" Wyott broke the silence surrounding us, and she ripped her hands away from me, surprised eyes flitting to mine.

"Of course not." She hissed and tore herself from me, striding back to the fire. She grabbed the canteen out of Wyott's hands and took a drink.

I joined them and sat across from Evaline and Wyott.

"I'm sorry I destroyed the courtyard." I said stiffly.

Without meeting my eyes she snapped. "It's fine."

Gone was the happy girl who'd been here minutes ago. Her wall was back up, her shield protecting her.

I tried not to let it upset me.

"We should probably end earlier today, though. I spent the entire day cleaning it."

My eyes cut to her again. "Cleaning what?"

She looked down at her hand as if suddenly finding it very interesting. "The courtyard."

Before I could respond Wyott did so for me. "Don't they have servants for that?"

And Gods-dammit, she swung him a wry smile and met his eyes. "They do, but my aunt preferred to punish me." We both quirked an eyebrow, but she only saw Wyott's. She elaborated. "She thought I did it."

Wyott and I scoffed at the same time. She shrugged. That was when I noticed the slump in her shoulders, the fatigue in her eyes. I'd been so excited to see her I hadn't noticed the faint signs of exhaustion until now.

"I'm sorry, Evaline." I murmured, speaking through the fire. "If I had known they'd punish you, I would've never done it."

She finally met my eyes, hers as piercing as the flames in the dark night. "Why did you?"

I swallowed. She'd closed herself off from me for the night. I couldn't tell her why I truly had done it, not when she'd already retracted into herself.

"Call it a stand against arranged marriages." Her eyes leveled on me, clearly catching my lie.

Wyott broke in and I was reminded why he was my best friend. "Historically, Maddox does have a strong opposition to arranged marriages." He nodded firmly as he spoke.

She just rolled her eyes and tilted the canteen back again, I tried not to pay attention to the way her throat moved as she drank. When she finished, she handed Wyott the container back, then shrugged. "It wasn't too bad." She paused, then added. "Except for having to deal with him watching me while I cleaned."

Him.

I knew who she meant and that same rage, icy hot in my throat, rose.

"Sounds like an asshole." Wyott remarked, breaking the tension that had coiled thick between us.

She snorted. "You have no idea."

I wanted to know what that meant. The mating bond ramming against the wall of my mind begging her to tell me.

But instead I rose. "I think we should call it a night then, you need to get rest and I'd say taking down a Kova is a good way to end the session."

She smiled and stood as Wyott moved to put out the fire.

By the time we'd walked her back to the edge of the castle property her body moved with utter fatigue and I knew I'd made the right call. I didn't try to speak with her alone like I had the last time, simply saying goodnight along with Wyott and watching her disappear into the darkness.

When we couldn't see her anymore Wyott and I turned and headed back toward the inn.

We were silent before he remarked. "I don't know whether I should be angry that you are so clearly malnourished that she was able to get a jump on you," he cut his eyes to me. "Or considering what kind of inhuman species she would be to have been able to get a jump on you."

I met his eyes, my own concerned.

"Wyott, I am underfed, but I'm not malnourished. She did catch me by surprise but..." I shook my head. "She's strong. And fast. I've never seen a human move like her before."

His gaze fell to the stones we walked along. "That's what I thought. The way she moved was so fluid. I've never seen a mortal move that way."

It had been four days since I'd seen her. We forced her to take a recovery break after two trainings, and cleaning the courtyard. Even if she was someone inhuman, she needed rest, and the break gave us the perfect opportunity to research.

Nathaniel told us that the castle library was open to the public every once in a while, and since the night Evaline tackled me there'd only been one thing on my mind; I had to figure out what other being she could possibly be. I was very certain that she was not human.

Wyott and I spent the entire walk there shooting ideas back-and-forth. He questioned whether she was really as strong as I claimed, or perhaps my judgment was clouded because we were mates.

I shook my head as we approached to library door inside the castle. "No, she is stronger than any human I've ever seen." I was careful not to use her name, as there were armed guards that had escorted us in. They left us to stand watch outside of the doors while we perused the shelves.

The library was large and sprawling and had several texts, most of which probably wouldn't be helpful for this particular question because mortals typically didn't carry texts on non-human beings. But it was still a library, so it was worth the time we'd spend researching.

That didn't make it any easier for me to concentrate, though, because I could sense her in the castle. I knew where her room was, but even if I didn't I'd be able to find it just by the pull of the bond alone. I had to constantly remind myself of why I was here in order to avoid wandering the halls to her room.

"Have you found anything yet?" I called to Wyott across the room.

He was at my side in a second. We were alone in the cathedral ceilinged structure. He shook his head. "No, there's really nothing here. It's mostly just histories and kingdom statistics. Tax and crop information. Things like that."

I pursed my lips. There had to be something in here about any kind of immortal or nonhuman being, I'm sure in her time in Kembertus Evaline had searched for answers too, trying to learn more about the species that killed her father. The thought still infuriated me, that she had been bitten. I was happy she somehow had survived, shocked, but still furious it happened at all. But I ignored it for the time being.

I wandered to a corner of the library, a section that neither of us had covered yet, and that fell slightly in the shadows, away from the light streaming in the windows and the candles that stood in the center of the room.

Deep in the corner, on the tallest shelf immediately I recognized the intricate spine of a lore glossary. I pulled the book out of its spot and turned, waving it at Wyott with a triumphant smile on my face.

We sat in the middle of the room at a large table and opened it. The only indication that it hadn't been opened in decades was the dust pluming out from between the pages.

"I guess it's a good sign that the lore book has been out of use, clearly they aren't too suspicious of immortals lurking in their city." Wyott said quietly.

I raised my eyebrows and nodded. "Thank the Gods."

It was common knowledge that almost no humans knew of our kind, or really of any nonhuman beings at all, but the world was vast and humans were unpredictable. If one of them did know what we were and suspected us, we'd be run out of Kembertus. And in no reality was that acceptable. I wasn't leaving unless it was with Evaline.

I flicked through the pages, trying to see what organization system was used. I sighed as I realized that it wasn't in any kind of order at all, not even alphabetical. It appeared the author and illustrator had simply entered beings into the text as they discovered their myths.

We went through each lifeform. Of course, the way the lore discussed them was in hypotheticals, simply a retelling of stories that had been passed down by generations. Most of them likely did exist, and Wyott and I had either already encountered them, or we would eventually, sometime in our lifespans.

The first section was dedicated to Nymphs, known for their affinity to live in and take care of nature. There was a picture of a mountain Nymph in the text, which looked just like any other human, besides the grayed skin and rock like structure jutting out from her shoulders.

Beside me Wyott snorted. "Remember that flower Nymph we met decades ago?"

I smiled at the recollection. "Near Correnti? Yeah. She was a talker."

Wyott shrugged. "She was just lonely." He was right. For the life of me I couldn't remember her name, only that she followed us for miles and only parted when we were exiting the forests. I don't think she stopped talking the entire time.

I snorted at the memory and turned back to the text, flipping the page.

Next were Fae. Their pointed ears gave them away, but they also had magical abilities. They were much like Kova in the way that they were immortal, but they didn't require human blood to sustain. We had never encountered them before, but that's likely because it was rumored they lived on distant land masses that pirates voyaged to. The closest we'd ever gotten to them is through stories passed through time. While Fae were stronger than humans and so was Evaline, she did not have pointed ears. I turned the page.

Next on the list were Sorcerers. They had an innate ability to wield magic that they were born with. Each Sorcerer or Sorceress was gifted with the ability to wield one of the four elements in this world; Air, Terra, Water, Fire. They could only wield one, but they could manipulate it in almost any way they chose.

Sorcerers could do other magic too, such as casting spells or creating enchantments, but there was not any lore I'd heard, or that was in this book, that mentioned a Sorcerer as being stronger than any normal human.

I shook my head. "She can't be that either."

Wyott scoffed. "Good, because it's extremely illegal here."

I nodded, not having thought of that.

In the Kromean Kingdoms having any sort of magical ability was prohibited. Usually men or women who were found to have those abilities were executed while the human villagers cheered from outside the castle, as the execution took place in the dungeons.

What the mortals didn't know was that before every execution, the kingdom had to get approval from the First Vasi. He was the reason that all Sorcerers and Sorceresses had to be killed, likely because he was afraid of anyone challenging his power as leader of our twin breed.

My father had always feared that there were worse intentions behind this Vasi practice, although he didn't talk about it with me. He'd never shared what his primary concern was regarding what cruel intentions the Vasi had, but I'd always speculated that perhaps he was trying to find a powerful enough Sorcerer or Sorceress to trap, to manipulate their powers and make them his own somehow, or to use their powers to exterminate the Kova, or at least to turn them into Vasi. I'd never voiced those concerns to my father, but I was sure they'd crossed his mind as well.

Before any executions, first word had to be sent to the First Vasi. He had to know what element of magic the Sorcerer had, what they looked like, and whether it was a man or woman. But as far as we could tell, each and every time a parchment had been sent to him regarding a Sorcerer, a raven always appeared within a few days with one word listed on the parchment.

Execute.

"Yes." I said to Wyott. "Thank the Gods."

Next were Sirens, but as fast as my eyes landed on the page I was turning it. Of course, she wasn't a Siren, she didn't have the fishtail that they all bore. Not only that, but she didn't even live close enough to a body of water big enough to hide a Siren, so even if somehow there was a magic that could hide a Siren's tail for a span of time, she wouldn't have anywhere to go when she had it.

The next page was Succubus and Wyott was laughing in my ear before I'd fully opened the page.

I shot him a look. "Shut up."

He just shrugged, a wide smile on his face. "I just don't think you can be partial to this ruling, so let me do it for you. She's not a Succubus."

I shook my head and turned the page, quelching the fire that lit my veins at the thought. Even though I found her intoxicatingly attractive, not everyone did. And even though the bond had a pull on me, it wasn't the same as dark magic that succubi pulled over any being they chose. But the idea of a Succubus, of Evaline being one, flooded my mind with thoughts I definitely should not be having over a woman I'd never even kissed.

But still, the thoughts didn't go away.

Shapeshifters were next. I'd never met one before, but I did see the words extreme strength etched into the parchment below the title. But Evaline wasn't that either, because shifters had telltale purple eyes. And while her eyes sometimes seemed otherworldly, they were most definitely not purple.

I crossed my arms and sat back roughly in my chair, feeling the wood strain against the movement.

Wyott pulled the book to his side of the table and continued to search through it.

"Maybe whatever she is hasn't been discovered yet." I said and shrugged. "By humans at least."

I didn't trust ravens to send a message to my father, I knew if any being in this world knew what Evaline could be, it was him. He'd been alive centuries and had traveled between our home and this land mass, among more distant ones, as well. But I couldn't for fear that the Vasi would somehow intercept it. I'd just have to wait until we got back to Rominia, if she ever came with me, to discover what she was. We had better literature there anyway. And more resources. Maybe our kingdom Sorcerer, Ankin, would know.

Wyott chuckled.

I turned to him. "What?"

He flipped the page to show me the winged being in the text.

"I think I'd notice those." I said.

He cocked his head. "I don't know, she sure wears cloaks a lot."

I heard a creak down the hall as we laughed and knew it was her before she entered the room.

I had the book pulled from Wyott's hands and re-shelved in the blink of an eye, running to stand behind the chair I'd been sitting in, and leaning over it with my hands planted on its back.

She wore lounging clothes, baggy linen pants that were beige in color and a white shirt that's short hem barely dusted the waistband of her pants. Her hair was pulled into a ponytail and it looked as if she'd just awoken from bed.

She eyed us and crossed her arms. "What are you two doing here?"

I smiled at her. "We were bored and came to catch up on our literature. I haven't seen a library this nice since I left my own back home." I shrugged, catching her eye. "Besides, what else am I going to do to pass the time until I see you again."

She rolled her eyes but I didn't miss the hint of blush that crept up her cheeks.

"Surely, in the centuries you've accumulated between the two of you," she started, whispering the word centuries so that the guards outside didn't hear. "You've grown bored of human texts."

Wyott burst out laughing and both Evaline and I turned to him with wide eyes, shocked by the outburst. He laughed and looked between us, the freckled tan skin crinkling around his eyes. He shook his head once he regained his composure. "Sorry," he waved. "I'm sorry." He shrugged. "It's just funny to me that you think that, because Maddox," he said, jabbing a thumb back toward me. "All he does when we're back home is read."

I rolled my eyes at him and pushed off the chair. "It is not all I do." I muttered, embarrassed.

Evaline's wicked smile widened, and she pulled out a chair for herself across from Wyott. She leaned her elbows on the table and I had to force myself to look away. Neither of them noticed me though, she was too busy leaning closer to him.

"Tell me. What does he read?" She tilted her head. "I'm thinking those crusty and dusty history books so that he can haughtily wag his finger and keep claiming 'I was there! They never get these things right.' When they misspell some General's name, or don't tell it exactly as it happened."

Wyott shook his head, a massive grin on his face.

She pursed her lips. "Hm. Okay. What about the mystery novels where he reads the entire book and only then claims he knew exactly who did it and how it was done from the first chapter?"

Wyott shook his head even harder, his smiling lips barely holding back the laughter that I knew was bottled inside.

She narrowed her eyes, opening her mouth to guess again.

"This is dumb." I interjected. "And I do not like this game."

Evaline only turned that smile on me, which immediately took anymore retorts out of my mouth and left my lungs just as empty.

"At least this game makes sense, unlike yours." Then she turned back to Wyott, hitting her index finger on the table. "Now I've got it. He only reads books written by men, because he doesn't think women can write as well."

I scoffed. "Please, do you really think I would ever think something like that?" I asked, and my voice only sounded partially desperate.

"No." Wyott squealed. "It's better." His face was growing red from holding his laughter in and I threw my hands up.

"What are we doing? Is the only way you two bond by embarrassing me?" I asked, shaking my head. "You just did this last week." I pointed at Wyott. "And you, you're supposed to be my best friend, and that means not spouting every last embarrassing detail of my life to everyone around us."

Wyott looked over at me, his eyes narrowed.

"I don't tell everyone." He said, waving to Evaline. "Only her."

She was nodding her head fiercely behind him.

I crossed my arms again and moved away from them, putting my back against the end of one of the bookshelves near the table. "Fine, but I want you both to know, I am not having fun."

"We don't care." They said in unison, and turned back toward each other.

She clapped her hands together. "Okay, this is it. This is definitely it."

He wriggled his fingers. "Give it to me."

"He doesn't read history books to gloat about what the author did or did not get right. He reads fantasy novels so that he can gloat about what beings are real or not, and whether the author got their traits or powers right." She sat back, throwing her hands in the air.

Wyott squeaked. "No."

She crashed forward against the table again and shouted. "How are none of those right?"

Wyott rubbed his hands together. "Are you ready for the answer?"

She nodded, balling her hands in fists in front of her.

Wyott placed both palms on the table, lifting and setting them back down with each word. "Maddox only reads romance novels."

I watched as Evaline's mouth dropped open. She quickly closed it, furrowing her brows, and tilting her head forward slightly. "No way."

He nodded. "It's true." He turned in his chair toward me, slinging one arm over the back of it. "Tell her Maddox."

I just rolled my eyes. "I told you, I don't like this game."

Evaline snorted. "You're telling me that, that," she said pointing at me. "Only reads romance?"

I narrowed my eyes. "What is that supposed to mean?"

She looked at me, deadpan. "Maddox, look at yourself. You're like… walking masculinity." She said, motioning to the swords and daggers hanging off me.

I rolled my eyes and looked away from them. I opened my mouth to speak but Wyott interjected, turning back to her. "It gets better."

She shook her head. "It simply cannot."

Wyott nodded. "Maddox only reads romance novels written by women."

But there was no burst of laughter from her like I'd expected, no slamming of hands on the table in hysteria. Instead, her face fell, her lips moved into an almost pout, and she turned her soft gaze to me.

"Is that true?" She asked.

I couldn't help the blush that flooded my face. I shrugged and looked away. "They're more wholesome than the ones written by men."

When she didn't say anything, I turned back to her, fully aware that my face was still very much red.

"That's not embarrassing. That's kind of…" she paused as if searching for the word. "Sweet."

CHAPTER THIRTY-FIVE

Evaline

After Wyott and Maddox left, I spent most of the day in my bedroom. I wasn't sure why I'd wandered into the library to begin with. I was supposed to meet my aunt in there before dinner, but that wasn't for hours. But after I'd woken up, I felt something pulling me to the room, urging me to go see what was in there. On some level I knew he'd be there. When he was, I couldn't ignore the uptick in my heart.

After we'd had our fun with Maddox, I realized I desperately craved those interactions. I loved joking with the two of them, especially when it was at Maddox's expense, because the way he always became so embarrassed was adorable. And after finding out what his preferred genre to read was, I couldn't help but start seeing him in a different light.

Maybe he wasn't just a ruthless Kova who loved a good fight and some witty banter. Maybe he had more to him than I really knew. And the more I thought about it, the more I realized that he'd been showing that side of him to me the entire time I'd known him, but my own preconceived notions about what Kova were, what men were, clouded that.

Maybe the problem wasn't that he was a Kova, or that he was a stranger, maybe the problem was that once again I had walls up, as I had my entire life, which only became thicker when my father died. Maybe

I needed to give him more of a chance. He was being a friend to me, I should do the same for him.

I fell asleep to those thoughts and awoke just in time to run downstairs to the library, once again, to meet my aunt.

She didn't comment on my lazy day of sleeping when I turned the corner of the door to see her sitting in the same spot Wyott had been only hours earlier. Hopefully she chalked it up to my residual exhaustion from clearing the wreckage in the courtyard.

I moved around the table to join her, sitting down and seeing that the table was littered with swatches of fabric and a few dishes among other things I couldn't see.

I couldn't stop the groan that emitted from me in time.

Her eyes narrowed. "Shut it, Evaline."

I did fight the eye roll that almost swept through me and begrudgingly sat beside her.

She spread her arms over the table. "Time to plan a wedding!"

"Aunt Therese, surely, you're talented enough to plan the wedding without me?" I said sweetly and shrugged. "I'll only slow you down."

She just stared at me, calling my manipulation. "You're the bride." I winced at the word. "And part of that title means helping to plan the wedding."

I just sighed in response.

We started with the swatches of fabric, of which she had countless. Different types, different colors. She asked for my opinions, as if she didn't already have her mind made up. She asked what color scheme I wanted, but when I said pink and blue her mouth tightened and she countered. "How about ivory and emerald?"

I just went along with everything she wanted. I couldn't possibly care less about the aesthetic of this wedding, as if that wasn't clear by my yawns every few minutes. Then we moved onto the dining ware.

I understood the fabrics. There were different colors to choose from, different textures that accentuated the colors differently. But dishes? What was the point? We'd just dirty them, hiding any patterns with food.

Why did we need to spend an hour choosing which porcelain would really set this wedding apart, when no one would even see it fully?

But I didn't argue. I just nodded along to everything she said, my mind falling back to my last training session with Maddox and Wyott.

I'd taken Maddox down. I knew I'd catch him off guard by outing that I knew he'd been the one to destroy the courtyard. But I didn't truly think I'd be able to tackle him so easily. I thought for a Kova that he'd be faster. That I'd catch him off guard, yes, but that I'd just bounce off his chest and fall onto the ground. It would have been humiliating, but at least I would have tried.

But I hadn't bounced off his chest. I'd brought him tumbling to the ground. And I'd drawn blood. Of course, it healed as soon as I pulled my blade away, but the point was that I was able to do it.

I'd already considered that perhaps he let me win, maybe to give me confidence.

But I knew that couldn't be true. Not when his expression had been so surprised when we landed. I couldn't get the image out of my mind. The whoosh of air that had expelled from his lips and coasted over my face. The feel of his hard body under me. I clenched my jaw as I recalled the way his teeth nipped my thumb. It'd been such an intimate move that it had shocked me.

As if she could read my thoughts and knew exactly what I was thinking, my aunt spoke, and for the first time it wasn't about decorations. "Evaline, while preparing for the wedding is important, it's more important to prepare for the marriage."

I nodded like I knew what that meant.

She folded her hands in front of her on the table and pursed her lips. "I know your mother died when you were young, and your father probably never talked to you about things such as this but…" My body tensed as I knew exactly what she was trying to say. "Part of being a wife is sharing a bed with your husband, which means more than just sleeping in it."

Of course, I knew about sex. She was right, my mom had died and my father would have simply never braved to talk to me about it. But I'd read enough romance novels to get the gist before I ever ventured into bed with men in Neomaeros. They'd been far more respectful than the men here, and it wasn't shamed like it was in Kembertus.

"I wanted to have this talk with you now so that you can prepare yourself for your wedding night, which is something I didn't get the luxury of." She said pulling me from my thoughts. "My mother waited until the night before my wedding to tell me about what it meant to lay with a man." Her eyes cast down. "Mothers normally don't tell their daughters until right before the wedding so as not to scare the women, but I didn't want to do that with you."

My heart actually clenched for a moment. This was a kindness she was giving me, our strained relationship aside.

"There are certain expectations of a wife, and one of those is not only to satisfy your husband, but also to produce him an heir. This is even more important for you, because someday Bassel will rule Vestaria, and he will require a son to carry on the legacy after him."

I nodded. "I understand how politics work." I muttered. I knew she was being nice, but I was unbearably uncomfortable.

She pursed her lips. "Do you know how children are made?"

I winced but nodded.

"Okay, well it's not just something that you do when you and your husband are attempting to create an heir. It's also something your husband will want regularly, because it brings him pleasure."

I did my best just to nod along, my eyes looking toward the door every few minutes. Begging someone, anyone, to interrupt us so that I could flee this conversation.

"It's important that you know that it can be painful. But it's our jobs as wives, specifically wives of powerful men, to grin and bear it. If the Gods are kind, your husband won't last very long. It will only take him a few minutes until he is done with you and falling asleep."

Tears welled in my eyes as she spoke, and it took me a moment to realize that they weren't even for me. Terror from the notion of marrying Bassel aside, I knew I had the ability to save myself before it ever got that far. But the way she spoke of this act, of what a marriage meant for her, was sad. Was this all she'd known for the nearly thirty years that she and Elijah had been married?

Her hand covered mine then. "I truly don't mean to make you cry. But it is better that you get this information now, rather than having to discover it all on your own." I just nodded, understanding that she needed that. "It might not even be that often. With how busy Bassel will eventually be with running Vestaria, or any traveling he might do since I know he's partial to it, you may barely even see him.

"But when he does come home, you will be expected to be ready and in his bed." She gave me a small smile then. "But eventually, as you age, and after you've hopefully given him a son, he'll come to you less and less." She shrugged. "It's natural for men to find a mistress that's far younger than them. It allows them to still get their pleasure and they won't be bothering you anymore."

I swallowed my surprise before she could see it as I allowed the vision of this type of marriage to take shape in my mind. Flashes of dark nights alone, crying in bed, and quiet misery lit my thoughts. This wasn't love, this was a business deal. And the thought of living the rest of my life with a man who didn't love me, but instead saw me as a means to an end, turned my stomach.

I'd seen some love. I'd seen it on my father's face, in his voice when he recalled memories of my mother, and I'd seen it between Aurora and Jacqueline. And only in this moment, in these warring images between what happy couples looked like and the desolate life that my aunt was describing, did I realize how badly I wanted it. I wanted what my father and mother had. I wanted what Aurora and Jacqueline shared. And I wanted it more desperately than I'd ever care to admit to anyone out loud.

I was pulled from my thoughts by her voice again. "But it's only natural that he finds a mistress. And you'll have more time to tend to the children, or do things that you enjoy." Her voice seemed wistful then, and I wondered what activities occupied Therese's days.

She went on to describe in excruciating detail exactly what it meant to lay with your husband, and I had to clamp down the fear that radiated through my chest.

My plan would ensure that Bassel and I would never consummate our marriage, that he would be dead and cold before that could happen. I was confident in my plan, in my strength and ability to fight. I'd overpowered Maddox for Gods' sake.

But no matter how hard I tried to remember my skill, to reassure myself that Bassel would never hurt me again, I couldn't help the shiver of doubt that coasted up my spine until I was sitting uncomfortably straight. What if my plan failed, what if I couldn't kill him in time, what if I couldn't kill him at all?

I felt the icy waves of dread wash over me.

CHAPTER THIRTY-SIX

Maddox

I was on edge, I had been since the moment I departed from Evaline in the library.

I hardly survived not seeing her for the few days before the library, and the day after wasn't any better. It made me question what life was like before I'd met her. Because all I did when I wasn't with her was think about each moment we had spent together. Thinking about what our future together would hold, when I'd tell her about the bond, and whether she'd ever accept it.

And as I stared into the fire, my hands wringing from where they hung between my knees, the same thoughts worried my mind as I heard her approach. Her image broke apart the darkness of the tree line and she came toward Wyott and I. As always, an effortless beauty.

Her black cloak flowed behind her as she walked, the hood hiding her sleek white hair. Her cheeks were red from the biting cold of night. I made a mental note to have her sit by the fire for a few extra minutes before we started.

"Good evening, Evaline." Wyott greeted her as she came into mortal ear shot. Her senses didn't seem to be heightened, so far the only deviations from a typical mortal we could find was her speed and strength. Still not that of a Kova, but exceptionally better than mortals.

"Good evening, Wyott." She reciprocated, not having looked at me yet.

She sat next to him and across from me, immediately reaching her hands out toward the flames.

"Is it too cold? We can pick a different time to train. The summer heat is still quite a way off for this time of night."

She clenched her jaw and shook her head.

"No, this is the only time I can get away with everything going on."

I nodded, my own jaw clenching at the mention of the wedding.

"Who is this guy?" Wyott asked and I shot him a glare. Did he think I wanted to hear more about the man currently engaged to my mate? He ignored me.

She shrugged, but there was a tightness in her shoulders. "A man from Vestaria."

Vestaria, a land full of entitled pricks. Rich beyond compare with a kingdom nestled on diamond mines so fertile with the glistening stones, that each day the miners went in with empty wheelbarrows and left with full ones.

I wasn't at all surprised.

"He's friends with your guardians?" Wyott continued.

She rolled her eyes. "Apparently he was friends with my cousin growing up, but they really got to know him right before the Spring Solstice Ball."

Wyott scoffed, asking the question for me. "So they're just marrying you off to some man that they barely know?"

A sad smile lit her face as she turned her stare into the fire. "Not just any man." She said with a roll of her eyes. "The future ruler of Vestaria."

My chest tightened at the words. "Bassel?" I asked, my voice rough.

She raised her eyes to meet mine and nodded. "Yes." The tightness in her voice, in her expression, told me she was done with this conversation.

I stood, and she did the same, while I threw a thanks to the Gods that she'd agreed to come with me and get away from Bassel.

"What do you want to practice today?"

She blinked at me. "I get to choose?"

I smiled at her. "Of course you can choose. I just wanted to practice the basics our first couple of times, but it's pretty obvious that you're more than competent with your fists and a blade." I shrugged. "Now I'm comfortable with practicing whatever you'd like."

A smile tugged at her lips for a second as she nodded. She took off her cloak while she considered. Her braid tumbled out of the hood and fell around her shoulder. My eyes fell there. It was full and long, and I considered what it might look like when it was completely untethered.

She was wearing black pants that hugged the wide contours of her body and a tunic that cinched at her waist. It was long sleeved and a dark blue, it made her eyes light up in the fire.

I tried not to let my eyes fall to the thigh that I knew held a dagger.

"While I love practicing with the dagger, I know how important it is to practice without them." I nodded, encouraging her to continue when she paused. "Can we practice what to do if I get caught without a weapon, when I'm subdued?" The tremor in her voice shook my entire being. Because there was a hint of desperation in her words, and I was afraid that she knew exactly what it felt like to be subdued, and that thought had my mind reeling.

I tried to keep my voice steady as I replied. "Of course."

We moved away from the fire, leaving Wyott sitting there quietly. I knew he could tell her mood indicated that it wasn't a night for joking around. He started sharpening his blade after he stoked the fire.

I didn't bother disarming, or making Evaline do the same.

I lifted my hands slightly, palms up. "What did you have in mind?" I elaborated when she quirked a brow. "There are a lot of different ways to be subdued. You could be tied to a chair, tied to a tree. Have your wrists tied, or ankles. Or an enemy could grab you by the wrist, or subdue you by holding your arms –"

"I get it." Her voice was small. She took a deep breath. "I think we should focus on getting out of holds when someone grabs you."

I nodded. I grabbed her wrist and stepped toward her, wasting no time.

"To get out of this, you need to aggressively swing your arm up and back into a windmill-like motion. It'll force your offender to twist their arm back too far, and they'll be forced to release your wrist."

She nodded and swung her arm back, breaking the hold immediately. Her eyes lit up. "That was easy."

I chuckled and grabbed the back of her upper arm, I walked her forward slowly as a captor would. "To combat this hold you should dip under my shoulder and spin behind me, it again forces my arm into an impossible angle and I have to let go."

She executed the move perfectly, popping up behind me, a smile on her face and her breath coming a bit faster.

"Are you even trying, Maddox?" She was being playful again and my heart jumped.

I smiled back at her. "Eva, the point is that you get out of these holds. I think I'm just a good teacher."

"Or maybe I'm an exceptional student." She said, ignoring my nickname for her.

I shook my head and rounded on her, holding her shoulder so she didn't whirl to face me.

"Why can't it be both?" I said softly as I wrapped my arms around hers, pinning them down. Her back pressed against my chest and I relished the feeling.

I heard her breathing stop.

"For this move, you need to use your weight." I said, low in her ear. "Slam your heel down on the foot, then as the attacker folds from the pain you have to do a couple moves simultaneously." She nodded and I watched from the corner of my eye as she bit her lip. I swallowed. "As I fold, throw your own hips back into mine and push off, turning and wrenching yourself out of my reach."

She nodded and took a breath.

Her heel came down and I bent as a human would at the pain. She moved fluidly as she threw her hips back and burst out of my arms. She whipped around to face me again, her braid reaching out and slapping me in the face from the movement. I felt a burst of pain on my cheek as it hit and looked at her as I straightened. Her eyes widened and she cringed.

"I'm so sorry." She said, her hand covering the hair at the base of her neck.

I laughed. "For what?" My fingers met my cheek and I pulled them away to find blood. My brows furrowed as I looked up at her.

"I'm so sorry, Maddox. I– I wasn't thinking when I whipped around." She pulled her braid around by the ending tail and held it there.

I shook my head. "You don't need to be sorry at all." I wiped my cheek with my sleeve and knew it was already done bleeding and had healed. "I guess I'm just confused about what happened."

Wyott was at my side in an instant.

"No fucking way." He said, his eyes zeroing in on her braid, then flicking up to her face. "Do you have something in there?"

She pursed her lips and nodded. "I braid a barbed wire into my hair every time I leave the castle." She looked down at her braid and used her fingers to brush away some of the hair so that the sleek metal peeked through.

"That's badass." Wyott said in awe.

She started to smile at him as I spoke. "No, that's fucking genius."

Her eyes flicked to me, but mine were still on her braid. I reached forward, gathering it in my hand and letting it rest there as I looked at the wire braided effortlessly into the white hair.

"I'd always wondered why you wore your hair in a braid constantly." I closed my hand around the braid, feeling the pricks of the wire poke into my skin. I loosened my grip before letting them break skin, not wanting to stain her beautiful hair. "You do this so no one yanks it?"

She nodded and her braid moved in my hand with the motion.

"Did your father teach you that?" Wyott asked beside me.

"Yes." She responded, too fast. It was a lie. And I knew it was by the increase in her heart rate, the catch in her voice.

But I didn't push her. I released the braid and stepped back. She took a breath. A smile cut over my face and I laughed.

She did too. "What?"

I shook my head but couldn't respond, and of course Wyott took it upon himself to do it for me.

"He finds that extremely alluring."

She furrowed her brows and looked at Wyott, a blush creeping onto her cheeks. "You think he finds the fact that I hide a wire in my braid attractive?"

Wyott nodded.

She rolled her eyes but I didn't miss the way they landed on mine for a second, searching.

I waved a hand at them and turned to walk back toward the fire. She needed to warm up. "What, a man can't find it attractive when a woman can defend herself?"

A snort. "Told you." Wyott said to her before I heard both of their footsteps behind me.

We sat around the fire and despite the cold, I saw a hint of blush on Evaline's face. We were quiet for a few moments, all likely aware of the tension pulling between Evaline and I. Sometimes I wished Wyott wasn't here with us. But I knew if he wasn't, he'd be moping by himself, back at the inn.

Evaline broke the silence. "Tell me about your home." She whispered.

My eyes flashed to hers, concerned with the lilt in her voice. It was different than normal, and when our eyes met, I saw the fear there. What was she afraid of, and why was she carrying it alone?

But Wyott spoke. "What do you want to know?"

She shrugged. "I don't know. What is it like? Where is it, even?"

"It's an island in the Madierian Sea." He responded.

Her eyes grew. "How close do you live to the ocean?"

Wyott spoke this time. "Maddox and I both grew up living with his parents, and the ocean is right outside their windows."

Her eyes grew even wider, somehow, and she turned to look at me. "That sounds like a dream. I've always wanted to see the ocean."

Wyott nodded and continued speaking about the different traits of Rominia. The volcano, the lush forests. The town where most of the Kova lived.

But all I could focus on was her extreme concentration on his words. She nodded along to everything he said, a smile on her face nearly the entire time. Her heart rate was rapid for someone who was sitting down. She was enjoying hearing about our home – no, she was downright wistful.

My own heart thumped out of rhythm in my chest as I considered that perhaps, for the first time, she was considering coming back to Rominia with us. Considering that perhaps we could be her future, her family. Even if she never saw me as a mate, and never realized what we were to each other. If I could get her to Rominia, then I knew she'd be safe for the rest of her life.

But one thing was certain. I had to get this girl to the ocean.

CHAPTER THIRTY-SEVEN

Evaline

I hadn't meant to whip Maddox with my braid, but I was thankful he wasn't upset. More thankful he seemed to like it. I couldn't stop thinking of the look of awe on his face, even as I was standing on a crate, stuffed into my wedding dress in Aurora's living room. I blinked and looked down. "Good Gods, surely it's not truly going to be this massive?"

The dress was exactly as I described it, massive.

It was ivory, with a corset top that cinched and then made way for what could only be described as a skirt so large that a small horse could fit beneath it. It was excessive. Layers of caging and tulle and silk stacked on top of each other.

"Would you stop complaining? You're being dramatic." She muttered up at me from where she bent below, grasping the skirt and pulling it so that it fanned out. "I want to see what it looks like with the under stuffing I added."

"Aurora, I look like an overturned bowl." My voice was incredulous.

A snort burst from her before she could stop it and she had to throw a hand onto the wall to catch herself from toppling over. "This is what your aunt told me to do." She said between breaths of laughter.

I crossed my arms. "Don't get me started on what my aunt tells people."

After steadying herself and pulling the last of the skirt out, she took a step back to evaluate the dress and cocked an eyebrow. "What happened?"

"I can't have this conversation while I'm on display up here."

She shook her head. "Fine. I'm done anyway." She helped me out of the dress and after I put on my own clothes. A long and layered, normal-sized, blue skirt with one side raised to tuck into the brown corset that held my waist over the cream top I wore. Its sleeves were small and rested off my shoulders with a tie closing the hole that would otherwise gape between my breasts. The front lacing leather corset ending just below my bosom. I positioned the skirt to hide the dagger around my thigh before rejoining Aurora in the living room where she laid out bread, cheese, and some fruit.

I slammed down into the couch and turned to face her. "She talked to me about sex."

Aurora nearly choked on the grape she was eating. "When?"

I reached for a strawberry and examined it as I spoke. "A few days ago, while we worked on some wedding planning." I took a bite and shook my head. "It was horrifically awkward."

Aurora snorted. "I bet."

She rose and walked toward the kitchen, throwing over her shoulder an offer for wine.

"Sure." I called back.

She came back with two goblets and the bottle, pouring us each a glass as she spoke. "What did she say?"

I took my glass from her and took a gulp. "She was giving me a warning for the wedding night." I cocked my head as I examined the deep maroon in my glass. "I think she was trying to be thoughtful. She said she didn't get this talk until the night before her wedding, and didn't have any time to prepare, so she told me now to give me time." I shrugged and looked up to meet Aurora's eyes. "She thought I didn't know about any of it because my father never talked about it, and my mother died young." I took another drink, the sweet taste of the wine slipping over my tongue.

"But you do know about it?" Aurora pushed.

I licked the remnant wine from my lips. "Yes." I laughed, "I wasn't always a royal woman." I waved a hand of dismissal. "Neomaeros was nothing like Kembertus. Women can do what, and who, they please there."

Aurora choked on her sip of wine with a fit of laughter. It sent me into one too.

When we calmed I smiled at her. "When you setup your shop there, you'll see."

She tilted her head onto the back of the chaise with a soft smile. "I can't wait."

We continued to discuss her plans for her Neomaeros shop, and her extension into the rest of the Madierian Kingdoms, and we drank until we'd finished a few bottles of wine.

We chatted while she made dinner, and when she refused to let me help, I continued to indulge in the wine even though she had stopped. I was having fun, and I didn't know how many days with Aurora I had left here, I wanted to enjoy them while I could.

CHAPTER THIRTY-EIGHT

Maddox

Just like the last time she'd visited me, I knew the moment Evaline was in the building.

Someone was with her, there was a second feminine voice, and that calmed my heart as I raced down the stairs.

"I'm looking for one of your newer guests," the voice said at the front desk. "Is there a Maddox here?"

I couldn't hear Evaline, only her heartbeat. A bit faster than normal.

I turned the corner of the hallway into the front room and as I stepped to see the young woman talking to Haekin, I heard Wyott approaching from behind. No doubt he heard me run downstairs.

The woman turned to look at me and relief washed over her face. "Maddox." She turned slightly to reveal Evaline slumped over on a bench against the front wall of the inn.

"What's wrong?" My voice choked as I stepped toward her.

The woman stepped into my path just as I was about to grab her. I recognized her as the friend Evaline had talked with at the Spring Solstice Ball.

"Nothing." She positioned herself between my mate and I. "Nothing is wrong with her, I mean. She's okay." My heart paced itself from the relief. "I'm so sorry," she shook her head. "We were at my house, drinking wine, and I guess I just didn't pay attention to how much she was drinking and..." We both turned to face her as she hiccupped. Her cloak hid most of her body, the hood hiding her face. Only the end of that braid poked out.

"I'm so sorry for coming here, but she needs to get home to," her eyes shot to Haekin before she whispered. "The castle." Her eyes coming back to mine. "Before sunrise, or she'll be in trouble. I'd take her back tonight but I can't walk her home in the dark alone and my wife isn't home –"

"It's okay, I'll handle it."

She sighed with relief, and as I made a move to step around her, she gripped my forearm, her nails digging in with the force.

I looked down at her. For a small woman her grip was impressive. The heat that lit her eyes was too.

"I'm trusting you because she trusts you." She hissed, her previously friendly tone lowered into a warning. "I don't like this – this leaving her with a man I don't know. I'm only doing it because she was explicit that you were to be trusted." I nodded, trying to ignore how that sentence alone warmed my veins. "But Maddox." I met her eyes once more, back from where they'd slipped to look at Evaline. "That girl has been through enough." Her voice caught on the last word, and a piece of me piqued. "If I find out you hurt her, I will come back here and slaughter you."

An empty threat, no doubt, considering her small stature. But I knew that she took it seriously.

I leveled my gaze with hers as I said, soft but stern. "No force in this world could ever get me to harm her."

Her eyes searched mine and she nodded, releasing me. She turned toward Evaline and knelt close. "Evaline." She whispered. "Time to stand up. Someone is here to see you."

I stood in front of her and she tilted her head up from where she must've been dosing off. A big smile lit her face. "Maddox."

I turned to the woman. "Do you need an escort home?"

She shook her head. "No, I live close." I nodded and she disappeared out of the inn, giving a cheery wave to Haekin.

I wrapped an arm around Evaline's waist and stood her up. To say she was unsteady on her feet was an understatement.

I turned to Wyott; he'd watched the entire exchange from the entryway. I flicked my eyes to Haekin, who tried to look like he hadn't been eavesdropping, and looked back at Wyott. His eyes flashed with understanding as he walked toward Haekin to compel him to forget what he'd seen and heard. I couldn't risk her getting in trouble if word got out that the niece of Lord and Lady of Kembertus was found drunk at an inn, being escorted upstairs by a man that wasn't her fiancé.

That word sent a low rage simmering in my chest but I pushed the feeling back.

Evaline looked up at me as I walked her toward the stairs and she said my name again in surprise, having already forgotten I was there.

"What are you doing here?" Her eyes were bright and glassy, her cheeks flushed. Then her eyes slid past me and she looked around. "What am I doing here?" She giggled.

I smiled at the sound.

"You're just going to sober up a little before we take you home." She nodded as we got to the first step. She looked at it as if it were the very wall surrounding this city, impossible to surmount.

She tried to lift her foot and when she started to fall out of my arms, I moved down and snatched her up into them. I scooped her legs out from under her and held her close to my chest, the fabric of her skirt flying up to meet us.

"Oh!" Her squeal of surprise filled the room.

I chuckled as we left Wyott behind.

She rested her cheek against my shoulder, staring up at me. I smiled down at her. "Do I have something on my face?"

She snorted and her breath cascaded over my neck, leaving goosebumps in its wake. "No." But she took a deep breath, letting the exhale come out as a sigh. "You just smell good. Like home." She raised her hand and placed it on my leather covered chest. "And leather." Her touch slid down the material and joined her other hand in her lap.

I clenched my jaw at the feel of her caress and how it reignited the low simmer I'd felt only minutes before, in a far different context. Now was not the time. I opened the door to my room, kicking it shut behind me and strode toward the bed. I set her on the side of it and knelt in front of her to remove her slippers. I tried my best to ignore the sleek length of her leg that popped out from the layers in her skirt.

I began removing the first shoe when I again felt her gaze on me. I smiled up at her. "What?"

She shook her head lazily, all her motions slowed down.

"Nothing." She said at first, then added. "I just noticed that this is the second time you've been on your knees in front of me."

I didn't have time to halt the wicked smile that lit my face as I spoke. "Eva, I assure you it won't be the last."

Her cheeks heated with the words and she turned her face away. I went back down to her shoes and heard the hitch in her breath.

I noticed what she was wearing for the first time as I moved to remove the second slipper. The brown corset that hugged her waist, her long blue linen skirt that should've covered her dagger but instead was thrown off to the side, revealing the gleaming silver there on her thick thigh, leather squeezing it gently just as I prayed to do one day.

It was a moment before I could force my gaze away.

My eyes roamed up and I felt her move. I watched as her hands raised to the button that held her cloak together. She released it and in one move flung her arms back, so it fluttered onto the bed behind her. I couldn't stop staring, and nearly unraveled as her fingers stumbled their way to the single tie that joined the two sides of her blouse. She loosed it so slowly that I thought I'd perish with the anticipation. When the tie was undone and each string fell straight against her chest, she opened the gap, revealing the cleavage barely restrained by the fabric.

"What are you doing?" My voice was hoarse.

She fanned herself. "It's too warm in here."

I could see that the flush from her face had migrated across her neck and chest, and I forced myself to look down as I removed her second slipper, trying to revert my thoughts to anything besides what the heat of her neck would feel like against my lips.

I stood up and moved through the room quickly, throwing all the windows open to allow the coolness of night to invade the room. I came back and stopped a few steps back from her.

She looked up at me and smiled.

And in that moment, I didn't need to even approach the bond, or tug, because I felt *her* tug. The sensation had me falling a step toward her, my lips drifting open to speak – when she jumped up from the bed.

"Do you hear that?" She asked, moving back to the seating area of my room and leaning near the windows.

I smiled. "Of course I do." She was referring to the tavern below us, the one next door that was connected to the inn. There was music being played outside for guests on their patio. It was a band of strings, and the tune they were playing was vibrant and quick.

She turned to me then. "Let's go dance." She walked forward, grabbing my hand, and dragging me to the door.

I stopped us before we made it there and tugged lightly on her hand so that she turned to face me. When she looked up at me there was nothing but anticipation on her face.

"We can't go dance, Eva." I said softly.

Her brows furrowed. "Why not?"

I smiled. "For one, you're not supposed to be seen out with me, now that you're engaged. Especially drunk." She nodded, understanding settling over her face. "And you don't have any shoes on." I added, chuckling.

She snorted and looked down at her feet. "Oh." She nodded. "I forgot about that." Then she pulled her hand from mine, and for a moment I was afraid she was angry with me, but instead she just looked around the room. She walked up to the chaise, which was the only piece of furniture near the fireplace. She put one foot on the base of it and pushed, and I watched as she sent it sailing across the room until it bumped back into the dining set behind it. The movement caused her to stumble back, too, and I crossed the room in a flash to catch her before she fell.

I couldn't help it, I burst out laughing. "What are you doing?"

She stood up from my grasp, her eyes gleaming as she turned and grabbed my hands, pulling me in the space she'd just cleared in front of the fireplace.

"I still want to dance." She said, pulling my hand to rest on her waist and taking the other in hers. "And if I can't go outside." She moved her other hand up and around the back of my neck. I shivered at the sensation of her hands on my skin. "Then we'll dance in here."

I could only smile and nod, pulling her body closer to mine and beginning to lead us. "I thought you hated dancing." I said to her, my voice low.

She cocked her head as she looked up at me, and I felt the end of her braid tickle my hand at her waist. "I did. Until I found someone who changed my mind."

I swallowed at her words, my hand on her side tightening and pulling her closer so that she was flush against my chest. I wanted to kiss her, needed to, but knew I couldn't. She wasn't in her right mind, and while I prayed the old adage that drunk words were sober thoughts was true in this moment, I couldn't be certain. I wouldn't take advantage of her.

Instead I opted for a joke. "Well, who is this mystery man?"

She just smiled and shook her head. "You'll never know."

I nodded. "As long as you're having fun, that's alright with me." Then I raised my arm to twirl her, and she spun, giggling as she went.

"I always have fun with you." She said as she landed back in my chest. "And Wyott."

"Good. That's all I've ever wanted." I whispered as I retook her waist in my hand.

Her wicked smile lit then. "I especially like learning about all the things you're so embarrassed about." She said before whispering. "Mad Axe."

I smiled and shook my head. "I'm going to ban Wyott from talking."

She laughed and rested her forehead against my chest. When she pulled her head back and looked up at me, there was unmistakable joy there. "No. How will I learn things, like what your favorite books to read are?"

I grimaced. "There's nothing wrong with a man enjoying romance novels."

She inclined her head, growing slightly more serious. "Of course there's not. I just never pegged you as a romantic."

I looked down at her, bringing our joined hands closer so that I could tuck a stray piece of hair out of her face and behind her ear with my thumb. "There's a lot you don't know about me." I said softly. My heart beat wildly in my chest. I hadn't held her like this since the Spring Solstice Ball. I knew the moment was fleeting, a drunken whim, but I desperately tried to cherish it regardless.

She nodded, holding her breath. "I know." Her eyes searched mine for a moment. "I'm sorry I misjudged you."

I returned our hands to the dancing position and continued to lead us. "There's no need to apologize. I can't even imagine how scary it must've been to see us, especially after everything you went through with your father's death."

She nodded, but changed the subject quickly. "Why do you read romance?"

I shrugged. "I've always liked them. Kova as a people just really value love, so when I was alone I'd find myself getting lost in stories about it."

She was quiet, and her voice was breathless when she spoke. "Have you ever experienced it?"

I twirled her again as the music outside peaked, and pulled her back into me, her smile flashing around the room as she spun.

"I've seen it. Basically everyone around me back home is –" I cut myself off before I said mated. "Married." I opted for instead, but then shook my head. "But I've never experienced it personally."

Until now.

"Me either." She whispered.

I dipped her then and she gasped, her braid just barely sweeping the ground below us. "You will." I whispered back, my eyes flashing to her lips.

257 |

She pursed them. "Do you think so?" She said, letting go of my hand and moving it to the collar of my shirt. Grasping there.

I stood us back up, both arms wrapped around her body and clutching her close to my chest, her face inches away. "Eva." I said, barely containing the emotion in my voice. "If love is what you want, you'll have it. An endless supply." I whispered, and this time her eyes watched as every word left my lips. I knew I shouldn't kiss her, but my control was waning.

"Maddox, can I ask you something?" She whispered.

I nodded, but before she could speak Wyott knocked on the door. I cursed under my breath and released her. I opened the door, letting him in, which was quite literally the last thing I wanted to do right now.

"Hello little miss lush." He said to her as he strode past me. For fucks sake, could he not tell I was on the cusp of a major breakthrough with her?

She laughed, a deep belly laugh, as he walked in with a tray in his hands.

Her eyes widened as she saw it and she turned, running for the bed and sitting on the side, raising one leg to fold onto the duvet as the other hung off.

He set the tray in front of her and removed the cover. Potatoes, beef, and greens lay steaming there. Along with a glass of water. She squealed and dug in.

"Good Gods, woman." He remarked as she stuffed the food into her mouth.

She started laughing but almost choked and had to wash it down with water. I cut a look to him and his eyes widened.

"Fuck, sorry." He said, finally understanding that his presence was no longer wanted. "I'll go." He raised his hands up in innocence. He turned back to Evaline. "I can't wait to make fun of you for this tomorrow." He said to her and she stuck a tongue out at him as he walked toward the door. "Good luck." He said with raised eyebrows as he left.

I was glad he was gone, but the moment with Evaline was over. I let her eat as I moved the chaise back toward the fire, taking a seat.

I leaned forward, my elbows resting on my knees, hands wringing in front of me.

What had she been about to ask me? Had I imagined her pull on the bond earlier? I tried every time I saw her, to near that bond that linked us together like a two-way tether of thoughts and emotions. Every time, I'd felt only a static of empty noise between the two of us. Not nothing, just not her reciprocation.

But just moments before, when she'd looked up at me with that smile, I felt that tug. I couldn't have imagined it. She trusted me, but more than that she was beginning to reach out to me, use the bond, without even realizing it.

The sound of her fork falling on the empty plate called me out of my thoughts. I strode toward her as she gulped down the water. I took the tray and set it on a side table.

When she finished drinking, I reached out. "Do you want more?"

She just nodded up at me and handed the glass over. I filled it up with the pitcher Wyott had left and handed it back to her. She gulped it down as I pulled a chair toward the bed, stopping a couple feet away to sit. She reached over then, straining to set the glass on the table along with the tray. Her skirt lifted to expose more of her leg. I gulped.

"Do you feel better?" I asked as she settled back into her seat on the bed.

She nodded. "Yes, thank you." Then as if a thought hit her. "Oh." She flung her hands into the air. "And tell Wyott thank you."

I smiled. "I will. Although you might want to take it back tomorrow when he gives you shit for it."

Her smile didn't falter as she leaned back on one hand and the other waved the words away. "I never drink. He can get over it."

I cocked my head. "Why did you?"

She let the other hand fall to prop her up on the bed behind her. "Why did I what?"

Her eyes were still glassy, her heart rate still out of pace. It'd be hours before she fully sobered.

"Drink."

Oh. She mouthed, then shrugged.

"I was talking to Aurora about a very unpleasant conversation I had with my aunt and wanted to ease some of the tension." Her eyes drifted to the ceiling as she talked, letting her head fall back and hang behind her.

I leaned forward, resting my elbows on my thighs. "What was unpleasant about it?"

She snorted. "My aunt was talking to me about sex for my wedding night."

Every muscle in my body hardened at the words, at the thought of him touching her. Especially because she didn't love him. Especially because he was a fucking Vestarian.

"Really." My voice was hard no matter how much I tried to soften it for her.

She nodded, and let her hands slide out, falling onto the mattress, one leg still dangling over the edge.

"Yes." She sighed when she landed, braid slung out on the bed beside her. "It was very awkward, but I think it was her way of showing she cared. She was trying to save me some pain, based on her assumptions."

The words clanged through my mind, she said them as if it would happen. But another set lit some small area inside of me. *Based on her assumptions.* I tried to ignore the way that thought sent a hot flash of want crawling through me and instead cleared my throat.

"But it doesn't matter either way, because you aren't marrying him, right?"

"Right." The breath of relief was coasting out of my lips when she spoke again. "Unless…" Her hands were fists at her sides.

"Unless what?" My words were sharp.

"Unless my plan doesn't work." She hiccupped.

I crossed the distance between us faster than she could comprehend, because she gave out a surprised breath as I sat on the bed and leaned over her.

My hand rested on the duvet beside her hip and I met her eyes as she stared up at me. "*Our* plan will work." I said, even though she hadn't told me what it was yet. "I will get you out of here, whatever it takes."

Evaline stared at my lips as I spoke, pulling her bottom one into her teeth. I clenched my jaw at the sight and gulped at the way she pressed her thighs together. An idea seemed to form behind those sultry eyes and she met my gaze.

"Will you do something else for me?" She asked, and her tone told me she already knew the answer.

"Of course." I could feel the heat from her body as I held myself above her.

"Take me, Maddox." She whispered breathlessly.

My brows furrowed. "I am taking you away, Eva. Just tell me when. I'll go right now, if that's what you're asking."

She squeezed her eyes shut and shook her head. "No. No, that's not what I meant."

"Then what —"

She opened her eyes and reached up to clasp a hand around my collar, lids dropping. "Take me." She tugged me an inch closer. The world slowed and everything but her became muddled around me.

"What?" I hardly choked out, heat creeping up the back of my neck.

Her other hand came up to slide along my chest. "Please." She leaned up, lifting her head off the bed.

I shook my head, the only thing I could do to clear my thoughts. Because inside my entire being was screaming at me.

Yes. Yes. Yes. Yes.

"Why would you ask me that?" My voice warbled with the effort of holding myself back.

Both hands knotted into my collar. Mine fisted as her fingers slipped through the opening of my shirt and touched skin.

"Eva." I warned.

"I want you." She murmured, one hand grasping the back of my neck and pulling me toward her.

This wasn't fair. Gods-dammit this wasn't fair. I'd gone weeks wrought with want for her, I'd been patient and honorable, and here she was whispering the words I'd prayed I'd elicit from her one day. And yet, I could do nothing. Not when she was under the influence. The Gods had a fucked sense of humor.

"I can't." I ground out against my will.

My instincts screamed at me. The bond raging in my head, slamming against the edges to get to her.

She hummed her disagreement. "Yes, you can." She sat up and I had to move back so she wouldn't knock our heads together. But her hands stayed planted on my neck, holding me as close to her as I'd allow. "I'm asking nicely." She crooned. My erection was barely restrained by my pants, and with each husky word they tightened. "Don't make me beg."

The way she said the words, the threat itself, sent a thousand thoughts through my mind in an instant. What I wanted to do with her, what she would sound like, how she'd feel around me. Before they could escape, before they could manifest into actions, into me pushing her back down onto the bed and burying my face beneath her skirt, I swallowed my self-hatred for what I was about to do and pulled her from me, lowering until our clasped hands rested on her knees.

I opened my mouth to speak, but soon realized there were no words. My lips were traitors, unwilling to say what I needed to. That I couldn't do this while she was drunk. That she had to stop, because my will wasn't made of Rominium. That if she kept speaking like this, touching me, I would break. And I'd hate myself forever for it.

But my silence only made her see another opening, and she flipped her hands in mine to hold them. "Don't you want me, too?" Her spine straightened as she spoke and the action only sent her blouse spreading wider against her chest, and without looking down fully, I could see that her nipples were hard.

A low growl shook through my chest and her hands only held mine tighter. I trembled as I responded, but only because the effort to restrain myself was so severe. "Yes." I ground out. "Yes." It was all I could muster.

Her hands moved from mine at the words, moving to her hair as her fingers flew over her braid, unraveling it.

"What are you doing?" I asked hoarsely.

Within a minute she had the wire removed from her hair, and it glinted from the dim light in the room as she leaned and threw it on the side table. She combed her fingers through her hair. It was white and silver, almost glowing in the darkness. It fell down in waves around her face. She watched me examine her, but then reached for me again. Her hands slid up onto the nape of my neck and she again pulled me toward her.

I planted a hand on the bed and stopped the movement.

"I can't, Evaline." But I groaned at the feel of her fingers winding in my hair, pulling softly. At this rate my heart was going to beat out of my chest. She released an exasperated breath. "If you won't do it for my pleasure, will you do it for my safety?"

My body stilled, the idea that there could be any threat against my mate's life lighting every instinct I had on fire.

"What are you talking about?" My voice was lethal.

She shivered and the thought that it was from my dangerous voice, that the violence woven through it might excite her, only sent more blood to my cock.

"Bassel would know what you were, if he saw you. Wouldn't he?" Her words were tactical but her eyes were forged by lust.

I ground my teeth and nodded my head. "Likely. He's set to inherit Vestaria, so he probably knows of the Kova and the Vasi."

She shrugged. "If he discovered that I spent the night in a Kova's bed, then even if my plan fails, maybe he won't want me." She pursed her lips. "As much."

My low growl vibrated the air around us. It was all I could do to stop myself from leaving her here, from going to Bassel and ripping his throat out. That she'd have any fear of him at all was too much, but that she'd have enough to be this concerned about it, that it would make her question whether I could get her out of Kembertus, that we'd be successful at all, was unacceptable.

But I just took a deep breath. "I don't care if I have to fight the Gods themselves, I will get you out of here unharmed. But we cannot do this tonight, Evaline. I can't do this."

"Why?" She whispered, her face inching closer.

"You're drunk."

She scoffed. "And?"

I let her pull me a beat closer this time, our lips were so close. Too close. "I won't do this when you're drunk. You aren't thinking clearly."

She let her hand dip into the back of my shirt, nails lightly scraping the muscles there. I shivered under her touch and felt my erection twitch.

"I'm thinking very clearly." Her voice was laced with want, and it sent a ravaged warmth through my body.

Now. Take her.

The bond pleaded in my head, every fiber of my being reaching for her.

"No, you're not." I whispered through a shaky breath. "You'd hate me for it." But my eyes had fallen to her lips. She bit the lower one and I was sure my teeth would shatter at the force of my clenched jaw.

"Please. Maddox."

The way she said my name, her voice sultry and breathless, had my hand sliding up into her hair, gripping the back of her neck, thumb tracing her jaw. I held her there, angling her eyes up to mine.

Her breath caught as she gave in to my touch and I heard her heart race in anticipation.

"I will not. Not like this." She opened her mouth to speak, but I cut her off. "Because when I do take you." My eyes dropped to her lips, then back up. "It will be because you want it. Want me. And it won't be when you're under the influence. When I'm inside of you," I growled at the words, the thought. "You will know with every part of you, every beat of your heart, that it is exactly where you want to be. Where you are meant to be."

By the time I'd finished talking her body was trembling and I didn't need to smell her arousal to know it was from want. Her hands tightened in my hair, nails bit into my back. I felt for the bond, and instead of the static I was used to, I felt her. I felt the longing thrumming through her. The exhilaration lighting her mind.

"Okay." Was all she said, breathless.

"Okay." I said back, wondering if she'd felt the bond too. I pulled back, away from the bond, and swallowed.

A breath shook from her lips and the sob she tried to quiet slipped out. My eyes flew to hers and I watched as a tear fell. My hand was already shifting to hold her face, my thumb catching the tear and wiping it away.

"What's wrong?" I choked out.

She shook her head in my hand, squeezing her eyes against the tears. "You better make sure I escape." Her eyes opened again, looking into mine.

"I will." The vow slipping through my lips without a second thought.

"He can't... you can't let him." I raised my second hand to brush the hair from her face and then held her there.

In my hands, the entire world. The reason for my existence. "I won't." The harshness in my voice, in this promise, seemed to calm her.

She nodded slightly, as much as she could in the hold of my hands. "Good." She breathed. "Good. Because he can't hurt me, not ag –" She cut herself off, eyes widening.

"Not what, Eva?" I growled, the only muscles in my body not locking up from the rage filling me were the hands that held her.

"Nothing." But I knew the fear that rolled off her wasn't from me.

"Ev –"

"Let it go." She whispered and grasped my wrists.

My eyes searched hers, searched for any clue as to what she was referring to, but –

Please.

The word roiled into my mind, filling the walls in my skull until all I heard was that word repeating over and over.

It wasn't my voice that filled my thoughts. It wasn't my voice that flowed down the bond.

It was hers.

CHAPTER THIRTY-NINE

Evaline

If I could, I would sell my soul to Mortitheos himself, if only to relieve the pain searing through my skull. Clearly, I'd overindulged, because the events of the night before were muddled in my aching head.

I peeked my head out from under the blankets and peered at the window, immediately hissing from the stark light of day. Pain reverberated through my skull from the overstimulation.

I rolled to face away from the window and curled into a ball, staring at the wall. I knew Aurora had taken me to see Maddox. I felt bad for worrying her, she'd been frantic over what to do. And when she was pacing in front of me, the only thought I could muster was that Maddox was right around the corner, and that he'd take care of me. I didn't know why the thought resonated with me, I just knew it to be the truth. I trusted him.

After Aurora dropped me off at the inn, my memories began to get fuzzy. I remembered sitting on Maddox's bed, remembered him helping me out of my shoes. But that was where my memories stopped. I just knew Maddox had ensured I got home safely, likely carrying me through the very window he'd entered when he came to visit before.

He must have taken off my corset before he put me to bed, but all my other clothing remained on.

The thought of what I had done last night, at the stupid things I may have said while under the influence, left a chill of mortification through me. Gods, I hoped I didn't embarrass myself.

I rose from the bed after a servant came and drew my bath. I knew the steaming heat of the water would dig deep into my skull and relieve some of the pain I was feeling. While I soaked, my nose the only part of me outside of the warmth of the water, I again tried to recall the night before. The darkness of Maddox's room. The way the glow of the fire glinted off his face. The way he looked on his knees in front of me, taking off my slippers.

It won't be the last.

The memory of those words slammed into me, breaking through a wall of wine-induced fog.

I tried to ignore the feelings those words, and the way he'd said them, stirred in me. Maddox was a flirt. Although I tried to remember more, I wasn't able to come up with any memories. But after I'd dressed and moved to begin braiding my hair, I realized that it too had been undone when I awoke.

I definitely didn't remember doing that. Perhaps Maddox did that too, so I wouldn't prick myself at night. I opened the drawer of the vanity and searched, but my wire wasn't in there. My heart rate increased as I stood and checked under my pillow, under my bed. Had he taken it? Did I leave it in his room? And for that matter, where was my dagger? I bit my lip as I turned throughout the room, searching to see if he'd left them anywhere. Surely, he wouldn't have left them out somewhere obvious, because he knew I had to hide them to avoid punishment.

I threw open the armoire and searched the clothes, but found them nowhere.

My eyes swept the room again and landed on a small decorative pillow on the chaise near the fire. That pillow usually adorned my bed, but it sat on the chaise exactly where I'd sat while Maddox had massaged my back.

An odd spark of heat lit my body as I moved toward the pillow, slipping my hand between the cushion and the arm of the sofa.

My fingertips touched cold metal –

A loud knock rasped at my door. I pulled my hand from the cushion and jumped up, but Therese was already entering the room before I could grant her permission, Bassel trailing behind her. His eyes roved me and my hands clenched around the throw pillow that I still held.

"Good… morning Evaline." He said the words as he took in my unmade bed and my still damp hair.

It must not have been morning.

"Good morning, Bassel."

"Bassel hoped you'd accompany him on a walk to the market today." Therese said, her eyes burning into me. Clearly she didn't like that I was just out of the bath and unmade myself, but considering she was the one who waltzed into my room without any warning, she could deal with it.

I shouldn't go. I didn't want to. But I didn't much have a choice, and it would be nice to get to go to the market. Maybe I'd see Aurora there.

Maybe I'd see Maddox.

The smile that raised from my lips wasn't entirely fake. "Sure."

He didn't look completely happy with my response, and I realized I hadn't been cheerful enough for his liking.

"Great." He said and extended his elbow.

Oh. He wanted to leave right this moment. I had to force my gaze not to fall down to the chaise, to the cushion that hid my safety nets. I ground my teeth and set the pillow down, moving to take his elbow. Therese followed right behind. She softly shut the door to my bedroom behind us and continued down the hall with us.

"Pretend I'm not here. I just cannot leave you two unchaperoned for too long."

Bassel nodded. "Of course, Lady Therese. Thank you for your company." Then he offered his other elbow. "But please, don't walk behind us." She was all too happy to run up and grab it, and I had to concentrate so that I wouldn't roll my eyes.

I knew she was only accompanying us because my assumed virtue had to be protected for the marriage, but I was thankful for it. The less time I had to spend alone with Bassel, the better. Now all I had to contend with was this migraine.

The sun was too bright when we walked out of the cover of the castle. I didn't bring my cloak, and I didn't need it. With the sun out in a cloudless sky, even in early spring the heat was enough to not warrant the extra layer.

Bassel seemed to notice the weather as well and looked down at my attire. I wore my black pants and a pale blue linen shirt. Matching intricately jeweled slippers were my only accessory since I was completely weaponless. Even my hair felt naked, as it draped down my shoulders in waves. My hair had already begun drying, and I was glad I was at least able to run a brush through it before they'd barged into my room.

"You look...comfortable." He remarked as he led us through the gardens. "Do you make a habit of not wearing dresses?"

I swallowed the venom that slithered up my throat, and saw my aunt straighten on his other side. Of all the times I'd fought her on wearing dresses every day, I assured her that men couldn't truly care about it. I didn't even bother looking over at her, unwilling to see the smug look that I knew adorned her face.

"I generally save dresses for special occasions." I lightened my voice as much as I could.

He nodded. "When we are married, you'll need to wear dresses every day. In Vestaria, no women wear pants. It is not the fashion."

It was a watered down way of saying that they weren't allowed to. I nodded, knowing any words I uttered would be laced with hatred.

As we neared the market I could already smell the freshly baked bread and pies from the baker's tent. My stomach grumbled. But if Bassel heard the noise, he didn't pay any attention. He just marched us right past the baker and toward the jeweler.

I ignored him as he droned on about all the diamonds he'd brought with him from Vestaria. How he'd sold them to the jeweler and wanted to pay a visit to see what pieces had been created from them. I think he believed I cared about such things. Therese surely did. She was conversing easily with him, and I was thankful for it. Maybe she should marry Bassel.

The smell of leather hit me before we came upon the blacksmith's tent, where I'd stood alone only a few weeks before, buying my dagger that felt like it had been mine for ages; where Maddox had saved me from punishment.

And as if the Gods had heard that exact thought, I saw that he stood near the entrance of the tent as we came into view. He was paying the blacksmith, quite a lot from the looks of it, his back to me. But as if he could feel my gaze, he lifted his head and looked over his shoulder. Dark gray eyes locked on mine in an instant. He started to smile before his eyes roamed to my partner, then they hardened.

Wyott appeared next to him, emerging from the tent. He always seemed to be able to tell when Maddox was on edge. His gaze followed the former's and landed on me, too. Wyott gave me a smile, and started to wave before he too, saw where my hand was tangled up.

Bassel and Therese, oblivious to the entire exchange, continued talking and walking, and as we passed the tent completely, I threw one last glance over my shoulder at Maddox, lips tugging up into a smile as I mouthed a thank you. I turned around before I could see his response.

Bassel, Therese, and I settled at the jeweler's tent for what seemed like hours. The jeweler was just as excited to talk about the diamonds as Bassel was, and I let my gaze drift away until it settled on Maddox, leaning against one of the buildings behind the grocer's cart. His arms were crossed as he stared at me. I stared back. He cocked his head to the side, and I knew what he was asking.

My shoulder hardly moved with the shrug, but I knew he saw it across the market. *I'm fine.* I tried to communicate with the wordless gesture.

He nodded once, and I knew his response. *Good.*

A wind cascaded toward me, blowing the hair that lay down my back and over my shoulders around my face and bringing the scent of the bakery back toward me. My stomach grumbled again, and Maddox glanced down toward it.

I just smiled at him. One side of his lips tugged as he relaxed. He drew an arm up to rub his neck. My eyes followed the movement and as they settled on his neck a warmth flowed through me. Images started to form in my mind's eye, working to come forward into view. Maddox's neck, my hand sliding up it, behind it. My hand sliding into his shirt, feeling the taut muscles there.

Gods.

In a rush, every second, every Gods forsaken moment from the night before re-established themselves in my memory. His arms around me while we danced. His clenched jaw and strained eyes as I begged him to have sex with me. His warm breath over my face when he declined. My eyes snapped back up to Maddox and I saw the concern on his face, the silent worry, as I felt my face pale.

Shit.

Shit.

What have I done?

I couldn't look away from him standing across the market. Was he mad at me? Would he still help me escape, or had I ruined everything?

He didn't look upset, he looked worried. I felt Bassel's hand loop around my waist and the action broke the trance I'd fallen into with Maddox. I turned toward Bassel, feeling Maddox's distaste for him even across the street, as Bassel led me away from the jeweler. My eyes met my aunt's, and I could see the fury sitting there. She hadn't seen my first dance with Maddox at the Ball, but she'd seen that.

Shit.

I didn't see Maddox again for the next hour, but I knew he hadn't left the market yet. We passed the baker's tent and I tried to go to it, I was famished. But Bassel tugged me away.

"I just want a quick pastry." I assured him.

He only rolled his eyes in response and continued leading me with his hand flattened on the small of my back. I suppressed a shiver from the disgust his touch conjured and held my breath.

"There's no time." He said without looking at me and continued on toward the stand where Aurora stood, selling dresses. I ground my teeth. At least I'd see Aurora. Her smile brightened as she spotted me, as if out of habit, but her expression suddenly became a touch grim as she greeted us.

"Good afternoon, Bassel." She said nodding at him. "Lady Therese." She said, lowering into a curtsy. Then flicking her eyes to mine. "And Evaline, how are you today?"

"I'm wonderful Aurora, how are you?" *I'm okay.*

Her smile returned. "Good."

And I knew she wasn't referring to her day.

Bassel took it upon himself to pick out five dresses to buy me, then made plans to have them delivered to the castle later that day.

"Of course Bassel, thank you for your business." Aurora smiled at him. "See you around, Evaline, Lady Therese."

I waved goodbye to her as Bassel led me to the aisle, finally he was letting me go home. We walked through the crowded street, having to compact close to one another, when he took the opportunity to put an arm around me, slipping his hand into the crook of my waist and pulling me ever so slightly toward him. A fury filled me, and a part of it felt foreign, as if the feeling wasn't wholly my own.

When Bassel departed from the Lady and I at the gates of the castle, he bowed and headed back into town, right for the inn. A cold shock chilled my skin as I realized he was staying in the same inn as Maddox. How many times had I been there now, how close had he come to seeing me?

Therese's claws in my arm ripped me from my thoughts as she pulled me into the castle and dragged me to my room.

"What are you doing?" I hissed, but she did not speak, only walking faster down the halls, nearly tripping on her dress.

When she opened the door to my room she threw me inside of it. Luckily, she wasn't very strong because it only resulted in me standing in front of her.

"Who was that man?" She hissed.

I pursed my lips, but otherwise tried my best to keep an air of ignorance. "What?" I asked.

She slammed the door shut behind us and folded her arms. "Don't play dumb with me, girl. Who was that man you were ogling? You know him."

Knowing my claim for ignorance was dead, I chose gaslighting instead. I sighed. "Yes, Aunt Therese. I have met him before. At the Spring Solstice Ball, where I danced with him. Don't you remember encouraging me to dance with the eligible bachelors there? It sure seemed as though you invited half the continent's worth of single men."

She narrowed her eyes. "There was something happening between the two of you, as if –" She cut herself off and the look in her eyes was pure rage. "Are you having relations with that man?"

I laughed, and it was only half in mortification as the memories of last night when I'd thrown myself at Maddox to do exactly that flashed through my mind. "No! Of course not."

She shook her head. "You better be telling the truth, because this marriage cannot fall through. It's embarrassing enough that you've been living under this roof for two years." She threw her hands up. "At twenty-four, six years after you should've first been on the market, and to still be unwed." She flattened her hands against her chest. "Do you understand how embarrassing that is for me, how that makes me look? That the Lady of Kembertus cannot even prepare her own niece, who is beautiful, for a proposal?"

My eyes widened with each word she said. I'd always wondered why she was so adamant that I be on the lookout for men, be accepting of their gifts and time, but I'd never known fully why until this moment. And to hear her say the words hurt more than I could've imagined.

"You care more about your reputation than you do about the rest of my life." I said. It wasn't a question, and each word dripped with venom.

She laughed. "Of course! It is every woman's responsibility to become wed one day, especially women in our positions, and that is how this world works. I am not the enemy."

I scoffed. "It is not how the world works, it is how your world works." I said, starting to shout. I jabbed my finger toward the window, toward where Bassel walked back through the city. "It is how his world works. But this is not the world my father wanted for me. He raised me in Neomaeros for a reason, and it wasn't just because he couldn't stand to be around you and Elijah." I hissed, fury fueling the rush of each word from my mouth.

She shook her head, an eerie silence falling over the two of us.

"You are a stupid girl, living in a fantasy." I clenched my jaw as she continued to speak, fists at my sides. "Your father is dead, Evaline." She shouted at me. "He has been for years. Whatever he wanted for you, died with him. This world you think exists out there for you, died with him. Because he was that world. He let you believe that you could live in a land where women have all these rights and privileges, while ignoring the very city he grew up in, and would have ruled, had your mother not been pregnant."

"Exactly!" I screamed, the audacity of her bringing up my father enraging me even more. "He knew they were having a child and he refused to raise it in this awful, Gods forsaken, shithole kingdom you call home!"

I expected her to hit me, almost hoped she would again because this time I'd return the blow. But instead, she laughed.

"Well." She said, sighing. "Good thing you'll be out of here soon. Off to Vestaria, and I won't have to deal with you anymore." She began walking toward the door, before she turned back toward me, her voice calm. "And Evaline? If you think Kembertus is bad, wait until you see Vestaria." She laughed again, tears in her eyes. "You'll pray for your days back here. And you'll regret every word you just said."

I didn't speak, focusing on keeping my feet in place so that I didn't run after her.

When she reached the door and opened it, she turned back one last time, her rage boiling over again as she shouted. "You are forbidden from leaving this castle until your wedding night! No more trips to the boutique, no more lessons with the orphan girls. For the next week and a half you will do nothing but fix that attitude for your wedding. If I catch you disobeying me, there will be severe consequences."

The fire in her eyes told me I didn't want to discover those consequences, and I didn't question it as she slammed the door behind her. All I could do once she left was let loose a scream that held every piece of anger and fear and misery that I'd been bottling since the moment I watched the light leave my father's eyes. I screamed so long that my throat was scratched, and tears streamed down my face. I turned and picked up a bust that sat on a side table near the door, turning, fully prepared to throw it at the window and shatter it into a million pieces.

But then I saw it.

On the bench near my window, the cherry pastry sat, and I knew exactly who put it there.

I was restless for the remainder of the day. All I could think about was everything that had occurred from the moment I arrived at the inn last night, until the moment my aunt slammed my door. But more pressing were the memories that returned while I was at the market with Bassel. What had I done? *Thrown yourself at Maddox.*

I rolled my eyes at the thought as I sat on the bench adjoining my window. The night was still muffled, but I knew I'd told Maddox I wanted him, begged him to have sex with me. I shuddered. What was wrong with me? Not only was it insane, but it was embarrassing. Mortifying. I'd been attracted to Maddox since the moment I saw him, but I hadn't acted on it, or voiced it. And here I was begging him to take me the moment I was under the influence.

I closed my eyes, and without wanting them to, the images formed behind them. I couldn't remember what he said in response, I just knew he'd said no. The only memories I could pull from the fog of the exchange was my white-hot desire and his refusal to touch me when I was under the influence. I couldn't help but thank the Gods for that. Not only because I would have regretted it, but because Maddox once again showed that he was unlike all the men I'd met before, namely Bassel. Everything he did, said, made me feel safe around him.

My heart clenched. I wasn't sure what to do with that information. With the knowledge that he made my heart thunder while also making me feel less alone, and more protected, whenever I was with him.

It's why I told Aurora to find him, even if I was drunk when I said it. I knew he'd take care of me, no matter how embarrassed I was now.

I leaned my head against the wall behind me. I hoped I didn't make things awkward between us, hoped he wasn't mad at me, or thought I was pathetic. And I tried to convince myself that the only reason I begged him to take me was to protect myself from Bassel, instead of acknowledging the kernel of truth that he affected me in ways I still couldn't understand.

I clenched my jaw as I watched the day turn into night, watched the stars come out and the fireflies light up the garden below me. I had no way of telling Maddox that I wouldn't be at our scheduled training session tonight. I knew I could easily sneak out of the castle, but the ability to do so wasn't the problem. I feared my aunt would be back tonight. That she'd check on me to make sure I was still here.

All I could do was get into bed and stare at the window, hoping that maybe Maddox would come through it, and I could tell him what happened.

But mostly, I was afraid that he wouldn't. Afraid that he'd think I was upset at him for the night before, and that I'd simply refused to go to the training session. And with that worry eating my insides, I dozed off.

CHAPTER FORTY

Maddox

I wasn't convinced that Evaline would show for our training session tonight after seeing her at the market. I knew the moment she'd remembered the night before, and she'd been mortified.

I clenched my jaw. I didn't know how much longer I could go without telling her the truth; what we were to each other. I knew I would be the one to beg this time, pleading with her to feel the same. Because I didn't know what I'd do if she didn't reciprocate.

But my fears that she was upset by the events of last night only deepened as minutes turned into an hour. My hands kneaded each other as they hung between my knees, bent over toward the fire.

"It's been too long." I hissed. I was scared, and it wasn't just at the idea that she somehow hated me. But that she was hurt, fallen in a ditch somewhere with a broken leg. Or incapacitated by that prick she had to call a fiancé.

"Maybe she's just running late, she does have to sneak out every time." Wyott offered, his voice even and calm as he tried to funnel that same energy to me. "Maybe she just got caught up."

I nodded. That had to be it, any other scenario was unacceptable because any other scenario meant she was hurt or that she hated me, and both of those made my heart ache.

After another half hour I stood in a huff, moving to the area where we regularly sparred, and started pacing.

"Mads, calm down." Wyott encouraged. "There's probably a logical explanation for this. Give her more time."

I rolled my eyes and continued pacing. "I'm trying." I said between clenched teeth.

Another thirty minutes passed.

I'd never been so unhinged in my entire life, no matter how many battles I'd fought in or how many armies I'd led. What was she doing to me? But I knew the answer. This is exactly how mates felt, often. Whenever they were without each other, or worried for the other's safety.

I stopped pacing then and lifted my head toward Wyott.

"I'm sorry." I said and he looked up at me, his eyebrows furrowed.

"For what?"

I waved my hands toward myself. "Look at me, I'm a mess. And this is after a couple hours of not knowing where she is, or what she's doing." His lips pursed and I knew he caught on to my thought. "Is this how you've felt for the last several months? Because if so, I am eternally sorry."

Wyott stood and brushed off his pants, moving toward me slowly and putting a hand on my shoulder. "Maddox, you are my best friend. My brother. I'd do anything for you, because I know you'd do the same. Don't apologize for pain you haven't caused. Yes, I feel like that, almost always. It gets easier over time. It also helps to know that she's somewhere safe. But you didn't drag me on this trip. It was my choice, and Cora knows that too. If I'm not with her, the only other place she'd rather I be is by your side, and that's exactly what I'm doing. For Rominia, for Kovarrin, and for you."

I swallowed the lump in my throat. Wyott and I were like brothers, we had been since we could form memories, but we hadn't had many talks like this in our existences. I wasn't sure if it was his kind words, the pressure I felt in my chest at not knowing where Evaline was, or the knowledge that my poor friend had felt this unbelievable pain for so long, but I had to fight to push back the tears.

I didn't respond, and knew he didn't expect me to. I just nodded, and he removed his hand from my shoulder and clapped. "But it has been too long. As the only one here who can be partial to this situation, I am officially worried. I think we should go check on her."

My eyes widened and I sighed. "Oh, thank the Gods."

I ran to the fire, dousing it in dirt to put it out. Once I was confident the embers would not relight, we ran. Only to the edge of the forest, this kingdom was still too small to do much more than that without being caught, and even this small burst was risky, but each beat of my heart urged me to find her.

When we finally got to the castle wall below her window, I listened. I could hear her rhythmic heartbeat, the even breathing, and knew she was asleep.

I turned to Wyott. "She's just sleeping."

Wyott nodded. "Do you still want to check on her?"

I pursed my lips. Of course, I did. But I was afraid that she stood us up on purpose, and if she was angry with me, I didn't want to cross any boundaries by going up there.

Wyott saw my hesitation. "It's still possible something has happened, like she's locked up or something, and she's just fallen asleep. We should still check."

I nodded, thankful for his validation, and after taking one sweep of lookout, I went up.

I was in her room in an instant, and Wyott was right behind. She was asleep, in bed and turned away from the window. She didn't look injured or incapacitated, and I didn't want to bother her.

I turned to Wyott, nodding at the window indicating that we should leave.

We hadn't made a sound, but of course she'd always be able to tell when I was around her. The pull of the bond could pull someone out of a sleep, and I knew that's exactly what it'd done when I heard her voice.

"Maddox?" It was raspy, groggy with the essence of sleep so freshly in her mind. My heart gave one big and painful pump as I turned toward her.

"I'm so sorry, I didn't mean to bother you, I just wanted to make sure you were safe." I whispered.

She was sitting up in her bed now, turned toward us. She nodded and ran a hand through her hair. "It's okay, I was hoping you'd come."

A flood of warmth filled me at the words, at the confirmation that she wasn't mad at me. She got out of bed and walked toward us, the light of the fire playing in her eyes.

"I've been forbidden to leave the castle until the wedding." She said as she walked toward us. She pulled a robe from the foot of the bed and over her arms. She wore sleep shorts and another top that barely reached her midriff. I swallowed the thoughts clouding my mind, about what she looked like just waking up from a deep sleep and what it would be like to experience it every morning, and cleared my throat.

"What happened?" I asked, following her to stand by the fire.

She shrugged. "Earlier when I saw you at the market, my aunt saw our interaction."

Wyott spoke quietly beside me. "Oh, shit."

My face paled at the thought that I'd gotten her in trouble. I took a step closer to her, hand raising to wrap around her elbow. "Did she hurt you?"

Evaline shook her head. "No, but as soon as we got back we got into a huge fight. She won't let me leave. I can't even see Priscilla or Megin." She said that last sentence to me and I could see the pain in her eyes. "I had no way of telling you that I wouldn't be able to meet you." She looked between the both of us, her arms folded around herself. "I'm so sorry for wasting your time tonight."

I shook my head. "Don't be absurd. You don't need to apologize."

She sat on the chaise near the fireplace, and the glow lit up her legs.

"Do you want us to compel her to let you leave?" Wyott offered.

She shook her head. "There'd be no use. She was screaming at me, half the castle likely heard it. And she probably already went and told my uncle." She shrugged. "The wedding isn't far off, I can deal with it until then."

"We can do the rest of our training sessions here." Wyott said, turning to look at me. "Right?"

I nodded. "Of course. We can be quiet, and we'll be able to hear if anyone comes to check on you and leave." I shrugged. "Or compel them."

A weight seemed to lift off her shoulders and she nodded. "Okay, thank you so much." She shook her head. "You guys do a lot for me, I'm not sure how I'll ever repay you."

Her words were sincere, but I knew Wyott's intentions by the smirk on his face as he went over to sit with her.

"You're going to be sorry you said that in about two seconds." I chuckled under my breath.

She looked at me confused, and as Wyott plopped down beside her, he bumped her shoulder with his. "How does it feel to be this trio's lush?"

Instead of shutting down or sneering at him, she shook her head and laughed. "What kind of world is this if a girl can't let go every once in a while?"

"I'd be inclined to agree with you if it wasn't so enjoyable to mock you for it." Wyott said, waving a hand toward her. "For a woman who is so straight laced and pent up all the time, it was fun seeing you let loose." He shrugged. "And I know you were mortified this morning."

She leaned forward, elbows settling on her knees, "Keep it coming, Wyott, but remember that I'll send it back a hundred times worse when I get some dirt on you."

I snorted. "You don't have to dig far."

Her smile whirled to me as she straightened.

"How are you feeling?" I asked, my eyes absentmindedly falling to her lips.

"I'm okay." Her voice softened. "I wanted to say thank you, all jokes aside." She looked at me as she said the words and then to Wyott. "I really do appreciate you both making sure I was fed and home safe." She shrugged. "I honestly don't know what I would have done if you hadn't helped. Aurora was panicked and there was no way I could get home in that state."

"Hey." Wyott said with an exaggerated shrug. "What am I if not a hero?"

"Annoying, for one." I mumbled, but turned my attention back to her. "You don't need to apologize or thank us, Evaline. We're always here for you."

Wyott nodded beside her. "It was no problem at all."

She smiled and thanked us again anyway.

"Wyott compelled Haekin to make sure he didn't remember you, so your secret is safe with us."

Her eyes widened. "I didn't even think of that, thank you." She said to Wyott. He shrugged.

There was a beat of silence before she turned to me, her voice soft.

"Maddox, I was wondering if I could talk to you privately?"

"Fucking finally." Wyott groaned and stood. "It's been days since I got a decent sleep thanks to you two."

He said his goodbyes and left us, disappearing out her window. She waited several minutes before speaking, no doubt waiting until he was out of his supernatural earshot, then she patted the seat beside her. I obliged.

"I can't even begin to apologize for my state last night —" She started but I cut her off with a hand on her knee.

"If you're going to sit here and apologize for being drunk, stop. We all go through it, there's no need."

She pursed her lips, wringing her hands in her lap. "I'm not just apologizing for being drunk…" She trailed off and took a deep breath, dragging her eyes away from mine. "I wanted to apologize for throwing myself at you. I don't know what I was thinking, but I'm sorry I put you in that position." The air left my lungs at the sight of her, my love, sitting here apologizing for asking to have sex with me. "I hope this doesn't change anything between us, or make you want to back out of helping me." A breath. "Because I'd understand if it did."

I covered her hands in mine, her eyes shooting to meet my gaze.

"You don't ever have to apologize to me. And nothing would ever stop me from helping you. And." I continued. "Nothing has changed between us. Everything's fine."

She nodded. "Thank you for not…you know."

The vulnerability in her eyes wrapped a fist around my heart. "Of course."

She bit her lip as she held my gaze, but mine fell to her lips, and I felt us both begin to lean in, her grip on my hands tightening.

But as if snapping back to reality, she pulled back and cleared her throat. "Instead of training today, I thought we could use this time to go over the plan for our escape."

I just clenched my jaw and nodded, trying to quiet my heart. "What did you have in mind?"

She turned back to face the fire, reaching her hands out toward it. "I want to wait until the day of the wedding to leave, like we discussed."

"Can I ask why?"

She straightened. "I just have something I have to do before I can go."

I just nodded; she didn't want to elaborate. "Do you know where you want to go?"

Her eyes fell to the fireplace. "No, I don't really have anywhere to go. I hadn't thought that far ahead yet."

I nodded, knowing that wherever she ended up, I'd be. "We can figure that out later." I said softly and she smiled up at me.

"How are we going to escape?"

I leaned toward the fire too. "We can go right over the wall."

A scoff erupted from her. "Maddox, it's taller than any building I've ever seen. What are we going to do, scale it?"

I laughed. "I think you sometimes forget that you're friends with two Kova." She nodded and smiled. "We can jump over it, so we'll have Wyott scouting the other side, you will meet me at the wall. All you have to do is walk straight west from our usual training spot. Another ten minute walk through there and the tree line breaks again. With the wedding, all the guards will be patrolling closer to the city. Even if there are any around there, we'll just compel them if they get too close."

"That seems too easy." She said softly.

"It will be, don't worry, nothing will go wrong. Wyott and I have gotten in and out of cities far more heavily protected than Kembertus."

She grinned as if she hadn't truly believed this was happening until this moment.

"Why do you look so surprised?"

She shrugged. "I just didn't let myself believe it was real until now."

I leaned and nudged her shoulder with mine. "I told you I'd take you away, and I will. Wherever you want to go. Whatever it takes."

Her expression changed as she tilted her head to look up at me. "Why?"

Every part of me ached to tell her. To confess that I'd loved her since the moment we met, that I felt it run deep into my bones. But even if she was beginning to trust me, it didn't mean she was ready to hear about the bond.

So instead, I opted for a joke. "What am I if not a hero?"

Her soft laughter filled my senses.

CHAPTER FORTY-ONE

Evaline

Aurora barely slowed to set down the wedding gown as she burst into my room and had me in the vice of her arms.

"I'm so sorry, Evaline, I'm so sorry."

My arms curled around her. She'd come to do another fitting for the wedding, but I was just happy to see my friend after being locked in here.

"Why are you sorry, I'm sorry!" It was the first time we'd gotten any time alone since the night I was drunk.

We pulled away but she didn't remove her hands from my arms. "I shouldn't have just left you with Maddox. I don't even know him! You hardly know him. I should've found a way to get you home –"

"Aurora, stop." I cut her off. "You did exactly what you should have. Maddox kept me safe, Wyott brought me dinner, and they got me home without a fuss. Everything was okay, and no one will ever know apart from the four of us."

She took a deep breath, her anxiety seeming to lessen. "Good, I was just so worried." We walked toward the chaise. "And then seeing you with Bassel at the market, I could barely stop myself from asking if you were okay in front of him."

We sat. "It's okay, everything's okay."

A smile finally lit her face. "Well good, now I don't have to murder Maddox."

I laughed at the absurdity of it. "What?"

She crossed her arms. "I made it very clear to him that if he hurt you, in any form, I'd march back to that inn and rip his throat out."

The laughter rolled through me, there was no stopping it as I clutched my stomach. The sheer thought of Aurora saying those words to Maddox ignited hysteria. I couldn't imagine what he must've been thinking. For a petite woman like Aurora to threaten an immortal creature without even realizing that's what she was doing.

But she joined me in the laughter anyway and it was several moments before we finally calmed down. I cherished the moment, because I knew my moments with her were running short. I only had a week left before the wedding, and I'd be gone. I pushed the thought away and stood as she helped me into the dress, so she could work on alterations.

"He's even more handsome up close, you know." She mused as she watched me.

I rolled my eyes. She didn't know the half of it. Of what I did. And in that moment, I realized just how much I needed to get that confession off my chest, to air out what I'd done to a trusted friend's ears.

"I asked Maddox to sleep with me."

If she'd been eating or drinking, she would have choked. She almost did, on air alone. "What?" Her hand melded to her chest, eyes wide.

I turned to fully face her. "I was drunk. I begged him, Aurora. It's mortifying."

She hardened. "Did...he?"

I waved my hand. "Gods no, thankfully." I could almost see the weight lift from her shoulders. "He refused, he said he wouldn't do it when I was drunk."

A wicked smile lit her face. "That sounds like he's considered it."

"Aurora!" I hissed.

She shrugged. "He clearly has an attraction toward you. He wouldn't have so quickly helped us if he didn't."

I considered it, but shook my head. "Surely, a man like him would already have someone he cared about somewhere else."

She cocked her head. "Clearly not. What married, or whatnot, man would spend so much time with a woman if he wasn't attracted to her?"

"If that was the case, don't you think he would've done something by now?"

She laughed, actually laughed, at that. "Evaline." She said incredulously. "You're not exactly the most approachable person."

I crossed my arms, but any rebuttal I had died on my lips. I knew she was right. I lowered my eyes.

"He wouldn't want to be with someone like that, like me. I'm cold inside, hard."

Aurora reached forward and grasped my arm. "No. You're not." I met her eyes. "You had something awful and horrifying happen to you, so you protect yourself. But that doesn't mean you can't be soft, too." Then she shrugged. "Or that someone who is hard wouldn't be worthy of love, for that matter."

There was a beat of silence between us.

"If you feel something for him, maybe you shouldn't marry Bassel." Her voice was quiet. "If you love Maddox, if you feel something for him, which is so blatantly obvious, if he loves you, you shouldn't marry Bassel. You should run."

I gulped, the lump in my throat hard and unyielding. "That's not possible."

I was in the bath when I heard my aunt's voice in my room, heard rustling of paper. I toweled off and slipped into a robe, and entered the bedroom to see boxes littering my bed.

"Hello, Evaline." She remarked, her voice tight.

"Hello..." Not only was my bed covered, but the chaise by the fireplace, the armoire, my vanity. Every space that wasn't the floor covered in decorative boxes, heaps of tissue paper peaking out of them. "What is all this?"

She lifted silk fabric from the box in her hands. "Some upgrades to your closet. Some dresses, some pajamas."

I nodded and moved forward, reaching into a box on the chaise. It was lacy, and frilly, and see through.

The breath choked from my lungs and I swung toward her. "Pajamas?"

She shrugged. "These are the pajamas married women have to wear." Gone was the concern she'd had for this aspect of marriage when she'd warned me in the library.

She spent the rest of the evening folding them delicately into my armoire and I knew it was to keep an eye on me.

By the time training was supposed to start, and Maddox and Wyott should've arrived, she was still in the room. I prayed to the Gods that they had enough foresight to listen before they came up.

They did, and when she left it was only a matter of minutes before they popped through the window.

"Finally, the Lady is ready." Wyott said as he strolled toward me, picking up one of the boxes that still had clothes in it.

I ripped the box away from him before he could see what was inside and rolled my eyes. "I am not a Lady."

He shrugged. "Could've fooled me. Gifts littering your room, living in a castle, hiding a dagger underneath all your pretty dresses. Sounds like a Lady to me."

Maddox just laughed beside him, and my eyes drew to the sound. Aurora's words filled my mind, but I pushed them aside.

"What's the plan for tonight?"

Maddox watched as I kneaded my hands together in front of me. "I think it's time we talk about what we might run into outside of the walls." I nodded. "Bandits, wolves, bears, and Vasi."

My stomach churned and I swallowed the fear surging within me. "My father always told me they usually didn't come this far inland." I shrugged. "But that clearly wasn't the case for us."

Maddox and Wyott exchanged a look, and he shook his head. "That was the case, but not anymore. I'm not sure what that Vasi was doing this far inland, but they've been seen on the mainland nearing mortal cities at the highest frequency in the last few hundred years."

I looked between them. "Why? And when? Recently?"

"We don't know why, but it started about two years ago and hasn't stopped." Wyott answered this time. "We just know they leave bodies in their wake."

I swallowed at the recollection of the Vasi's body on the ground after I'd decapitated him.

"What happens if we run into them?" I kept my gaze locked on Maddox.

"We kill them, on sight." He said firmly. That's what I hoped he'd say. "In all my years, I've never met a decent Vasi, and I'm not going to hesitate to gauge their innocence, when I have you to think about. I won't jeopardize your life." The words covered me, sliding over my skin as they reverberated through my head. "We fight first."

I nodded. "We're going to practice killing a Vasi tonight?"

"Yes. Are you ready?" He asked and I nodded. I moved closer to him, about to take off the long robe that I wore over my linen pants and shirt. "Leave your robe on." He threw over his shoulder as we walked to the center of my room. "It simulates a cloak, and you need to practice what it's like to fight with all that extra fabric on."

"Okay."

He turned and faced me, reaching to pull my dagger from its holster, his fingers sliding over the length of my thigh as he did so. I shivered and his eyes lifted to mine. I stayed silent as he brandished the dagger between us.

"There's only two ways to kill Vasi or Kova." I nodded, my father had told me about them.

"Cutting off their head or ripping out their heart." I whispered.

He nodded. "Obviously ripping out the heart is usually something other Kova or Vasi do, since we're the ones who are strong and fast enough to do it without being killed first. So you should focus on decapitation."

I was going to say something then, to let him know that I'd already done it. But he came up behind me, moving my hair forward to rest on my chest, exposing my neck, and all thoughts evaporated at his touch.

"Do it from behind. This will be the safest way, because it'll be harder for them to reach you."

I just nodded as he reached his arm around me. He held my dagger in his hand and laid the cool metal along the side of my neck.

"From here, cut. Deep. And keep pulling until you feel the spine. Don't stop and don't hesitate." His words were urging and quiet in my ear. "Hold their hair."

His hand slipped into mine, at the nape and I shivered.

"So that when you get through the spine you can use it as leverage to pull the knife through the rest of the way."

He tried to keep his voice even, but I noticed the way he pushed his body into mine as he spoke. He moved away from me then and I released the breath I'd been holding.

"That's just with a small dagger though." He said, handing me my dagger back. I sheathed it. "With a sword, you'll want to have a powerful swing and do it in one blow, the sword's length away." I nodded. "Are you ready to practice?"

Wyott was watching us from the chaise. I looked between them and pursed my lips.

"I'm happy to practice." I started, of course the first time I'd done it had likely been a fluke. "But you should probably know that I've already done this."

I couldn't say the words, that I'd sliced my dagger through the neck of the Vasi who had bitten me, but I saw the dawn of realization in Maddox's eyes as he took a step closer to me.

"You're the one who killed that Vasi?" He asked, his words soft.

I nodded, brows furrowing. "I didn't have much of an option. My father was incapacitated."

Maddox's eyes slid to Wyott, who looked equally as surprised.

"Evaline that is…" Maddox shook his head. "I've never heard of a human killing a Vasi one on one."

I stayed silent, allowing them to digest this information as they needed.

"How did you do it?" Wyott asked, sharing another look with Maddox.

I shrugged. "He was biting me." At the words Maddox stiffened. "Then my father came up behind him and attacked his back. His focus broke for a moment, and I jumped on him." I raised my hand toward Maddox. "I did the same strategy you just showed me, it's what my father taught me, too. But I did it from the front, and I climbed on top of him."

Maddox just raised his brows and shook his head. "That is very impressive." His praise was kind, and stirred something within me, but I couldn't take much pleasure in it. It wasn't a night I liked to remember, and Maddox seemed to understand that.

"But I can't imagine how frightening it was." He reached for my hand and held it gently. "I'm sorry you had to go through that alone." He whispered, and I knew he meant all of it. The whole night, including watching my father die. He pulled out one of his sparring swords. "Can we still practice? It'd make me feel better."

I nodded.

He pulled another for himself and backed a few strides away from me.

I blocked his swing and we launched into a spar as quietly as we could. It ended with both of our swords at kill shots. Mine at his neck and his at my gut.

"You're too close." He whispered. He was right, I wasn't using the full length of the sword to keep him away from me, I'd bent my arms and come in closer to land the sword where I wanted it.

We continued like that for some time before Wyott jumped up.

"Okay, my turn."

A smile widened on my lips as he strode toward me, excited to spar with him for the first time.

We clashed until my arms grew tired, and Maddox called it a night. As they strode to the window he threw one last concerned glance at me.

"Are you okay?"

I nodded, a smile on my face. The activity had lifted my spirits.

Wyott turned to me, too. "You did pretty good, but it's unfortunate we couldn't practice decapitation with melons or something. It's not perfect, but it would've been the closest we got to the real thing."

A wicked smile lit my face and I cocked my head. "You mean the closest thing, besides practicing on you two?"

His face fell. "Now, why do you have to say things like that? It's incredibly unsettling."

But I just laughed.

CHAPTER FORTY-TWO

Maddox

Wyott and I spent most of the next day gathering supplies for the journey.

We bought an extra canteen so we'd all three carry our own, even though they were all for Evaline. We bought dried fruits, and an extra satchel for her, since I doubted that she owned one. By the time we made our way to the blacksmith's shop the sun was beginning its dip under the clouds.

"Good evening, boys." He said, as we walked in. I wondered if he'd miss us when we were gone, what with how much money Wyott and I had spent between the two of us.

"Hi Marshall." I offered as we approached the counter of his store. The back door behind him opened up into his workshop, and I could smell the waves of heated metal wafting in between the cracks in the walls. "We were in the neighborhood and wanted to stop by."

He nodded and looked behind me to where Wyott already began browsing his merchandise. I could've rolled my eyes, he certainly didn't need anymore weaponry, but he wasn't the sort to walk out of a metal shop empty handed.

Then Marshall's eyes flicked back to mine. "I'm glad you stopped in, actually. I finished your project early."

He bent and pulled out a heap of leather, folded in on itself, and set it on the table. Wyott was beside me in an instant.

Marshall slowly removed each flap of the leather wrapping, exposing the beautiful obsidian colored dagger it held.

"Fuck." Wyott breathed.

It was gorgeous, and exactly what I asked for.

"It was difficult at first, learning how this foreign metal works, but I made it work." Marshall started, bringing his hands over his work of art. "This curving was difficult but I think it came out beautifully." He said, his hand hovering over the cross-guards. "And the blade itself is strong, I tested it multiple times. It shears everything from hide, to meat, to bone." He laughed. "I even tried it with metal armor and chains, it slices right through with enough force."

I smiled. "Thank you so much. It's everything I asked for and more."

His eyes beamed with the compliment, the face of a man who found pride in his work.

Wyott crossed his arms. "Now I want one."

I rolled my eyes and turned to him. "No. This is a one of a kind piece, and you already have enough weapons."

He rolled his eyes too and sulked off, mumbling under his breath. I handed Marshall the purse and he shook his head as it fell into his hand.

"This is too much." He said after feeling the weight of it.

I held a hand up. "Nonsense, not only is this a beautifully made dagger, but it's going to be protecting the most important person in my life, so it's worth every coin and more."

He just smiled at me and nodded. "Thank you."

After we left, one of the few times Wyott had done so empty handed, we headed back to the inn.

We both heard my stomach growl.

"Maddox, what the fuck." His expression was stern. "You still haven't fed?"

I ignored him as we walked.

"It's been over four weeks since the last time. You need to feed."

I sighed. "I tried, a couple weeks ago."

He shook his head. "What do you mean you tried? There isn't any 'try' in feeding, you either do or you don't." He waved his hand. "And don't give me any of this bullshit that you couldn't get it down. I know it's unpleasant, gross even, but you have to get over it —"

I spun toward him. "It's not unpleasant." I hissed. "It's not even gross, it's impossible."

He narrowed his eyes. "What does that even mean?"

I wiped a hand down my face. "It means that I tried to feed from two different humans, and both of their blood felt like I was drinking fire. It burned all the way down. I had to choke it up and spit it out to get the feeling to go away."

His face paled.

I threw my hands. "Say something. You had so much to say about my eating habits a few seconds ago."

Wyott's hands came up to rest on the hilts of his swords on each hip. "I've never heard of that before." He said lightly, shaking his head. "But it doesn't sound normal."

I scoffed. "No shit."

I turned and we started walking again.

"You have to feed from her then, Maddox."

My eyes cut to him. "You know I can't do that, Wyott. Not right now, not when she just started opening up to me. I can't tell her we're mates yet. She'd implode."

He sighed as the light trickling out of the inn appeared a few hundred yards ahead. The inky black of the night creeping in.

"If you don't feed soon, you're going to be too weak. You're going to start getting even more irritable than normal, you're going to get weaker, you could even snap and lose control."

"I know the risks." My voice was low and lethal.

When a Kova waited too long between feedings they ran the risk of going feral. Of draining a human dry and making the transition to a Vasi, their eyes turning red and their soul marred for life, never the same.

I took a breath. "I won't let it get that far, I promise."

We stopped in front of the inn, pausing before going inside.

"You better keep your word, because I won't watch you go through that when the solution is literally beside us." We were best friends, and I knew he meant the words as he said them.

"I promise." I looked down. "And I need you to make one, too."

He cocked his head in question.

"If something happens to me somewhere along the way." I shook my head. "With all these Vasi sightings…" My words trailed off.

"I'll take care of her." His voice was sad as he said the words.

"Please. You have to get her to Rominia, if they kill me. Even if they take me alive, you are to run. Leave me behind and get her home, safe."

He swallowed, and I knew it went against every part of him to promise such a thing. "I promise."

CHAPTER FORTY-THREE

Evaline

The wedding was four days away. With each hour that passed, taking me closer to the ceremony, I felt like I was being buried deeper in the sand that counted down the minutes. I tried to ignore my anxiety as I spent the day with Aurora and Jacqueline for the last time.

My aunt didn't know they came to the castle as my friends. She thought they were only around to work on the wedding gown with me. When I left Kembertus, I didn't want her questioning them about me, they'd have nothing to do with it.

We made the most of our time, knowing it would be the last that we'd spend together for, potentially, the rest of our lives. We reminisced on the last year of our friendship. We laughed about the lengths my aunt was going to for this wedding. We drank the wine I'd requested from the kitchen, and this time I paid attention to how much.

Aurora practically burst with the news that she'd received that morning from Neomaeros, that Lady Margot herself sent — they'd be honored to review her business inquiry in one month's time. It would give her plenty of time to prepare for the shop opening next summer.

I could've cried at the news, and eventually we all did. We cried over the distance that would mar our lives, the difficulties in communicating we'd face. But we didn't say goodbye, not as they left my room. We'd do that at the wedding, and I wanted to put off the finality for as long as I could.

After they left, though, I was a wreck, crying into my pillow and rubbing my swollen eyes. I'd fought for so long to leave this place, but now that the time was quickly approaching, I began to realize how many people there were that I truly loved. Jacqueline, Aurora, Priscilla, Megin… I couldn't bear to think about life without them, but the thought of what their lives would be like after I did what needed to be done was painful.

I sat up in my bed. I couldn't stay in the castle any longer. It had only been a week of being cooped up in this room, but it was enough. Therese be damned, I was leaving. It was late enough anyway, deep into the night, and I didn't think she'd come check on me. She hadn't at all since she'd locked me away. Probably afraid of another screaming match.

I quickly dressed in my boots, pants, a long-sleeved tunic that fell to hide the dagger I strapped to my thigh. I threw my hair quickly into my braid, weaving in the wire as I went, and was headed for the window within minutes.

I scaled the castle wall and took the long route to my father's grave. I needed to see it one last time before I left, and I didn't know if I'd get another opportunity before the wedding. I ran through the woods to that side of town, sure to keep my footfalls as light as I could and my breathing quiet.

As I reached his grave, I fell in front of it, trying to keep myself as low as possible. I didn't anticipate anyone walking through the cemetery at this time of night, but you could never be too careful. I didn't love being out in the dark, unless it was the quick trip to a training session, but I felt safe with Maddox and Wyott. Here, I was sitting out in the open waiting for anyone to stumble upon me.

But as soon as I sat and looked at the glass casing on the grave, I realized why I'd wanted to come so badly. The locket my father used to wear with the painting of my mother inside was the only remaining piece of her that I had. I couldn't leave Kembertus without it.

I began pulling at it, but the late-night dew that rested on the glass made my hands slip clean off.

"Gods-dammit." I hissed. I pulled my sleeves up over my wrists and hands, doing my best to dry the glass off.

I pulled at it again, but still had no luck. I pulled my dagger out, turning it in my hand so that the butt of the blade angled down. I slammed it into the glass once.

Gods, that was too loud.

And still nothing. Not even a crack in the glass.

What was this thing made of, diamonds?

I tried once more but then gritted my teeth. This was definitely too loud. Anyone walking by would come looking to see what was going on. I huffed and re-sheathed my dagger, raising my head to look around me. Still no one, thankfully.

I sat back and looked at my father's headstone. Running my fingers over the engravings, as I always did when I visited. I knew I shouldn't speak out loud so as not to be caught, so I projected my thoughts at him.

It's happening, Pa. I'm finally leaving. Just a few days, and with a Kova no less. I smiled. *He says he knew you, and I hope that's true. But he hasn't given me any reason not to trust him yet.*

A flutter went through my chest at the thought that I did trust Maddox, implicitly. I turned my thoughts back to the headstone.

You were right. He's good. I don't know where I'll end up, but it'll be somewhere better than here. And if Maddox and Wyott opt to stick with me, it'll be safer, too.

I laughed to myself at the idea that this could really happen. I could really leave, finally, and get my freedom. I could travel with Maddox and Wyott, who had become my friends in the last month, and I could only laugh at the irony that I'd been afraid to listen to my father's advice. After his death, after my bite, I'd sworn that any bloodthirsty creature I came upon would meet my blade if I had anything to say about it. But in reality, here I was. About to run off into the woods with two of them.

The smile on my face was wiped off as I heard a noise somewhere behind me. A scuffle of some sort. I ducked behind the stones surrounding me and peered around their sides.

Please, Gods, no. I prayed, because the same feeling of dread washed over me as the night Bassel and Lonix attacked me.

"We know you're here, kitten. We heard you giggling." I froze as the familiar, drunken, voice of Bassel floated to me.

How? My heart thudded faster as I asked the Gods. *How could this happen twice?*

And for that matter, how had I been so stupid to come out here in the middle of the night?

I gritted my teeth and recalled the dagger on my thigh. I unsheathed it silently, and began moving. They were behind me somewhere, more than just Bassel by the sound of the footsteps, and I was closer to the forest. If I could crawl between the headstones, I'd make it there. Then I'd be covered enough to sprint back to the castle.

I began to move, weaving in and out of the headstones as quietly as I could.

"Come out and play." Another voice slurred and I swallowed. What was it with men and their liquor making them become animals?

I crawled faster, I only had three rows of stones left before I made it to the short span of grass, before the cover of trees. I heard a noise behind me, closer than I thought they'd be, and looked back while I crawled.

It was a mistake, because I didn't see the vase of flowers sitting at the base of a headstone when my hand jostled it, sending it reeling sideways. I turned and watched as it slammed into the headstone. There wasn't enough force to shatter it, but enough to cause a loud thunk that reverberated through the painfully quiet night.

"Over here!" One man hissed, a different voice again.

He was close, and I heard all their footsteps bounding toward me. I didn't have a choice now as I stood up and began running toward the trees, vaulting over headstones and weaving through others. I was so close, and I knew these woods better than the ones I was in the first time

Bassel attacked me. If I made it to them, I'd be safe, there was no denying that. I knew exactly what trees to dodge and what logs fell where. My heart ravaged in my chest. Three more strides and I was free.

One.

Two.

The wind was knocked out of my chest as a man caught me, turning and slamming my back into a tree. I gasped for air, my dagger fell from my hand at the impact, and I began thrashing. But in an instant another man was there too, and both pushed me up against the trunk, one on either side.

"What a turn our night has taken." The one on the left breathed.

"And here we were thinking we'd be alone out here." The man on the right snickered. "But now the night has gotten much, much more fun."

"Who do we have here?" Bassel said as he came closer, and I saw the way he swayed from the effects of the booze. When he saw me, a smile lit his face. That same, cruel smile, he'd given that night. "Everline!" He slurred my name in surprise, mispronouncing it.

My jaw clenched at the realization that, once again, Bassel had simply stumbled upon me, alone, in the middle of the night. The Gods had a sick sense of humor.

He came closer and closed the small circle around me that he and his friends made.

"This is my betrothed! Isn't she lovely?" He asked the others. They all reeked from liquor.

He reached forward and stroked the back of his hand over my cheek.

"She certainly is." The one on my right purred and I felt his hand on my braid, tugging only the bottom tail of it, no thorns reaching there to ward him off.

"What a shame that we can't have our fun with her." The one on my left crooned, his hand tightening over my arm and shoulder. He turned to Bassel. "Unless you aren't attached?"

I could only watch as I tried desperately to form a plan. I could knee the one on my right in the groin and bend, maybe getting enough space to grab the dagger that sat at my feet, and while he bent, slit the one on my left's throat. Saving Bassel for last, making him watch what his betrothed was capable of.

And the blood in my veins warmed, surged, preparing each muscle and each ligament for battle. My heart raced. But I couldn't move, the fear holding an icy grip around my throat until I couldn't speak at all.

"Oh boys." Bassel said as he too stepped forward. "You know I'm the sharing type." He crooned. "But we have to keep her face pretty, the wedding is this weekend."

And he was on me, pushing me closer into the tree, my arms pinned there and the ache in my wrist rising to remind me what he'd already done to my body once. I shook with fear as they surrounded me, in the same position I had been two years ago when it was only Bassel and Lonix.

Silent tears flowed down my cheeks as I could only watch. Couldn't even tell them no, frozen in fear. There was no way I could fight off three of them, not really. All the training in the world with Maddox would never allow me the skill to fight three grown men, drunk or not, while the trauma from that night shook through me.

I closed my eyes as I felt their breath on my face, tried to ignore the disgusting words they said and the threats they made. The plans they had for the future in Vestaria, where Bassel assured them that they could have more fun than they would tonight. The tears flowed faster as I escaped into my mind, thinking of every good thing that'd ever happened to me, unable to go through this a second time.

But instead of recalling morning horse rides with my father, or the laughing fits I'd had with Aurora and Jaqueline only hours before, gray eyes filled my mind. And the crinkles around them when he smiled. The black hair that adorned his head, and the dusting of it that covered his chin, the curve in his nose. I thought of those pouted lips that I wish I had kissed when I had the chance and how he'd spun me when we danced.

I felt the hands of the drunken men grip me tighter, one falling to my waist.

But in my head I was back in Maddox's room, at the inn, the night I was drunk. He was pulling me in, until I was completely in his arms, protected there. And the more I thought of him, the clearer the image became. The more I pushed into my mind for the sound of his voice, the feel of his skin, the smell of him washing over me, the more it felt like I was in front of him, sitting on that bed with him.

So I reached forward, touching a hand to his face.

E…Evaline?

My eyes shot open at the sound of his voice in my head, so clear and so real it surprised me – shocked me so violently that it shook me from the cages of my mind. The fear paralyzing my body disintegrated as I pushed the hands away from me.

No. No. No. Stop! Get off of me. I shrieked, and it was a moment before I realized I said the words in my head, and it felt as though something stirred with them. But I ignored it as the grip of fear around my throat melted away until I was screaming out loud.

"No! Get away from me!"

And this time I didn't just think about fighting back. I pushed the one on my left off of me, affording myself a second to duck down to snatch my dagger from the ground before he pounced right back.

I gripped the dagger hard this time, brandishing it between the men as all three of their eyes widened. But based on the sneer's that twisted their faces, the sight of the weapon only infuriated them.

I struck to the right as I'd planned to, but before I could swipe for the other, he bent from the pain from my blow and swiped my arm along with him, dragging my weapon down. I tried to yank my arm up, to recover my only defense, but the distraction allowed the left one to push me harder into the tree.

"Please!" I screamed before my voice was cut off.

My breathing was choked against his grip, and against the panic rising in my mind. I kicked out wildly, landing a blow on Bassel who stumbled and slammed his head into a tree opposite us, sliding down the bark as he slumped, knocked out.

I couldn't relish the small victory as the other man recovered and stood again, grabbing for me. I swung out, trying to connect my blade or fist with anything at all. The man holding me tightened his grip on my throat and I choked, my hand flying for his face. I dug my fingers into his eyes and he screeched, pulling his head out of my reach.

A wheezing breath sounded and it took me a moment to realize it was mine, the edges of my vision began to prick with a fuzzy black cloud, shadows filled my peripheral. But I didn't stop flailing, even if I could hardly see anything anymore.

And as the last of my breath exited my lungs and my legs began to give out, I heard Maddox say my name again.

Only this time it wasn't in my head.

CHAPTER FORTY-FOUR

Maddox

"Evaline!" I screamed as I sprinted through the cemetery, vaulting headstones toward the sound of her ragged breathing.

But she didn't respond and as I ran closer, and saw her surrounded by multiple figures, I could see why. My blood boiled at the sight of the man's hand around her throat, the other pulling her dagger from her now limp hand.

They both whipped their heads to me and I didn't hesitate. I grasped the hair of the man holding her and slammed his head into the trunk of the tree. His skull crunched, and I let him drop.

I filled the space he'd occupied beside her, his grip on her throat being the only thing that had kept her standing. I slipped an arm around her waist, pulling her to me as I reached for her dagger in the other man's hand. He swiped it out, toward both of us. I couldn't defend myself as I shielded her with my body, protecting her from the blow. It landed in my side, the dagger digging deep. When I barely grunted, he looked up in shock, and I ripped her blade from my side and head butted him.

He hissed and stumbled back a few steps.

I felt her stir against me, coughing to clear her previously blocked airway, hands coming up to feel at her own throat.

In one move I sheathed her dagger back into its holster and turned her to face me, tilting her chin up to see her better.

"Are you okay?" I choked out. She just nodded, wide eyed.

We both turned at the sound of the man coming back, having recovered from the headbutt. I pushed her behind me and heard her sharp intake of breath at the sight of the man who lay, dead, behind us. But she stayed against me, hands fisting in the back of my shirt as I pulled out the hatchet at my side, sending it soaring through the air until it found its home in the approaching man's forehead.

He stopped and his eyes widened as the blood began pouring between them, in them. He fell to his knees, and then onto his side, dead.

Evaline shook behind me and I turned. My hands cupped her face, and she didn't pull away when my thumbs swiped her cheeks.

"What happened?"

Her eyes were still wide, she just shook her head, her mouth opened to speak but no words came out. Tears began to fall again, replacing the previous tracks down her cheeks with fresh saltwater.

But Bassel stirred, I'd almost forgotten I'd seen him there, slumped. I let go of her and stalked to him, picking him up by his collar and pushing him against the tree he sat at. His eyes fully took in the scene around us and he began to scream, but I covered his mouth. When I lowered my face, we locked eyes, and he shrunk back into the tree behind him. I knew he'd recognize a Kova's eyes if he ever got close enough to us, and the question of how much he knew about Kova, Vasi, rose within me. Letting go of his collar I dragged a dagger from the holster on my chest and placed it against his neck.

Evaline found her voice then. "Stop!" She hissed. I whipped my head back to her, waiting for her command. "He saved me." She proclaimed, but underneath my hold even he seemed surprised. I turned back to look at him, but she continued behind me. "He tried to stop them, and they knocked him out, that's when you showed up." Her voice was shaky, and her heart raced, and on any other day I'd take that as an indication of lying. Considering the circumstances, I didn't think her heart had stopped racing for a moment since she was attacked. I had no choice but to believe her, and as much as I wanted to gut him just for playing the role of her fiancé, I re-sheathed my dagger as she came to stand at my side again.

"Can't you just compel him to forget about all of this?" She whispered, her hand reaching to touch mine and Bassel desperately shook his head, eyes afraid.

I set my jaw against my instincts and turned to catch his eyes, capturing her hand in mine as I did so.

"You will forget this night ever happened. You will go back to your bed and go to sleep. All that you remember is going to the tavern and leaving early. On your walk home you hit your head, and that's where the injury came from." His eyes glazed over, and he nodded.

I felt her catch her breath beside me. I turned to look at her and then back to Bassel.

"You will kill any man who ever lays a hand on her against her will." He nodded and her grip on my hand tightened, I released him. He ran away, heading straight for the inn.

I took a deep breath as I turned to face her fully. "Are you okay?" I repeated my previous words and she nodded.

"I think so." She said, pulling her hand from mine and sliding them down her body, as if checking for injuries.

I shook my head and reached forward, a hand catching her cheek again.

"No." I started. "I mean are you okay?"

Realization flashed through her eyes as she understood what I meant. Her eyes shielded before me, her wall going back up as she nodded again.

She cleared her throat. "Yes, I'm okay." She said softly. "I just wanted to see my father's grave before I left. I wanted to take the locket with me. Sorry you had to save me."

I knew she hated it. The idea that I'd had to save her, that she didn't do it herself. I just smiled at her, my thumb coming up to swipe over her cheek. I took a mental note of the locket I'd have to get to her.

307 |

"You never have to be sorry for that." I shrugged, trying to lighten my tone. "Besides, if I hadn't come along, you would've done the job for me. I'm just selfish that way."

We both knew it was a lie, not because she wasn't capable of killing them, only because she'd been on the cusp of passing out from lack of oxygen. But the words did as I intended, and she snorted out a small laugh, her lips tucking up in a smile. She brought a hand up to hold my wrist.

"Thank you."

I nodded and dropped my hand from her face, letting my wrist slip through her grip until I was holding her hand in mine.

"We have to leave, before anyone sees the bodies."

She looked around, as if remembering for the first time that there were two dead men at our feet.

She eyed the one who'd held her throat, his skull cracked open as blood still spilled out. His eyes open and empty. Then she moved to the other, further down the path. His mouth hanging open and the ax still protruding from his skull.

I held my breath, afraid she'd be disgusted. Be upset with me for killing them, or worse yet, be scared of me. But she released my hand and strode forward until she was standing over the man with the hatchet protruding from his skull. Evaline reached down, one hand holding his skull as the other wretched the metal from his head.

My breath caught as she straightened and wiped the blade over her leg, the blood swiping off, and strode back to me, her eyes locked with mine the entire time.

She stopped in front of me and replaced the ax into its holster on my hip and looked up at me.

"Can't have a Mad Axe without his *hatchet*."

The laugh rumbled through my chest and I reached forward, slipping an arm around her and pulling her to my chest as if I'd done so a thousand times. I couldn't help the movement after the relief washed over me, not only that she was okay but that she didn't cringe at this violent side of me. She didn't pull back, just caught herself against me. One hand on my chest and the other falling to my side. She gasped and pulled that hand back, bringing it into her line of vision. My red blood coated her hand.

Her eyes shot to mine. "You're hurt."

I shrugged. "I don't care."

She narrowed her eyes and pulled me.

But she didn't aim for home, the castle. After peeking her head out to ensure we were unseen, she turned right, and headed to the inn. Wyott had been asleep when I left, and I hadn't woken him when I raced to find her. But as we walked up the stairs past a sleeping Nathaniel, Wyott stood with his arms crossed in front of my door, no doubt smelling the blood.

He regarded us for a moment.

Evaline and I walked down the hall, her grip was tight on my hand as she tugged me along. I was fine, but she insisted we get a better look at the wound.

"What the *fuck* happened to you two?" He said as his eyes landed on the blood staining my shirt.

"Oh, wouldn't you like to know." She hissed at him as she pulled me past him and into my room. "You know you talk a big game for someone who was nowhere to be found when the actual fighting took place."

She mocked him, but I knew under the light tone was a hint of actual concern.

He followed in behind us. "Well I was sleeping." Then he turned to face me. "Why didn't you wake me?"

She pushed me to sit on the chaise in front of the fire and I smiled at the dominance.

"She was being attacked at the cemetery, I heard her and went to help. There wasn't time." She listened while she gathered the pitcher of water from a side table and a towel from the bathing chamber.

His eyebrows rose. "You heard her?" We both knew my hearing didn't extend that far, not half a city away. But she didn't know that.

I nodded and met his eyes.

"I heard her." Through the bond.

His eyes widened with recognition and he just nodded. I flicked my eyes to the door, urging him to leave as she reappeared from the bathing chamber.

"Well, I can see you are both alive, so I guess I will go back to sleep."

He threw me a glance before he left, indicating that I'd have to tell him the whole story tomorrow, and shut the door behind him.

She crouched in front of me, and I opened my legs so she could kneel between them. She set the pitcher beside her and began pouring some on the cloth, then looked to me.

"Take off all those weapons." Then nodded her head to my chest, clearing her throat. "And your shirt."

I obliged silently, the only sound was the crackle of the fire and the thud of my sheathed weapons on the floor. Finally, I removed the shirt and threw it into the fire, it was too ruined to wear again. She cleared her throat as I did so, but her eyes weren't on the fire. They scanned my torso, my chest, my arms. So quickly any lesser creature wouldn't have caught it. I couldn't help the smile that pulled on my lips as I placed my hands behind me on the chaise, leaning back to give her better access to the wound. The movement seemed to shake her from her thoughts, and she straightened so that she was standing on her knees. She leaned forward and placed her long fingers beside my wound and I hissed.

Her eyes cut to me. "Oh the gaping wound in your side doesn't hurt but my hand next to it does?"

I chuckled and stared down at her position bent over my wound. "It doesn't hurt, your hands are just freezing."

She rolled her eyes and continued working. She dabbed the towel around the wound, cleaning the skin. I wanted to tell her that this was pointless, that it would be healed by the time I woke up, in the next few hours likely. But I quite liked watching her work. Especially when she was this close, on her knees and between mine. Plus, I'd already told her all of this on the walk.

"What happened?" I probed again; my voice quiet.

She paused and her eyes flicked up to mine before falling back as her hands started again.

"I snuck out to go see my father's grave. I spent my last day with my friends today and needed to get out of the castle." She shrugged. "The men wandered into the cemetery and found me. I tried to run but they caught me."

My hands fisted behind me.

"What did they do?" My voice was lethal.

"Not much. They didn't get far." Her voice was clipped, and I dropped that line of questioning.

"And Bassel helped?"

She swallowed and nodded. "Yes, but it didn't do anything. Then you showed up."

I considered her for a moment, but she stood then, grabbing a larger towel from the bathing room and coming back to kneel between my legs. She piled the towel beneath the wound and carefully poured the pitcher over it, cleaning any debris from the wound itself. The towel caught the excess water and she dried the rest around it. She shrugged, sitting back on her heels and setting the towel on the ground beside her.

"That's really all I can do without any supplies."

I smiled at her. "That's okay, you've done more than enough."

She took a deep breath and swept her braid off her shoulder, letting it fall onto her back.

The movement had my eyes falling to her neck, where the purple blemishes in the shape of a hand already bloomed. I was straightened in an instant, hands reaching for her. I tilted her head up gently with one hand, my other lightly trailing my fingers over the bruise. She hissed.

"You're hurt." I'd known he had been strangling her, but with how calm she'd been since then I didn't think it was this serious. Surely there was internal damage too. She cleared her throat again, and I realized that she'd been doing that since we left the cemetery. Guilt filled me as I realized she'd been in pain this entire time and had kept it from me.

"Eva." I whispered, my eyes roving the bruises marring her skin.

311 |

"It's fine." She whispered back, and I felt her eyes on me.

"It's not fine." I seethed, sliding down until I kneeled on the ground beside her. I moved toward the fire, pulling her with me. Using the light of the crackling flames to see the bruises clearly. My jaw clenched at the sight, and the bob of her throat. I was glad I'd killed him.

"How bad does it hurt?" She started to shake her head but I cut my eyes to her. "Don't lie. Not to me."

She shrugged instead. I lowered my head to meet her gaze. I searched her eyes, her face, for any indication of pain, but there wasn't any. A thumb absentmindedly swiped over her lower lip and her breath stopped at the move.

My voice was low as I spoke. "You don't have to be so strong all the time. Not with me."

"I get by just fine." She said just as soft.

I clenched my jaw and let my hands drop from her. I sat back on my own heels. "Let me heal you. It'll make the pain go away."

She looked at me warily. "You said you didn't have magical powers."

"I don't, but a Kova's blood can heal injuries."

She scoffed. "I am not drinking your blood, Maddox. That's disgusting."

I nodded. That was fair. "I know it sounds gross, but it'll just be for a minute, and you need to heal. There's internal damage. That's going to be painful for weeks if you don't."

Her eyes widened. "But the wedding is only a few days away, I can't walk around with a massive bruise on my neck. There's no way to hide it."

I reached for her hand. "Then let's leave tonight."

She pulled her hand away. "No."

My brows furrowed as I tried to wrangle my frustration. "Why?"

"I have unfinished business here; I can't leave until then."

I sighed. "Fine."

She cast her eyes toward the fire. "I can't have a massive bruise on my neck though. My aunt might postpone the wedding until it's healed."

I tilted my head. "If I knew another way to help you, to take the pain and the bruising away, I would. But I don't."

She considered another minute before sighing and nodding her head. "Okay." She said, meeting my eyes again.

I nodded and moved to stand but she caught my hands, stopping me. "Where are you going?"

I sat back down. "To get Wyott."

She scoffed. "For what?"

"Drinking blood from a Kova is very intimate." I didn't know any other way to put it.

She shook her head. "Even more reason for Wyott not to be here, that sounds incredibly awkward."

"You don't understand the way it'll feel for me." I pursed my lips. "It'll be hard to control myself. And I'm weakened right now."

I meant the lack of feeding, but her eyes fell to my wound. It certainly didn't help my situation, but it wasn't the main contributor to my weakening willpower.

"I can handle myself, Maddox." She said, her eyes raising to meet mine.

I hesitated. I didn't lie, it was intimate to drink from a Kova, but usually it could be overlooked. But a mate. That bond would make the moment infinitely more arousing.

"Are you sure?"

She nodded.

I sighed and pulled her dagger from her thigh, placing it in her hand. "Wha –?"

"In case you need to stop me."

CHAPTER FORTY-FIVE

Evaline

I watched as Maddox brought his wrist to his mouth, canines elongating in order to bite the flesh there. It was the first time I'd ever seen them. His teeth looked ordinary, like mine or any other human's, normally. But I watched, just as I had when the Vasi had bitten me, as the two sharp teeth simply lengthened, their points sharpening. I wondered if I should be afraid, if it would have been a normal reaction to shy away at the sight, after my own attack from another immortal with identical fangs. But I couldn't find any fear in me.

I only stared, my heart rattling in my chest. Maddox's eyes never left mine as he released. Blood stained his lips and he straightened his arm toward me.

I shifted to get a better angle on his wrist. I turned my back to the fire and slid into his grasp. He rested his other arm on his muscled thigh, and I did the same with my right hand that still held the dagger he'd pressed into it.

I clasped my left hand around his thick forearm, fingers unable to meet around it due to the sheer size of it.

"Remember, stab first. Ask questions later." He murmured low beside me and I snapped my narrowed eyes at him.

"Would you shut it? I get it. You're going to go feral. I don't need another reminder." This was awkward enough. Between my pounding heart in my ears and the heat radiating from both the fire, and his body, I could hardly stand to focus on anything but the task at hand.

His chuckle vibrated through where our skin met. "That's not what I'd call it, but yes, you get the point."

I looked back to his wrist and the blood that dribbled out of the wounds. I didn't know what was more alarming. That I was preparing to drink blood from someone, or that every fiber of my being was begging me to do it. Like this was the most natural thing I'd ever done. Like this was okay.

I took a deep breath and lowered my mouth over his skin, closing my eyes.

Maddox went still beside me. The first drops slid past my lips, and I awaited the foul taste. But instead, it tasted sweet. Like sugar and maple and spiced plums.

I took a long drag and he shivered with a moan. I'd never experienced anything like the sensation it gave me. As if the blood rushing past my lips, filling my mouth and sliding down my throat, was addictive. It was sweet, it was smooth. And I could immediately feel the healing magic of it warming my throat, my skin. The pain slipped away as I took another pull.

Maddox hissed and squeezed my hip. I didn't protest, lost in the intoxicating drug that was his blood. I did my best to inhale but didn't dare break my lips away.

Maddox pulled me closer, into his chest, so that I sat on his lap. My back pressed against his hard muscles. His wrist was still held against my mouth, but his other arm was wrapped around my abdomen, hand fanning out over my waist and rib cage.

I could spend the rest of my life trying to articulate the feel of his blood filling my stomach, seeping into my own veins, but I'd never do it justice.

It was the crackle in the air after a thunderstorm. It was the first sips of wine, when the buzz roved from the lips and through the rest of the body. It was falling asleep in the backyard as a child, warm air wrapping around you and rendering a blanket unnecessary.

I pulled my mouth from his wrist and laid my head back against his shoulder, taking a deep breath.

Gods.

"Eva." He whispered in my ear; his lips brushing the hair against it.

The dagger dropped from my hand and its clanging filled the room as I straightened again and pulled his wrist back to my lips, both of my hands holding him close. As my lips slipped over his skin he groaned and I felt his head fall forward, resting against the back of mine.

I could feel the stirring of something hard beneath me, feel the way he pushed against me. The movement curled something deep within and I moaned, the sound muffled by his arm.

Maddox growled and I felt his lips on the back of my neck. Felt his light kisses, the graze of his teeth gently against my skin. I moaned again, taking a drag as I felt his tongue against me.

"Eva." He groaned before I felt the hand that clung to my waist slide down, land on my thigh. I opened my legs without hesitation. The movement sent him shuddering, his voice husky in my ear. "My Eva."

I moaned in return, adoring the nickname for the first time since I'd known him, and took another drag. I felt his head nod through his lips on my shoulder, and for the first time realized he'd dragged the fabric down with his teeth.

His hand on my thigh was rising, so, so close to the core that had been aching for him, for Gods knew how long. His fingers trailed along my inner thigh, and I bit harder in anticipation.

Maddox growled and his lips were at my ear again. "Please." He choked out as his hand rose ever closer. His breath was hot on my ear, and I shivered against it, against his fingers on my leg. "Please."

I could only moan in response as I pulled another gulp from his wrist. His hand on my leg fanned out then, grasping at the inside of my thigh and my heart ravaged in my chest. Just a few more seconds and he'd be there, touching, and I'd let him, beg him to do so —

There was a loud bang, and I was ripped off of him.

"What the fuck is wrong with you?" Wyott's voice hissed above me. I felt his arm wrapped around my stomach, my feet off the floor.

I opened my eyes for the first time, my heart still racing in my chest and saw that I was clear across the room from Maddox.

He knelt in front of the fire, his chest heaving as his eyes, totally black, stared in mine. That coil deep within me wound tighter at the image of him there. Shirtless, breathless, staring at me with nothing less than lust. I bit my lip and watched as his eyes fell down my body, as his hands clenched into fists. Even from this distance I could feel the wave of want that swept from him.

"Maddox." Wyott hissed. Both Maddox and I jolted at the sound. Even with Wyott holding me, we'd forgotten he was there.

Maddox released me from the heat of his gaze. "I had it handled." His voice was rough as he glowered at Wyott.

Wyott carried me to the bed, setting me on it as he moved to Maddox, dropping onto one knee and evaluating his friend.

"The fuck you did. She could've drained you Maddox, and you almost let her."

The words shook through me. "What?" My voice was quiet across the room.

They both turned to look at me. "I said you almost drained him dry, he's already weak. You could've killed him." Wyott hissed at me.

My face paled and I leaned to meet Maddox's gaze around Wyott's shoulder.

"Is that true?"

Maddox took a breath and shook his head. "I'm fine." But it was his turn to lie about his injuries.

Wyott hissed and shoved a water pitcher into Maddox's hand. "At least drink this, since you won't drink anything else." Maddox took the ceramic and guzzled it down, but not before giving Wyott a pointed look.

"I'm going to go find you something to eat, it'll be better than nothing." Wyott said and then turned to face me. "Don't do that again. Not in his condition."

I just nodded and he closed the door behind him.

Maddox finished the pitcher and threw it onto the chaise beside him. He looked up at me and smiled, raising his uninjured hand. "Come here."

I listened, walking over to him and placing my hand in his. He lightly tugged and I fell onto his lap, my legs on either side of his hips. His arm curled around my back and I wrung my hands between us.

"Why didn't you tell me to stop?" My voice barely above a whisper.

He smiled and pushed my hair away from my face. "I told you I'd have a hard time controlling myself."

I furrowed my brows. "Control yourself from attacking me. You didn't tell me you wouldn't be able to push me off when you needed me to stop."

He lowered his injured hand to brush his fingers along my throat, eyes roving the skin that I knew no longer bore bruises.

"It was worth every moment." The sound of his voice moved something within me, and I grasped the hand on my neck to survey the damage of his wrist.

Two pin pricks of blood sat there, droplets falling away. Instinct moved me forward until I'd swiped my tongue over the two points. Maddox just watched me, his arm around my back curling tighter, but when I pulled away both of our eyes fell to his wrist and watched as the dots healed. I gasped and looked to Maddox, who looked equally surprised, but his voice was level as he shrugged.

"I told you I heal quick."

I just nodded and let go of his wrist, facing him fully. "Are you okay?"

He nodded. "I'm fine." I sighed, knowing he was lying. He chuckled. "Isn't it frustrating when someone lies about their pain?"

I narrowed my eyes. "That's not fair, I didn't nearly die."

He rolled his eyes. "Wyott was being dramatic, I didn't almost die."

A breath shuddered through me from relief. "Are you okay?" I repeated.

He reached forward and kissed my forehead. "Yes." He whispered. "I just need some rest. Let Wyott take you home when he gets back. I'll see you for our last training session before our departure."

Wyott opened the door then, a tray of food in his hand. He narrowed his eyes at us, gauging whether I'd fed off Maddox again. But I just stood and Maddox did the same. Wyott led him to the table to eat and rest, and I followed him out of the room.

CHAPTER FORTY-SIX

Evaline

My heart raced through my chest as I paced around my room, waiting for Maddox and Wyott to come to my window for the last training session before we left. I'd felt uneasy since I'd left Maddox the other night. And the trip home with Wyott hadn't made it any easier. The entire walk to the castle he remained silent. Not speaking to me, hardly even looking at me, as we walked.

The guilt rose in my throat and I tried to speak, but the lump that'd formed made it impossible. So instead, when we got to the castle wall below my window, and he'd turned toward me, expecting me to jump onto his back, I pulled away and scaled the wall myself. I heard him curse below me, but I didn't care. If he couldn't give me the benefit of the doubt that I didn't intentionally hurt Maddox, then I wouldn't ask for his help.

But as I waited to see them, to see Maddox, that same unease shifted through me. It wasn't because I was uncomfortable, or upset, or hurt. It was from the confusion plaguing my mind. Maddox had refused to touch me before, but now everything was different.

Not only that, no man had ever made me feel this way before, and it'd begun to get to me. Because I wished he'd just tell me if he had some sort of affection for me. Gods knew I'd never make the first move. For all I knew, he was just one of those men who showered every woman they came across with affection. I'd look pathetic if I confessed any sort of attraction to him, just for him to reject me. Then how would I get out of Kembertus?

I swallowed the concern that skulked up my throat and whipped to the window as I heard a noise. My eyes shot around the room but wound up back at the window where only Wyott stood. Dismay rolled through me, but I said nothing as I watched him walk closer.

He raised his head and I met his eyes. "Maddox is at home, resting. There's no use in him coming here and wasting energy when he needs to focus on gaining it back."

I just nodded and cast my eyes down.

"I'm sorry, Wyott." I said, moving to sit on the chaise in front of the fire.

He sighed and came to sit beside me, grabbing my hands and pulling them into both of his. I met his eyes. "You don't need to be sorry; you didn't know. And I shouldn't have taken it out on you." Another breath. "It's just that Maddox can't think clearly when it comes to you, and he put himself in danger when he offered his blood to you without anyone there to ensure you stopped when you'd healed, and didn't take any more than necessary."

I shook my head. "I told him not to get you, he tried. But he told me it was to protect me, not him. And I thought it would be mortifying, even more so if you were there. So I told him no. But that's only because I thought it was for my benefit, not his."

He nodded and his eyes softened. "I know." He let go of my hands, moving them to hang toward the fire and sat back. "You can trust him, you know." He said, swinging his face to the side, toward me.

I nodded, staring into the fire. "I know, I do."

He shook his head. "No, not just with your life. With everything. You can trust him with everything."

I clenched my jaw at the words and considered for a moment if Kova possessed some ability to read minds considering my whirling thoughts before he'd gotten here.

I pursed my lips and nodded.

He seemed to get the hint and switched the conversation to our plan. He'd obviously discussed it with Maddox, but wanted to iron out the last details before the wedding came the day after tomorrow.

"I will wait over the wall, just to make sure it's safe. Maddox will wait just inside the wall, past our usual training spot. You'll come join us when the bell tower chimes its fifth ring." I nodded. Five o'clock is what I'd told them, but I knew it wasn't true. But how could I tell them to wait a few more hours until I had the chance to kill Bassel? Especially since they knew he was the future ruler of one of the kingdoms.

I knew it was a gamble, to stand them up for our meeting time, but I didn't have any other choice. I'd have to hope they'd wait for me, that they wouldn't abandon the plan once they'd realized that I was hours late. But after Maddox had adamantly asked so many times to confirm that the wedding wasn't going to happen, I couldn't very much tell him that it was, and ask them to wait for me.

"We'll have to travel overnight in order to get far enough ahead of them that they won't be able to catch us." He turned to meet my eyes. "That means you will be severely fatigued."

"What about Maddox? You said he's already weak?"

He shrugged. "He's fine now, still weak in terms of Kova strength, but far superior to any mortal who might try to stop us. He'll rest tomorrow too and should be almost fully recovered, apart from needing to feed."

I nodded. I assumed he'd do that before we left, and then he'd be fine.

We spent the rest of the evening sparring with fists and daggers. I took him down a few times, he took me down a few more times. He wasn't as fast as Maddox, but what Maddox had in speed, Wyott had in strength. And for a moment I considered what they might be like working together on the battlefield. Every now and then I'd be concerned that someone would hear us, but he assured me that he couldn't hear anyone around my room.

When he headed for the window I realized this would be our last time training in Kembertus. I felt the nostalgia already floating over me, but pushed it away. He swung a leg out the window, that goofy grin that usually adorned his face reappearing.

"See you in two days, my Lady."

I rolled my eyes, but the smile was on my face. I felt relieved that he wasn't upset with me anymore. "I'm not a Lady."

He nodded in understanding. "Ah, yes. Of course. Not a Lady." He turned to start exiting the window, then threw over his shoulder. "Just the bride."

CHAPTER FORTY-SEVEN

Maddox

I groaned from the fullness in my abdomen and from the feeling of being cooped up. I threw the tray across the room, having finished it, finally. It landed among all the others Wyott had made me eat in the day, to recover since Evaline fed on me, the small pile of them beginning to heap next to the door. Of course, he knew it didn't offer the same effect blood would, but it did provide some nutrition, which, like he'd said in front of Evaline the other day, was better than nothing.

I growled in annoyance. Wyott was my best friend, but I was beginning to think he'd forgotten that he wasn't my father.

I was upset with him for scaring Evaline like that. I'd hardly spoken to him since he'd taken her home that night. But my ears perked when I heard him enter the inn, because I knew he was coming back from training with her.

I was still annoyed at that too, that he insisted I stay here instead of go to see her. Because I'd told her I'd be there. But I knew it was likely best that I not waste any energy on that when we did have such a long journey.

I felt fine, I truly did. I'd rested and eaten enough to refuel myself; it just took longer than it should have. I felt back to normal, just as I'd felt when I'd crushed the skull of the man who'd strangled her. But I didn't have time to let that upset me again, because Wyott was strolling into my room.

"Are you done sulking, yet?" He sat across from me.

"Are you?" I asked.

He rolled his eyes. "Fine, I apologize. I didn't mean to scare Evaline, but I was scared." He said, leaning forward. "You almost willingly walked off the cliff without so much as a rope. I should've been here, and you know it."

I nodded and sighed. "I realize that now, yes, you should have been here." I shook my head. "But at the time, she seemed so disgusted by the thought, and with the way blood tastes to humans, I figured it'd be a task on its own just to ensure she drank enough to heal herself. Not that she'd devour it."

Wyott leaned back in his chair again. "You two are quite odd."

I rolled my eyes. "Thanks."

He shook his head. "No, I don't mean it like that. Just that you're abnormal. First of all, I've never heard of a Kova's mate being non-Kova, so that in and of itself is strange. But to her, the blood should have been disgusting, but it certainly didn't seem that way." He paused, staring at the ground. "When I walked in, Maddox, the two of you curled into each other like that. Her mouth on your skin…she enjoyed it. And I don't just mean the feeling of the magic from the blood healing her, but I mean she savored the taste."

I nodded. I knew this too, all of it. We were not a normal pairing, and thus everything that had happened since was not normal. Her affinity for my blood, abnormal strength and speed, my inability to drink from anyone else since I'd met her.

He shrugged, standing to leave. "You need to consider telling her, very soon. You need to feed, and if she isn't freaked out from feeding from you, surely she wouldn't freak out if you fed from her." He walked toward the door and turned to face me, waving a hand over the pile next to the door. "I'll send someone to clean this up." Then he turned his eyes to me.

"And you're officially off bed rest." His eyes flashed. "Don't do anything stupid."

I was out my door before I heard his own door shut. I wanted to go see her, but knew she'd likely already be asleep after her training with Wyott.

We wouldn't be here much longer, and I didn't want to risk not getting it in time. I went straight to the cemetery, straight to Wallace's grave.

I knelt in front of it and rested a hand on top of the stone. "My friend, I hope you'll forgive me for not being here to stop her attack completely." I said, referring to the last time I'd been here. "But I will do my best to stop every other in the future."

I grasped the glass casing that held the locket and twitched my wrist, the glass seal breaking off the stone immediately. I plucked the locket out and looked down at the photo that was still visible.

I didn't know Wallace when he was married, he must've met Evaline's mother after we defended Neomaeros together. I hadn't asked Evaline about her yet, but by her absence and this locket at his grave, I could only presume she'd passed, too.

My love had gone through too much pain in her time in this world and I'd do everything I could to prevent anymore, even if it killed me. I swept my hand over the picture. She looked eerily like her mother. I smiled down at the photo.

"I'm sorry you didn't get forever with her here, Wallace." I whispered to the grave. "But I pray you get that now, in the Night."

CHAPTER FORTY-EIGHT

Evaline

The day had passed so quickly it was hard to keep up with it. Between the servants, my aunt, and Aurora sweeping into my room every hour to check on me, confirm last minute details, or in Aurora's case, have one last fitting, there'd hardly been a minute of being alone.

But my aunt had left around eight o'clock, urging me to go to sleep early to ensure I was rested for the big morning, just hours away.

But I hadn't, and at ten o'clock, I knew no one would bother me, with the castle on orders by my aunt to leave me alone. I'd blown out every lamp and candle in my room, only the glow of the fire lighting it dimly, so that they'd think I was asleep if they happened to pass by.

My heart raced, anticipating everything that would happen tomorrow, and I couldn't find a way to take my mind off it. I'd been pacing my room, shying away from where my massive dress hung in the corner, awaiting the festivities.

I sat by the fire, and scratched at the wool pajamas I wore. I looked down at the plaid shorts and button down top. The rough fabric irritated my skin. My head angled to the armoire, where I knew the new pajamas my aunt bought me lay. I bit my lip and stood up, moving to ease the drawers open gently.

They could hardly be called pajamas. They were pieces of clothing made for a man's gaze, items women would certainly only wear to appease their husbands. But as I ran my hands over the fabrics, I pursed my lips at the softness of them. As I felt the fabric of the clothes I currently wore itch my side again, air hissed between my teeth and I grabbed a set from the drawer to begin changing.

I kicked my flannel set toward the hamper.

I pulled on the soft shorts that certainly lived up to their name. They were a light blue, made of a material like silk in both look and feel, that stretched over my bottom. The hem of the shorts only covered half of my ass as the rest lay bare, exposed. I blushed and pulled the top on. It had an empress silhouette, the waistline cinching right below my breasts before the fabric fanned out over the rest of my torso. The hem of the small dress almost covered the barely there shorts.

The material was equally as soft and stretchy but completely transparent. I blushed at the sight of my breasts in the transparent fabric, the only thing hiding my nipples from plain sight was the single embroidered flower on each side, lined up perfectly to cover them. The top was a paler blue than the shorts were.

I brushed my hair over my shoulders and onto my back, the long waves settling there. I'd never really examined my body like this, usually just undressing and redressing, without ever glancing at the mirror while naked. Not that I was naked now, but I was nearing it.

I ran my hands down the small straps adorning my shoulders, small, embroidered flowers lay there, too. Down, pasts my breasts, I felt where my waist dipped in and then my hips jutted out. I turned slightly, eyes falling to my ass that was totally exposed at this angle of twisting, the dress lifting and the shorts hardly covering anything. I'd never noticed how plump it was before, but now I understood why I frequently caught men staring at it.

In the flickering light of the fire, I could see the pale white stretch marks around the sides and bottom of each cheek.

My eyes were so focused on that lower area of my body that I didn't notice him standing there until his reflection in the mirror caught my eye. I jumped, whirling around, one hand clutching at my heart that was racing out of my chest.

Maddox stood there, eyes black, lips parted. He'd snuck through the open window, evidently, and I cursed myself for not hearing it. But I couldn't devote much energy to that, not when his eyes were raking over my body. Not when I could feel his stare. The hot gaze swathing over my neck, tugging at my breasts, down to my lower half. I was frozen as his eyes slowly, so slowly, raked back up and met mine.

"Eva." He whispered; his voice hoarse.

I jolted, remembering what I was wearing, and snatched the pale blue silk robe, the final piece of the set, from the armoire behind me, wrapping it around myself and tightening the straps.

I looked down and wrapped my arms around myself.

"You could've at least knocked, you know." I tried to hiss it, to let venom leak into the words, but I couldn't. Not when I was so relieved to see him standing there, healthy, and not in pain.

He stalked toward me, stopping only when he was a breath away, lifting his hand to catch my chin and lift it until my eyes met his. "I'm sorry, I didn't mean to…I didn't think you'd be wearing…" He shook his head. "I knew you'd still be awake, I just wanted to see you."

"It's okay." I said, too fast, and he smiled.

He took a shaky breath as his eyes dipped down to where the short robe hid what we both knew he'd just seen. Everything. "You're beautiful." He breathed, eyes meeting mine again, his thumb smoothing over my jaw.

But I didn't respond to the compliment, couldn't acknowledge it. "Are you okay?"

He let his hand fall back down to his side and nodded. "Yes, I'm sorry if Wyott alarmed you. I was always okay. You don't have anything to be worried about."

I reached up, touching my fingertips to touch his cheek, just below his eye. He shivered.

"Then why are your eyes still black?"

"What?" He asked softly, brow furrowing in confusion.

I dragged my eyes from where I touched him, up to his eyes. "Your eyes, when Wyott pulled me off you they were black. And they still are. Is that because you haven't recovered yet?"

He gave a small chuckle and shook his head, catching my hand in his as he pressed a kiss to my knuckles. "No." He said, gaze alight. "I believe they were black for an entirely different reason. Then, and now."

I just nodded and pulled my hand from his, walking toward the chaise. Anything to get a deep breath that wasn't coated with the smell of him, amber and leather. I sat and he watched me. I scooted to one side and patted the empty seat beside me.

Silently, he crossed the room and sat beside me. He looked so out of place in my frilly room. The room was covered in pinks and blues. The bed in silk and cushions. Even the chaise he sat atop was pink.

He leaned back on his hands, his long legs stretched out before him, ankles crossed. He looked completely at ease, if not totally out of place. A shadow of black in a room full of pastels. His size alone would've set him apart, hulking over the seat beside me. His broad shoulders taking up most of the space.

A log in the fire fell and jerked me out of my trance. I realized I'd been staring at him, but also realized he'd been doing the same to me.

I was tucked against the arm of the lounge, my back against it as I had one leg pulled up onto it, crossed underneath me and the other hanging off the side, my toe meeting the ground. The fire danced off the light blue of my silk robe, or at least the small area that it covered. It was long sleeved, but the length of it was nowhere near as protective. In my position, with a leg wrapped underneath me, my legs spread open, I'd made sure the robe was long enough to cover everything important, falling until it just barely kissed the cushion below me.

That's where his eyes were when we both jumped from the sound of the fire. His faded a bit grayer as we stared at each other for a beat.

I shook my head. "I didn't know I could've killed you. I'm –"

He cut me off and snatched the words from my mouth. "Please, stop apologizing. There's no need. I was okay, I am okay."

He turned and slid a leg up to mimic the position I was in until his leg pressed up against mine. The rough fabric of his black pants met the smooth, bare skin of my leg and made my stomach tingle.

I looked down to my lap, where I twisted my fingers and picked at the skin around my nails. "I guess I just got carried away." I breathed.

He caught my hands in his. "Are you okay?" His gaze was full of concern.

I took a deep breath. "Well, I assume you're asking about the blood part, considering you can see my neck is healed." I tried to lighten the mood, but his eyes didn't falter. I sighed. "Yes, I'm fine. It was just all very odd and overwhelming. What's blood supposed to taste like?"

His eyes flickered at that, but I couldn't tell from what. "To me, blood normally tastes bitter, almost like coffee with just the slightest spoonful of sugar in it. Not enough to sweeten the flavor, but enough to bite back some of the bitterness." I nodded and gulped, but he continued. "I've heard most humans find it to taste like metal, what they'd imagine rust tasting like."

I felt my hands shake in his, and he tightened them. That's what it tasted like when I got a papercut and licked it. It's what I expected, before. He let several seconds pass, not forcing me to speak.

I opened my mouth. "It didn't taste that way to me." I whispered, furrowing my brow.

His hand came up, the backs of his fingers caressing my cheek. "Everyone is different." Was all he said. He didn't ask what it tasted like, didn't tell me I was deranged.

I took a breath. "It was sweet." His eyes pierced mine, intently. "It didn't taste like coffee at all, or metal, it tasted like sugar and maple. It tasted good. That's why I couldn't stop." His eyes shifted at the confession. I felt a traitorous tear begin to well in my eye. "Is there something wrong with me?" I didn't realize I was squeezing his hands until he did so back.

"No." He said, matter of factly. "It was likely the healing power of the blood that made you crave it, the pain in your neck urging you to."

I nodded, convincing myself to believe him even when I knew I'd continued drinking far after the pain in my neck had dissipated. I wiped my tears away and took a deep breath. "You didn't come for training." It wasn't a question.

His eyes softened. "I know, Wyott insisted I stay back, and I knew it was for the best. Besides, I had to give you the chance to take him down a few more times, I couldn't be the only Kova you conquered. It's not good for my ego." He joked. "Or Wyott's."

I laughed, throwing my head back. He smiled at me, bringing the crinkles up around his eyes. We stared at each other then, our smiles wide across our faces, before his lessened as his eyes took in something behind me.

I turned, my wedding dress hanging there. "Believe it or not, it was bigger. I made them take the extra layering and cage from the skirt off."

But Maddox's face wasn't joking anymore, his eyes no longer jovial.

"But you're not wearing it, right? We're leaving before the wedding." The second part wasn't a question, but a statement.

I nodded, hating every second I spent lying to him. "Right." I whispered.

As I looked at him, his eyes still unable to leave the ivory fabric behind me, I thought of what life might be like if I stuck with him, and Wyott. If I didn't veer off from them like I intended, but traveled to Rominia, saw what it was like. Saw the ocean for the first time.

And the idea ignited something inside of me, an excitement I didn't realize I was capable of anymore. But with the knowledge that this new life, the one I'd begged the Gods for, for so long, came the feeling of finality, that I'd be leaving this kingdom, and everyone I loved inside of it, forever, in the wake up something awful.

I swallowed. I didn't want them to be collateral damage.

I reached for Maddox's arm as an idea formed in my mind.

His eyes flashed to mine. "What?"

"Would you do something for me?" I whispered.

"Anything." No hesitation.

I gulped. "Can you compel people for me?"

He let my question settle in before his brow quirked. "Of course. I will, but why?"

I looked away, trying to hide the tears that pricked my eyes.

"When I run away tomorrow, the first thing my guardians will do is go find my friends." I looked back at him, ignoring the sting of tears I still felt in my eyes. "I can't let them be collateral damage."

He nodded, his eyes softening. "When do you need me to do it?"

I took a deep breath. "Now. It's the only time we have."

He nodded and stood, pulling me up to join him. "Go, get changed. It won't take long and then you need to go straight to bed. You won't get much sleep during our travels."

We made it to Aurora and Jaqueline's house quickly. Maddox picked the lock of the front door and we snuck in silently. I pulled him toward their room, but left him in the hallway; I'd call him when I was ready.

I opened their bedroom door and saw only Aurora sleeping there, tears already pricking my eyes at what I had to do.

Jacqueline must be spending the night at the Orphanage, perhaps Lillian had gotten sick again.

Jacqueline's absence worked in our favor since we'd only have to compel one at a time. I went to the bed beside Aurora, and gently jostled her awake.

"Aurora." I whispered.

She stirred for a moment before she opened her eyes, and when she did, she jumped back. A hand flying to her chest. "My Gods, Evaline, you startled me."

I smiled but the tears were still obvious, and when she saw them, she sat up in bed, pulling me to sit in front of her. "What's wrong?"

I shook my head and grabbed her hands. "Aurora." I whispered. "You were my friend when no one else was. You were there for me when I was my weakest, and never asked for anything in return." The tears came harder, until I was sobbing in front of her. "And now I wish I could repay you somehow, but I have nothing to give." I shook my head as another sob wracked my frame.

"It's okay." She whispered, her voice calming but with a hint of tears in it as well. She brushed some hair out of the line of tears on my cheek. "What's going on?"

I took a deep breath and met her eyes. I needed to get it done, I couldn't keep dragging it out when I still had to have this conversation with Jacqueline, too.

"You and Jacqueline are the very best friends I could've ever asked for, and I didn't deserve you." She shook her head and started to speak, but I cut her off. "For the rest of my life, I will carry you with me. And I pray to the Gods that I'll see you again, someday. But until then, I must protect you."

She cocked her head, confusion clouding her eyes. "What do you mean?"

My chin quivered as I took a deep breath. "Aurora, tomorrow I'm going to do something that everyone will deem horrible, but I promise I have my reasons."

She straightened, hands gripping me tighter. "You're running away?" And through her voice, through the way her eyes lit at the words, I realized she was happy for me.

I clenched my jaw. "Yes." I nodded. I wanted to tell her about Bassel so desperately, but if I did Maddox would hear, and he'd stop me from going through with the wedding. "You and Jacqueline helped me so much in my time here, and now it's my turn to protect you. I brought Maddox here with me."

She shook her head, her eyes cutting to the door. "Evaline, you brought a man to my home in the middle of the night?" There was concern in her voice, but not anger.

"Yes, and I'm so sorry, if there was any other way, trust me I wouldn't have bothered you. But when I leave tomorrow, you and Jacqueline could be in danger."

Her eyes widened. "Danger from whom?" She said quietly.

I shook my head. "My aunt and uncle are not the good people they try to display to the kingdom. Some have seen their dark side before, me most of all, and when I leave tomorrow, the first thing they're going to do is come after everyone I've ever spoken to, looking for answers."

She clenched her eyes shut, pressing her fingers to them. Guilt ran through me, I didn't mean to upset her, but I was only trying to do what was right for my friends. She took a deep breath and looked at me.

"Why would the Lord and Lady harm me, or Jacqueline, just for knowing you?"

I took a shuddered breath. More tears sprung in my eyes as I looked between hers. I wanted to tell her, I considered it. But it wouldn't do any good. She'd forget about me soon enough, and the truth might scare her.

"They'll see my running away as treason, it'll be a slight to them and Vestaria. They'll stop at nothing to find me, and while I'd hope they wouldn't hurt innocent people just because they knew me, I'm not willing to take that risk with the people I love. Do you understand?"

She was quiet for a moment, staring at me, contemplating. But she gave a nod. "Maddox is here? Now?"

"Yes. He has gifts..." I trailed off, trying to think of the right words. "He has the ability to make people forget certain things."

She gasped. "He's a Sorcerer of some sort?"

I nodded. "Something like that. It's the only reason I brought him. Please, please let him make you forget me."

She shook her head vehemently and sat back. She started to speak, but cut herself off. I knew she was running through my previous words, the fear I had over what my aunt and uncle may do, and understood why

I was suggesting this. She cast her eyes down at our joined hands as she thought.

"What if I never see you again?" Her voice was soft.

I swallowed the lump in my throat and took a shaky breath. "Then that likely means you'll be safe."

She lifted her eyes to meet mine again, and this time there were tears. She took a deep breath. "Okay." Then shook her head. "I hate this. I hate that you're in this position, that loving you has put Jacqueline and I here. I hate all of it. I don't want to forget you, Evaline. But I can't put my family in danger." She gave me a small smile. "But I can't bear the thought of you being married and living with that man in Vestaria either." She took a deep breath. "He won't alter any other memories? Just the ones of you?"

I nodded. "Of course not, he'll only change the ones of me. And I'll be here the entire time."

Aurora nodded, seeming more at ease, before coming forward and pulling me into a hug. Her grip was tight, but so was mine. The embrace of two friends who didn't have nearly enough time together.

"May the Gods watch over you, every day." She whispered in my ear.

I nodded against her hair. "May the Gods keep you and Jacqueline safe, every day." I whispered back.

"Even if I don't have memories of you anymore, I'll miss you. I know I will."

I clenched my eyes shut against the tears and nodded again. "I'll miss you every day."

We separated, taking shaky breaths, and I pulled the robe from where it hung off the post of her bed. I handed it to her and she shrugged it on.

"Now." I turned to the door and whispered, knowing he heard me.

The door creaked open, and Maddox walked through it, smiling at Aurora. "Good evening, Aurora." He said to her as he approached.

She nodded at him. "Good evening, Maddox."

The world was silent as Maddox kneeled on the ground beside us, turning to face Aurora.

"What do I have to do?" She asked him.

"I just need you to make eye contact."

She nodded, meeting his eyes. But before he could speak, she interjected quickly, hand reaching out and wrapping around his shoulder. "You'll keep her safe, right?"

Maddox's jaw clenched as he nodded. "With every breath I take."

Aurora looked at me, giving me one last smile. "I love you." She whispered.

"I love you too." I said, through the tears running down my face. She looked just as sad as I, and in that moment I saw the future she and Jacqueline could have together. Happy, in love, the family I'd always wanted someday. They'd flourish in Neomaeros, and I thanked the Gods she'd get away from Kembertus, eventually.

"Wait." I said, grabbing her arm before Maddox started. She turned toward me; brows furrowed. "When I was attacked, it was traveling between here and Neomaeros." She nodded, confused. "When you and Jacqueline travel there for the new store, bring every guard you can afford. It's dangerous, more dangerous than you know. Tell them to kill any attackers by decapitating them." I whispered, tears aching in my eyes.

She jerked her chin down. "I will." She turned back to Maddox and he held her gaze, similar to the night he'd compelled Bassel. I saw the moment she fell into the same trance. He began the compulsion, exactly as we had discussed it.

"You are going to forget how close you, and everyone you know, were to Evaline." His voice was even, comforting. "You will remember that you knew her, that you were polite with each other, and often helped her pick out dresses, but that is it." My bottom lip quivered the more he spoke, and I felt his hand move around my calf that hung off the bed. "You will forget every personal detail Evaline has ever told you about herself and her life. If anyone asks how well you knew her, you will tell them that it was not well, and that she was more of a customer than a friend."

Aurora nodded along with each new word he spoke.

"If anyone asks you where she is, you will tell them you have no idea. You never spoke with her about anything personal. Tell them that you aren't sure why the Lady had such an impression that you were friends, that you only saw Evaline as an acquaintance." I pressed my lips together to fight back the tears. "If anyone questions why Evaline would say she was coming to see you so often if you weren't friends, tell them she never came to your home to see you. Only your store. Tell them she must have lied about her real destinations. When traveling outside a kingdom, bring as many guards as you can afford. If there are attackers, kill them by decapitation." He said, reinforcing the information I'd told her since she wouldn't remember it anymore. I sighed, I'd so easily forgotten that all memories of me would be wiped. Maddox pursed his lips and added one more note. "You will only remember the extent of your friendship with Evaline if I, and I alone, tell you to remember. Until then, forget." She nodded. "Now lie down, and go to sleep." He said softly and she did, in an instant.

My body shook from holding back tears, but Maddox only grasped my shoulders and lifted me from the bed, guiding me out of the room, and toward the door.

We locked it behind us and went to the Orphanage. He recited the same lines to Jacqueline, and to Megin and Priscilla. Thank the Gods each girl had their own room in the home.

By the time we got back to the castle I was shaking so violently with the silent sobs that Maddox picked me up and held my body with one arm as he moved up the castle wall to my window. When he entered my room he took me straight to the fire, my skin turned cold from being outside so long. He tried to stand me on my feet, but I crumpled beneath the weight of my pain, my guilt.

He lowered both of us to the floor as he pulled me on his lap, and let me sob into his neck. One arm curled around me while the other moved up and down my arms and legs, trying to warm me up.

Eventually the shaking subsided, and the tears dried. When I could finally breathe, I realized that my face was pressed to the skin of his neck and his scent overpowered that of the fire beside me. But I didn't move when I'd finished mourning, and he didn't make me.

My eyes felt heavy, and they ached from the effort of crying. I snorted into his skin.

"What?" He asked softly.

I pulled my head back and shook it, looking at him. "My eyes. Therese isn't going to like how swollen they are tomorrow."

He smiled at me and moved forward to lay soft kisses on each of them. I held my breath. I would never be able to get used to his touch.

"She'll get over it." He shrugged. "And it won't matter, because you'll never see that altar anyway."

I forced a smile onto my face and nodded. He stood, bringing me along with him. I hated that I had to keep this from him, despising each lie I told him more than I thought I would. But I didn't want to hear or see his judgement, didn't want him to know that this was something I had to do.

He searched my eyes, and I knew he was searching for the lie. But instead of speaking he just stood both of us up, his arms still around me. I could only watch as he pushed some hair behind my ear.

"We'll be waiting for you at five o'clock."

I nodded.

He moved to turn but I caught his wrist. He turned back toward me. My mouth was open, poised to speak, ready to tell him that I'd be late. But as he spun back to face me, his eyes black and one long curl falling over his dark skin, scars lit up by the flames, I couldn't find the words.

In that moment, all I wanted to do was tell him everything, but most of all, tell him who Bassel was to me. What he'd done. What I planned to do. Maybe he'd understand. Maybe he'd help make sure I pulled it off. Maybe he'd see me.

But maybe he'd kill Bassel, the likeliness of it had crossed my mind more than once. Especially after my attack in the cemetery. It was why I'd lied and told Maddox that Bassel had saved me, because I didn't want him to kill Bassel. I didn't want that taken from me.

Or maybe he'd stop me.

Or maybe he'd be disgusted.

I swallowed the confession, the words I wanted to say. I couldn't take the risk. "I have to take care of something before I can leave." I confessed and his brow furrowed. I shook my head. "Before you offer, no. It's nothing you can assist with. I must do it alone."

His jaw tightened.

"But there's a chance it'll make me late." More of a certainty that it would, but I didn't say that. He opened his mouth to speak, but I cut him off. "If I'm late, please wait for me."

His eyes blazed. "Of course, I'll wait for you."

I took a breath but continued. "But don't come looking for me."

He shook his head. "If you skip out on the wedding, they're going to search for you. If I think something's happened, I won't be waiting to come find you."

I squeezed his arm. "Maddox, I need you to trust me. Only come searching for me if dawn breaks."

He scoffed, and I knew he thought that was too late, but he must've understood the demand in my eyes. He swallowed whatever he'd been about to say and gave a curt nod. "Fine."

"Thank you." I breathed, a sudden wave of relief washing over me.

He noticed and softened his expression. "But I will see you tomorrow." He started, "And we will run away from here."

I just nodded.

"Okay." He breathed. "Get some rest tonight, Eva. We have a long journey ahead of us."

"Okay."

Then he reached down, and placed a kiss on my forehead, my eyes fell closed. When they opened again, he was gone and my window shut.

I awoke with a start, going from completely unconscious to alert, heart racing, in one instant.

My aunt walked in at that moment, beaming, with a tray in her hands. "Good morning, Evaline!" She sang, her voice lilting up as she swept into my room.

She set the tray over my lap and lifted the lid. Eggs, fruits, and pastries littered the plate. Fresh squeezed orange juice, water, and coffee all present as beverage options.

My jaw dropped. "What's all this?" I asked, she'd never, in all my time here, brought me breakfast in bed.

She shrugged and moved to the wedding dress, running her hands over it. "It's your wedding day, the most important day in any woman's life. You should go into it well fed, and caffeinated."

I just blinked at her. I'd never seen her this happy.

She left me alone to eat, telling me she'd send a servant in to draw a bath. I had to force myself to pick up a pastry. My stomach was in knots as I thought about my plan, how the day would go, the anxiety surging up my throat and closing it. But I knew it was important to eat now, as much as I could before we began the journey.

After I cleared the plate I felt sick so I turned on my side and laid back down into bed, staring through the window. In my mind's eye, I imagined every move I'd make. How I'd lead Bassel to the honeymoon suite. Each strike I'd send out and how they'd feel. I considered every counterstrike he might make, how I'd defend myself before swiping out an offensive move.

I did that until I fell asleep, being awoken by the servant lightly tapping me, telling me the bath was ready.

I bathed, again imagining how the night would progress. I had to be reminded to leave the bath when the water grew cold. The haze around me wouldn't lift and it was like I was stuck in a waking dream.

Hours passed before Therese returned, but they could have been minutes to me. I didn't hear a word she spoke, and it wasn't long before I was a doll in the chair. I sat in front of my vanity while my aunt did my makeup, lining my eyes and thickening my eyelashes with black powder. She dusted the inner creases of my eyes with a pearly white and dusted the rest with a light rose pink.

The only thing left was my hair. When she touched it I opened my mouth for the first time. "I want to do my hair myself."

She paused, clearly not a fan of the idea. "Are you sure?"

I nodded. "My mother would've done it if she was here. I want to do it myself, alone."

Yes, it was incredibly manipulative, and morally wrong to use my mother's death as a reason to be alone, but I had to be manipulative, and I didn't have time to feel bad about it.

She slowly pulled her hands back, clasping them in front of her chest.

"Okay." She said, her tone too sweet. She left and ushered the servants along with her.

I moved quickly, afraid she'd change her mind and come back. I left more hair out of my braid than I normally would, allowing the pieces to wave down the sides of my face, framing it nicely. I paid careful attention to each swipe of hair I pulled into the braid, ensuring I had a loose weave that would be thick and full. When I got to the tail, I grabbed the wire and wove it in effortlessly, as I'd done a thousand times before.

I plucked and picked out pieces to fluff out, and then moved to my window. I grabbed the vase of fresh flowers my aunt had brought me, and plucked some out, weaving them in as well. I knew that she'd like that.

I poked my head out of my room, and, as I'd guessed, she was not far. She ushered Aurora in and they assisted me into the dress.

As they layered the dress on me, I stood still, lifting my braid out of the way and allowing them to move me as they needed. My chest ached with the effort of slowing my breathing, but I could feel the sob that was rushing to the surface each time I looked at Aurora. The painful sorrow was like a white-hot prod on my heart each time she gave me one of her customer service smiles.

She'll be safe this way. I reminded myself, the only thing I could do to keep the tears at bay.

They paused when they'd finished, taking in the sight. The dress was ivory, pairing nicely with my white hair. The neckline was a straight across my chest, adjoining the sleeves that began falling down my shoulder. The rest of the sleeve was tulle, puffed and transparent, cuffing at my wrists.

The skirt was plain, and I knew they'd done so on purpose, allowing the top of the dress to be the star. The skirt was satin layered upon tulle, giving it the shape to sit out, falling into a bell shape, instead of the bowl I'd originally had.

It was beautiful, and I was beautiful in it, but the day wasn't for beauty. It was for death.

CHAPTER FORTY-NINE

Maddox

I leaned against the city's wall, heart rate as high as the bricks above me. It was nearing five o'clock, and I knew Evaline would join me soon. I took a deep breath. It was all happening. Everything that I had wanted since the moment I saw her face. Everything I had prayed for since I met her.

I couldn't help the smile that tugged on my cheeks. I'd never been more excited for anything in my entire existence. I'd take her away from this Gods forsaken kingdom, away from her harsh guardians, and this sham of a wedding. I'd take her wherever she wanted to go, and I'd stay with her there. Until she was ready to be with me, really be with me. Until hopefully one day she was ready to go home to Rominia.

I closed my eyes and allowed myself to imagine it. Watching her walk the beaches with the ocean breeze stirring her hair. The hair that could fall down her back, unbound from that barbed braid, because she'd always be safe with me.

I looked at the sun. It'd passed the high point in the sky hours ago. I knew soon, any minute, I'd hear the bell tower chime five times, and then she'd be here. We'd probably hear the tower chime again, once they realized she was missing, but we'd be long gone before they realized she left the city.

I looked down at the present I'd gotten for her. My grip shook with every minute that passed and my ears strained for any sound to crack through the trees before me. The smile on my face wavered as I instead heard the bell tower start to chime.

But it wasn't the five chimes for the hour I'd expected. It was longer, a different melody.

My head snapped up, heart thundering harder than before. "What the fuck?" I hissed.

"Are those...wedding bells?" I heard Wyott say on the other side of the wall.

"Yes." I growled. My breath came fast, chest heaving. What did this mean? Was she in trouble? Did she need me?

"Maddox." He warned, hearing my anxiety rush. "Calm down, I'm sure she's on her way."

I shook my head, even though he couldn't see it. "No. Something is wrong, I can feel it."

He sighed. "She asked you not to look for her, she promised she'd come."

But the only thoughts that ran through my mind were the worst scenarios. That they'd found her dagger and taken it from her. That they'd forced her into that dress and shoved her down the aisle. That she had no way of protecting herself and was moments away from reaching down the bond, just like she'd done the night she'd been attacked, screaming for me.

"You promised you'd wait." He hissed, his tone was a warning. But I was already running.

I slowed my pace to match a human's as I broke through the tree line, my head swiveled as my eyes tried to search for the crowd. I hadn't bothered to ask where the wedding was intended to take place, I thought we'd be long gone.

The bells continued to chime as I ran for the castle, it seemed the most likely venue, and the bond beat with a rhythm of its own in my head.

Go. Go. Go. You're too slow.

But I couldn't run any faster without outing myself as nonhuman. By the grace of the Gods, I made it to the castle quickly.

The streets had been desolate, every citizen seemed to be in attendance. I snapped my head to the sound of chatter and knew I was on the wrong side of the castle.

I ran to the opposite, where the rose garden stretched. When I rounded the corner and saw the large gathering of people, I scanned over the affair.

Bassel stood in a tailored tunic, dress pants, and brand-new boots, in front of a trellis that arched over the hedged garden. Roses in shades of pink, red, blue, and purple littered the bushes around him. There were dozens of guests seated, and dozens more standing on the outskirts, watching.

I clenched my jaw and swallowed past my dry mouth, walking slowly to join the crowd.

Where is she?

I surged through my mind, feeling for the bond. If I could only grasp it, know she was alive, unharmed, I'd be okay. Then I'd find her, and we'd get the fuck away.

I felt it shiver, knew I was close, and just as I found it, I heard the stringed quartet begin the bridal procession.

All heads snapped back toward the entrance of the aisle, and I turned there, too.

She stood in her white gown, as beautiful as I'd ever seen her, a bouquet of flowers clutched in her hands. But she wasn't under duress. She wasn't even being dragged down the aisle as she began to move.

No.

She was alone as she strode down the petal littered grass, the smile on her face visible even through the veil that floated over it. With every step closer to him, the vice grip of fear on my heart tightened until I couldn't breathe.

As she went further down the aisle, I turned, facing her back. I caught the eyes of Therese in the first row of seating, her eyes drifting away from the bride to find mine. Her brows pulled together and I watched as she recognized me as the man Evaline knew from the market. The reason Evaline had been locked in the castle.

I expected her to scowl, to stand up and demand I leave. But instead on her face I saw the slightest twinge of pity, of sorrow, deep within her eyes, and that's when I realized that my emotions had gotten the best of me, contorting my face until everything I felt was evident.

Devastation.

I could only watch in horror as the ceremony progressed. A sick torture to put myself through, but I couldn't look away. The removal of her veil. The exchanging of their vows. The words of the officiant. At any moment, this would stop. At any moment, I'd wake up from the worst nightmare I'd ever had.

I waited for her to turn to me, tell me to take her away. And I would've swept her up into my arms, dress and all and run faster than any of these mortals could process. And we'd run. We'd never look back.

But she didn't.

I felt the anguish simmer off her, saw the fake smile she so desperately tried to maintain. The bond ravaged inside me. Indicating my mate was in trouble. Urging me to save her, but it didn't appear that she was forced.

I knew I shouldn't try to connect with her down the bond. Knew it would only scare her. Knew she still didn't comprehend that I'd already done it the night I'd saved her from those fucks in the cemetery. But I couldn't help it. I shoved the question through, unsure if she'd even hear it.

What are you doing?

Her posture tightened and her eyes flicked to mine without having to search the crowd. But they only widened when they saw me, her skin paling. A flash of heat lit my skin, trying to communicate all my thoughts through one simple look.

But she turned back to Bassel.

I watched as she did the one thing I'd been silently begging her not to do. Over and over and over until it sounded like a drumbeat in my head. I didn't send it down the bond, maybe this was what she wanted.

Don't kiss him. Don't kiss him. Don't kiss him.

Because that would seal the vow, unite them as one, and I couldn't handle that. I couldn't watch my mate, the love of my life, the reason I'd been placed on this miserable plane, swear her life, her love, to this mortal. To this wretched man that she'd sworn she didn't love.

But the wind stalled, the bond quaked, and my heart hardened as their lips met.

CHAPTER FIFTY

Evaline

I could barely remember a moment from the time I walked out of my bedroom, until we entered the reception hall. Only the panic in my chest as I felt Bassel's lips on mine and the guilt that'd swept through me when I saw Maddox standing among the throng of observers. Everything else had passed by in a fog.

Even with the reception halfway over, I was stunned, and in a haze. All the ridiculous toasts and speeches were done, I'd barely heard a word before people were moving onto the drinking and dancing.

I regretted my decision more and more with every hour that had passed. The talking, the lying, the smiling. Good Gods, I didn't think I'd smiled so much in my entire life. My acting was draining, and I was afraid that I wouldn't have the resolve to execute my plan's end when the time came.

If you looked through the window, you might be able to fool yourself into thinking it was just another Ball. It was decorated in the same manner. The same band played. The same pillars stood around us. But it was far different than the last time I'd been in the ballroom.

I was far different.

I strode toward the pool at the base of the stairs. I needed a moment to myself. If I could sit for a second, clear my head and stare at the fish lazily swimming content in their granite prison, surely I would –

My thoughts cut off as I felt him here with me. Not Bassel, Maddox. I raised my eyes and saw him standing in the shadow of one of the pillars at the edge of the party.

His eyes, while sullen, were pinned on me fiercely, and only darted away to point toward the kitchen door, before landing back on mine. He moved then, and I knew he was requesting I follow.

I contemplated ignoring him, to choose not to follow him because he'd found me when I told him not to, even though a piece of me begged my legs to move, to turn and run – no sprint – after him, and do absolutely whatever he told me.

I considered letting him stand in the kitchen alone, waiting for me to walk through the door until he realized I wasn't coming. Gods, for the first time all night, the thought of plastering a smile on my face and engaging with my guests sounded enjoyable, compared to having to go face him, lie my way out of another plan with him.

I inhaled deeply, jaw aching from the tension in it as I exhaled harshly. *Gods-dammit.*

I sighed and turned to follow him. I didn't have time for this, if we were caught I might not get the time alone with Bassel that I needed.

I looked behind me as I turned the corner to the back entrance of the room, sweeping the crowd to see if anyone was tracking my movements.

Then I swallowed, focused on the kitchen door, and turned the knob. My gown hardly fit through the door's frame, I had to force it to ripple over itself as I strode into the room.

He stood with a hand holding open the door, a towering figure of shadows and rigid shoulders.

I clenched my jaw and walked past him. I stopped beside the large wooden table in the center of the kitchen, freshly washed dishware piled high on the end behind me. I almost wondered why the kitchen was empty, but of course I knew. Maddox would've compelled every remaining worker to flee when he entered.

With movements so torturously slow it made the day tick by slower, I swear it, he stepped forward and softly closed the door. I held my breath as Maddox turned to lean his back against it, crossing his arms and looking me dead in the eyes. He didn't speak, and I wasn't sure if I should. I steeled myself for his rage. For the anger I knew was coming my way. But I had my own frustrations with him. He promised not to come looking for me until dawn.

You promised you'd never see that altar. I reminded myself.

"Why are we here?" He asked, his tone even.

I didn't feign ignorance. I knew he wasn't referring to our current location in the kitchen. When I didn't speak, he pushed away from the door, the wood moaning from the impact. I straightened as he stalked toward me, his black eyes never leaving mine.

He stopped in front of me, head dipping low so his face hovered inches above mine and I tilted my own up to meet his eyes.

"Why are we at your wedding?" He stepped forward and I backed away from him. Not from fear, from guilt. "Why did I have to stand by and watch as you married him?" His voice dropped even lower. My back hit the edge of the tabletop. He pinned me there, hands dropping to rest on the table on either side of my waist.

My thoughts spun and anxiety crept through me. This was it. This was the moment I knew was coming. Where everything would fall apart and I'd be left alone to pick up the pieces of my own mistakes. He'd leave, Wyott would leave, and I'd be stranded with best friends who no longer remembered they loved me once. I'd be alone. Again.

The thought scared me more than it ever had in the past, the idea of losing him, and I only shook my head.

His face was inches away as he stared down at me with furrowed brows, and I waited for him to yell. To tell me he was done with this arrangement. To hate me. But he only gave a shake of his head, black eyes searching mine.

"You lied." He croaked.

I could've handled hatred. I could've handled rage. What I couldn't bare was the catch in his voice, the fear in his misting eyes.

"I told you to trust me." I whispered, blinking away the tears that I couldn't help from forming after seeing his own.

He squeezed his eyes shut, shaking his head. The table behind me groaned from how tight his hands gripped it. "It's hard to have faith in that vow, after watching you swear a sacred one to him."

My fists clenched at my sides. "I can't tell you everything. I can't give you what you want right now. But I can promise you that I will meet you at that wall," I lowered my eyes to the floor, unable to maintain his gaze when I spoke the next words. "If you're still in this with me."

His hands rose from my sides until they were tangled in the back of my hair, angling my face up to meet his.

"I will be in this with you until the moment you ask me away." He ground out. "Nothing will ever change that." I realized some tears had fallen when his breath flitted over my face. "Do you understand?" He asked, his voice was gruff.

I could only nod my head, not trusting myself to answer. I didn't know what I did in this life to warrant the Gods putting him in my path, but I didn't deserve it. I didn't deserve him.

A silent moment passed with our wordless gaze before he spoke.

"I need you to answer one question." He said and I saw fury churning slow and hot behind his eyes.

"Yes?" I whispered.

"Did you always plan to have this wedding?" The words sounded as if they burned when he said them.

"What?" I asked, taken aback.

"I'm not going to repeat a question we both know you heard." His voice was devoid of emotion, and I recognized the wall behind his eyes. It matched my own.

"No." I answered. His eyebrows raised. "I mean, yes, but –"

"There is no 'but'." He said, his voice so low it rumbled through me. His hands moved then, dropping to my waist, hauling me to sit on the edge of the table as he stood before me again.

"Gods." I hissed at the sudden move, my own hands gripping his shoulders for stability.

His gaze never left mine as he took something out from behind his back and slammed it onto the table mere inches from my hip.

I looked down. Beside me, in the midst of the ruffles of my wedding gown, was an upright dagger, stabbed into the table. And through my dress.

But that was merely an observation and not a concern, because the only thing I found myself focused on was the beauty of the blade beside me.

He must've taken my gasp as an invitation to elaborate.

"I was going to give it to you when you met me at the wall, but now seems as good a time as any." He said softly. My heart did a painful thump as I realized he didn't believe me anymore; didn't think I'd truly come meet him tonight.

When I didn't reach for it, could only stare, he gripped the handle and ripped it from the table. He flipped it in his hand and offered the hilt to me. It was extraordinary. Entirely made from Rominium, it appeared.

The blade was nearly eight inches alone, far longer than my current dagger, which felt entirely unworthy as it rested against my leg. The cross-guard was unlike any I'd ever seen. The metal curled up on one side and crossed to curl downward on the opposite.

My palm opened and my gaze fell to the hilt. Leather wrapped around the metal for comfort in my hand, but my eyes landed on the finest part of the weapon.

At the tip of the handle, right on the butt of it, lay a blue-green gem. It was large, larger than the diamond on my hand. Instead of the sharp end of the gem set inward, it was reverse set so that the flat part of it melded to the handle, and the sharp end faced out. The color was vibrant, unlike any stone I'd ever seen. It almost looked like –

"Your eyes." Maddox whispered above me, and it was only then that I realized he'd been staring at me the entire time.

I shook my head in confusion.

He nodded to the dagger in my hand. "The gem. I requested it be added because the color matches your eyes."

I squeezed my eyes shut, not believing what he was saying. I opened them and met his. "You had this made for me?"

Something flashed in his eyes so quickly I couldn't tell what it was. He cleared his throat and gently flattened the dagger, so that it lay atop my open-faced palms, as he ran his hand over it, and subsequently, me.

"I had it made for you." He confirmed. My eyes followed his fingers as they drifted to caress the jewel. "Madierian Sea blue topaz." He identified it. I held my breath as he looked up and tilted his head, examining me. A hand coming up to swipe his thumb along my cheek, just below my eye. "Because it's the color of your eyes."

I clenched my jaw as he lowered his hand over the blade again, this time tracing over the cross-guards.

"Curved cross-guards." He started before his hand met my waist, sliding down the slope of it until it rested on the crest of my hip. I bit my lip at all the thoughts flooding my head, the urges aching through my body. This was distracting, he was distracting, but I didn't stop him. "Because it matches the contour of your body."

I pursed my lips, it was all I could do to lock away the moan that almost slipped out at his words.

He dropped to his knee then. Pulling my ankle up so that it popped out of my dress.

"Maddox." I hissed in surprise, but couldn't even fool myself away from thinking I wished he'd do more. Couldn't pretend I didn't want his lips on my skin again, just as they had been when I drank from him.

I felt cool leather against my leg as he began strapping a new holster to my calf. He raised his eyes to meet mine and flashes from the night I'd been drunk played in my mind. *It won't be the last.*

Inside, I was a wreck of want as his fingers tightened the harness to my leg, slipping over my skin, his eyes never straying from my own. While trying to calm myself I reacted too slowly to the surprise of his hands sliding up my opposite thigh to where the other dagger was holstered.

I gasped. "Maddox."

His hands stopped above the dagger, so very close to the space between my legs that begged for his touch, poised to detach the scabbard along with the sheathed knife. His eyes cut to mine.

"Eva." His voice was rough, uncontrolled. "Say my name like that one more time and there'll be far more than just my hands hidden beneath this dress."

I couldn't tame the flame his words caused to burn deep within my body. My jaw made an audible noise as it slammed shut.

With slow hands he removed the scabbard and blade. He caressed the skin down my leg to attach the sheath to the new holster. I didn't know why I was surprised when he snagged the new dagger from my hand and drew the scabbard from somewhere behind him, and worked his way back up my leg.

This time he attached the scabbard first and then slid the knife in, letting the blade kiss my skin as he slid it into place, gaze locking with mine once more.

I hissed between my teeth, but we both knew it didn't hurt.

No, it did quite the opposite.

"And finally." He whispered. He straightened and leaned close to me again so that only a breath could pass between us. "The entire dagger is made from Rominium." His eyes fluttered down to rest on my lips and I felt the move as much as I saw it. "To always remind you of me."

He gathered my head in his hands again and drew me close. His hands around my jaw, in my hair, tightened as he tipped my head back to face him fully. He moved into my spread legs until his hips met mine. I watched with bated breath as his eyes focused on my lips and he slowly leaned in. I let my own flutter closed as I felt his breath mix with mine, knew what was coming next.

But his lips only grazed mine, never landing fully, as he whispered. "It should have been me."

He moved, and I felt something cold touch my collarbone, felt cool air hit me. When I opened my eyes, he was gone.

CHAPTER FIFTY-ONE

Maddox

My heart was in my throat as I stormed from the kitchen, unseen. Stormed through the gardens, through the forest, and to the wall where I would continue to wait for her. The ghost of her touch still buzzed on my lips.

The lump in my throat was painful, hard and unmoving, and I knew it was from the anger, the rage that filled me. At the thought that she'd lied. That perhaps she did love Bassel. That maybe that was the reason she'd spared him that night in the cemetery.

But the emotion that roiled through me the most as I stood at the wall, arms crossed and waiting, was fear. Fear that she wouldn't come. That she'd stand me up again. That this all had been some sick joke played on me by the Gods and Goddesses.

That they wanted to watch as they gave the son of the First his mate, dangled her in front of him, showed him how amazing and beautiful and wonderful she could be, that their life together could be, just to rip her away.

Wyott's voice pulled me from my worsening thoughts.

"What happened?"

My own voice was raw. "She married him."

CHAPTER FIFTY-TWO

Evaline

My breath shuddered through me as I felt at my neck for what Maddox had left there. My lips pursed and tears sprang in my eyes as I realized it was the locket from my father's grave.

I gritted my teeth to dispel the tears. I had to pull myself together. I couldn't allow my feelings for Maddox to deter my revenge.

I hopped off the table, dress billowing back out around me. Sliding my hands down the front of the corset I took a deep breath and tried to forget the feeling of his hands on my legs, his lips on mine.

I urged myself to stop thinking about him.

I took a deep breath and righted myself.

It was time.

My eyes locked on the door of the kitchen, thinking about how my father would prepare for a battle when he was a soldier. How he'd widen his stance, hold his chest high, and pray to the Gods. To the Goddess of Bloodshed, in particular. The Goddess with dominion over war and destruction. I closed my eyes.

"Vestari." I prayed. "Please grant me the grace of your speed and the might of your strength."

When I opened my eyes, the room seemed brighter.

I made my way back into the ballroom where I found Bassel laughing with a few other men. His hand was wrapped around an entire wine decanter, and the liquid sloshed around the edges, almost brimming over with each swing.

I knew I wouldn't have to do much. Just be in sight. I meandered close to his group until his eyes caught me, and I knew I had him. His drunken smile lopsided and he left his conversation abruptly. I ducked a spray of wine that flew from his bottle. He wrapped an arm around me and pulled me against him.

"I think I'm ready to start our honeymoon." He slurred.

A satisfaction swelled inside of me. He made it so easy.

"That sounds lovely." I gathered Bassel and set his wine down on a nearby table as I led him out of the doors.

I threw one last look back at Aurora and Jacqueline. They looked happy, laughing together as they moved on the dance floor. An ache rocked my chest.

They're better off without you. I promised myself.

My eyes swung to my guardians at the center of another group, all bellowing with laughter. A moment of guilt swelled inside of me. I knew the consequences they'd face over my actions. They'd never truly cared about me, but still I felt remorse. They'd find the letter I'd written hidden underneath the pillow on my bed.

With a clench of my jaw, I turned back to the hallway, and we left the gathering. Our room for the night was in the guest wing of the castle. My aunt and uncle only used it for our most high profile guests, but I guessed that this was just as big of a deal.

As we neared the bedchamber, Bassel spoke. He'd been oddly quiet this entire walk. "Evaline, my wife." He started, and tightened his arm around my waist. "I have been waiting for this day for so long."

I opened the door to our room and allowed him inside. He passed the threshold and continued talking.

"You have no idea how hard it's been to wait for this night, especially after seeing you in all those perfect dresses." I swallowed the bile in my throat and quieted the fear his words raised.

You can do this. I shut and locked the door and heard his snicker behind me.

"That's my kitten. Lock the door."

I took a deep breath against the frame, needing to steel myself for one moment before I turned to face him. Before we started.

"I've already told the staff to steer clear of this room, I don't want any interruptions." He slurred.

I could've laughed. I could've cried with giggles at the words. In all my life, I'd never thought killing a man and getting away with it would be so easy. But his ill intent had finally worked out in my favor, and I was ready to take advantage.

With no interruptions, came no witnesses.

I finally turned toward him and noticed the room for the first time. It was expansive. There was a large, perfectly made, four poster bed against the back wall, its white duvet contrasted starkly with the dark walnut of the frame. A fireplace crackled in one corner of the room, with a chaise placed in front of it, an armoire against the wall, and the door that I knew led to the bathing chamber on the other side.

He looked small in the massive room, and I knew I looked smaller.

But as I took in the details of the layout, my plan formed. For the last time I'd ever have to do so, I allowed my mask to slide into place as I smiled at him. I walked closer, placing a hand on his chest and pushing him back toward the bed.

A surprised breath passed his lips and he jolted as the backs of his legs hit the frame. I slid my hand up to his shoulder and pushed him to sit down. He fell to the end of the bedding, a post from the bed stretching up above us to the right.

The plan was strong, I knew he'd never see it coming. But that wasn't what had the panic rushing through me. It was his scent overwhelming my senses, his smirk that kept growing.

Be strong now. Now it matters most.

I gritted my teeth and stood between his spread legs, thankful for the thick space my dress created between us.

He swept his eyes up to mine, covering the length of my body as he did so. His stare was hungry. Too hungry, and too thirsty for power, and exactly the look that had been on his face the night of the attack. When I imagined how this night would run, I'd been afraid of that moment. Of that second where I saw the real him, just as I had that night two years ago. Afraid that it would freeze me in fear, lock my muscles and joints as it had in the cemetery.

But seeing the dangerous gleam in his eyes and flashing back to when I'd seen it in that forest had the opposite effect. I wasn't afraid. I wasn't frozen. I was excited. Every pump of my heart pushed more energy out to my body and I was ready for the fight, ready for the revenge, ready for the kill.

I smirked at him and raised my left hand to brush some hair away from his forehead. His eyes drifted to my lips.

"Oh, Bassel." I said softly as his hand settled on my left hip in response, pulling me closer. I trailed my hand down to his neck, spreading it over the skin, my thumb resting on the center of his throat. His eyes drifted closed. "If only you knew how long I've waited for this night, too. All the things I've dreamed of doing to you."

He shuddered beneath my hand, and I felt his throat bob with a gulp.

My right hand moved just behind my thigh, fingers crawling over my leg to pull the dress up silently, slow.

"Tell me." He whispered, his hand on my hip tightening.

"Where's the fun in that?" I grinned. The tulle was gathering up by my wrist, and fingers were beginning to ache from pulling the fabric up.

A smirk played on his lips, eyes still closed. "It builds the anticipation."

A quiet laugh left me, the breath floating over his face. "Maybe that's true." I crooned. He leaned forward slightly, eyes beginning to open. My hand on his throat moved up to grasp his jaw, turning it away from me slightly as my lips met his ear. "But don't you think the anticipation of what might come next is better?"

A sigh of approval rumbled his chest. "Yes." He licked his lips. "Yes."

My fingers met the flesh of my thigh, finally. They prodded down, finding the handle of the dagger Maddox had just gifted to me.

The hand on Bassel's jaw fell, scaling his body as it made its way across to his left hand. He leaned into me again. My hand circled his wrist. "Do you want to know what's better than the anticipation of what happens next?" I said, low in his ear. I pulled the dagger out of its sheath, so slow it was painful.

"Fuck, yes." He croaked.

I smiled. "Being in control of it." In a flash of speed, I threw his hand back against the post beside him and brought my dagger forward, embedding it through the flesh of his palm and deep into the wood.

A gasp left my lips at the same time he screamed, and I stumbled away from him. That dagger was exceptionally sharp.

He stood, turning so that he saw for the first time that he'd been impaled against the bed.

"What the fuck is wrong with you?" He shouted, head whipping around at me. His chest heaved with the shock, with the pain, and I saw the sheen of sweat that broke out on his forehead.

I only laughed.

His other hand raised to prod the skin around his wound, a sob escaping him as the blood trickled down and fell to the floor. When Bassel looked back at me his eyes were filled with tears and I watched as connections formed in his mind. My heart raced as I awaited his memories to flood back, to remember exactly who I was.

But instead, I heard his laughter fill the room. My smile faded, confidence slipping for a moment.

The smile that drew on his face was the same as that night, smug and violent, and it didn't make any sense. But all the same, he settled it on me. "You're smarter than I thought you were." He tightened his jaw and gave his wounded hand another look. "I didn't fucking see that one coming."

I took another step away from him. "You've underestimated a lot of things about me."

He looked back up at his hand, wiggling it to gauge the damage. He gasped, cursing, and shook his head. When he looked back, that smug smile remained. This didn't make sense, none of this made sense. He should be afraid, should be shaking in fear. If he knew who I was, knew why I'd dragged him here, he shouldn't be laughing.

But he was. "How did you figure it out?" He asked, leaning back against the bed, gritting his teeth.

I tilted my head up. "I knew the moment I saw you at the Spring Solstice Ball."

The situation no longer felt like it was in my control, but I didn't have a choice. I had to move before he freed himself and I was caught trying to fight in this dress. I ripped the sleeves off the sides, tugged them from my wrists and let them fall to the ground in a whisper.

His eyes narrowed. "That's not possible."

I bent to pull my other dagger from my calf and scoffed as I reached behind with both hands and cut the tie of the corset that held me in place. The ribbon unfurled immediately and I pulled the bodice until it was so loose the dress fell to the floor and puddled around my feet.

I twirled the dagger in my hand, looking down at it. "Nothing could have prevented me from remembering you the moment I saw you again." My voice was low, deadly.

He shook his head. "What the fuck are you talking about, we'd never met before I came here." He hissed.

This was confusing. He was confusing. Why would he ask me how I'd figured it out, if he didn't remember me? I stopped the dagger so that it pointed directly at him. "You know that's not true, so why try to lie now?"

His brows furrowed, his hand still hanging in the air. "We met at the Ball. A month ago." He reiterated.

I shook my head, flipping the dagger in a reverse grip so that the blade was clutched against the skin of my forearm, and folded my arms behind my back.

"I can't pretend I didn't find it alarming that you didn't remember me at the Ball. I could almost be offended." I tilted my head. "But perhaps your lack of memory says more about your habits than it does of my presence."

"Evaline, I don't know what you're talking about." He tried to be calm. "We've never met. I thought you discovered the real reason I married you, not that you recognized me."

I shrugged, ignoring his words. Whatever horrific reason he had for marrying me didn't matter. We wouldn't be wed for long.

"I know that you made a lasting impression that night." I said.

He threw his head back in aggravation. "What night?" He shouted.

"I remember the smell of liquor on your breath." I bent down to pick up the dress I'd discarded. It was heavy in my hands. "I remember how it was so dark that I could hardly see anything but shadows." I moved to the chaise, laying the dress over it delicately. "I remember the feel of the tree against my back as I was pinned to its bark." I smoothed my hands over the fabric and turned to face him again. "And I remember the sound of Lonix's nails scraping down his throat as he died."

Recognition flared in Bassel's eyes and he stood straighter, skin paling, eyes the size of saucers. He was afraid.

"It's...it's you." The fear in his voice shocked me. But what shocked me more was the pleasure it filled me with.

My smile turned wicked. "So you do remember." I waved the blade in the air. "Isn't it easier to tell the truth?"

He shook his head violently. "No. No. Let me go, I don't know what kind of dark magic you possess, but let me go."

I scoffed. "Just because a woman knows how to fight, doesn't mean she possesses magic, you fucking misogynist."

His body started trembling. "It wasn't just your strength. It was your eyes."

My lips curled back into a snarl. "My eyes were begging for you to stop, like my lips would have been doing if you had taken your hand off of them."

He squeezed his eyes shut tight, shaking his head. "You killed Lonix."

I didn't have time to consider the words because he seemed to find his courage then. "And I'm not afraid to kill you before you can kill me." Then he reached up and grasped the black dagger, ripping it out of his hand as he screamed.

I couldn't find it in me to be afraid. My heart only raced, preparing for battle. A smile stretched on my face as I bounced on the balls of my feet. "Well, I would be lying if I said I hadn't hoped you'd try."

He growled, rushing forward, toward me. I dropped into my stance, and easily side stepped, pivoting to face him again.

"Too slow." I mocked.

His eyes were alight with fury as he came forward again, and instead of stepping away, I ducked, reaching up to catch his daggered fist and swipe my blade over his thighs, slicing a deep gash over them.

He roared and fell away. "You stupid bitch." He said, gasping at the pain.

I shrugged as I stood. "Can't be that stupid if I fooled you for the last month." I brought my left hand up, wriggling my fingers at him. The diamond on my hand flashed.

He straightened, wincing against the strain from his wounds, the desperate look of a wounded deer as he faced a wolf in his eyes.

Bassel came at me again, and this time punched me in the face with his free hand. Something I hadn't been expecting, my eyes only on his dagger.

I reeled back from the blow; my ego more injured than anything. He swiped his dagger, but I was too far out of reach to kill. His blade swept air over my face before nicking a slice down my brow.

I jumped back up with a wicked smile on my face. "I applaud your effort, Bassel, but still not enough." I cocked my head.

"I'm going to kill you, you fucking whore." He hissed. "Vasier's orders be damned."

He lunged for me then, but I squared my elbow and shoved toward his throat. He stumbled back a step, gasping for air, and I took the opportunity to spin around, kicking the dagger from his hand. It flung across the room, the metal clanging across the floor.

I tried to run for it, but his hand wrapped around my braid and he yanked me back. Hard.

I laughed as he screamed before spinning to meet him again. I lifted a leg, stomping dead-center into his chest, and kicked him back.

He flew back and fell onto the ground. He groaned but didn't move, and I took my time picking up the Rominium dagger. I let out a low whistle as I stepped down onto his chest. He whimpered below me, flexing both of his injured hands, as if he could do anything with them, moving like he might try to stand.

I bent toward him, my voice dripping with venom that only revenge could produce. "You fucked with the wrong woman, the wrong daughter." I hissed down at him. He stared up at me, nothing short of terror reeling from him. I angled my dagger, poking him directly over his heart.

"Gods, have mercy." He begged, and I did smile at that.

I gave a humorless laugh. "The Gods used up all their mercy when they saved me that night. There's none left for you."

"I'm sorry, I –"

"It's too late." I whispered, and swung the blade up and over his throat.

The blood spurted from it, spraying my chest, my hands, my dress. I straightened and moved away from him. Watching him struggle, his wounded hands trying to clasp the wound shut. It didn't take long for the movement to stop, for the light to leave his eyes.

And when it did I moved to the bed. The duvet was perfect and white, until I swiped my daggers across it, stark red staining the fabric.

I smiled as I considered that Bassel had probably hoped for blood to stain the sheets tonight, when he thought he'd take the virginity from the pure young woman.

But it was never going to be my blood that would spill, and I certainly wasn't pure.

CHAPTER FIFTY-THREE

Evaline

I was prepared to leave after killing Bassel, I'd donned a cloak from the closet and was halfway to the window. I knew Maddox would have my satchel with my spare change of clothes. But I wanted everything I had of value to go with me over the Kembertus walls. I had my daggers and the locket around my neck.

But one item was missing.

I gritted my teeth and ran toward the door. No one was in the hallway when I peeked out. Bassel truly did encourage everyone to stay clear of our room.

I took one last deep breath and strode out. I kept my head down, hood drawn, but knew I'd be fucked if anyone saw me. The idea scared me, but knowing my father's sword would spend the rest of its days in Elijah's possession was worse.

I tried to keep track of every window around me as I moved, a failsafe so that if I was caught I could go right for it. I got to the corner of the hallway that connected to the rest of the castle and paused. I was only one hall away from my uncle's study, so close. But if he was in there, which he almost always was, I'd be executed before morning.

My heart beat loudly in my ears, almost as loud as the thoughts of my father screaming at me to turn around, and I rounded the corner.

I ran, my feet as quiet as they could be against the granite. I heard voices down the adjoining hall and ran faster. I couldn't stop to listen as I got to his door, only wrenched it open and spun myself inside.

When I turned around, I breathed in relief to see the room empty. I locked the door behind me in hopes that it would at least slow anyone coming in and stepped into the room to turn to the fireplace.

Natalia stood there, her hand wrapped around a feather duster, poised against a vase. Her eyes widened as she took in my appearance. With my cloak covering my body, and the hood falling down to cover the cut on my brow, I hoped she couldn't see anything damning. I paused for a beat before opening my mouth to speak, but she did first.

"I haven't seen anything." She said in a rush, hands raising in innocence. She shook her head. "I'll walk out and come back in an hour." She moved slowly around me, heading for the door. "No one saw me come in here. I never saw a thing." She said again, urging me with her eyes.

She got back to the door and I turned, facing her. She raised her ear to listen, hand on the knob. Before pulling on the handle she turned back to me one last time. "May the Gods be kind." She whispered, and I didn't have time to respond as she slipped out.

Tears pricked my eyes and I tried my best to blink them away at the act of kindness. I moved back to the door, locking it again behind her, and did my best to calm my shaking breaths. A part of me wished I could stay, that I could run after Natalia and reforge the friendship we could've had.

But there was no going back. And, maybe in the morning she'd regret helping me, after she discovered she'd let a murderer flee. But no one had seen me enter this study, and no one would see me leave. She would be safe, and if she chose, she could tell them I threatened her. But it wouldn't matter, because I'd already be gone.

I dragged one of the chairs to the fireplace and stood atop it, reaching to grab my father's sword from where it was displayed over the mantle, beside its intricately embroidered scabbard. As I pulled it away, I saw that the holster was attached to it.

367 |

Thank the Gods.

I swung the holster around my hips, below the cloak, and cinched it tight.

The climb down from the window was harder than the one from my room, there were less places to catch my feet or hold onto with my hands. And doing it all in such a small dress was the hardest part. My knees went raw from scraping the brick.

But the moment my slipper clad feet hit the ground I started running. I didn't stop until I reached the cover of the trees, knowing I'd meet Maddox soon. I slowed my pace as the canopies hid me, my heart pounding against my chest.

I stopped for a moment and took a deep breath and it was as if every emotion I was capable of feeling hit me at once.

Shame. Pride. Anger. Joy. Pity. Hatred.

I cycled through them in my brain until I landed on the one that stood out.

Loneliness.

As I walked the tears started streaming down my face before I could stop them. I was alone.

I was in the process of abandoning my best friends and the only family I had left in this world. I knew Maddox and Wyott had become my friends since we'd met, but I knew I couldn't tell them about what I'd done. They could be disgusted, enraged. They were supposed to be good, and I was afraid they'd abandon me once they discovered that I wasn't.

I was alone.

Like I had been since the moment my father took his last breath. Like I was the night of my attack. Like I was when I killed Bassel.

I approached the clearing near the wall where Maddox and I planned to meet. I stepped out from the protection of the trees, and saw him for the first time, stationed near the wall rising a hundred feet above him. He leaned against it with his arms crossed as if he was waiting for a friend at the tavern instead of waiting for a fugitive.

He must have been lost in thought because it was a second before his head whipped toward me. And with his eyes on me, sharp even across the span of dozens of feet, that same ache settled in my chest. Here I was, having to lie to him, again.

I walked toward him, my satchel of clothes sat at his feet, but he left it and cut the distance between us.

"You came." He whispered as he stopped in front of me, eyes searching mine, a slight smile tugging on his lips.

I nodded. "I told you I would." I looked up at him and the sight of his smile sent a wave of butterflies through me.

His smile widened and he raised a hand to swipe his thumb over my lower lip. My breath caught.

"I was afraid you'd stay." He whispered. I could only stare up at him, see the way the stars glistened behind him. His eyes raised to meet mine now, his hand slipping away. "Is everything taken care of?"

"Yes. Thank you for waiting."

He opened his mouth to speak, that lazy smile still evident, but before he could his body stilled and his pupils dilated. "Why do you smell like blood?" His tone was chilling, like the night he'd seen the hand print on my face.

I gritted my teeth. I hadn't thought about that. I could hide the sight of Bassel's blood coating my dress. I couldn't hide the smell from a Kova.

I swallowed. "It's nothing. We have to go." I made a move to go around him but he stopped me, stepping forward and catching my face in his hands, examining me. My hood slid away from my face in the movement and his eyes landed on the cut I knew I had on my brow.

"What happened?" His hands held me tight, eyes darkening.

I sighed and shook my head. "It's nothing, please. We have to go."

Maddox's jaw ticked under the tension before he released me and started walking past me and back toward town.

"Where are you going?" I hissed, following.

"To kill him." His voice shook and I saw the tension build in his shoulders as he stormed away from me.

I groaned and jolted forward, grabbing his arm and whipping him around before he could disappear into the trees.

"You can't do that."

He took a step closer and I had to tilt my head up to meet his hot glare. "I refuse to leave Kembertus until he's paid for your blood, with his." He growled.

He was too angry to reason with. I couldn't argue my way out of this one. I couldn't tell the entire truth, but I could offer a piece of it. I reached up, catching his face in my hands this time, and pulled his gaze back to mine. "I need you here. I need you with me."

Maddox's jaw clenched before his eyes softened. He closed them for a moment, taking a deep breath, and when they opened again they were a shade lighter. "Okay." He whispered.

I turned, taking his hand and dragging him back to the wall. I needed to change and we needed to leave before anyone found Bassel's body or noticed I was gone.

We were a few feet from the wall when a gust of wind blew past me, and he stiffened. He halted and tugged my hand until I whipped around to face him.

"I smell too much blood for a small cut on your eyebrow. Are you hurt?" He asked, his hands already moving to tug on the collar of my cloak. My hands fumbled up to move his away, if he saw my slip there'd be no denying it.

"I'm fine. Just forget about it."

He furrowed his brows and shook his head. "I can't just forget about it Evaline. What did he do to you?" He stepped forward again and pulled my hood off my head.

I back stepped away from him. "Maddox, stop." I hissed and turned to reach for my satchel, unfastening my holster and dropping the sword onto the ground. "I need to change, and we need to leave." I fumbled through my bag, looking for clothes to change into.

"You couldn't tell me why we stayed for the wedding. You couldn't tell me why you married him. Now you can't tell me this?" His voice shook and I knew he was making an effort to soften it.

I shook my head, dropping the bag onto the ground. I turned to face him fully and his brows were raised, waiting for my response.

"You don't want to know." I said, crossing my arms.

He raised a hand to pinch the bridge of his nose. "Evaline, what are you even saying? Of course I want to know. If he hurt you, he shouldn't be breathing."

That caused a breath to shake through me and I felt tears begin to prick the backs of my eyes. I wanted to tell him, but I was afraid. I didn't want to lose him. I looked up at Maddox and shook my head.

"You won't see me the same." I whispered.

His face fell as he stepped closer to me, his hand reaching for mine. "I'll never judge you." He raised my hand to kiss my knuckle. "There's nothing to be afraid of, ashamed of. If he hurt you, you can tell me."

I sighed and took my hand from his. "You don't understand." My hands raised to the few buttons at the collar of my cloak, working to undo them. If it would get him over that wall, I'd tell him.

His eyes watched my hands work. "Then make me understand." He said as I started on the last button. "Make me understand what he did to you. Make me understand why you went through with the wedding, only to run away with me." He shook his head. "You're Bassel's wife."

I slid the cloak away from my chest and off my shoulders, dropping onto the ground below me, exposing the blood that speckled my dress.

"And now I'm his widow."

There was a moment of silence as Maddox's eyes drank me in, then a strangled breath left his lips.

His eyes traveled down my chest, where I knew in the cold of the night my nipples poked through the fabric of my silky slip. Down the white speckled with red. To my thighs where the hem hardly covered anything. Over the holster that sat there, sporting the weapon he gave me. Down over my second dagger, to my feet.

"Eva." It was only my name but it sounded like a confession on his lips.

The way he stood rigid, the way his eyes enveloped me like I was the finest piece of art he'd ever seen, the way his hands balled at his sides.

A warm heat flushed over my skin and an ache began between my thighs. The same one he'd caused over and over.

He moved. His eyes held mine as he advanced and flattened one hand over the soft material on my stomach, pushing me until my back hit the cold stone of the wall behind me.

My breath hitched in my throat. "What?" It was a whisper on my lips.

His hand roamed to slide in the crook of my waist. His other landed on my collarbone. I looked down to see my chest was splattered in blood as well. His hand slid down, between my breasts, almost catching on the fabric there, almost sliding inside. I took a sharp breath and felt his wash over my face, I looked back up to meet his eyes.

"You can't say things like that, and wear things like this." He tugged on the hem of my dress, eyes exploring my body again. "And expect me to be able to control myself."

My breath shuddered. The warmth crept along my skin everywhere he touched, everywhere he looked. My mind fogged and I didn't know what to say, but in this moment, in his arms, I needed to know what he meant. After so many soft touches from him, so many sweet words. I needed him to voice what he wanted.

"Control yourself from what?" It was so quiet. If his senses weren't heightened he wouldn't have heard it. His hand slid along my thigh, toying with the edge of my holster. My back arched absentmindedly, pushing my chest toward him.

"You." A deep groan shook him and reverberated through my body until it ended between my thighs. I gasped at the sensation and he closed the distance between us.

His hands held me tightly while the rest of his body pushed me into the wall, his face nosing into my neck. His breath over my skin burned like sparks and my heart rate spiked. My hands balled at my sides. His lips trailed over the sensitive skin of my neck, down to my collar bone. Not kissing or nipping. Just moving across me light as a feather.

A soft moan escaped me at the sensation as he pushed himself harder against me. I felt that he was ready against my stomach and need coiled low in me. I heard him take a deep breath and his fingers trailed to rest on my hips. I felt him smile against me.

"He was afraid." The words were soft, but I could hear a tinge of admiration. "I can smell it."

The revelation was something I knew, but coming from Maddox's mouth, in a tone of wonder, it further fueled the fire within me.

An uncontrolled breath left my lips. "I know."

He pulled away just enough to meet my eyes. "You look like a Goddess." He whispered, nearly against my lips. "The Goddess of Bloodshed."

I raised my chin to look at him. "I prayed to her for strength."

"You didn't need it."

A gust of wind blew past us, kissing the buds that poked even harder through my dress. He glanced down and dug his nails into my hips. "Eva." His breath came in short spurts. "If you don't want this, you need to tell me. Because I'm losing it." His voice quaked. "And I need you. And I've needed you for so long." He shook his head. "So push me off and walk away." I didn't move as he leaned down, his breath caressing my ear. "Tell me to stop."

I opened my mouth and didn't hesitate. "I don't want you to."

His moan was desperate and the sound lit my soul as he closed the distance between us and caught my lower lip in his. We stayed that way for a moment, neither moving as we just enjoyed our first kiss that I didn't realize until exactly this moment I had been waiting for since the moment we met. I swung my arms over his neck and pulled his body closer to mine and he tilted his head, deepening the kiss and pulling my hips against his.

His mouth was soft against mine and the energy that passed between us had my lips parting for him, moaning against the feel of his tongue as he pushed me harder into the wall, as if he couldn't get close enough to my body.

My hands dropped to his shoulders and I grasped him, pulling him against me just as hard as he was. His lips moved down over my jaw and to my neck. He kissed the sensitive skin there before I felt his teeth graze over it. Not hard enough to draw blood, just to elicit a moan.

My nipples scratched against the inside of my slip and even though it was the softest material, the friction was agonizing. Teasing and slow. So were his lips on my neck, trailing down to the dip in my collar bone and then back up to the other side. I tried to arch my back even more, press my chest against his, get any relief, but there was none. I let my hand fall down to his.

I pulled his hand from my hip and he started to pull away, to look at me as if I was pulling him off of me, to stop him from touching me.

No.

His eyes locked on mine as I dragged his hand up to my breast.

"Eva." My name was a moan on his lips as his eyes drew black. I wove my fingers through his hair and pulled his lips back to mine, and as they met I felt his hand fan out over my breast, thumb sliding over the bud. He swallowed my moan as his tongue slid into my mouth. His thumb didn't stop and the tension it created was addictive, coiling deep within me.

He slipped his other hand under the hem of my dress. His fingers trailed my skin until his fingers wrapped around my bare hip.

The heat was rising inside of me and it was almost intolerable. His fingers on my skin, his thumb teasing my nipple, the other screaming for attention. I sucked his lower lip between mine and bit down. His curse was lost to my tongue and he grabbed me, picked me up, and pressed me against the wall. I wrapped my legs around his hips on instinct and his hard length pressed right against the very spot that ached for him.

My eyes widened and his name fell from my lips. He held me up above him, his face almost at perfect height as he dipped his mouth and his tongue flattened over the fabric covering my other nipple.

A groan escaped me as I watched his mouth close over it.

He looked up at me and broke his mouth away long enough to whisper. "Be quiet, my Goddess."

A strangled laugh filled the air. "Don't be blasphemous."

His lips raised into a smile before they closed back around me and my head rolled back against the wall. He quickly released one hip and slid under my dress to my other breast. I had to bite my lip to keep from screaming as he pinched the nipple in his fingers. He grumbled his approval against the silk.

This was the most beautiful agony I'd ever experienced.

My head came forward again and I looked down at him as he lit my body on fire.

"Kiss me." It was breathless.

He straightened to his full height and I watched his eyes land on my cut again, brows furrowing.

"You're bruising." He hissed even as his hands tightened around me.

I shook my head. "I don't care." I whispered, breathless from his touch.

With both hands hidden beneath my dress, I watched as Maddox's canines elongated just as they had the night I fed from him. But this time he bit his own lower lip until blood shone in the moonlight.

He didn't need to explain his intentions as he moved. I dropped my head and kissed him, sucking his lower lip between mine. He shuddered below me and groaned against my mouth. His blood was just as I'd remembered it, smooth and sweet as it slid down my throat. I felt the pain ebb on my brow immediately and forced myself to pull away from him, swiping my tongue over his wound before fully pulling away and watching as it healed in front of me.

His eyes were black and I watched as they dropped to my lips before he came forward and swept his tongue over them, removing the blood that must've remained there.

Maddox's hand found its way to my inner thigh and my breath caught in my throat. His large hand wrapped around my thigh and he slid it forward until his thumb met a different bud.

His lips silenced my scream before it could fill the night.

He moved his thumb in slow circles and I swear to the Gods I had never experienced such bliss, in the haze of my pleasure I pondered how none of the men I'd been with in the past had found this bundle of nerves. Maddox pulled his lips from mine and I let my forehead fall against his as his thumb moved.

His eyes watched my face but mine drifted closed, my lip between my teeth.

"Does that feel good, my Goddess?" His voice was thick and made the swirl of his thumb even sweeter.

All I could do was whimper in response.

"Tell me how good it feels."

My mouth dropped open as his pace quickened and I moaned. "It feels so good." I opened my eyes to see his had fallen to my lips.

He lifted his gaze then to meet mine as his thumb stopped.

I sucked in a breath and lifted my head from his, the demand to continue stopping in my throat as his fingers pulled from my thigh and I felt them slide along me.

"My Eva." He groaned and his brows furrowed as if he was in pain. "You're so wet for me."

"Yes." Was the only whisper I could muster.

His hand that had been on my breast fell to my waist, holding me in place against the wall.

Slowly, he slid a finger in, easing the ache I'd felt for too long. A moan took me a second later as he fully sheathed his finger and pressed against me.

"Fuck." A breath shuddered through him, wracking through his body.

While his finger began to slowly move, his thumb met the bundle of nerves again. The combination untied me, his thumb rubbing circles as his hand pumped in and out, and my breaths came fast.

"Maddox." My voice was breathless.

He shuddered around me. "Yes?"

"I —" The words were stolen from my mouth as he increased his rhythm. I took a breath. "I'm going to scream."

I knew I was. If he continued, it was impossible that I remained quiet. I'd give away our position and I'd do it happily if it meant he didn't stop.

I saw the swell of pride in his eyes as he reached forward and caught my lips in his.

And I did scream, but he muffled the noise with his kiss.

I wove my hands in his hair, pulling him closer to me. But he was going too slow, a rhythm that had been perfect a moment prior now too agonizingly slow to appease the fire he ignited. I rocked my hips against his hand, and the moan of approval that I caught from his lips drove me to continue. It felt as if he curled his finger inside of me and I came undone.

This scream he seemed ready for, squelching it before it could escape. My entire body locked and relaxed somehow at the same time and I pulled his hair and bit his lip so hard I tasted blood again.

But he only kissed me harder and pumped his finger faster as I rode the wave of bliss right off a cliff, for all I cared. Because in this moment he was everything, this was everything.

When the wave passed, I was exhausted, muscles aching more from the pleasure than from my entire fight with Bassel. I pulled my lips from Maddox's and went limp in his arms, my breathing ragged and my pulse pushing against my neck.

He slowly removed his hand and the absence was immediately noticed. I leaned my head against the wall as I watched him bring his hand up, sliding that finger between his lips, my mouth dropped open at how the sight struck a chord in me. His eyes held mine as he sucked the taste of me away, and when he removed his hand, his eyes were the darkest they'd been the entire night. He drew his head closer to mine and I allowed mine to fall forward off the wall, above him.

"So sweet." He whispered and I shivered. He leaned forward and caught my lips in his again, this time just a soft, sweet kiss.

"We have to go." He whispered.

I nodded and he loosened his hold on me and set my feet on the ground. Maddox watched me as I bent to unfasten the holster at my calf and I gasped when I felt his hands on my thigh, undoing that one for me. I looked up at him, like I was embarrassed. After everything we just did, his touch still shocked me. He smiled at me and pulled me to stand.

He looked around to ensure we were still alone while I grabbed my clothing from my satchel and pulled my trousers up, tucked my slip in. Finding my long-sleeved tunic and sliding it on. I reattached my holsters with their blades and slid on and tied my boots. Finally, I threw on my cloak that I had in my bag, leaving the one I'd stolen from the honeymoon suite in the dirt.

When I straightened and slung the bag across my body, Maddox's stare was on me again. "Ready?"

I nodded. Maddox held out his hand and I took it. He turned to evaluate the rise of the wall. In a moment he would sling me over his shoulder like I had just done with the bag, and jump over it. With his back to me I took the time to bring my second hand up, fingers touching my swollen lips. He turned and smiled at me, and when my breath caught, it wasn't for the kiss.

Not the kiss. Not his hands. Not the orgasm. No. All I could think about was what Maddox didn't do tonight. What he didn't do when he found out what I'd done to Bassel.

He didn't ask why.

CHAPTER FIFTY-FOUR

Maddox

When I landed on the other side of Kembertus' boundary a new hope had sprung in my chest. Hope that on this side of the wall, Evaline might finally let her own crumble completely. Allow me in, let me love her. I let Evaline slide off my back, my heart still beating through my chest. I'd imagined kissing her, touching her, the feeling of her so many times, but it paled in comparison to the act.

Her smooth skin, her hands gripping onto me, the moans she made. Now, walking beside her quietly in the woods, approaching where Wyott stood waiting for us, I could feel myself getting hard again.

She was everything. Everything I'd ever dreamed my mate could be, everything I'd hoped she would be. Too hard for her own good, but soft in my hands, falling apart around me.

I clenched my jaw as the feel of her around my hand re-entered my mind. I'd wanted nothing more than to open my pants and sink into her, make her scream louder than she already had, and I think she might've let me.

But I didn't want our first time to be rushed. To be quick against a cold wall when we had to be quiet. I wanted to have all night with her. I wanted to hear her soft sighs, and the way she moaned my name while I sent her rolling through orgasm after orgasm.

I wanted her to remember that first time always, how soft and slow and perfect I knew it would be, so that in a few years, when I fucked her against a tree in the woods on a trip I knew we'd take, when I showed her the world she'd been kept from, she'd know that I would want her under any circumstance, fast or slow, hard or soft, with every breath I took.

She spoke to Wyott. He'd just gotten back from scouting farther out into the forest, making sure it was safe. As I turned to look at her, breaking myself away from my thoughts, I could feel her withdraw into herself a bit already, and I could only imagine the thoughts filling her mind. She built walls from allowing anyone in, except her friends. She was open with them, and even with Wyott. I saw her smile and laugh at his jokes in a way she didn't do with me.

I'd been afraid it meant she wasn't attracted to me, but now I knew that wasn't true. She guarded herself from me, and it hurt. Not because my ego couldn't handle it or because my pride needed her to need me. But because I knew she was only doing it to protect herself. Afraid I would hurt her. I was the last person she'd ever have to worry about that with. I'd light the world on fire to protect her, and I'd fight a war on my own if that's what it took to keep her safe.

I just wish I could tell her that. But I knew it was too soon. She didn't even know Kova had mates.

"Maddox, we need to move." Wyott broke me out of my trance.

I nodded and we started to walk, but Evaline stayed put.

She met my questioning glance and turned her attention to Wyott. "Wyott, I have to tell you something."

He quirked an eyebrow at her.

"I killed Bassel. They're going to come after me." Her gaze fell to me now. "So if you both want to bow out of this arrangement, I understand."

My little mate. My heart ached inside of me. Hadn't I just shown her my loyalty, my admiration?

But before I could speak, Wyott's snort filled the air. "That's all?" He rolled his eyes and waved a hand off. "Most days we do that before lunch."

It was an exaggeration, for sure, but it did what I know he intended. Evaline laughed and the sound lit my soul.

We moved through the night, heading toward the River Brawn until we could make it to Neomaeros where I knew we'd be safe enough to recover until she was ready to travel again.

I could tell Evaline was dragging by the time the morning threatened to break. She'd had an exhausting day that started early. She'd been on her feet throughout the whole ceremony and reception. She'd killed Bassel and then began this trek.

We couldn't stop and build a camp too close to Kembertus, though. We had to push to keep moving long after I knew she was spent. While she never complained, or showed any outward indication of fatigue, I could see her eyes struggle to remain open and the small yawns that would crest her mouth every few minutes.

We were near a lake, an entire night's journey away from Kembertus, so if we didn't build a fire, we'd be safe to stop for a few hours. I stopped walking and Evaline almost ran into me.

Wyott nodded when I looked at him. He knew she needed to rest, too.

"Why'd you stop?" She asked, looking up at me. The bags under her eyes couldn't lie.

"You need to rest."

She shook her head. "No, I'm fine I promise."

I smiled at her, hand lifting to caress the dark circles under her eye. "You don't need to pretend with us, Eva. We can tell you're tired, and you should be. Rest now so we can travel throughout the rest of the day."

She opened her mouth to protest, but Wyott cut her off. "You know there's no point in arguing with him."

She groaned and agreed. I cleared an area on the thick grass for her to lay and set my pack down for her to use as a pillow.

"Sleep here, we'll scout the area to make sure it's safe. I'll wake you in a few hours."

She shook her head. "Don't you need to rest, too?"

I shrugged. "Kova don't need to as often as humans do. Wyott and I will be fine for now."

She nodded and I watched as she sank onto the greenery, resting her head back on the pack and looking up at me, eyes so tired.

"Thank you." She whispered and closed her eyes. "We need to find shelter soon; it's going to rain."

My brow quirked up as I looked toward the clear, blue skies. "It doesn't look like it."

She sighed sleepily. "It will. My wrist aches when there's a storm coming. It's never healed properly from a break."

I smiled at her and shook my head. "We'll deal with that if it happens."

I didn't walk twenty feet away before I could hear her breathing had slowed and she'd fallen into a deep sleep.

CHAPTER FIFTY-FIVE

Evaline

I woke up to raindrops hitting my face.

I sat up, seeing Maddox sitting a few feet away. A smug smile lit my face as I looked to him.

"I told you."

He shook his head with a smile. "I guess you have some extra abilities of your own." He walked toward me and offered his hand. I took it and let him help me up. My heart felt like it was soaring, despite the droplets landing on my head, and I knew why. My nap was dreamless, and for the first night since my attack, there wasn't even a glimpse of the nightmare that so frequently plagued my mind.

"Where's Wyott?"

Maddox didn't release my hand as he led me to the shore of the lake, guiding me to sit on a rock beside it. I did so. "He's scouting ahead, I think he got bored." He pulled a handkerchief from his satchel and I snorted, he raised his brows at me. "What?"

"I never took you for a man who carried around a handkerchief."

He smiled at me as he dunked it into the water of the lake. "I stole it, if it makes you feel better."

I nodded. "That definitely seems to be more in character for you."

He laughed and kneeled on one leg in front of me, I froze.

"What are you doing?" The flashes of the night before running through my mind as I looked into his eyes. His lips on mine, on my neck, on my breast. His hands sliding down my body, inside me. I flushed.

His hand, that'd been on its way to me, hung in the air as he paused. "We have to wipe all this blood off of you, if we run into anyone it'll look mighty suspicious."

The realization that I still had Bassel's blood coating my chest and neck dawned on me and I nodded.

He dabbed at the part of my chest that was visible with the tunic on.

I looked to the water while he worked. My mind slipping back to that room where I'd ended a man's life. I tried, sincerely tried, to feel bad about it. Each moment since I felt my blade cut through his skin. But I couldn't. Who knows how many other women he'd done this to previously, or that I'd saved from the same fate?

"Are you thinking about it?" Maddox whispered, but even though his voice was low I still startled.

I turned to face him, meeting his worried gaze. "Yes."

He dabbed the handkerchief again, wringing out the blood that had already gathered in it. The pink drops fell into the lake, the color dispersing immediately. He brought the towel back up and moved to my neck.

"Was it your first?" His voice was so low.

I hesitated, Bassel's words filling my mind. "You killed Lonix." He'd said. It was impossible.

"Yes."

Maddox's other hand came to tilt my chin away, exposing the side of my neck for him. "You can talk about it with me, you know." My jaw clenched. "I will never judge you."

I fought back the tears that tried to spring in the back of my eyes. There was something wrong with me, because in that room I'd been high on retribution. I'd smirked at Bassel, mocked him, baited him until I killed him. And I'd relished the sound of his gurgling breaths, the swipe of my blades on the duvet.

But reality had set in, and I was ashamed. Not because I'd killed him, but because I'd enjoyed it. And I didn't know what that said about me.

My father never spoke about killing that way. Perhaps it was because that was different. He was a soldier. He followed orders. He had no personal vendetta for the men he killed. He didn't even know their names. Whether they had families they were leaving behind as he plunged his sword through their heart. He felt every life he took deep in his bones, and he carried it with him until he died.

I struggled to consider what he must think of me. What he'd say if he could see me, hear my thoughts.

Would he be disgusted? Appalled?

"Eva." Maddox whispered again, bringing my chin back to face him. I realized I hadn't responded to him.

"I'm not ready."

He just nodded and tilted my head to the other side and finished wiping the blood from me.

When he was done, we stood, Wyott coming up the lake bank towards us.

"Ready?"

That evening, a few hours before sunset, we were still trekking toward the Madierian.

Every hour the Kova on either side of me would look at me, and try to pretend they weren't, to check to see if I needed rest. But I pushed forward as much as I could, not wanting to slow us down. They'd shove the canteen into my hand every hour, too, ensuring I was hydrated. They'd pass me dried fruits and bread, anything to give me nutrition on the walk.

But they were handling me with care. Not speaking about anything, glancing at me like I'd break.

Finally, I snapped.

"If you look at me like a little girl who lost her pony one more time, I will drive a dagger through your heart."

There was a silence before Wyott heaved a sigh of relief.

"Oh, thank the Gods. I was worried we'd lost you there for a minute." He shoved my shoulder as we walked. "But glad to see we still have our little sadist."

I laughed along with him, relieved for things to be back to normal. No, I wasn't entirely okay after Bassel. But I would never get better if the two of them tiptoed around me.

"You're usually quite the gab, Wyott. I'm sure it's been killing you not to talk this entire trip."

He rolled his eyes at me playfully, but then nodded. "Yes, please, anything. I'm losing my mind, I'm so bored."

I laughed and peered at Maddox. He smiled down at me. "Can you tell me more about Kova?"

I said the words to Maddox but, of course, Wyott interjected. "Of course. We are one half of two beings that were given life and immortality by the Gods. Maddox's father was the first to be given the gift of being a Kova, which is why he's the leader of our people."

I nodded. "What do you call him, Lord, King?"

Maddox laughed beside me. "He would sooner die than have anyone call him those names."

Wyott smiled. "He prefers to be called by his name, Kovarrin. But if he must be referred to by his title as our leader, he goes by the First." I nodded. "The other set of beings who were gifted immortality are the Vasi. They kill to feed but we," he wobbled his thumb between the two of them. "Only drink enough from humans to survive."

I nodded. "Doesn't it hurt them?"

Maddox spoke. "We always compel them first, that it won't hurt. It turns the pain center of their brain off while we feed, and after, we heal the wound."

My face paled. "They drink your blood to heal the wound?"

He shook his head. "No, our saliva can heal small injuries, like the wound of the bite." I nodded. That made more sense. "When we walk away, they are exactly as we found them, despite maybe being a bit lightheaded. But nothing some food and water won't cure."

I turned to Wyott as he started to speak again. "There's also the matter of how we're created. While Vasi and Kova can both be born, either by two full blooded parents or one full blooded parent and a mortal, there's also a transition option."

I raised my eyebrows and he continued. "Kova can turn into Vasi, if they drain a mortal of all their blood, killing them. It damages the thin veil in all our souls, what alters us from becoming monsters, and their soul never recovers. They transform into Vasi in mind and spirit, and their eyes change color."

I looked between them. "Have you guys ever known anyone that turned?"

Maddox answered this time. "No, just scary stories our parents told us growing up."

I nodded. Wyott continued. "Even though Kova can turn into Vasi, it's not mutually exclusive. Vasi can't turn to Kova, because –"

"Their veil is already torn." I finished for him.

"Yes," he nodded.

"What about humans?"

Maddox looked down at me. "Humans can turn into Kova, yes. If a mortal makes the transition, the default is always to a Kova, but as Wyott already explained, they could then turn into Vasi."

I nodded.

"It's not common." Maddox added, and I saw Wyott snap his head, giving him a look.

I ignored it. "Do you know anyone that's changed?"

Maddox regarded me. "Yes, a few friends over the years."

Wyott jumped in with the answer to my next question. "It's a relatively easy process, but not one that happens by accident too often." I turned to him. "A Kova or a Vasi must drink the human's blood, not a lot, just enough to get into their own system. Then the human must drink the Kova or Vasi blood, which is a mixture of the two. Without this mingling of bloods, there is no transition. So usually it's a time-restricted process."

"You said Kova could be born from a human and a Kova, does that happen often?" I tried to make the question as nonchalant as possible, angling it to Wyott instead of Maddox. Trying not to indicate the real question I was asking.

Do humans and Kova ever pair?

But as Wyott opened his mouth to speak, his eyes flashing up to Maddox as if he was asking permission, both of their eyes snapped behind us.

"What the fu –?" Wyott started.

I turned along with them, and in a flash of movement Maddox snapped his hand in front of me, hand clasping the butt of a dagger in mid-air, the blade an inch from my face.

I gasped at how close I'd almost come to being killed. Before I could have any other reaction Maddox swiped me behind his back, shielding me.

"What kind of cowards attack from behind?" Wyott called out, stepping in front of us, too.

Five men emerged from the greenery around us.

"Won't be calling us cowards when we're fileting the meat off your bones."

Wyott laughed and Maddox, who I would've thought acted in the same way in fights, was silent. Stone cold still as he protected me.

CHAPTER FIFTY-SIX

Maddox

My heart thundered in my chest as I watched the men standing before us. Not at the impending fight, not at the fact that we hadn't heard them approach, but from the realization that my mate's life had almost ended because I stopped paying attention to our surroundings.

I'd been so focused on her question, whether Kova and humans had children together, that I'd drowned the rest of the world out. It wasn't until I'd heard the blade whizzing behind her that I'd realized she was in danger.

"I'd sincerely love to see you try." Wyott shot back at the man standing in front.

The man rolled his eyes, nodding the tip of the dagger in his hand to point at each of the men beside him.

"There are five of us, and two of you. No amount of extra weapons," he said, swirling the dagger in the direction of Wyott's full armory. "Will save you."

I heard Evaline scoff and sidestep out from behind me. "You're so quick to count me out, boys?"

A collective chuckle rang from the men before their eyes ran over her frame. Both her daggers were out of sight, her tunic covering the one on her thigh and her tall boots covering the one on her calf. Her sword hung proudly off her hips.

She gave a curt nod and pursed her lips. "You'll regret laughing, because you've just made it personal."

I didn't have time to find her confidence attractive, even though it was the sexiest thing I'd ever witnessed, because my eyes were roving the holsters of every man in front of us, searching for the one with an empty sheath for the dagger I held in my hand, the one that almost killed Evaline. The man to the left of the one who'd been speaking, on his chest. An empty sheath.

In one quick movement I brought my arm back then forward, snapping my wrist. A second later the man gurgled up blood as the dagger I'd thrown stabbed him, right next to the sheath it was meant for.

"I think you dropped that." I hissed at them, but they were all already in motion.

The four remaining men charged, and so did Wyott and I. I sent my arm cascading behind me, hoping to sweep Evaline back, but she was too fast, running forward and swiping the blade I'd given her from her thigh.

Two men were on the right, near Wyott. The leader was directly in front of me, leaving one man charging Evaline alone.

I bit back the fear in my gut and swallowed the urge to throw her over my shoulder and run. But if she could take Wyott and I down, and kill Bassel, she could hold her own.

I turned my attention as Wyott collided with the two men, his sword drawn.

As he swept the blade over one man's gut, spilling his entrails in front of him, he shot out his other and punched the second in the face, knocking him back a few feet.

While he pushed to pursue that man, I collided with the leader. Leaning to the side to miss his overhead swing of his sword, I shoved my dagger up, into his throat.

I turned to Evaline as I heard Wyott end the life of the second man he fought behind me.

She was a picture of divinity, crouched in her stance, circling with the man who leered at her as if this was all a joke.

Wyott came to stand beside me and it was then that the man realized he was the last remaining. He turned, fear in his eyes, looking to Wyott and I, worried we'd attack him from the rear.

I shook my head. "Don't look at us, we wouldn't kill you from behind." I waved a hand toward Evaline, who hadn't taken her eyes off the man's sword. "We're here to watch the show."

The man's eyes grew but he turned and began circling Evaline again.

I clenched my jaw as I watched her move, my eyes falling to the Rominium dagger in her hand. I wasn't sure if she chose it over her sword because it was a faster pull, or because she had only been practicing with daggers lately, but I couldn't hide the way seeing her use the dagger I'd given her heated my blood. In a moment of battle, she chose the dagger that was given to her by me. She chose me.

But the worry won out, I'd rather her use the sword compared to her dagger which was only the length of her forearm. A sword would reach closer to the man, but keep her out of his blade's sweep. I swallowed the panic, I knew she could do it. I knew she was fast enough, strong enough.

She circled him and I could see the light in her eyes, shining more than it had since she climaxed with my finger inside of her.

A smile formed on my lips.

He swiped the blade out, aiming for her face. She fell to the ground, landing flat on her back, then twisted, using her upper body as leverage on the ground as she swung her legs in a semicircle, knocking his legs out from underneath him.

He yelled at the impact, falling on his stomach, his sword fallen a few inches away.

As agile as a cat she punched up until she was crouching over him, her foot holding him down.

She bent her head toward him, a smile playing on her face. "I didn't make the promise about killing you from behind." Then plunged the dagger into his back, driving where she knew his heart lay inside.

He died within seconds, and she stood, turning toward us. I knew a smile lit my features and as she caught my eyes, she returned it.

"That…" Wyott started beside me. "Was the single most impressive thing I've ever seen you do."

She turned her smile to him, walking toward us as she wiped the dagger over her leg.

"Scratch that," he said. "Most impressive thing I've ever seen any mortal do… ever."

Her smile grew at the compliment, and I knew it was because his complimented ranked her over the men he'd fought with, including her father.

"Thank you." She said, coming to stand beside us, but her eyes dragged to me, waiting.

"A Goddess." I said, low. Her eyes flickered, and I knew the nickname stirred the memories of the night before.

"You're letting your blasphemy show again."

We continued our journey after dragging the men into the brush, not that it did anything to hide their blood that smeared the path. Evaline and Wyott bickered about nonsense.

"I'm just saying, you have more weapons on you than you will ever use. You could give me a bandolier." She made her case.

He scoffed. "You kill two men, and now you think you're a warrior worthy of these beauties?" He asked, waving his hands over his holsters.

"Yes, I think I made that abundantly clear." She retorted, and I had to hide my snicker.

Wyott rolled his eyes. "Listen, my Lady, let's take down more than one person at once, and then we'll talk."

She just laughed, shoving him in the side, and cast her eyes up to me. I knew she was searching, asking me to interact. I'd been silent on the walk since the fight. And it wasn't because we killed those men, it was because she'd almost died, in my arms, and she still didn't know about the bond. All I could do was retrace every interaction we'd had in the last handful of weeks that we'd known each other.

She'd been hesitant around me, though it had gotten better after she fed from me, but she hadn't spoken of our kiss once. If she couldn't even speak about the intimate moment we'd shared, how was she going to react to being told she was a mate? To learning that Kova even had mates?

But as she looked at me, I saw the shadows below her eyes, and knew she was tired.

"We need to find a place to camp. We're far enough away and we could all use some sleep."

Wyott nodded and veered, and I knew he was hunting a meal.

I clasped Evaline's hand and tugged her after me. "Let's go look for a campsite."

She nodded and didn't pull her hand away.

After finding a suitable spot, far enough from the path that we felt safe, we started gathering firewood. Eventually Wyott came back with a rabbit, and we prepared it, cooking it over the fire until we split the meat between the three of us.

I volunteered to take the first watch, and they both fell asleep soon after. I stared at the crackling flames, running through every variation this conversation could go, when Evaline learned she was my mate.

She could be happy. She could be angry. She could run.

I'd spent hours thinking up ways to tell her, and each one left a pit of anxiety deep in my gut. But I needed her to know, even if she rejected me. I took a deep breath and vowed that I'd tell her once we made it to the next town, when she'd had a proper meal and slept in a proper bed. I needed to feed, badly. And I knew Wyott would continue pushing me to tell her until I did.

If I –

But my eyes shifted to Evaline. Moments before, she'd been sleeping soundly, but she suddenly began whimpering, and as I drew closer I realized she was crying in her sleep. My heart raced, seeing her in any pain was unbearable.

As I sat beside her, she started shaking.

CHAPTER FIFTY-SEVEN

Evaline

I felt myself fall down. Further and deeper into what seemed like an endless pit of darkness. Pain rippled up my wrist as I landed, catching myself on the brittle bones. The grass below my hands a comfort, as I was glad to no longer be slipping through time and the blackness of a void.

But the eyes that danced above me were not comforting. They gawked at me, trailing over my skin in a different type of assault. Their eyes were hungry and greedy. Brown and green pools of filth and disgrace. Their expressions peeled back in shows of aggression.

Then it was their hands.

They roamed my body, searching for somewhere to tie a rope. One found its way to my mouth and covered it, but on my skin the hand dissolved until it was billions of particles, sliding like sand past my lips. It coated my tongue and dried my mouth. Sinking back into my throat and clogging it. I couldn't make a sound as I watched the men over me. My lips moved but no noise came, no whimpers or cries or shouts.

Just silence.

I was being dragged, the dirt and grass and leaves piling into the back of my shirt as it rolled up and the men pulled me closer and closer.

The only noise was their heavy breathing, puffs of a disgusting need. A need for power, for domination, for superiority.

Then a voice.

A voice entered my mind, and I couldn't tell if it was my own.

"Evaline."

No, it wasn't my voice. But my name sounded natural coming from it. As if the owner had said it a thousand times before.

"Evaline, you're in danger."

That was quite obvious.

The men continued to drag me. The few feet that we'd spanned felt vast.

"You can protect yourself."

The voice was urgent and I struggled with placing who I heard. In the haze that covered me I couldn't place it, couldn't even tell if it was deep or high pitched.

The men grew closer and I knew my reckoning was near. I felt my body shake, jolting against the hold on me as I fought against my attackers.

Yes, I could protect myself. Where was my dagger? My fingers straightened and palpated my thigh to find it. My hand only met the soft flesh of my leg, the handle that would usually be there, gone.

"You don't need knives. You are the weapon." The voice was rushed, like it was losing time with me. "Evaline, please understand."

The ground below me shook with the men's laughter, reveling in their power over me.

"Evaline, please." The voice was morphing, not the same as before but still unidentifiable.

"Wake up, please."

I made the mistake of looking up at the men who grew closer. Their eyes swallowed me and I began to tumble again, sinking into the grass and falling into their eyes, the only anchor their hands on my ankles.

"Wake up!"

Another set of hands shook me, but I shook within them. My body roiling to escape the holds that imprisoned me.

"Evaline!"

A desperate gasp of breath pulled through my lungs as I whipped into an upright position, nearly knocking heads with Maddox who knelt over me, his hands still on my shoulders as they heaved for air.

Not yet having escaped the nightmare, Maddox's hands on my body were an affront, and I swiped out violently, knocking his grip from me and kicking my feet to scoot away from him.

"Don't touch me." My voice shook.

"Okay." Maddox's voice was soft and patient and he kept his hands to himself.

My eyes opened, I didn't remember shutting them again, and they found his. They were gray and soft and comforting. Concern pulled his brows together. The crackle of the fire reminded me of where I was. Another shaky breath left my lips.

"I'm sorry," I whispered, no longer meeting his eyes. My heart finally began to slow, the remnants of the nightmare slipping away.

"What was your nightmare about?" His voice was quiet.

I craned my neck to look over his shoulder. Wyott slept, oblivious I hoped, on the other side of the fire, facing away from us.

My gaze came forward to focus on Maddox. "Nothing."

He pursed his lips and stared at me. I knew he wanted to fix me. To help me through my trauma, but I didn't know if I was ready to tell him. Even though the thought had crossed my mind before, I still didn't know if I was ready.

"Evaline."

I released a huff and stood up, trying to hide how unsteady I felt, and began walking away.

"Where are you going?" He asked as he followed.

I shook my head, ducking a branch that was in my way. I stumbled through the roots between trees, I wasn't on a path, just walking blindly through the night. I wished I had Maddox's vision, able to see perfectly even in the darkness.

"Where are you going?" He repeated, right behind me. He didn't stop me, just followed.

"Leave me alone."

"So you can get lost in the woods by yourself? No."

I took a deep breath and huffed.

Finally the trees thinned as we entered a clearing. It was small, but there was enough room for the two of us to stand without the claustrophobic threat of the canopies overhead.

I walked a few paces into the field and sank to my knees, my hands catching me as I kneeled on all fours. The nightmare was so vivid, just as real as the night of my attack. They always were, but normally once I awoke, reality grasped its hold onto me and I was able to distinguish between the two.

But waking up in the same environment as my attack had been, a forest in the middle of the night, made the fear sink in deeper. My fingers dug into the grass and I heard Maddox above me, knew he must've been asking a question but all I could hear was my own breathing.

I realized I was hyperventilating.

Tears streamed down my face and the hard lump in my throat made it impossible to breathe. No air could get past it, and I kept taking in short, choppy, breaths. I felt like I was suffocating, like I was Lonix and instead of watching him struggle to breathe, I had taken his place.

"Evaline." Maddox's voice was concerned and before I knew it, he was sinking down behind me and pulling my chest up to clear my airway, his muscled thighs spread around my own. He held me against his own chest, his hand on mine, just above my heart. "Just take in deep breaths." He coaxed me quietly, lips at my ear.

I couldn't do what he asked, it was impossible, and I feared I'd pass out soon.

But Maddox was steady behind me and over-exaggerated his own breaths. Lifting his shoulders to inhale, and sinking with each exhale, taking my body with his as he did so.

"Please Eva, take one big inhale for me." He sounded afraid.

But I did as he asked. It was painful and as the lump in my throat fought against the breath, I thought it would burst out of my neck from the pressure. But I broke past it and the lump dissipated. A ragged breath left my lips and I started to take an even slower, deeper breath.

"Yes, sweetheart. Yes." He praised.

Maddox stayed behind me, hand on my chest and the other wrapped around my torso, holding me against him. We stayed that way for several minutes until my rhythm was back to normal. I questioned why I didn't remove myself, why I didn't get up the moment I could breathe again. But I knew the answer. Being in his arms again felt right. It felt like the most innate thing I had ever done.

But then he spoke. "What was your nightmare about?" His tone was soft, but it still struck a chord in me. He didn't understand what he was asking. This wasn't a nightmare about what might've happened if I was still married to Bassel, or reliving his death. This was my trauma, the most private thing that had ever happened to me.

And right now I didn't know if I could give that to him.

I ripped myself from his arms and stood up, striding away from him and closer to the center of the clearing. I heard him stand behind me, start to follow.

"Just because you walk away from me doesn't mean you can avoid this conversation." He said quietly, but I could hear the frustration in his voice.

I whipped around to face him, and he halted. "Maddox, drop it."

"I won't, I've been patient every step of the way with you. But you were crying, you were shaking in my arms. I want to help. Please. Please tell me." His hands were on his chest, pleading with me.

We stared at one another. Neither budging.

I ground my teeth and looked past him, past the trees lining the way behind him. The sky above us was vast, stars pins in the sky as if they were needle points in one of Aurora's embroideries. The wind blew past, shuffling the small hairs that evaded my braid.

"It must have been something terrifying for you to react that way." Maddox's voice had softened, he took a small step toward me. "Why did you pull away from me like that? Who hurts you in your dreams?"

The hard lump began to form in my throat again as tears threatened the backs of my eyes. I swallowed and looked back at him.

"Why do you need to know so badly?" I had to concentrate to keep my voice even.

"Because I care about you, Evaline." He took another step closer.

I shook my head. "You hardly know me." I whispered.

Pain flashed through his eyes, pain that seemed so out of place but so genuine. "I care about you. Why isn't that enough?" His voice was rough this time, stern.

Anger broiled within me, bubbling up to the surface as I stared at his clenched jaw and dark eyes. He was right, he'd done nothing but prove how loyal he was to me, how much he cared, every step of the way. But I think that's what angered me most. Because who was he to save me? Why did he feel so strongly and care so deeply? Why had he chosen me?

Gods know I didn't deserve it.

"Just because you care about me doesn't mean you get to know the worst things that have ever happened to me, the worst twenty-four hours of life."

His eyes softened and his arms fell to his sides as he looked down. "You're right."

I had taken a breath, ready to counter whatever argument he put forth, but the breath stuck in my throat at his response. "What?"

His eyes raised to meet mine, pained. "You're right. I don't get to know everything about you, even if I want to. I understand you don't want to tell me." He took another small step toward me. "But I only want to know so I can help take away the pain. I need you to tell me how I can be here for you."

My anger dissipated. He was being sincere, and I realized that my anger stemmed from the fear he'd hurt me. Because I knew that I didn't deserve him, but he was still here. After everything. And now he was vulnerable, telling me words I didn't know I wanted to hear until they left his lips.

A rush of emotion hit me. It entered my lungs as I inhaled. The feeling seeped through my pores, into my blood, and coursed through my veins. It smoothed the lines on my face, the creases that had formed from the anger that settled there. It relaxed my shoulders and unclenched my fists. It rested in my heart, squeezing it painfully.

I released a shudder of a breath.

I began to tell him what happened. Every detail, not just the vague information I'd given him so far. Not just that I'd been bitten by the Vasi and that I'd killed it. As I spoke, I raised my eyes to meet his again, gauging his reaction.

I told him how I'd attacked the Vasi to save my father, how he'd been impaled. Maddox took another step toward me as I described what it looked like to see my father mortally wound himself, pulling off of that tree, just to save me. I told him what my father had said before he died, that I'd taken the locket and sword with me when I fled, my hand raising to caress the necklace as I spoke.

Then I told him about the next night. How I was dead tired and starving, how I was caught in the path. Maddox's eyes hardened. I explained how they pulled my braid, that I vowed that night that I would never be grabbed by it again. He went rigid as I spoke, but only listened.

I told him how they'd broken my wrist and his eyes had flashed in recognition. I told him how I fought against them but still couldn't break free. I didn't realize tears were streaming down my face until I felt the cold air against them. Maddox took another step toward me, until he was right before me. I told him how Lonix died, his death making just as little sense in my recounting as it did that night, but Maddox didn't move away, didn't relax, only listened.

"The other man ran off. I was left there alone with a dead body, but I just brushed myself off and walked away. Physically fine other than my broken wrist, but that night still haunts my dreams. My wrist is a constant reminder, aching occasionally. I thought the nightmares would go away, at least, after I —" I stopped myself.

A silence fell over us.

Maddox spoke for the first time in several minutes. "It's okay." He said softly.

I took a shaky breath. "That night, at the Spring Solstice Ball, when my aunt and uncle introduced me to Bassel," I started, looking up to meet his gaze. "That wasn't the first time we'd met."

His gaze hardened. "Please don't say it."

"I hadn't seen Bassel since that night, since I watched him run off." My voice grew rushed, words tumbling from my mouth as if I needed Maddox to understand, needed him to hear me. "But that's why you thought I looked uncomfortable when I danced with him. That's why I was thankful when you stole me from him, even if I didn't know you, and even if you were a Kova. That's why I asked you to help me train when my aunt confirmed my fears, that they were marrying me off to him. They didn't know what happened, the only people I'd told was Aurora and Jacqueline. And even then, they didn't know that Bassel was the second man that night. I never told anyone." I took a breath, replenishing for my next words. "But most importantly, that's why I had to lie to you. That's why I had to go through with the wedding, even though it hurt you."

My voice grew thick, the clump tried to reform and steal my words. "I knew it was the only way I'd get time alone with him, the only chance I had to kill him." I pleaded with Maddox silently through my gaze, begging him to understand. "And I needed to do that. I had to do that to stop the nightmares. To stop him from walking this continent, thinking he could take any woman, at any time, and harm her like that." My voice was shaking and I rushed my words together. "It's why I had to lie and I'm sorry, because you've done nothing but help me and I'm sure it was frustrating when I changed the plans, and you were so upset and so hurt at the wedding but I had to —"

Maddox moved forward, closing the short distance between us. He reached up and held my jaw in his hands, silencing me.

"Shh." He whispered. "Please stop." His voice raw. "Please stop apologizing for things that aren't your fault."

I was silent as I looked up at him through the wavy lens of my tears. He tilted his head toward me and one of his black curls landed on his forehead.

"Evaline, none of what happened to you is your fault. Those men who thought they had some right to put their hands on you, they're at fault. They're at fault for taking your voice, breaking your bones, instilling a burden in you that you don't deserve to carry." His eyes switched between mine, this time he was the one begging. Begging me to hear his words. "And I'm at fault." My brows furrowed. "I'm at fault for not trusting you, not trusting your plan, even if I didn't know it. You didn't deserve my anger, even if I thought it was justified at the time."

Maddox swiped his thumbs gently over my lips until they rested on my cheeks.

"And Bassel's death," he shook his head, clenching his eyes shut against whatever images were flooding his mind. "He's damned lucky it was you who killed him."

I shook my head as much as I could in his embrace. "What do you mean?"

He opened his eyes and they bore through me, cold and hard and black. "If I had known what he'd done to you, what you had to go through that entire month of being forced to be near him, to kiss him at the ceremony." His last words were a growl. "Bassel wouldn't have even made it to the wedding. Because if I had known, my Eva." The words made my stomach flip. "I would have strapped Bassel down. He would've been alive when I sliced off the ears that heard your screams and ignored you. He would have watched as I cut off the hands that held you down and stole your voice." Maddox's thumbs caressed my cheeks, moving in soft circles. "He would've screamed as I gouged out the eyes that watched you struggle and did nothing."

I didn't understand why these words, these violent words, were comforting me. Why they sounded like a proclamation of love rather than a promise of death.

"And only when I was bored of hearing him beg and scream, would I have killed him, slowly. And still, it would not have been enough."

I took in a sharp breath at the words, watching as Maddox's eyes trailed my face. Caressing my skin as it drifted over my features. A look of adoration in his eyes.

Finally, I found my voice. "I didn't need saving." My voice shook so that the statement didn't come out nearly as confident as I would've hoped.

Maddox smiled, a genuine smile. One that reached his eyes and warmed them. One that pulled me in and held me there. "No. You didn't. And you don't." He agreed, and then whispered. "But that doesn't mean I don't want to."

The weight Maddox's words hit me then. And not just his words here tonight. But all of them. Everything he had said to me since the moment we met.

His offer to train me, to help me escape the city. His gentle demeanor when I was drunk, his refusal to sleep with me while under the influence. The rage in his eyes when he found me at the wedding. The rage that wasn't rage; it was devastation. Hurt from watching someone you care about kiss someone else, promise their life to them. His praise when I downed him in a spar, his admiration when he found the spikes in my braid, the hurt that laced his words tonight.

Maddox cared about me.

And I reciprocated. Maybe these feelings that had been whirling inside of me since the moment I met him were all accumulating to something. Maybe this was how love worked. Maybe love was the sum of all the tiny moments between two people. A graze of a hand, a whirl on the dance floor, a flick of a braid. Maybe you didn't need to see love, or grow up around it, to know what it was. Maybe all you had to do was feel it with someone who made you feel whole again. Someone who took all the dark parts of you and worshiped them.

Maddox's eyes were on me as my head whirled with thoughts. But I was tired of thinking, of building walls to protect myself from him.

And for the first time in my life I did something without thinking about the repercussions. Without care for what anyone else thought. I did something simply because I wanted to.

I reached up, grabbed his collar, and pulled his lips to mine.

Maddox was surprised for only an instant. He froze for half of a breath.

Then he moved. He slid his hands to cup my head, cradling the back of my neck, tilting my head up so that he could deepen the kiss. He groaned against my lips, against my tongue. My hands dropped to rest on his chest, balling the fabric in my fists, pulling him closer. He bit my lip gently, and I moaned into his mouth. A growl rumbled in his chest at the noise and he curled an arm around my back. Maddox held his body against mine. His other hand dropped from my head, past my shoulders, down to my waist where he grasped and pulled me even closer to him. I reached up, wrapping my arms around his neck and tangled my fingers into his hair.

The kiss was fierce. It was wild and desperate. Maddox's lips fell down my jaw, his teeth grazing the skin along my neck.

I moaned loudly as my head fell back, my body turning to mush in his arms. The exhaustion from the day, from the nightmare, taking over as I surrendered into him. He supported my weight and pulled me tighter. One hand dropped down my leg and encircled the back of my knee, pulling it up to loop around his waist. The motion caused me to rub against him, where he was hard and ready.

"Maddox." I said breathlessly and tugged on his hair, pulling his lips from my neck and back to mine.

This time I ensnared his bottom lip in my teeth, biting and pulling him toward me. I tasted blood, his sweet blood, and a deep growl rang from his chest. His hand that held my leg over his hip moved to my ass as he pulled me closer to him and I rolled my hips against his.

A shiver ran through him and he pulled away, resting his forehead against mine.

"Eva." The murmur sent a flutter through my heart.

I opened my eyes and looked up to meet his eyes. "What?" Breathless.

He closed his eyes for a moment and let my leg drop off of him, moving both hands up and around my back as he pulled me against him.

"We have to stop." He whispered, eyes still closed.

A heartbeat passed and I nodded. It was dangerous to be out here like this at night, we knew better. I bit my lip and tried to slow my breathing.

"Evaline." He hissed as he pulled away slightly and clenched his jaw. "That is not helping."

I shook my head, confused. "What isn't helping?"

His hand raised to swipe a thumb over my lip, his eyes watching intently. "Biting the lip I want to sink my teeth into."

I breathed. "Oh."

Then he moved forward and kissed me softly. A kiss I was ready to fall into again. But instead he steadied me and pulled away. The loss of his touch instant. I took another deep breath and smoothed my tunic over my torso, hands moving up to wipe over my face, willing the blush in it to go away.

When I looked up, he was watching me. He smiled at me, and I couldn't tell if he looked happy or in agony.

"Ready?" He held a hand out. "We need to get some sleep for our journey tomorrow."

I nodded and put my hand in his. I knew he could see better in the dark, and there was no way I could find my way back to camp.

Maddox turned, still holding onto me, and led me into the trees.

Chapter Fifty-Eight

Maddox

I awoke to Evaline sprawled on my chest, her face buried in my neck. After we'd gotten back to camp, she hadn't wanted to sleep alone. I smiled at the feel of her against me, her body totally relaxed as her breathing was rhythmic and slow.

I took a deep breath, closing my eyes again. Not wanting to start the day yet. But a shadow fell over my face, and when I re-opened my eyes Wyott stood over us, arms crossed.

"It's time to tell her." He whispered.

I suppressed a growl. "I will. Once we get settled into the next town."

We both knew I needed to feed, desperately. But I didn't want to push her faster than she was comfortable. She stirred on my chest and Wyott walked away. When she lifted her head to look at me, she smiled.

"Good morning." She whispered.

I tucked her hair behind her ear. "Good morning."

We spent the day traveling. I knew we'd run into a town soon, and when we did, I'd feel safe staying there for the night. We were far enough away from Kembertus that no one near would have heard of Evaline.

While Kembertus had likely already sent word to Vestaria and Arlomandrah, they wouldn't bother with the small towns along the way, or the Madierian Kingdoms. I doubted Kembertus would send guards so far to search for her.

Evaline stayed close to me as we traveled. She didn't pull away when our hands met while we walked, or when I found an excuse to touch her.

Once again, she and Wyott were bickering back and forth.

"I'm sorry, Wyott. I don't see it."

He scoffed. "You don't think I can pull more women than Maddox?"

Her eyes slid up to me, a smile in them.

She shook her head. "No, you're far too arrogant."

He rolled his eyes. "You don't know what you're talking about."

She shook her head. "I'm a woman, and we're discussing a woman's attraction to the two of you. I think I'm the only one who knows what they're talking about."

His words were quick and unthoughtful. "Well then how did I find my mate before Maddox found his?"

My head snapped to him, and so did hers.

A beat of silence passed. "…What?" Her soft voice was laced with shock.

Wyott's eyes grew, but he tried to play it off. "Oh, did I forget to mention that yesterday? Yes. Kova have mates."

She shook her head, in disbelief. "You just so happened to leave out that huge piece of information?" Her body grew rigid.

"I didn't think about it." I could see the tension building in her shoulders, could hear the increase in her heart.

"How does it work?" She asked and I saw her hands clench into fists at her side.

"The Goddess of Fate assigns each Kova their mate before they're born, she weaves the thread that links all those fated together."

Evaline nodded, and I could feel her sidelong stare. "That seems like an awfully big deal."

He nodded, and his eyes grew glazed as I knew he thought of the day he met Cora. "It's the most important day of a Kova's life."

She smiled at him. "Your mate is back home, in Rominia?"

He looked at her, coming back to reality, and nodded, his eyes sad.

She nodded as everything he'd said processed. She looked sidelong at me. "You have a mate, too?"

I hesitated. Because yes, I had a mate. You. I wanted to scream. But I couldn't, not with those wide, scared eyes staring at me. But I couldn't lie. Wyott had just confessed it.

I nodded. "Yes."

Something changed in her eyes. She gave one nod and turned away. She carried on small, quiet, conversations with Wyott when the town came into view.

It was small, quaint. But it was better than making Evaline sleep on the forest floor for another night.

CHAPTER FIFTY-NINE

Evaline

I moved through the world in a haze of anger. Mate.

He had a mate and he didn't tell me. Worse yet, he had a mate and he'd spent the last few days kissing me as if I was the air he breathed. He turned to me now, like he could hear my thoughts. His brows knitted with worry. But then he turned back to the innkeeper, booking three rooms for us just for the night. I breathed a silent sigh of relief, thankful to get away from him, get a chance to breathe when the air wasn't pulled from my lungs every time he looked at me.

He turned and handed me my key, letting his hand slide along mine as he did so. "Your room is—" He started, but I cut him off.

"Yes, I can listen to directions too." I hissed, before pulling the key from his hand and walking toward the stairs.

I heard his sigh but didn't turn around.

After I shut my door I turned the lock, placing my forehead against the door as I took a deep breath.

It hurt, this crack in my chest that felt like it was ever widening.

But the anger hurt more. Pulling at my throat, flushing my skin, until it was unbearable, and I moved to take a bath, if only to drown out the sound of my whirling thoughts.

I sunk into the water and realized why I really wanted to bathe. With Maddox's superb hearing, I knew he'd hear the moment it happened, but maybe, in the depths of the water, it would be too muffled.

I sunk into it, and sobbed.

After my bath I passed the time by lying on the bed, a cold, damp towel over my eyes. I'd be damned if Maddox saw the red rings around the edges, the swollen lids.

I'd just finished dressing when I heard a knock at my door. I sighed, knowing who it would be.

I bent, taking my time to finish tying my laces and fastening my holsters before I opened the door. He could wait.

I wore a pair of tight black pants, my black boots pulled up to the knee. I didn't need to wear a long sleeved tunic or my cloak since we were only going to dinner downstairs at the tavern, so I opted for the only decent shirt I'd packed; white with capped sleeves that fell on the edges of my shoulders and a black corset, tightened around my waist.

I touched my hair, ensuring my wired braid was in place, and strode to the door.

Maddox stilled when he saw me, eyes falling to my chest. I hadn't bothered tying the strings to close my top, leaving the cleavage visible above the corset. My chest was on display, as well as my sleeveless arms. His eyes continued down to my daggers that were no longer hidden and the sword that hung from my hips. He opened and closed his mouth but didn't speak.

"What do you want?" I asked, tone disinterested.

His eyes snapped up to mine then, and he swallowed. "I came to get you for dinner."

I grabbed my key off the side table and walked out, Maddox moving out of my way. I locked the door behind me and didn't wait for him to lead me down the stairs.

In the tavern below, I saw Wyott seated at a table. I swallowed an annoyed grumble at the realization that I'd have to sit beside Maddox.

I fell down into the chair.

"Aren't you just a ray of sunshine this evening." Wyott grumbled at me.

I rolled my eyes and we ordered dinner.

Wyott and Maddox spoke, mostly about how they were going to buy some horses. Thank the Gods. I could get away from them much easier if I had a horse below me. A pang of sorrow beat through me at the thought. It had only been days before when I'd been afraid of losing Maddox, of he and Wyott walking out of my life, but here I was prepared to do just that.

How could he kiss me, say the things he'd said, if he'd had a mate at home? Wasn't mating for life? It certainly didn't seem like the type of relationship that would be worth ruining through infidelity.

The worst part to all of this was how much I cared.

I'd let myself care, since the day I'd met Maddox. It had slowly built, and I'd come almost completely undone when he'd kissed me against the wall. For Gods' sake, just last night I'd contemplated whether I loved him.

I bit back the tears that were almost ready to come on again and I felt Maddox's stare. I wanted so badly to glare at him, to hiss at him to leave me alone, but I knew if I looked up, the tears would be unstoppable.

Wyott rose, heading for the bathroom. I swallowed and pushed the remaining bits of my dinner around on my plate.

I froze as I felt Maddox's hand cover the one that held my fork.

"Evaline." He said softly. "What's wrong?"

I didn't look up at him as I spoke. "Nothing."

"Don't lie."

I cut my eyes to him, anger seeping through. "I'm not."

His brows furrowed, his hands sliding from my hand to my forearm. "You have barely said a word to me all day. You haven't looked at me once."

"I'm fine." My tone was flat.

His eyes hardened and then he blinked. "I think I know what's wrong. I wish you'd just talk to me about it."

I laughed. "I don't."

He opened his mouth to speak, but Wyott rejoined us then, craning his head as he sat.

"Have you seen the waitress? I wanted another ale before I went upstairs for the night."

I shot up, Maddox's hand sliding off me in the process.

"I'll get them." I strode to the bar and leaned on it, my elbows resting on the wooden, albeit sticky, bar top. I caught the eye of the barkeep and held up my fingers.

"Three ales please."

She nodded before turning away.

As I turned to stare straight ahead, I saw a motion to my left. I cut my eyes to a man moving from a few feet away to stand directly beside me, mimicking my pose and leaning on the bar.

"I've never seen you around here before." He remarked.

And I almost scoffed, almost rolled my eyes and told him to leave me alone. But I felt it then, Maddox's heated gaze on my bare skin. Felt his fury rolling through the room as if it filled my own head. And instead, I smiled.

"Probably because I've never been here before."

The man smiled back, his hazel eyes sparkling beneath his arched brows. "I can tell, I would've remembered a pretty face like yours."

Heat radiated from Maddox. I turned to face the man, leaning my right side against the bar. "And how do I know you don't say that to every woman you meet?"

He smiled, his eyes falling to my chest for a heartbeat as he turned to face me. "I guess you'll just have to trust me."

I smiled and popped my hip forward, my thigh along with it, nodding down to my dagger. "Can't you tell? I have trust issues."

He moved closer, his hand moving toward my thigh, ready to place it there and slide it up. "Well I guess we will have to –"

"If you plan on keeping that hand," Maddox spit out behind me, heat simmering off his chest. "Then I suggest you *fuck off.*"

The man didn't even look back toward me as he spun on his heel and all but ran away.

I rolled my eyes, ready to whirl around and scream at Maddox, but he fanned his large hand over my back and pushed me. Down the hall, toward the stairs that led to the bedrooms.

Rage flashed through me as I marched up the stairs, the weight of his hand on my back never easing. As we crested the top he pulled the key to my room from my pocket, the heat of his fingers over my hip sending a traitorous blush up my neck. With one hand he unlocked my room, dipped us into it, closed the door and spun to pin me against it.

"What is your problem?" He bit out, hands on either side of my head, caging me there.

I crossed my arms. "I'm sure that I don't know what you mean."

He made an effort to swallow whatever words he'd been ready to spew back. His eyes were black again, and I knew this time it wasn't from lust.

"Evaline, use your words. Talk to me."

I responded by turning my head away from him, peering at the floor beside us. Too fast for me to avoid, he clasped his hand around the back of my neck, thumb on my jaw, angling my face back to his. My heart skipped in my chest.

"Do you think I enjoyed watching you flirt with him?" His curly hair had fallen forward, tendrils falling into his face. I had to bite back the urge to wind my fingers through them, to pull him to kiss me.

"I think," I hissed. "That's a conversation you should have with your mate."

His eyes flashed and I watched the muscles in his jaw tick. "No one has ever tested my patience, like you." He said, his voice wavering with anger.

I leaned forward; eyes narrowed into slits. "Then leave."

He leaned forward, too. We were so close I could feel his breath flitting across my face. "No. I won't leave, ever. Not unless you truly want me to."

My eyes hardened, my fists clenching. "Consider this your sign. I want you to go." I lied.

His hand on my neck tightened and his eyes flashed. "No," he growled, his eyes falling to my lips before meeting mine again. "You don't."

His lips crashed onto mine before I could stop it, pushing me against the door with his body.

I swung my arms forward, ready to push him away, beat his chest. But when they landed my hands only fisted into the material there and pulled him closer. The kiss was rough, aggressive. Both of us fighting the other for dominance. Breathless and harsh. He bit my lip and I moaned, the sound sending his hands sliding down my body until they rested on my hips. I had to catch myself as he spun me, pushing me against the door so the length of his body covered mine. My hands were on the wood as I felt every inch of him down my back, the curve of him around my ass.

His lips met my ear. "You can't hide from me." He said, low, his hand slipping forward and moving between my legs.

I gasped.

"I can see – smell – how your body responds to me."

His voice was gravelly and hard, every word adding ammunition to the fire building within me. His fingers slid forward more, somehow finding my clit through my pants that covered me. He swirled his fingers around it.

I moaned, tossing my head back so that it rested against his shoulder.

"Or have you already forgotten what it felt like to have me inside you?" One hand teased me while the other tightened on my hip.

I bit my lower lip trying to muffle the sounds escaping them.

"How you fell apart around me." He growled, lips moving against my skin. "And that was only my *hand*."

He pulled my hips against his, my ass grinding against the hard length there.

I groaned, pushing off the door to spin in his arms and as soon as I faced him, he was on me. Replacing himself over me, the heat of his body pressing me into the door. He ripped his mouth from mine and angled my face to look at him.

"You want me." His hands slid down my body, resting on the curve of my waist, eyes falling there for a moment. "And I want you."

My breath caught at the words, and he took the next one as his lips covered mine, dominating me as he stole my air. When his lips slid over my neck his words replayed in my head. Over and over and over.

And I want you.

I felt the tears sliding down my cheeks before I realized I was crying, Maddox's lips at my collar bone now. He may have wanted me, but he was fated to another. And what kind of person did that make him – make me – to stand here ravishing each other?

Wyott's sad eyes filled my mind, the eyes of a man lost without his mate. Shouldn't that be how Maddox felt? Is that how his mate felt, back home? His lips moved down, kissing the dip between my breasts, teeth pulling on my shirt, about to drag it down.

"Stop."

I only had to say it once and his body stilled, lips off my skin as he straightened, removing his hands.

When he saw the wet trail of tears down my cheeks his brows knitted. "Eva, what's—"

"Wrong?" I finished for him, eyes radiating heat. "Nothing that can't be fixed. If you haven't noticed, I've survived worse than getting caught up in the promises of a stranger, while another woman waits for him at home."

I didn't wait to see his reaction, didn't give him a chance to speak.

I whirled and ripped the door open, but just as he did the first night I went to his inn in Kembertus, he raised his hand over mine and slammed the door shut.

"Just ask the fucking question, Evaline." His voice was a collage of frustration and restraint. "That day at the market, I told you I'd never lie if you asked me a question." His breath was hot on my neck. "So ask me."

I ground my teeth as I turned around to meet his gaze, at least this way I could shove him away from me so that I could actually flee the room this time.

"I know all I need to." I hissed, trying to quell the rage inside of me.

His eyes were stormy as he gave a shake of his head. "You think you do, but you don't. And you're too afraid to ask."

My fists tightened and I could feel the prick of my nails against the skin of my palm. I knew he was baiting me, trying to pull me to ask who his mate was. I'd never pegged Maddox as sadistic, but clearly he wanted to ravage my emotions. Force me to learn more about the woman he was with, the woman who wasn't me.

I didn't want to know her name, didn't want to have one to loathe for the rest of my life. To haunt my dreams more than they already were.

But my curiosity got the best of me, or perhaps he was just good at pulling it out, because I swallowed the rage and spoke. "Is she alive?"

His chest was still moving with the restraint, and I didn't know if it was for his desire or anger. "Yes." He said, and I felt the little hope I'd had in my chest fall.

Something was wrong with me, surely, because I shouldn't feel sorrow at the knowledge that the love of his life, some innocent woman somewhere, wasn't dead.

"Ask the next one." He pushed, his voice softening.

Tears pricked my eyes and my breath shook. I knew I shouldn't ask, that the answer would only hurt, but I had to know.

"Do you love her?" My voice was quiet, and I did my best to remove all semblance of emotion from it, as if he couldn't see that I was crying.

Something flashed behind his eyes and his brows twitched to furrow. "More than anyone could possibly love another."

I looked to the ground, one of my tears falling and hitting the hardwood floor between his boots, and mine.

Maddox's hand wrapped around my cheek again, raising my head up to meet his. "These aren't the right questions. Ask me what you want to know."

One day, when I'd left this world and was met by the Gods, I would ask why they put me through this. Why they let me fall for a man who'd always seemed so good and caring, but turned out to be so cruel.

I refused to ask her name, he wouldn't pull that from me. But perhaps if I knew how long they'd been together, when they met, I could walk away with the knowledge that I had no claim for him. If they'd met decades ago, a century ago, how could I ever compete?

I swallowed the lump forming in my throat and blinked back the tears. "When did you meet?"

The words were hardly out of my mouth before he was holding my face in both hands, answering the question he'd so desperately wanted me to ask.

"A month ago." His eyes flicked between mine. "When she tried to pickpocket my dagger."

A shuddered breath released from my dropped jaw before I had the chance to stop it, my eyes widened and the tears dried.

"It's you, Evaline. It's always been you." He whispered, thumb tracing my cheek.

Fury, delight, rage, and disbelief all stampeded to the surface as I planted my hands against his chest and shoved him with all my might.

He stumbled back a few paces, closer to the four poster bed behind him. There wasn't a hint of shock on his face, he'd anticipated that I'd respond this way, he only caught himself and straightened. A beat of silence passed between us as I tried to calm my breathing.

Finally, I found my voice and poked an accusatory finger at him. "Don't lie."

He took a small step toward me. "I'm not."

It couldn't be. It simply couldn't be. He couldn't be my mate, nor I his, for all this time and I had no idea.

But even as the thought crossed my mind, I knew it was flawed.

This last month I'd been plagued by questions of how I could feel this otherworldly attraction to him, why his voice sent shivers down my

417 |

spine, why his touch sent heat back up it, why every minute of every day I felt the urge to find him.

Maybe I didn't consciously know it to be true, I didn't know Kova had mates at all, but my body knew the entire time. And that knowledge, that confirmation that this was true, that he was telling the truth, sent another wave of anger crashing through me.

I looked up at him, from where my gaze had fallen to the ground in concentration, to see a look of concern on his face. His brows furrowed, his eyes soft. His stupid fucking gray eyes that meant he was a Kova, that meant he had been fated a mate, that mate who was me.

He was silent as he watched me process his confession, the one he *dragged* out of me. When he could've just told me himself.

How fucking could he? How could he know this secret about me for weeks and never bother to share it? How could he see the way I felt about him, when I threw myself at him when I was drunk. When I was scared that I nearly killed him when I fed from him. When I kissed him the night of the wedding. How could he know the way I felt about him, and not tell me?

I crossed the distance between us, his eyes tracking every step, and slammed my hands against his chest again, pushing him back a few more feet closer to the bed.

"You lied!" I screamed at him, my rage and desire and fear all boiling over as I yelled. "This entire time, you lied to me!"

He shook his head, and his calm demeanor ground against my patience.

"No, I didn't lie. I just kept it from you until now. I didn't want to scare you, we had just met." I listened to his words but none of them made the rage fall to a simmer. "You were going through so much, I just wanted to help you, to get you out of Kembertus."

I scoffed and barked back at him. "And this is how you do it? You make me ask questions about another woman I thought existed, knowing that hurt, just to find out it was me?"

He ground his teeth, finally, *finally*, his anger was beginning to meet my own again.

"I wanted to make sure you were ready when I told you. Ready to hear the truth."

I laughed, a short, maniacal, laugh as I took another step toward him. The bed rising behind him.

"And what? You thought I'd cry and fall into your arms, forget that you've kept this from me the entire time we've known each other and that everything would be okay?"

He took a step closer so that we were chest to chest, his eyes churning with frustration. "I thought you would understand that I have been in love with you since the moment I saw you. I thought you'd remember that I've done what was best for you at every turn. That I've tried to keep you safe, to make sure you felt protected, and always remembered that I was here for you. I thought you'd take a fucking breath and know that I haven't done all of this just because I knew your father, not just because I wanted to help you escape, but because I am desperately and endlessly in love with every part of you."

He was shouting by the end, his tone didn't match his confession at all. The anger outpouring from him didn't match the weight of adoration that his words carried.

And the more he spoke, the more I realized that he was right. That I should've given him the benefit of the doubt. That I should've understood that he'd done nothing so far the entire time I'd known him besides show his dedication to me. And by the end of his spiel, his confession that he loved every part of me, I remembered his face when I downed him in a spar. When he danced with me at the Ball. When he saw me covered in Bassel's blood.

Maddox loved me. But more than that, he loved, and accepted, every *part* of me. The dark and the light. The bad and the good. The broken and the whole.

And without another thought, without another breath, I flung my arms around his neck and pulled myself onto my toes to kiss him.

He growled at the contact but didn't pull away. He wrapped his arms around my body and melded my chest to his. His lips devoured mine, just as they had only minutes before out of anger. But now the anger was gone from both of us. This was simple, desperate, need. This was love. This was lust. This was the answer to the question we'd both had the entire time we'd known each other.

What if we both felt the same way?

Maddox's tongue found mine and I struggled to breathe against the fury of our kiss. One second my feet were on the ground, and in the next Maddox had lifted them slightly off and whirled us around to set me down again. I felt the hard wood of the bed post behind me, felt the intricate ridges of it dig into my back as he pushed me against it, felt his erection press against me. Show me that he was just as ready as I was.

I tore my lips away to get a breath, but he'd already lowered his over my neck, his hands fumbling over the front strings of my corset to untie it. My hands found the front fasteners to the swords holstered on his back and worked to undo the latch, and a moment later the thud of their impact on the floor sounded throughout the room, barely noticeable over our hungry breaths and desperate moans.

Maddox wasn't moving fast enough on my corset, and as I wrapped my hands around his jaw and dragged his lips back to mine, I whispered. "Just fucking rip it."

I swallowed his growl of approval as our lips met, as my tongue slid against his and without needing a second more, his fingers grabbed on either side of the corset's ribbons and tugged.

The release of pressure around my waist was immediate as he pulled it from me and sent it sailing across the room.

"Thank the Gods." He mumbled against my lips. "You look ravishing in the garment, but it's not made for easy access."

I laughed, but it was quickly cut off by his hands under my shirt, lifting the white fabric over my head until my chest was exposed to him. His eyes looked over my naked breasts, a muscle in his jaw twitching, before he lowered his head over one.

I moaned as I felt his tongue swipe out over one of my nipples, his hand quickly finding the other, and my entire being vibrated with both my pleasure, and his groans against my skin.

"I will never tire of that noise." He said and I hissed as I felt his teeth graze the bud. "Or that one."

A giggle broke past my lips as fire lashed through my body, stemming from everywhere he touched me. His lips and hand on my breasts, his other on my hip, tugging it toward him.

"You're a tease." I said breathlessly after another moment, fully aware that there was one area of my body that was begging for his attention, aching for it.

He straightened and grabbed my jaw, angling my gaze up to meet his. "If you want something, Eva, all you have to do is ask."

A smirk lit my face as my eyes danced between his. "Why don't you feel for yourself how badly I want it?"

His eyes darkened as he pushed me harder against the bed post and lowered one hand to pull at the tie of my pants. I gasped as I felt his fingers hit my core, slide along it. He shivered and I heard the deep rumble in his chest. Maddox angled my head up to his until I was tilted completely back against the pole behind me. His thumb ran over my bottom lip before tugging it open, and just as his tongue plunged in, his finger did the same.

I groaned against his mouth and held onto his shoulders for support as his finger moved in and out, slow at first with the sweetest friction, before moving faster.

My nails dug into his shirt, pulling him closer to me even though nearly every part of him touched every part of me.

It was better than the wall, better than being out in the cold with the threat of being found weighing on my mind. In the safety of the bedroom, I could give myself completely over to Maddox, let him untie every worried knot inside of me until I was a mess in his arms.

"Gods." I hissed when I felt him slip in another finger and tightened my grip on him because the pleasure rolling through me was weakening my knees.

421 |

His teeth nipped at my lower lip in response and I growled into his mouth, the pain of the bite complementing the pleasure of his fingers in a perfect symphony of touch.

I rolled my hips against his hand, the butt of his palm hitting the bud so expertly that moans were bubbling from my lips and being swallowed up by his faster than my own breathing.

Maddox used the hand that wasn't hidden beneath my pants to haul my wrists up and press them against the wood above me, holding them above my head and against the post while he crashed his mouth against mine again, his hand intertwining with mine. When he added a third finger inside me, I broke my lips from his and gulped a few breaths. Maddox's mouth fell to my neck, biting and licking, as his hand moved faster inside of me, against me.

I knew the moment he curled his fingers to hit the sweetest spot, because my hips bucked against his hand on their own accord and a guttural sound escaped me.

"That's it, my Goddess." Maddox said against my neck. "Come for me." His voice held a snarl.

His words only intensified my pleasure as his fingers sped to hit to the spot harder, quicker. My breathing was erratic, desperate, and I wrapped my fists into his shirt to hang on for dear life as the orgasm crashed through me.

A slew of moans danced on my tongue as his hand continued moving until I was only gasping, holding onto him for support, and he slowly removed his hand.

I opened my eyes and watched as he slid the fingers into his mouth. The sight had me biting my lip and that low desire curling again. He licked his fingers clean, eyes never leaving mine. I shivered under his gaze. It was black and heavy and communicated everything that he didn't have to say.

That he'd been waiting for this for weeks. That he'd dreamed of this moment just as I had.

He watched me raise my fingers to run over the tie around his collar before I tugged at the bottom of his shirt. He pulled it over his head and tossed it behind him. The dim glow of the firelight danced across his dark skin, and the shadows it cast only enhanced the ridges of the muscles that scrolled over his chest, arms, and abdomen.

My mouth watered at the sight and I laid kisses on this chest, my teeth dragging down until I was on my knees, fingers twisting over the fastener of his pants.

Maddox's hands were on my arms the moment he realized what I was trying to do, I looked up at him, confusion contorting my brow, as he stood me back up and dropped to his own knees.

"Absolutely not." He said as his fingers made quick work of all three holsters adorning my lower half. I watched with bated breath as he undid all of them until the thump of the leather wrapped blades hit the ground. Maddox looked up at me, his hands my waistband. "I have waited far too long to taste you, all of you, for you to go first."

A squeak of anticipation fell from my lips at the words, at what he might do next. I'd been with men, but all of them were more concerned with their pleasure than mine. None of them had ever gotten on their knees for me, none had ever kissed me at my core, and as Maddox pulled my pants down, and I kicked out of my boots, I realized that's what he was preparing to do.

When I was standing in front of him completely naked he looked over the length of my body. His eyes snagged on a few areas. My lips, my breasts, all the way down until he was at the apex of my thighs. Slowly, so fucking slowly, Maddox wrapped a hand around the back of one of my knees, and pulled it until it was hanging over his shoulder.

He moved the other hand up and flattened it over my ribcage, pushing me into the post behind me. I realized he was trying to steady me against the wood since I was balancing on one leg.

Maddox looked at my core, his lids dropping and his chest heaving, taking a deep swallow before he met my gaze.

"I want you to pay attention, my Goddess, so that the next time you question my loyalty, you'll remember exactly how much I worship you." He never broke eye contact as he lowered his mouth over me, and my body jolted.

His tongue started at my clit, moving against it in a slow rhythm, swirling his tongue around it. It was the purest bliss I'd ever felt.

"Fuck." I shuddered under his touch.

His response was a grumble deep in his chest. As Maddox's tongue lapped against me, I made a mental note to add this to one of the many reasons I was thankful for him.

His hand on my ribcage slid up until he had a nipple between his fingers, and as if the ecstasy of it wasn't enough, his tongue moved down, and in one motion licked from the base of my opening all the way back to the bud.

I jolted forward against him, another curse on my lips.

My hands slid into his hair, tugging on the curls as he, again, moved his tongue low. Only this time he dipped inside.

"Gods, Maddox." I hissed and tugged, perhaps a little too hard.

He growled against me and only moved faster, sliding his tongue in and out just as his fingers had done only minutes prior. I didn't know what afterlife would be like in the Night, but this had to be close to the bliss it promised.

Before I could process that his hand holding my thigh over his shoulder had moved, his fingers were inside of me. His tongue moved back over the bundle of nerves, twisting smoothly as his finger moved in and out to graze that sweet spot.

My head rolled back onto the post behind me as curses and moans and Maddox's name fell from my mouth at a rate I couldn't control.

"That is so fucking good." I rasped as his fingers moved faster, his tongue keeping up the pace. I could hardly breathe, but had enough breath to sing my praises back to him.

His growl rumbled against my clit and I cried out at the sensation.

"Don't stop." I gasped. "Please, don't stop." He obliged and continued his quick pace until I was shivering and jolting and nearly falling from the release wrecking me.

Maddox stood just as my lone knee started to give out. Both hands grabbed my face and hauled it to his as he kissed me roughly, tongue and teeth scraping over my lips.

The kiss was fast and hard and exactly what lit the fire beneath my skin for the third time.

"Pants." I gasped against his mouth, having no other energy to complete a full sentence. But it didn't matter, because he understood. He tore through the fastener and the rest of the holsters until the fabric, weapons, and his boots, were discarded on the floor. Naked in front of me, with the dying light of the fire behind him, he'd never looked more like a God.

My eyes lowered to his erection, which was finally free of his pants. He was well endowed, something I knew from all the times I'd felt it pressed against me, but it was far different seeing it in person.

Once again I tried to drop to my knees, but before I could, Maddox was picking me up. "There's no time." He said hoarsely before whirling us until he was seated on the edge of the bed, with me on his lap. "I need you now."

My knees were on each side of his hips and I felt his hard length against me, the feeling sending a shudder through me.

I pulled Maddox's gaze to mine, my hands wrapped around the back of his neck, and saw a thousand feelings rolling behind his eyes.

He was breathing heavily, his lips glistening in the dim light, and his hands tightened around my hips. I rolled them lightly against him, felt it twitch below me, and watched the pleasure sail over his face.

His brows pulled together as he spoke, trying to maintain his composure. "Are you sure?"

A smile widened on my face at the words, after everything we'd already done, he still wanted to make sure I was okay.

I only nodded as I reached behind me, picked him up in my hand, and lined us up together.

He shivered under my touch and I heard him hold his breath as our skin met. I bit my lip as I sank down onto him. I went slowly, it made for a more delicious friction, but truly I just wanted to feel every part of him.

My mate.

My Maddox.

He sucked breath through his teeth and clenched his eyes shut as I moved down, his fingers digging into my hips. When our hips met again his eyes shot open, wide and blinded by lust, as they looked up to meet mine. Mine matched and my jaw had dropped open.

"Gods, Evaline." He rasped. "I don't think you've ever looked so beautiful."

Instead of answering I raised again, before falling back down. I continued to move against him slowly, lost in the pleasure of the friction and the feel of him inside me.

His hands started to guide me even though I'd break stride every few pumps to swirl my hips. When I did that, he swore.

Maddox's hands moved up my back until he had a grip on the back of my neck, helping me to move against him. The faster I moved, the harder it was for me to keep pace, and as I bounced against him, curses and moans falling from my own lips, I realized I couldn't maintain this pace sitting straight up.

I planted my hands on his chest and pushed until he laid back onto the bed.

He growled at the move and lowered his hands to rest on the tops of my thighs. I kept mine on his chest, leaning over him now as I moved.

"Right there, sweetheart." He grunted as I was able to move him deeper against me. Inside a small part of me lit at the praise, and I moved faster against him. He groaned in response, digging his head back into the bed. "Fuck."

He gasped as I moved, and before I knew what he was doing one of his hands moved forward and his thumb was swirling over the bud at the apex of my thighs.

My arms gave out at the pleasure and I caught myself against his chest. Maddox sat up again, locking one arm around me as he flipped us around until I was pinned beneath him.

He lowered his head to kiss me, his thrusting making it hard to keep our lips against each other as we both panted. He groaned and a thrumming started in my head. Deep in my mind where it felt as if someone else resided. Like the night of my attack at the cemetery. Like the wedding when I heard Maddox's voice in my head.

As the pleasure coiled inside of me, I smiled at the thought that there was a place for Maddox in my mind, that perhaps he'd been there all along.

But before I could ask him what it was, or tell him I felt it, a spike of pain flashed through the back of my head.

I hissed, throwing my elbows beneath me to get off my barbed braid.

Maddox stalled and his eyes widened, hand moving behind my neck. "Are you okay?" His eyes lit with concern.

I nodded. "I'm sorry, I didn't think to take my braid out." I whispered, but the pain was gone, and all I wanted was for him to get moving again.

"It's not bleeding at least." He started to pull away. "Let's remove it to be safe."

One of my hands grasped his arm before he could pull away.

"No." I hissed. "No, don't stop. Please, I just won't lay on it."

His brows knitted with confusion and he opened his mouth to speak, likely to disagree with me again, but I wriggled my hips against his, wordlessly begging him to move. His jaw clenched and he groaned.

Maddox straightened to kneel and pull out. I was sitting up in protest, a demand to resume on my lips, when he took both of my legs and tossed them to the side. His hands were on my hips, finishing the spin, as he pulled them toward him once more, only this time I faced away from him.

I smiled against the duvet of the bed, exhilaration sparking beneath my skin.

CHAPTER SIXTY

Maddox

My entire body shook as I eased back into her. It was unreal, the entire night had been. Evaline arched her back and pushed her head into the bed as I started thrusting against her, the duvet muffling the sound of her moans.

I had played this moment in my mind a million times in the last few weeks. What it would be like to taste her, how she'd react when I told her the truth, what it would feel like to be inside her.

This had all gone far better than I ever anticipated. I knew she'd be angry when she learned that I'd kept our bond a secret from her. I just hoped she'd see reason, understand why I'd done what I'd done.

It took her a few rageful moments to get there, but she did. I didn't blame her, I just wanted her to see, feel, how much love I had for her. That this was real, and it wasn't a game or a lie or a joke.

I wanted all of her, every piece inside that she tried to hide from the world, and I wanted it until the day I fucking died.

But watching the firelight bounce off the smooth of her skin, the arch of her back, the way she fisted the sheets around her head until her knuckles were almost as white as her hair, drove me closer and closer to the edge.

At the thought of her hair my eyes fell to it, the braid was fallen to the side, but I didn't want to risk another ounce of pain for her. I reached one hand forward, wrapping the braid around my fist, and balanced my fingertips against the back of her shoulder. I didn't pull on her hair, I knew that was the reason she had the barbed wire in the first place. I just held the thorns away from her body, and let them prick into my hand instead. I could feel that some of them had already broken through the skin, but the slight twinge of pain only heightened the severe pleasure spiraling through my body, emanating from my cock that was fully sheathed into her at the moment.

She moaned as I moved and finally tore her lips far enough away from the blanket so that I could make out what she was saying.

"Harder." She bit out and my fist involuntarily tightened around the braid, a growl ripping through my chest as I followed my Goddess's demand.

She squeaked out a moan and turned her head slightly to look back at me. The sight tore a hole through my chest and I vowed that I'd do whatever she told me to for the rest of my existence. I'd fight a war if she asked me, but most of all I'd do this every day if it was what she wanted and I'd do it so fucking happily that I might begin to think I was dreaming and that none of this was real.

Her mouth had fallen open, gasps and moans and curses dripping from it at an impressive rate. I'd be lying if every single one of them didn't further fuel the pride riding just as high as my ecstasy was.

My mate chose me.

She wanted me.

She was screaming my name.

I realized, for the third time, that her pleasure was my top priority, but in this position, with one hand holding her braid and the other guiding her hips, I couldn't reach down like I wanted to.

"Touch yourself, Eva." I rasped and felt my erection twitch when she didn't hesitate to obey. Her eyes rolled into the back of her head as she did so, and I moved faster, but I refused to climax until she did.

I could feel the pressure building, the tightness growing in me, and knew I was close. I clamped down on my jaw, teeth feeling as if they'd shatter, and moved harder. Evaline threw her head back. Every muscle she had tensed, and the pulse of her around me, of her orgasm rolling through her, sent my own over the cliff.

I growled her name as the ecstasy shuddered through my entire body, my own muscles tensing and every nerve in my body lit with the power of a roaring fire.

I shivered when it was over, Evaline melting into the bed below us, her breaths still irregular.

I slowly eased out and wrapped an arm around her, moving us to the top of the bed and under the covers. When she settled against me, our heads resting on the pillows but our arms wrapped around each other, I reached forward and kissed her forehead.

She gave a small hum, exhaustion already settling into her. Before she could fall asleep, I reached behind her with one hand and made quick work of undoing her braid that was flung on the pillow. There was a bit of my blood on her silver hair, but it was dried, and we could wash it tomorrow. I knew there was no way I'd get her out of this bed.

I threw the barbed wire on the side table behind her and pulled the blankets up over us. When I finished she was smiling up at me, her ocean eyes beaming with contentment and joy.

"What?" I asked, a smile lifting on my own face.

She released a happy sigh and shook her head.

"Nothing. I just..." She trailed off, her eyes scanning over my face. She shrugged. "I'm happy." She met my gaze again. "It's been a long time since I could say that."

It was hard to put the feeling that swept through me into words. Because it wasn't as simple as happiness or elation or bliss.

It was gratitude.

I was so fucking thankful for her, thankful for the Goddess of Fate for sending her to me, thankful for Evaline for finally seeing and understanding all that I wanted for her. That I loved her.

If the cost of this moment, of her in my arms and the taste of her still on my tongue, was a couple centuries of longing, of being alone, then I'd gladly pay it a thousand times over.

I wasn't sure if it was because I was the son of the First, or if the Gods just wanted to give me a particularly blessed existence, but I was the luckiest Kova, man, in the entire world at this very moment.

I realized I never responded, so I gave her a soft kiss on the lips.

"Good." I said, my breath mixing with hers. "I'll spend the rest of my existence making sure you always are."

Evaline smiled, and a flash of tears swelled into her eyes.

"What's wrong?" Every protective instinct I had immediately ignited.

But Evaline just smiled again and blinked the tears away. "I love you, Maddox." She whispered and I swear my heart stopped in my chest. "Until the end of my days, I love you."

My arms around her tightened, my heart throbbed, and the bond in my mind quaked. "I love you, Eva." I whispered back. "Until the end of my days," I littered a few kisses over her face before pulling back and looking into her eyes. But I realized that wasn't good enough. I wouldn't only love her until the end of my life, I would continue loving her far after. Years, centuries, after I was gone from this world and only a faint memory in some Kova's mind. While I was in the afterlife, hopefully with her in my arms. "Until the end of my days, and in the Night that follows."

The words lifted her cheeks and her arms around me tightened, before she pulled me in for a kiss.

The sunlight streaming through the windows woke me, and when I opened my eyes I saw her there. On her side facing me, blankets clutched up to her chest, her long silvery white hair covering the pillow beneath her.

I moved closer until I lay right before her. I reached up and brushed the stray strand out of her face and behind her ear.

I had never loved anyone so completely, so thoroughly. She stirred, smiling at my touch on her cheek. Her eyes eased open and caught mine.

"Good morning." She whispered.

"Good morning, beautiful." I whispered back, relief washed over me at her lack of regret. She scooted closer and I wrapped my arm around her, pulling her to my chest, our naked bodies flush together.

She kissed me, hands on my cheeks. "How do you feel?" I asked.

She smiled. "Amazing."

I released a breath and kissed her again. "Good." I had to fight every minute of last night to make sure I didn't use too much strength on her, didn't harm her in anyway. I knew she couldn't be human, but she still seemed to feel pain the same way. Still seemed just as fragile.

I heard the birds outside and knew we needed to start moving, but I could think of nothing worse than leaving her bed.

I sighed. "I need to go soon."

She breathed. "For the horses."

I nodded, my forehead resting on hers. "Yes."

She placed her hand fully on my cheek, staring at me. I could tell she had a question, and I didn't blame her.

"How did you know?" She whispered. She didn't need to clarify, I understood what she was asking. It was only natural to be curious.

I took her hand in mine. "For Kova, there is no denying the bond. No mistaking it. When our eyes met in that inn lobby, I knew."

She nodded. "I think I've known this entire time, too. Not consciously, I didn't even know anyone was truly ever fated to another, but I think my body always knew."

I ran my fingers past her cheek, into her hair. "It was the bond. As soon as we were near each other, close enough to sense one another, the bond between us woke up." Realization flashed through my mind, and I wondered why I'd never thought about it before. "Back when Wyott and I were traveling to Kembertus, the closer I got, the more anxious I was to get there."

Her brows furrowed and she nodded. "The day before we met, when I was eating dinner with my aunt and uncle, I felt that too." She swallowed and cast her eyes down. "I think I felt the bond last night, I felt it like it was humming in my head."

I nodded. "I felt it too. Mates have a bond, it's like a tether that binds them together, soul to soul, mind to mind. When they choose to, they can send thoughts and feelings down the bond to each other." I took a breath. "It's how I heard you that night when you were being attacked in the cemetery."

"And how I heard you at the wedding."

I smiled at her quick learning. "Yes."

Wyott's hands slammed on the door in an impatient knock.

"Mads, we have to get going." I ground my jaw, annoyed with his interruption. But I knew he likely wanted to get a move on because he was hopeful we'd be heading back to Rominia soon.

There's no doubt he heard Evaline and I last night, and now that she knew we were mates, he likely figured she'd be happy to go back to Rominia, and that he'd see Cora soon.

Guilt swept through me and I sighed, turning back to Evaline.

"I have to go. We must prepare to leave, we have to keep moving."

She took a deep breath and nodded.

I pulled myself, very reluctantly, away from her and dressed. She watched me from where she clutched the sheet over her body.

When I finished I crossed the room, leaning down to kiss her.

"I will only be gone a few hours. We just need to buy horses and get more supplies, then we'll leave." She nodded. "Think about any more questions you may have, I'll answer anything and everything when I get back. And I'm sure Wyott will be happy to tell you about absolutely everything mate related, he's never let me live it down that he found his long before I met you."

Evaline laughed and smiled. "Okay."

I kissed her again and moved to the door.

I turned back one last time to take it in, what she looked like the morning after a night of being together. How she smiled at me from the bed, looking every bit as soft and vulnerable as I knew she would be when she let me in, then I turned and left.

"How'd she react?" Wyott asked as we walked to the stables. Since he probably heard most of what happened last night, unless he left the inn to go on a walk, I knew he was only humoring me. Giving me a chance to talk about the exact event I'd been waiting decades for.

A smile lit my face. "About as well as you'd expect her to." I shrugged. "She was angry at first, but she understood why I'd waited. We talked a bit about what the bond was, but then you came and we left. But last night, she said she was happy, and that's all I could've hoped for."

Wyott clasped a hand on my shoulder. "I'm happy for you, Maddox." We turned and continued walking. "It's about time you caught up to me." He said, bumping his shoulder with mine.

I laughed and shook my head, unable to even fake annoyance today because I was soaring. After so many years, so many decades, waiting for this moment, this woman, I'd finally found her. And protected her from a harmful kingdom, got her to safety, and now had finally gotten to tell her the secret that had been eating away at me for weeks.

I took a deep breath.

"It's overwhelming, isn't it?" Wyott asked as we turned up the street for the stables.

I nodded. "It really is. Everything feels different now, I hadn't been expecting that."

Wyott smiled. "It's because the bond settled. When you told her, when she accepted it, it shifted into place, permanent."

I nodded. "I know, I just spent so much time pining over finding my mate, I never really stopped to consider what it would be like when I finally got to be with her."

Wyott smiled at the ground as we walked, not far from the stables now, able to hear the horses whining from here.

"Wait until the first time you feed from her." He said, shaking his head, his brows raising. "It's unlike anything you've ever experienced."

I snorted. "Even if it's not, I'll enjoy it. I need to feed, regardless."

He nodded his head, a roll in his eyes. "No shit, I've only been saying that for a month."

I just shook my head as we made it to the stable doors. Nothing, not even Wyott's concern, would damper my mood this morning.

CHAPTER SIXTY-ONE

Evaline

I smiled as I watched Maddox leave, shutting the door behind him.

But I stayed still, now that I was alone my mind started going over everything that had happened in the last twenty-four hours. Mates.

I'd been upset when I thought he had another mate, but it was me. I was his destiny. Picked by the Goddess of Fate, Rominiava herself to spend the rest of our lives – my life, rather – together. I felt the smile slowly fall from my face. How would that work exactly? I was a mortal, and he was not. He'd live centuries more, and at best I had a handful of decades left. Would he force me to be a Kova? Would I want to turn?

And what did mating even mean? Did this mean I was automatically… what? A wife?

I took a deep breath, feeling my skin flush, my hands slowly falling away from holding the sheet to my chest. Did this mean I'd have to go to Rominia with him? What if I hated it, would he leave with me?

I stood from the bed. Could he hear my thoughts?

When they choose to. He'd said. When mates choose to share, they could send it down the bond. My cheeks heated, listening in my mind for any inclination that I wasn't alone. It was quiet, a kind of static filling my head when I searched for that tether.

I felt it start to rise within me, that panic.

I moved from the bed, finding the clothes I'd worn before strewn about the floor and redressing in them. Before I realized what I was doing, I'd gathered what few belongings I had together, shoving them into my bag.

How could I be a mate?

I found my holstered weapons and strapped them on.

I'd never had a man in my life like this, a partner I was in love with. In one night I went from a single woman who only had herself to worry about, to being bonded to a Kova. And he was a member of his island's ruling family. What did that mean for me?

My head whipped around, searching for my cloak. There, draped over the chaise. I threw it on, clasping it around my neck.

Finally, my eyes landed on my barbed wire on the night stand. I sat on the bed, fingers shredding through my hair, pulling it into a braid faster than ever before. I grabbed the bag and slung it over my body, and made for the door leaving my torn corset on the floor.

I rushed from the room, the inn, the tavern, as fast as I could. I hardly passed anyone as I did and turned left out of the door. The stables were to the right, across town. I remembered the innkeeper telling us that.

But to the left, forest.

I felt the rush of guilt as I fled, but I just needed some air. A chance to think out in the open when the walls of the room weren't closing in on me.

I tripped my way through the trees until I made it to a small creek, its dribbling the only sounds filling the air. I nearly collapsed at the edge, catching my hands on my knees as I doubled over and struggled to breathe. Another panic attack, another hyperventilating fit, only this time Maddox wasn't here to calm me down.

He wasn't here because I'd left. I'd left him behind, if only to get some clarity.

But as I bent over in the woods, urging my breaths to slow down, to deepen, all I could think about were all the expectations I'd just fled from in Kembertus. Being a ruling Lady someday, having a husband who only wanted an heir from me, not able to have a life of my own.

Did I only flee one prison to end up in another? Would Maddox force me to marry him, to give him an heir for his family's power? What if he made me stay in Rominia, locked on the island and completely isolated from the landmass I'd grown up on?

By the grace of the Gods, the panicked fog that clouded my mind cleared for an instant. One instant which was long enough for me to see myself, see what I was doing, see reason.

I was running. It was exactly what he was afraid of. And I fell right into it, into my old habits of leaving when things became difficult, when I gave others the power to hurt me.

I felt my breathing start to even out.

I had given Maddox the power to hurt me, and that was terrifying. And I knew that fear of abandonment, of restriction, of being broken completely again after Maddox had just started molding my pieces back together, was what had fueled my flee.

Maddox had only shown me that I could trust him, with every single act he'd done since the moment I met him. He'd protected me, armed me, and helped me escape. He wouldn't have done that only to force new expectations on me. I owed him the chance to explain his plans, explain what it would mean, if anything at all, that I was his mate.

I straightened fully. I took another deep breath, my breathing almost completely back to normal. I felt my pulse even out.

As I took another breath, feeling like myself again, a smile slipped onto my face. Everything would be okay.

I turned on my heel –

A man stood behind me. Tall and muscular, his red hair shaggy on top of his head. I inhaled at the sight of him. "Gabriehl?"

He smirked. "How nice of you to recognize me, cousin." He took a step closer, his hands hidden beneath his cloak.

Panic, real panic, enveloped me. But I slipped a smile on my face to hide it. "Well your portrait is strewn all across the castle. Your parents talk about you all the time."

He nodded, looking down at the ground between us. "How are they?" There was no way he could know what happened. Not this quickly.

"They're great. I know they miss you, though."

His eyes cut up to me. "I'm sure they do, but they understand that I can't be cooped up in that city all the time. I'll spend enough time there once my father dies and I take over as Lord of Kembertus."

I nodded. "I'm sure the city will be lovely with you as its leader." I barely even knew him, only the stories from his parents, but the lies kept slipping from my lips as he advanced. I didn't understand why he was here, how he was here, but I had to give myself time to figure a way out.

He cocked his head. "You know I've never seen you in person before, but you look exactly as I pictured. Just like your mother."

I tried to play off my surprise. I laughed, shaking my head. "A lot of people tell me I look just like her."

He nodded. "You do. But you never got to know her, or even have a mother." He cocked his head. "Do you know how many times my mother wrote your father, begging him to bring you to Kembertus so she could raise you?"

I pursed my lips. "Well she got her wish."

He smiled. "But is it really the same? You were already grown, already too stubborn for her to really have any connection with you."

My smile was tight. "We had a great relationship."

How could he know all of this? "I know I've never met you in person, but that white hair, those blue eyes. I'd know you in any crowd."

I nodded, eyeing him.

"And what funny timing, having just heard from my parents this morning." I stilled. "Surely you didn't think they'd just let you flee?"

My own hands were beneath my cloak, hidden. I calculated the distance between my sword and my hand. Too far.

"You killed one of their esteemed guests, the man they betrothed you to, no less."

My eyes hardened as I gauged every step he took.

"Did you know Bassel was my friend?" He shook his head. "One day he'd rule Vestaria, and I, Kembertus. Do you know the plans we had?" He cocked his head. "The plans we had for you?"

My heart seemed to speed up at those words. Why had I expected to escape, to live a life free anywhere else?

"What are you going to do?" I ground out.

He took a step toward me, and I took one back. He shrugged. "I have options. There are a few bounties on your head."

He took another step toward me but this time I backed up, and ran into something hard. Hands covered me and I tried to jump from them but the arms wrapped around me, holding me hostage.

Six more men moved from behind me, where they must have been sneaking up throughout the entire conversation. I recognized one from the tavern, the one who'd flirted with me.

Gods how could I have been so dumb. How long had we been trailed, how long had they been watching us?

Gabriehl gestured to the men. "I hope you don't mind. I brought some friends."

I thrashed against the arms that held me. "Gabriehl, let me go. Please, please. You have to believe me, Bassel was —"

"I don't particularly give a fuck what Bassel was or wasn't. He was a friend, a business partner, and now he's dead." He scoffed. "I'm not going to lose out on our plans, on the deals we'd made, just because you went and killed him."

I opened my mouth to speak but the man holding me brought his hand up, covering it.

My eyes widened as the familiar feeling of hands clasping my mouth shut rolled through me. I thrashed against him, whipping my head to free myself, but it was no use. I tried to breathe but his hand cut off all supply of oxygen through my nose and my mouth.

As the black shadows began to dance at the edges of my vision, a similar feeling to the night Maddox had saved me, all I could think about was him.

How he loved me, and how I ran. Tears filled my eyes as I realized that he'd come back to the inn and think I left him. A sob rolled through me, only speeding up my fainting spell.

I tried to push through my mind, to feel close to him as I had the night of my attack in the cemetery, but there was nothing.

And the last thing I remembered doing as the men hauled me away, almost slipped totally into unconsciousness, was easing the dagger he'd given me from my thigh and dropping it on the ground.

CHAPTER SIXTY-TWO

Maddox

Wyott was outside with the three horses as I strode into the tavern and up the stairs to get Evaline. Wyott and I already had all our belongings, so once Evaline was ready we would ride.

But when I got to her door it was cracked open, and my heart leapt from my chest.

I eased it open, poking a head inside. Her bed was still disheveled as it had been when I left this morning. My eyes coasted the floor, all the weapons and clothes that had littered there earlier were gone save for the corset. My eyes flashed to the bathroom, and I ripped the door open, looking for her. It was empty.

I pulled the drawers of the armoire open, nothing.

Finally, my eyes snapped to the nightstand where I'd thrown her wire the night before. Bare.

I fell to my knees in the middle of her room and felt the very visceral pain of my heart cracking in my chest.

She left me. Exactly what I was afraid of happening, happened. I waited too long to tell her, or maybe not long enough. I fell forward and caught myself, my hands holding me up from the floor as my body convulsed. Rage and fear and sorrow all roiling through me until I couldn't breathe. Until I couldn't feel anything but the buzz of loss.

I squeezed my eyes shut and willed the pain to go away, willed my lungs to breathe. She left and there was no way she'd survive out there on her own. Not forever.

My eyes hardened as I straightened. I had to find her, had to protect her at the very least. Even if she rejected the bond, even if she decided she hated me, I couldn't let her die just because she didn't want to be my mate. I took a deep breath as I walked outside, I'd have to track her.

Wyott's eyes widened when he saw me, and I knew I didn't have to tell him what happened. He just rode alongside me as we took the three horses and headed straight for her scent. It was hard to keep up with, the wind from the quickly approaching thunderstorm skewed it until I could barely trace it.

I couldn't hear her heartbeat. I'd already tried for the bond, but there was only a static more desolate than the one from before. This wasn't like before, where it was caused by her ignorance of the bond. This static was fainter, hardly discernible, and caused by the distance between us. I tried to stamp down on my fear, because I knew what that meant. It meant that even if she was in trouble, calling out to me down the bond, I wouldn't hear it. She was too far.

We landed in a small clearing beside a babbling creek. I dismounted and looked around, a growl loosing from my lips as my hands fisted in my hair. Her scent ended at the water. How the fuck was I supposed to find her? Would she even want to be found?

"Maddox." Wyott said quietly, a few feet away.

I turned, he kneeled on the ground, looking down at something.

"Everything will be okay." He whispered as I approached, but knew better than to touch me.

When I came up beside him I saw what it was, and fell to my knees for the second time that day.

Because I could've dealt with her leaving me, I could've dealt with this pain for the rest of my life, if it meant she was safe. If it meant she was living her life somewhere else, somewhere with a man who made sure she was happy, made sure she was safe.

But I stared down at the dagger I'd given her, dropped in the dirt. The black Rominium glinting off the sun that was quickly getting encroached by the storm clouds ahead. I knew she wouldn't have left it behind willingly, whether it was a gift from me or not, she wouldn't have gone into these woods a weapon down. She was stubborn, but she wasn't stupid.

No.

But she would have dropped it here for us, for me, if she'd been taken against her will. She would've left it here as a message, a sign. A plea to come find her.

I looked up, scanning the woods around me. The green canopies becoming only greener with the static of the storm roiling above us. There were no signs of movement, that anyone had been here.

Thunder cracked through the air and it was a moment before I realized it wasn't thunder at all, but my scream. And the more it ripped my throat apart the louder I roared. Because I hoped whoever had my Evaline, would hear me, and I hoped wherever they were, they were afraid.

TURN THE PAGE FOR A SNEAK PEEK OF...

Made
&
Marred

THE FATED CREATIONS

BOOK TWO

CHAPTER ONE

Evaline

"Good morning, sunshine."

A voice lulled through my dreams, and I realized I'd been tossing and turning in my sleep. I almost smiled, almost sighed in contentment from waking up beside Maddox. But before my eyes could flutter open, or I could even anticipate seeing the glow of the morning sun cascade over his bare chest, and touch the skin that stretched over the tight muscles on his torso, I felt it.

An ache in my lungs. It was sharp and rhythmic, lulling for one moment before crashing back down on me again. Reminiscent of the stories my father would tell me of the waves that crashed on the Madierian shore.

I tried to groan, but realized I couldn't make any sound at all. My chest was compressed, air evading my lungs as it was knocked out every few moments in tide with the pain. The discomfort stretched to my chapped lips, behind which my tongue lay listless in my dry mouth. I tried to wet it, to close it and swallow, but was hindered by the cloth that filled my mouth.

Tears stung the edges of my eyes as I opted to take deep breaths through my nose, but only the faintest amount flowed through. My clothes were damp, my hair stuck to my face, and I knew even without looking at the saturated dirt below us that we'd traveled through a storm.

When I opened my eyes, I had to concentrate to recall the recent events.

Maddox and I were mates.

I'd panicked and fled.

Gabriehl found me.

And now he was taking me... Gods knew where.

I winced as the horse I was slumped over jolted forward.

The ache in my lungs reverberated through my ribs. How long had I been draped here like this?

"There she is." Gabriehl remarked from a nearby horse.

I stilled.

I didn't bother trying to speak, just listened to the stamp of hooves around me, straining my eyes to look around despite my limited visibility with my head angled toward the ground.

"That must've been some dream you were having." A different man said above me, the one whose lap I was draped over.

My eyes widened as I knew exactly what he was talking about, my dreams of my last night with Maddox, and I bit back the tears that threatened to fall. I still had the dagger hidden in my boot, but I could no longer feel my father's sword at my hip. I could at least fight with the dagger when the time came. For now, I just had to focus on surviving.

The horse jostled me roughly again and I nearly slid off, before the man's hand came to grip my waist. I squeezed my eyes shut as he held me against him.

I took a deep breath, or as deep as my bondage would allow, and tried to clear my mind. I didn't know how long I'd been knocked out, but I knew we'd be hours ahead of Maddox.

What would he think when he got back to the inn and realized I was gone?

He'd think I left. I had. But I could never truly leave him, not anymore. I'd fled as one last act of selfishness. My last ditch effort at protecting my own heart. His confession could have gone a thousand different ways, but in each of them, I would have gone back, I was going back, when Gabriehl stopped me.

I had just needed a few moments of clear air, of being alone with my thoughts. Of being away from Kembertus, Therese, Bassel. Even Maddox. I needed one moment where the only person I had to answer to was myself. One moment where there was no more pretending, no more lying about my plans or maintaining the walls that I tried so hard to hold steady over my heart.

So much had happened in the last month. Most of it jammed into the last week, alone. I'd just needed time to process it. But I was happy Maddox and I were mates. I loved him.

Realization hammered through my mind as I remembered the bond. The bond that I could talk to Maddox through. I squeezed my eyes shut, and searched in my mind. Having no idea what I was looking for, but searching nonetheless. It was as if I was crawling through the darkness. My hands outstretched, searching the ground for that tether. As if it was a physical chain I could find and tug.

After several minutes of nothing I could've cursed myself.

I should've at least asked how the bond worked before I ran away. I only knew that I somehow used it the night Bassel and his friends attacked me in the cemetery. I squeezed my eyes shut once more, trying to remember what I'd done that night. I'd tried to escape, to flee into the happy memories of my mind. I'd pictured Maddox sitting on his bed, the way we'd been the night I was drunk and he took care of me. The night he said no to me, even though I begged. The night he chose what was best for me over what he wanted.

I'd reached out to him that night, as if I could touch him through my memories, and he'd heard me. I steadied myself, trying to stop the slight tremor that had started rolling through my body, and tried to replicate what I'd done then.

I pictured the two of us last night, when he'd proved his loyalty. I pictured the way he looked at me as if I was a portrait of divinity, the way he promised to love me even when we were dead. Replaying those moments over and over, reaching out again and again, waiting to feel that same stir in my mind as I had the night I used the bond.

But there was nothing. Only static.

"When are we going to stop for camp?" One of the men behind me asked, interrupting my concentration.

"We can't risk the men she was with catching us. If they found she was gone and picked up horses, they could be right on our tail. We have to push through the night." I heard Gabriehl say, and noticed for the first time the orange swatch of light that coated the land below me. It was sunset.

I'd been gone for hours, near the entire day, and Maddox was nowhere to be found. There was only static in my head, settling over the bond until I couldn't reach him. Heartache settled in my chest as I realized Maddox wasn't coming for me.

From the moment I'd met him, I'd feared trusting him. I pushed back against his attempts to get close to me, to show him who I really was, to let him love me. Afraid that it'd be a mistake, that it'd leave me vulnerable to being hurt. Being betrayed.

But my greatest mistake wasn't trusting Maddox, it was leaving him.

"How would they catch up to us? We're heading southeast and they're heading either northeast or east. We're far enough now that they would've diverted their path." The man whose lap I was on rumbled above me.

I stilled and felt my already dry mouth desiccate.

Southeast. Why did that strike such fear within me?

My fatigued brain wracked through every map I'd ever seen throughout my life, picturing the small town Maddox, Wyott and I had been in, between Kembertus and Neomaeros, right on the cusp of River Brawn, and what lay southeast of it.

Not Arlomandrah, that was south. Not Vestaria, thank the Gods; that was straight east. And definitely not Kembertus, which is where Maddox was likely headed, something these men already thought.

"I'd rather be safe than risk having to deal with any more interruptions in this deal. Bassel dealt with most of the details, I don't want to risk being late for the exchange." Gabriehl hissed at the man.

I thought back to the history lessons my father taught me about the Kova and Vasi. They didn't live on the mainland, at least not the majority of them. They lived on their own landmasses. My brow crinkled with effort as I thought back to what I'd never seen on those maps as a child. Rominia. That's where the Kova resided.

But where did the Vasi?

"Humans don't believe in the monsters who lurk in the night." My father's voice filled my head. A lesson he'd given me once.

His lesson had continued. "But they do fear those that lurk in the depths of the oceans. Sea monsters don't exist, but they've taken the blame for the Vasi's bloodshed." Tears stung my eyes.

"The Kromean Sea houses the landmass where the Vasi reside. They overtake pirate and trading vessels, draining those aboard while they make their way to Brassillion on ships that dock in the port south of Vestaria. They kill so frequently there, that at certain times of day, in certain shades of sunlight, the color of the water is altered by the blood. One day, the humans named it accordingly." His words echoed in perfect memory in my head, and I realized that silence had fallen over the men around me as Gabriehl had been sharing a similar story, the reason they couldn't risk tardiness. I could sense their unease.

"Have any of you ever been to Blush Bay?" One whispered.

I gritted my teeth, doing my best to ignore the way they sank into the fabric in my mouth and the vile, dank, taste of it.

Why would they take me to Blush Bay? It was a major Brassillion port, but what did that have to do with me? I'd never been before, and my father never mentioned going either. I just knew the lore that surrounded it. That Vasi roamed there.

Gabriehl was taking me to someone, collecting a bounty for him and his posse. But who would want me in Blush Bay?

Going back to Kembertus, to give me up to his parents would make more sense. I embarrassed them in front of one of their allies, and the other kingdoms once word spread in time. Taking me to Vestaria made even more sense. I killed the heir to the kingdom, I'm sure Bassel's parents had several tortures planned, and with a kingdom atop a diamond mine, they surely could pay a heavy bounty.

Taking me to either of those kingdoms made perfect sense, which is why, if Maddox was looking for me, that's where he'd be headed. If he hadn't already given up and turned back for Rominia, back to his life as a member of the Kova ruling family.

But taking me to Blush Bay didn't make any logical sense –

My skin paled, my heart felt as if it stopped even as I jostled atop the horse's back, as every thought, interaction, memory I'd ever had regarding the Kova or Vasi flashed through my head at once.

My attack, my father's death, the stories he'd told me as a child, the information I learned from Maddox and Wyott.

No. My voice was but a whisper in my mind. *Please, Gods. No.*

I tried to calm myself, to think through the information logically.

Maddox's father's name was Kovarrin. He was the first Kova to ever exist. He was the First.

My eyes widened, staring at the shifting ground below me, as my heart raced, realizing that the immortal species was named after the First. After Maddox's father. It seemed so obvious now, but I'd never considered it. Maddox had never mentioned it.

Another memory flashed forward faster than the former, and all I heard was Bassel's threat during our fight the night I killed him.

"I'm going to kill you, you fucking whore. Vasier's orders be damned."

For the first time since I'd woken up slung over this horse, I throttled myself. Shifted my body and attempted to roll off. I shrieked and screamed as much as my parched throat would allow. I swung my head and bit down against the dirty cloth in my mouth.

"I'll be damned." Gabriehl chuckled from his horse, and based on the sound I knew he turned to face me. "I guess she does know whose bounty we're collecting."

Bassel wasn't supposed to kill me, but he was willing to defy orders to survive.

Vasier's orders.

Vasi.

Acknowledgements
from the Author

Thank you to my husband for being my rock this last year. I've been a mess who spends too much time on her computer, and forgets what she's saying halfway through a sentence, but you never complained. You watched me spiral in 2021 planning the wedding, in 2022 preparing Bound & Barbed for publication, now we get to do it all again in 2023 for Made & Marred! (It's funny because it's true). I love you endlessly, thank you.

To my family who has been a steadfast support system my entire life, thank you. Each of you have taught me that the struggle is always worth it, if it's for something you love. Thank you for your unwavering belief in me.

Thank you Carolann for letting me bounce ideas off you for weeks on end through many overly-long video messages. You were the first reader who believed in Bound & Barbed, and without your confidence I'm not sure how I would've carried on past the first draft.

This book would not have published in 2022 if it wasn't for Ari Annachi, owner and editor at Padma Katha Press. Thank you so much for sharing your extensive publishing knowledge with me and for talking me through the several breakdowns I had along the way. Thank you for being my critique partner, web designer, editor, and friend.

Thank you to Saumya, Bianca, Aamna, and Daniel for helping make this book look beautiful on the inside and out. Thank you to my entire ARC team, for whom there are too many to list. Thank you to everyone else who helped Bound & Barbed along the way; Alisha, Amanda, Scott, Jesika, Ruthie, Ayla, Emma, Madeleine, and Jodi.

Finally, thank you, Reader, for taking a chance on an Indie author. Perhaps most importantly, thank you for joining me as we go back to our vampire romance era. What a time to be alive.

About the Author

Samantha R. Goode is an author from Cleveland, Ohio. She's been an avid reader and writer since she was young, and has a bachelor's degree in Creative Writing from The Ohio State University.

She spends her free time reading, writing, re-watching the same few shows countless times, and spending time with her husband, corgi, collie, and cat.

Find out more about her or her works on www.samanthargoode.com or @samanthargoode on Instagram and TikTok.

Printed in Great Britain
by Amazon

28486604R00263